Drama,

Adventure,

Romance

This illustrious collection spans the
incredible variety of subject matter and styles
associated with the short story.

Twenty-two masterpieces have been selected
from the best of world literature for their
dramatic or narrative excellence, convincing
characterizations and masterful evocation
of mood. Ranging from long to short,
light to humorous, romantic to bizarre, all are
stunning examples of the short-story form.

Such classics as "The Necklace," "The
Devil and Daniel Webster," "The Luck
of Roaring Camp" and "Haircut" make this
book an invaluable volume for students
and lovers of great literature.

A POCKET BOOK OF SHORT STORIES

Edited and with an Introduction by
M. Edmund Speare,
A.B., M.A., Harvard University
Ph.D., Johns Hopkins University

WASHINGTON SQUARE PRESS
PUBLISHED BY POCKET BOOKS NEW YORK

A Washington Square Press Publication of
POCKET BOOKS, a division of Simon & Schuster, Inc.
1230 Avenue of the Americas, New York, N.Y 10020

ISBN: 0-671-50982-9

First Pocket Books printing March, 1941

98 97 96 95 94 93 92 91 90 89

WASHINGTON SQUARE PRESS, WSP and colophon are
registered trademarks of Simon & Schuster, Inc.

Printed in the U.S.A.

COPYRIGHT NOTICES AND PERMISSIONS

CONTENTS

vii

INTRODUCTION

THE DESIRE to tell stories and to listen to them is one of the qualities inherent in all human nature, and the storyteller's art is perhaps the oldest of all the arts in the world, and the best-beloved. Egyptian tombs of 6,000 years ago have delivered up imaginative accounts of domestic and social life inscribed in papyri. Greek and Roman bards sang the glories of their gods and heroes in narrative form; ancient India had its fables; the Persians excelled in legends and folk tales; the ancient Orient gave us the lavish Arabian Nights' Entertainments; the Bible is a repository of every conceivable kind of short story. The Italian *novella* of the Middle Ages (short prose fiction perfected by Boccaccio) and the French *fabliaux* (humorous and 'earthy' stories, they were) were well known to the English through Chaucer's *Canterbury Tales*. Even Shakespeare made use of the brief 'novels' of his contemporaries Thomas Lodge and Robert Greene in some of his plays. And Deloney's simple narratives of Elizabethan middle classes and Overbury's *Characters* of 1614, were followed by the picaresque tales of Defoe, the story-essays of Addison and Steele, and the contributions in *The Rambler* of 18th century Samuel Johnson. By the beginning of the 19th century, when the *genre* for the first time attained its place as a dignified art, the short-story form thus had a long history behind it.

Ours is the great generation of the short story. The growth of the newspaper, the development of the magazine, the universality of popular education with its increase in human curiosity—most of all, the increasing tempo of modern life, its speed of living and competitive pressure—gave this literary type its greatest encouragement. Here is the people's literature, and the most democratic of all forms of writing because it offers a means for the use of every conceivable sort of plot or character or background. It is just the right length in a world of tumult and hurry; it is a form that presents things succinctly and graphically; it is the type of writing most easily understood by every kind of reader. Men of our own country—Washington Irving, Hawthorne, and most of all, Edgar Allan Poe—gave it, in the early 19th century, its highest development. Poe is the undisputed father of the present-day short story, and his is still the classic definition. Says Poe:

> A skillful literary artist has constructed a tale. If wise, he has not fashioned his thoughts to accommodate his incidents; but having conceived, with deliberate care, a certain unique or single effect to be brought out, he then invents such incidents—he then combines such effects as may best aid him in establishing this preconceived effect. If his very initial sentence tend not to the outbringing of this effect, then he has failed in his first step. In the whole composition there should be no word written, of which the tendency, direct or indirect, is not to the pre-established design. . . .

In Somerset Maugham's succinct summary of Poe, this might be read as follows: A good short story is a piece of fiction, dealing with a single incident, material or spiritual, that can be read at a sitting; it is original, it must sparkle, excite, or impress; and it must have unity of effect or impression; it should move in an even line from its exposition to its close.

Examine even the limited collection of stories in this anthology and you will conclude that this is the most flexible of all forms; one may put almost anything into it, from the lyrical exposition of a single mood to a plot that attempts an analysis of the most complex human emotions. The essential quality of the short story is its *economy*. Like the portrait in a miniature compared to the landscape painted on a great canvas, here everything must show intensity of concentration, a squeezing of a slice of life into the narrowest of compasses, and yet every intricate detail must be seen clearly. In this art-form, every word, every phrase, counts; every detail becomes part of a comprehensive whole and leads to one unified impression, an impression that was articulate in the author's mind clearly and completely before he set his first word down on paper. Most of all, like a good race horse, to hold the reader's attention the short story must get off to a good start It's the start and the finish that count, and the beginning, the right beginning, is usually the harder for the creator to obtain. In the hands of the amateur here is where the catastrophe usually occurs. Ellery Sedgwick, former editor of *The Atlantic Monthly*, illustrates this humorously from an account of a short-story class that met at Harvard. Says Sedgwick:

> It was at a time when Russian literature of a particularly dismal type infested the minds of young men. The proletariat were called on to furnish all the characters, and the successive themes invariably represented deepening crises of poverty, illness, and general misery. The instructor was no doubt a kindhearted man (all teachers are), but the drab monotony of his students' stories overmastered his sympathy. "For Heaven's sake," he said, "give me variety. Mix in a few aristocrats with the populace and don't begin your story with some platitudinous affirmation of the brutality of life. Begin dramatically."
>
> The students took him at his word. When the class met again, the story first to be considered began with the dramatic note: " 'What insolence!' cried the Duchess, rising in alarm. 'Take your hand off my knee!' "

In making a selection of representative short stories for this volume, I chose most of the material from among the writings of the last decades in both America and England because, first, in these two countries the *genre* has been developed to its highest form by men and women of genius, who gave it "a character and a currency it had never had before"; and, secondly, because the book is mainly designed for our own readers.

No attempt has been made to select necessarily the most celebrated stories by these twenty-two important writers, least of all to select the greatest stories of all time or from every important nation—an impossible feat for a single collection like this. My purpose rather was to bring together a representative collection of stories (with some contrast of subject matter and style from Russian, German, and French writers), which have given much entertainment to a great many discriminating readers, which show distinguished imaginative power and obvious technical skill and dexterity.

The first principle in assembling the collection was that each story had to be direct, dramatic, surprising, gripping in the intensity of its interest; each had to move swiftly in one unbroken line from the first moment when curiosity was aroused in the reader to the end when that excited curiosity was completely satisfied. Only those stories were included whose characters were convincing and alive. The second factor was to present as large a variety of mood as possible, a balance of matter and manner. Here are stories long and short; serious and grave stories are mixed with light and humorous ones; and next to rugged tales of love are tales of the bizarre and the unusual. To make the scope and mood the more emphatic, the countries and the authors have been mixed together without reference to divisions of class, nationality, or type of story. There are no excerpts or deletions; short or long, each story is as it was written. By reading many contrasting writers, all of them acknowledged masters of the form, we can see how sensitive personalities react in their own ways to the various aspects of life.

The arrangement of the tales is in reverse chronological order. Those from the most recent writers, whose language and matter seem the truest and most absorbing to our own time, appear first; those farthest away from our own days lose something in intensity and rapidity of narration, but gain the compensatory qualities, in their leisurely telling, of a more natural humor, a less·bitter irony, and the revelation of a greater depth of knowledge of human nature.

All told, these varied narratives illustrate Sir Philip Sidney's dictum about a good storyteller: "With a tale, forsooth, he cometh unto you; with a tale which holdeth children from play, and old men from the chimney-corner."

M. EDMUND SPEARE

A
POCKET
BOOK
OF
SHoRT
STORIES

ERNEST HEMINGWAY (1898–1961)

THE KILLERS

THE DOOR of Henry's lunchroom opened and two men came in. They sat down at the counter.

"What's yours?" George asked them.

"I don't know," one of the men said. "What do you want to eat, Al?"

"I don't know," said Al. "I don't know what I want to eat."

Outside it was getting dark. The street-light came on outside the window. The two men at the counter read the menu. From the other end of the counter Nick Adams watched them. He had been talking to George when they came in.

"I'll have a roast pork tenderloin with apple sauce and mashed potatoes," the first man said.

"It isn't ready yet."

"What the hell do you put it on the card for?"

"That's the dinner," George explained. "You can get that at six o'clock."

George looked at the clock on the wall behind the counter.

"It's five o'clock."

"The clock says twenty minutes past five," the second man said.

"It's twenty minutes fast."

"Oh, to hell with the clock," the first man said. "What have you got to eat?"

"I can give you any kind of sandwiches," George said. "You can have ham and eggs, bacon and eggs, liver and bacon, or a steak."

"Give me chicken croquettes with green peas and cream sauce and mashed potatoes."

"That's the dinner."

"Everything we want's the dinner, eh? That's the way you work it."

1

"I can give you ham and eggs, bacon and eggs, liver——"

"I'll take ham and eggs," the man called Al said. He wore a derby hat and a black overcoat buttoned across the chest. His face was small and white and he had tight lips. He wore a silk muffler and gloves.

"Give me bacon and eggs," said the other man. He was about the same size as Al. Their faces were different, but they were dressed like twins. Both wore overcoats too tight for them. They sat leaning forward, their elbows on the counter.

"Got anything to drink?" Al asked.

"Silver beer, bevo, ginger-ale," George said.

"I mean you got anything to *drink?*"

"Just those I said."

"This is a hot town," said the other. "What do they call it?"

"Summit."

"Ever hear of it?" Al asked his friend.

"No," said the friend.

"What do you do here nights?" Al asked.

"They eat the dinner," his friend said. "They all come here and eat the big dinner."

"That's right," George said.

"So you think that's right?" Al asked George.

"Sure."

"You're a pretty bright boy, aren't you?"

"Sure," said George.

"Well, you're not," said the other little man. "Is he, Al?"

"He's dumb," said Al. He turned to Nick. "What's your name?"

"Adams."

"Another bright boy," Al said. "Ain't he a bright boy, Max?"

"The town's full of bright boys," Max said.

George put the two platters, one of ham and eggs, the other of bacon and eggs, on the counter. He set down two side-dishes of fried potatoes and closed the wicket into the kitchen.

"Which is yours?" he asked Al.

"Don't you remember?"

"Ham and eggs."

"Just a bright boy," Max said. He leaned forward and took the ham and eggs. Both men ate with their gloves on. George watched them eat.

"What are *you* looking at?" Max looked at George.

"Nothing."

"The hell you were. You were looking at me."

"Maybe the boy meant it for a joke, Max," Al said.

George laughed.

"*You* don't have to laugh," Max said to him. "*You* don't have to laugh at all, see?"

"All right," said George.

"So he thinks it's all right." Max turned to Al. "He thinks it's all right. That's a good one."

"Oh, he's a thinker," Al said. They went on eating.

"What's the bright boy's name down the counter?" Al asked Max.

"Hey, bright boy," Max said to Nick. "You go around on the other side of the counter with your boy friend."

"What's the idea?" Nick asked.

"There isn't any idea."

"You better go around, bright boy," Al said. Nick went around behind the counter.

"What's the idea?" George asked.

"None of your damn business," Al said. "Who's out in the kitchen?"

"The nigger."

"What do you mean the nigger?"

"The nigger that cooks."

"Tell him to come in."

"What's the idea?"

"Tell him to come in."

"Where do you think you are?"

"We know damn well where we are," the man called Max said. "Do we look silly?"

"You talk silly," Al said to him. "What the hell do you argue with this kid for? Listen," he said to George, "tell the nigger to come out here."

"What are you going to do to him?"

"Nothing. Use your head, bright boy. What would we do to a nigger?"

George opened the slit that opened back into the kitchen. "Sam," he called. "Come in here a minute."

The door to the kitchen opened and the nigger came in. "What was it?" he asked. The two men at the counter took a look at him.

"All right, nigger. You stand right there," Al said.

Sam, the nigger, standing in his apron, looked at the two men sitting at the counter. "Yes, sir," he said. Al got down from his stool.

"I'm going back to the kitchen with the nigger and bright boy," he said. "Go on back to the kitchen, nigger. You go with him, bright boy." The little man walked after Nick and Sam, the cook, back into the kitchen. The door shut after them. The man called Max sat at the counter opposite George. He didn't look at George but looked in the mirror that ran along back of the counter. Henry's had been made over from a saloon into a lunch counter.

"Well, bright boy," Max said, looking into the mirror, "why don't you say something?"

"What's it all about?"

"Hey, Al," Max called, "bright boy wants to know what it's all about."

"Why don't you tell him?" Al's voice came from the kitchen.

"What do you think it's all about?"

"I don't know."

"What do you think?"

Max looked into the mirror all the time he was talking.

"I wouldn't say."

"Hey, Al, bright boy says he wouldn't say what he thinks it's all about."

"I can hear you, all right," Al said from the kitchen. He had propped open the slit that dishes passed through into the kitchen with a catsup bottle. "Listen, bright boy," he said from the kitchen to George. "Stand a little further along the bar. You move a little to the left, Max." He was like a photographer arranging for a group picture.

"Talk to me, bright boy," Max said. "What do you think's going to happen?"

George did not say anything.

"I'll tell you," Max said. "We're going to kill a Swede. Do you know a big Swede named Ole Andreson?"

"Yes."

"He comes here to eat every night, don't he?"

"Sometimes he comes here."

"He comes here at six o'clock, don't he?"

"If he comes."

"We know all that, bright boy," Max said. "Talk about something else. Ever go to the movies?"

"Once in a while."

"You ought to go to the movies more. The movies are fine for a bright boy like you."

"What are you going to kill Ole Andreson for? What did he ever do to you?"

"He never had a chance to do anything to us. He never even seen us."

"And he's only going to see us once," Al said from the kitchen.

"What are you going to kill him for, then?" George asked.

"We're killing him for a friend. Just to oblige a friend, bright boy."

"Shut up," said Al from the kitchen. "You talk too goddam much."

"Well, I got to keep bright boy amused. Don't I, bright boy?"

"You talk too damn much," Al said. "The nigger and my bright boy are amused by themselves. I got them tied up like a couple of girl friends in the convent."

"I suppose you were in a convent."

"You never know."

"You were in a kosher convent. That's where you were."

George looked up at the clock.

"If anybody comes in you tell them the cook is off, and if they keep after it, you tell them you'll go back and cook yourself. Do you get that, bright boy?"

"All right," George said. "What you going to do with us afterward?"

"That'll depend," Max said. "That's one of those things you never know at the time."

George looked up at the clock. It was a quarter past six.

The door from the street opened. A street-car motorman came in.

"Hello, George," he said. "Can I get supper?"

"Sam's gone out," George said. "He'll be back in about half an hour."

"I'd better go up the street," the motorman said. George looked at the clock. It was twenty minutes past six.

"That was nice, bright boy," Max said. "You're a regular little gentleman."

"He knew I'd blow his head off," Al said from the kitchen.

"No," said Max. "It ain't that. Bright boy is nice. He's a nice boy. I like him."

At six-fifty-five George said: "He's not coming."

Two other people had been in the lunch-room. Once George had gone out to the kitchen and made a ham-and-egg sandwich "to go" that a man wanted to take with him. Inside the kitchen he saw Al, his derby hat tipped back, sitting on a stool beside the wicket with the muzzle of a sawed-off shotgun resting on the ledge. Nick and the cook were back to back in the corner, a towel tied in each of their mouths. George had cooked the sandwich, wrapped it up in oiled paper, put it in a bag, brought it in, and the man had paid for it and gone out.

"Bright boy can do everything," Max said. "He can cook and everything. You'd make some girl a nice wife, bright boy."

"Yes?" George said. "Your friend, Ole Andreson, isn't going to come."

"We'll give him ten minutes," Max said.

Max watched the mirror and the clock. The hands of the clock marked seven o'clock, and then five minutes past seven.

"Come on, Al," said Max. "We better go. He's not coming."

"Better give him five minutes," Al said from the kitchen.

In the five minutes a man came in, and George explained that the cook was sick.

"Why the hell don't you get another cook?" the man asked. "Aren't you running a lunch-counter?" He went out.

"Come on, Al," Max said.

"What about the two bright boys and the nigger?"

"They're all right."

"You think so?"

"Sure. We're through with it."

"I don't like it," said Al. "It's sloppy. You talk too much."

"Oh, what the hell," said Max. "We got to keep amused, haven't we?"

"You talk too much, all the same," Al said. He came out from the kitchen. The cut-off barrels of the shotgun made a slight bulge under the waist of his too tight-fitting overcoat. He straightened his coat with his gloved hands.

"So long, bright boy," he said to George. "You got a lot of luck."

"That's the truth," Max said. "You ought to play the races, bright boy."

The two of them went out the door. George watched them, through the window, pass under the arc-light and across the street. In their tight overcoats and derby hats they looked like a vaudeville team. George went back through the swinging door into the kitchen and untied Nick and the cook.

"I don't want any more of that," said Sam, the cook. "I don't want any more of that."

Nick stood up. He had never had a towel in his mouth before. "Say," he said. "What the hell?" He was trying to swagger it off.

"They were going to kill Ole Andreson," George said. "They were going to shoot him when he came in to eat."

"Ole Andreson?"

"Sure."

The cook felt the corners of his mouth with his thumbs.

"They all gone?" he asked.

"Yeah," said George. "They're gone now."

"I don't like it," said the cook. "I don't like any of it at all."

"Listen," George said to Nick. "You better go see Ole Andreson."

"All right."

"You better not have anything to do with it at all," Sam, the cook, said. "You better stay way out of it."

"Don't go if you don't want to," George said.

"Mixing up in this ain't going to get you anywhere," the cook said. "You stay out of it."

"I'll go see him," Nick said to George. "Where does he live?" The cook turned away.

"Little boys always know what they want to do," he said.

"He lives up at Hirsch's rooming-house," George said to Nick.

"I'll go up there."

Outside the arc-light shone through the bare branches of a tree. Nick walked up the street beside the car-tracks and turned at the next arc-light down a side-street. Three houses up the street was Hirsch's rooming-house. Nick walked up the two steps and pushed the bell. A woman came to the door.

"Is Ole Andreson here?"

"Do you want to see him?"

"Yes, if he's in."

Nick followed the woman up a flight of stairs and back to the end of a corridor. She knocked on the door.

"Who is it?"

"It's somebody to see you, Mr. Andreson," the woman said.

"It's Nick Adams."

"Come in."

Nick opened the door and went into the room. Ole Andreson was lying on the bed with all his clothes on. He had been a heavyweight prizefighter and he was too long for the bed. He lay with his head on two pillows. He did not look at Nick.

"What was it?" he asked.

"I was up at Henry's," Nick said, "and two fellows came in and tied up me and the cook, and they said they were going to kill you."

It sounded silly when he said it. Ole Andreson said nothing.

"They put us out in the kitchen," Nick went on. "They were going to shoot you when you came in to supper."

Ole Andreson looked at the wall and did not say anything.

"George thought I better come and tell you about it."

"There isn't anything I can do about it," Ole Andreson said.

"I'll tell you what they were like."

"I don't want to know what they were like," Ole Andreson said. He looked at the wall. "Thanks for coming to tell me about it."

"That's all right."

Nick looked at the big man lying on the bed.

"Don't you want me to go and see the police?"

"No," Ole Andreson said. "That wouldn't do any good."

"Isn't there something I could do?"

"No. There ain't anything to do."

"Maybe it was just a bluff."

"No. It ain't just a bluff."

Ole Andreson rolled over toward the wall.

"The only thing is," he said, talking toward the wall, "I just can't make up my mind to go out. I been in here all day."

"Couldn't you get out of town?"

"No," Ole Andreson said. "I'm through with all that running around."

He looked at the wall.

"There ain't anything to do now."

"Couldn't you fix it up some way?"

"No, I got in wrong." He talked in the same flat voice. "There ain't anything to do. After a while I'll make up my mind to go out."

"I better go back and see George," Nick said.

"So long," said Ole Andreson. He did not look toward Nick. "Thanks for coming around."

Nick went out. As he shut the door he saw Ole Andreson with all his clothes on, lying on the bed looking at the wall.

"He's been in his room all day," the landlady said downstairs. "I guess he don't feel well. I said to him: 'Mr. Andreson, you ought to go out and take a walk on a nice fall day like this,' but he didn't feel like it."

"He doesn't want to go out."

"I'm sorry he don't feel well," the woman said. "He's an awfully nice man. He was in the ring, you know."

"I know it."

"You'd never know it except from the way his face is," the woman said. They stood talking just inside the street door. "He's just as gentle."

"Well, good night, Mrs. Hirsch," Nick said.

"I'm not Mrs. Hirsch," the woman said. "She owns the place. I just look after it for her. I'm Mrs. Bell."

"Well, good night, Mrs. Bell," Nick said.

"Good night," the woman said.

Nick walked up the dark street to the corner under the arc-light, and then along the car-tracks to Henry's eating-house. George was inside, back of the counter. "Did you see Ole?"

"Yes," said Nick. "He's in his room and he won't go out."

The cook opened the door from the kitchen when he heard Nick's voice.

"I don't even listen to it," he said and shut the door.

"Did you tell him about it?" George asked.

"Sure. I told him but he knows what it's all about."

"What's he going to do?"

"Nothing."

"They'll kill him."

"I guess they will."

"He must have got mixed up in something in Chicago."

"I guess so," said Nick.

"It's a hell of a thing."

"It's an awful thing," Nick said.

They did not say anything. George reached down for a towel and wiped the counter.

"I wonder what he did?" Nick said.

"Double-crossed somebody. That's what they kill them for."

"I'm going to get out of this town," Nick said.

"Yes," said George. "That's a good thing to do."

"I can't stand to think about him waiting in the room and knowing he's going to get it. It's too damned awful."

"Well," said George, "you better not think about it."

STEPHEN VINCENT BENÉT *(1898–1943)*

THE DEVIL AND DANIEL WEBSTER

IT'S A STORY they tell in the border country, where Massachusetts joins Vermont and New Hampshire.

Yes, Dan'l Webster's dead—or, at least, they buried him. But every time there's a thunderstorm around Marshfield, they say you can hear his rolling voice in the hollows of the sky. And they say that if you go to his grave and speak loud and clear, "Dan'l Webster—Dan'l Webster!" the ground'll begin to shiver and the trees begin to shake. And after a while you'll hear a deep voice saying, "Neighbor, how stands the Union?" Then you better answer the Union stands as she stood, rock bottomed and copper sheathed, one and indivisible, or he's liable to rear right out of the ground. At least, that's what I was told when I was a youngster.

You see, for a while, he was the biggest man in the country. He never got to be President, but he was the biggest man. There were thousands that trusted in him right next to God Almighty, and they told stories about him and all the things that belonged to him that were like the stories of patriarchs and such. They said, when he stood up to speak, stars and stripes came right out in the sky, and once he spoke against a river and made it sink into the ground. They said, when he walked the woods with his fishing rod, Killall, the trout would jump out of the streams right into his pockets, for they knew it was no use putting up a fight against him; and, when he argued a case, he could turn on the harps of the blessed and the shaking of the earth underground. That was the kind of man he was, and his big farm up at Marshfield was suitable to him. The chickens he raised were all white meat down through the drumsticks, the cows were tended like children, and the big ram he called Goliath had horns with a curl like a morning-glory vine and could butt through an iron door. But Dan'l wasn't one of your gentle-man farmers; he knew all the ways of the land, and he'd be up by candlelight to see that the chores got done. A man with a mouth like a mastiff, a brow like a mountain and eyes like burning anthracite—that was Dan'l Webster in his prime. And the biggest case he argued never got written down in the books, for he argued it against the devil, nip and tuck and no holds barred. And this is the way I used to hear it told.

There was a man named Jabez Stone, lived at Cross Cor-ners, New Hampshire. He wasn't a bad man to start with, but he was an unlucky man. If he planted corn, he got borers; if he planted potatoes, he got blight. He had good-enough land, but it didn't prosper him; he had a decent wife and children, but the more children he had, the less there was to feed them. If stones cropped up in his neighbor's field, boul-ders boiled up in his; if he had a horse with the spavins, he'd trade it for one with the staggers and give something extra. There's some folks bound to be like that, apparently. But one day Jabez Stone got sick of the whole business.

He'd been plowing that morning and he'd just broke the plowshare on a rock that he could have sworn hadn't been there yesterday. And, as he stood looking at the plowshare, the off horse began to cough—that ropy kind of cough that means sickness and horse doctors. There were two children down with the measles, his wife was ailing, and he had a whitlow on his thumb. It was about the last straw for Jabez Stone. "I vow," he said, and he looked around him kind of desperate, "I vow it's enough to make a man want to sell his soul to the devil! And I would, too, for two cents!"

Then he felt a kind of queerness come over him at having said what he'd said; though, naturally, being a New Hamp-shireman, he wouldn't take it back. But, all the same, when it got to be evening and, as far as he could see, no notice had been taken, he felt relieved in his mind, for he was a religious man. But notice is always taken, sooner or later, just like the Good Book says. And, sure enough, next day, about suppertime, a soft-spoken, dark-dressed stranger drove up in a handsome buggy and asked for Jabez Stone.

Well, Jabez told his family it was a lawyer, come to see

him about a legacy. But he knew who it was. He didn't like
the looks of the stranger, nor the way he smiled with his
teeth. They were white teeth, and plentiful—some say they
were filed to a point, but I wouldn't vouch for that. And he
didn't like it when the dog took one look at the stranger
and ran away howling, with his tail between his legs. But
having passed the word, more or less, he stuck to it, and they
went out behind the barn and made their bargain. Jabez
Stone had to prick his finger to sign, and the stranger lent
him a silver pin. The wound healed clean, but it left a little
white scar.

After that, all of a sudden, things began to pick up and
prosper for Jabez Stone. His cows got fat and his horses sleek,
his crops were the envy of the neighborhood, and lightning
might strike all over the valley, but it wouldn't strike his barn.
Pretty soon he was one of the prosperous people of the
county; they asked him to stand for selectman, and he stood
for it; there began to be talk of running him for state senate.
All in all, you might say the Stone family was as happy and
contented as cats in a dairy. And so they were, except for
Jabez Stone.

He'd been contented enough for the first few years. It's a
great thing when bad luck turns; it drives most other things
out of your head. True, every now and then, especially in
rainy weather, the little white scar on his finger would give
him a twinge. And once a year, punctual as clockwork, the
stranger with the handsome buggy would come driving by.
But the sixth year the stranger lighted, and, after that, his
peace was over for Jabez Stone.

The stranger came up through the lower field, switching
his boots with a cane—they were handsome black boots, but
Jabez Stone never liked the look of them, particularly the
toes. And, after he'd passed the time of day, he said, "Well,
Mr. Stone, you're a hummer! It's a very pretty property
you've got here, Mr. Stone."

"Well, some might favor it and others might not," said
Jabez Stone, for he was a New Hampshireman.

"Oh, no need to decry your industry!" said the stranger,
very easy, showing his teeth in a smile. "After all, we know
what's been done, and it's been according to contract and

specifications. So when—ahem—the mortgage falls due next year, you shouldn't have any regrets."

"Speaking of that mortgage, mister," said Jabez Stone, and he looked around for help to the earth and the sky, "I'm beginning to have one or two doubts about it."

"Doubts?" said the stranger not quite so pleasantly.

"Why, yes," said Jabez Stone. "This being the U.S.A. and me always having been a religious man." He cleared his throat and got bolder. "Yes, sir," he said, "I'm beginning to have considerable doubts as to that mortgage holding in court."

"There's courts and courts," said the stranger, clicking his teeth. "Still, we might as well have a look at the original document." And he hauled out a big black pocketbook, full of papers. "Sherwin, Slater, Stevens, Stone," he muttered.

" 'I, Jabez Stone, for a term of seven years——' Oh, it's quite in order, I think."

But Jabez Stone wasn't listening, for he saw something else flutter out of the black pocketbook. It was something that looked like a moth, but it wasn't a moth. And as Jabez Stone stared at it, it seemed to speak to him in a small sort of piping voice, terrible small and thin, but terrible human. "Neighbor Stone!" it squeaked. "Neighbor Stone! Help me! For God's sake, help me!"

But before Jabez Stone could stir hand or foot, the stranger whipped out a big bandanna handkerchief, caught the creature in it, just like a butterfly, and started tying up the ends of the bandanna.

"Sorry for the interruption," he said. "As I was saying——"

But Jabez Stone was shaking all over like a scared horse.

"That's Miser Stevens' voice!" he said in a croak. "And you've got him in your handkerchief!"

The stranger looked a little embarrassed.

"Yes, I really should have transferred him to the collecting box," he said with a simper, "but there were some rather unusual specimens there and I don't want them crowded. Well, well, these little contretemps will occur."

"I don't know what you mean by contertan," said Jabez Stone, "but that was Miser Stevens' voice! And he ain't dead!

You can't tell me he is! He was just as spry and mean as a woodchuck Tuesday!"

"In the midst of life . . ." said the stranger, kind of pious. "Listen!" Then a bell began to toll in the valley and Jabez Stone listened, with the sweat running down his face. For he knew it was tolled for Miser Stevens and that he was dead.

"These long-standing accounts," said the stranger with a sigh; "one really hates to close them. But business is business."

He still had the bandanna in his hand, and Jabez Stone felt sick as he saw the cloth struggle and flutter.

"Are they all as small as that?" he asked hoarsely.

"Small?" said the stranger. "Oh, I see what you mean. Why, they vary." He measured Jabez Stone with his eyes, and his teeth showed. "Don't worry, Mr. Stone," he said. "You'll go with a very good grade. I wouldn't trust you outside the collecting box. Now, a man like Dan'l Webster, of course—well, we'd have to build a special box for him, and even at that, I imagine the wing spread would astonish you. He'd certainly be a prize. I wish we could see our way clear to him. But, in your case, as I was saying—"

"Put that handkerchief away!" said Jabez Stone, and he began to beg and to pray. But the best he could get at the end was a three years' extension, with conditions.

But till you make a bargain like that, you've got no idea of how fast four years can run. By the last months of those years Jabez Stone's known all over the state and there's talk of running him for governor—and it's dust and ashes in his mouth. For every day, when he gets up, he thinks, "There's one more night gone," and every night, when he lies down, he thinks of the black pocketbook and the soul of Miser Stevens, and it makes him sick at heart. Till, finally, he can't bear it any longer, and, in the last days of the last year, he hitches up his horse and drives off to seek Dan'l Webster. For Dan'l was born in New Hampshire, only a few miles from Cross Corners, and it's well known that he has a particular soft spot for old neighbors.

It was early in the morning when he got to Marshfield, but Dan'l was up already, talking Latin to the farm hands and wrestling with the ram, Goliath, and trying out a new trotter and working up speeches to make against John C. Calhoun. But when he heard a New Hampshireman had come to see him, he dropped everything else he was doing, for that was Dan'l's way. He gave Jabez Stone a breakfast that five men couldn't eat, went into the living history of every man and woman in Cross Corners, and finally asked him how he could serve him.

Jabez Stone allowed that it was a kind of mortgage case.

"Well, I haven't pleaded a mortgage case in a long time, and I don't generally plead now, except before the Supreme Court," said Dan'l, "but if I can, I'll help you."

"Then I've got hope for the first time in ten years," said Jabez Stone and told him the details.

Dan'l walked up and down as he listened, hands behind his back, now and then asking a question, now and then plunging his eyes at the floor, as if they'd bore through it like gimlets. When Jabez Stone had finished, Dan'l puffed out his cheeks and blew. Then he turned to Jabez Stone and a smile broke over his face like the sunrise over Monadnock.

"You've certainly given yourself the devil's own row to hoe, Neighbor Stone," he said, "but I'll take your case."

"You'll take it?" said Jabez Stone, hardly daring to believe.

"Yes," said Dan'l Webster. "I've got about seventy-five other things to do and the Missouri Compromise to straighten out, but I'll take your case. For if two New Hampshiremen aren't a match for the devil, we might as well give the country back to the Indians."

Then he shook Jabez Stone by the hand and said, "Did you come down here in a hurry?"

"Well, I admit I made time," said Jabez Stone.

"You'll go back faster," said Dan'l Webster, and he told 'em to hitch up Constitution and Constellation to the carriage. They were matched grays with one white forefoot, and they stepped like greased lightning.

Well, I won't describe how excited and pleased the whole Stone family was to have the great Dan'l Webster for a guest, when they finally got there. Jabez Stone had lost his hat on the way, blown off when they overtook a wind, but he didn't take much account of that. But after supper he sent the family off to bed, for he had most particular business with Mr. Webster. Mrs. Stone wanted him to sit in the front parlor, but Dan'l Webster knew front parlors and said he preferred the kitchen. So it was there they sat, waiting for the stranger, with a jug on the table between them and a bright fire on the hearth—the stranger being scheduled to show up on the stroke of midnight, according to specification.

Well, most men wouldn't have asked for better company than Dan'l Webster and a jug. But with every tick of the clock Jabez Stone got sadder and sadder. His eyes roved round, and though he sampled the jug you could see he couldn't taste it. Finally, on the stroke of 11:30 he reached over and grabbed Dan'l Webster by the arm.

"Mr. Webster, Mr. Webster!" he said, and his voice was shaking with fear and a desperate courage. "For God's sake, Mr. Webster, harness your horses and get away from this place while you can!"

"You've brought me a long way, neighbor, to tell me you don't like my company," said Dan'l Webster, quite peaceable, pulling at the jug.

"Miserable wretch that I am!" groaned Jabez Stone. "I've brought you a devilish way, and now I see my folly. Let him take me if he wills. I don't hanker after it, I must say, but I can stand it. But you're the Union's stay and New Hampshire's pride! He mustn't get you, Mr. Webster! He mustn't get you!"

Dan'l Webster looked at the distracted man, all gray and shaking in the firelight, and laid a hand on his shoulder.

"I'm obliged to you, Neighbor Stone," he said gently. "It's kindly thought of. But there's a jug on the table and a case in hand. And I never left a jug or a case half finished in my life."

And just at that moment there was a sharp rap on the door.

"Ah," said Dan'l Webster very coolly, "I thought your clock was a trifle slow, Neighbor Stone." He stepped to the door and opened it. "Come in!" he said.

The stranger came in—very dark and tall he looked in the firelight. He was carrying a box under his arm—a black japanned box with little air holes in the lid. At the sight of the box Jabez Stone gave a low cry and shrank into a corner of the room.

"Mr. Webster, I presume," said the stranger, very polite, but with his eyes glowing like a fox's deep in the woods.

"Attorney of record for Jabez Stone," said Dan'l Webster, but his eyes were glowing too. "Might I ask your name?"

"I've gone by a good many," said the stranger carelessly. "Perhaps Scratch will do for the evening. I'm often called that in these regions."

Then he sat down at the table and poured himself a drink from the jug. The liquor was cold in the jug, but it came steaming into the glass.

"And now," said the stranger, smiling and showing his teeth, "I shall call upon you, as a law-abiding citizen, to assist me in taking possession of my property."

Well, with that the argument began—and it went hot and heavy. At first Jabez Stone had a flicker of hope, but when he saw Dan'l Webster being forced back at point after point, he just sat scrunched in his corner, with his eyes on that japanned box. For there wasn't any doubt as to the deed or the signature—that was the worst of it. Dan'l Webster twisted and turned and thumped his fist on the table, but he couldn't get away from that. He offered to compromise the case; the stranger wouldn't hear of it. He pointed out the property had increased in value, and state senators ought to be worth more; the stranger stuck to the letter of the law. He was a great lawyer, Dan'l Webster, but we know who's the King of Lawyers, as the Good Book tells us, and it seemed as if, for the first time, Dan'l Webster had met his match.

Finally, the stranger yawned a little. "Your spirited efforts on behalf of your client do you credit, Mr. Webster," he said, "but if you have no more arguments to adduce, I'm rather pressed for time . . ." and Jabez Stone shuddered.

Dan'l Webster's brow looked dark as a thundercloud.

"Pressed or not, you shall not have this man!" he thundered. "Mr. Stone is an American citizen, and no American citizen may be forced into the service of a foreign prince. We fought England for that in '12 and we'll fight all hell for it again!"

"Foreign?" said the stranger. "And who calls me a foreigner?"

"Well, I never yet heard of the dev—of your claiming American citizenship," said Dan'l Webster with surprise.

"And who with better right?" said the stranger with one of his terrible smiles. When the first wrong was done to the first Indian, I was there. When the first slaver put out for the Congo, I stood on her deck. Am I not in your books and stories and beliefs, from the first settlements on? Am I not spoken of still in every church in New England? 'Tis true the North claims me for a Southerner and the South for a Northerner, but I am neither. I am merely an honest American like yourself—and of the best descent—for, to tell the truth, Mr. Webster, though I don't like to boast of it, my name is older in this country than yours."

"Aha!" said Dan'l Webster with the veins standing out in his forehead. "Then I stand on the Constitution! I demand a trial for my client!"

"The case is hardly one for an ordinary court," said the stranger, his eyes flickering. "And, indeed, the lateness of the hour——"

"Let it be any court you choose, so it is an American judge and an American jury!" said Dan'l Webster in his pride. "Let it be the quick or the dead; I'll abide the issue!"

"You have said it," said the stranger, and pointed his finger at the door. And with that, and all of a sudden, there was a rushing of wind outside and a noise of footsteps. They came, clear and distinct, through the night. And yet they were not like the footsteps of living men.

"In God's name, who comes by so late?" cried Jabez Stone in an ague of fear.

"The jury Mr. Webster demands," said the stranger, sipping at his boiling glass. "You must pardon the rough appearance of one or two; they will have come a long way."

And with that the fire burned blue and the door blew open and twelve men entered, one by one.

If Jabez Stone had been sick with terror before, he was blind with terror now. For there was Walter Butler, the loyalist, who spread fire and horror through the Mohawk Valley in the times of the Revolution; and there was Simon Girty, the renegade, who saw white men burned at the stake and whooped with the Indians to see them burn. His eyes were green, like a catamount's, and the stains on his hunting shirt did not come from the blood of the deer. King Philip was there, wild and proud as he had been in life, with the great gash in his head that gave him his death wound, and cruel Governor Dale, who broke men on the wheel. There was Morton of Merry Mount, who so vexed the Plymouth Colony, with his flushed, loose, handsome face and his hate of the godly. There was Teach, the bloody pirate, with his black beard curling on his breast. The Reverend John Smeet, with his strangler's hands and his Geneva gown, walked as daintily as he had to the gallows. The red print of the rope was still around his neck, but he carried a perfumed handkerchief in one hand. One and all, they came into the room with the fires of hell still upon them, and the stranger named their names and their deeds as they came, till the tale of twelve was told. Yet the stranger had told the truth—they had all played a part in America.

"Are you satisfied with the jury, Mr. Webster?" said the stranger mockingly, when they had taken their places.

The sweat stood upon Dan'l Webster's brow, but his voice was clear.

"Quite satisfied," he said. "Though I miss General Arnold from the company."

"Benedict Arnold is engaged upon other business," said the stranger with a glower. "Ah, you asked for a justice, I believe."

He pointed his finger once more, and a tall man, soberly clad in Puritan garb, with the burning gaze of the fanatic, stalked into the room and took his judge's place.

"Justice Hathorne is a jurist of experience," said the stranger. "He presided at certain witch trials once held in Salem. There were others who repented of the business later, but not he."

"Repent of such notable wonders and undertakings?" said the stern old justice. "Nay, hang them—hang them all!" And he muttered to himself in a way that struck ice into the soul of Jabez Stone.

Then the trial began, and, as you might expect, it didn't look anyways good for the defense. And Jabez Stone didn't make much of a witness in his own behalf. He took one look

at Simon Girty and screeched, and they had to put him back
in his corner in a kind of swoon.

It didn't halt the trial though; the trial went on, as trials
do. Dan'l Webster had faced some hard juries and hanging
judges in his time, but this was the hardest he'd ever faced,
and he knew it. They sat there with a kind of glitter in their
eyes, and the stranger's smooth voice went on and on. Every
time he'd raise an objection, it'd be "Objection sustained,"
but whenever Dan'l objected, it'd be "Objection denied."
Well, you couldn't expect fair play from a fellow like this
Mr. Scratch.

It got to Dan'l in the end, and he began to heat, like iron
in the forge. When he got up to speak he was going to flay
that stranger with every trick known to the law, and the
judge and jury too. He didn't care if it was contempt of
court or what would happen to him for it. He didn't care
any more what happened to Jabez Stone. He just got madder
and madder, thinking of what he'd say. And yet, curiously
enough, the more he thought about it, the less he was able
to arrange his speech in his mind.

Till, finally, it was time for him to get up on his feet, and
he did so, all ready to bust out with lightnings and denun-
ciations. But before he started he looked over the judge and
jury for a moment, such being his custom. And he noticed
the glitter in their eyes was twice as strong as before, and
they all leaned forward. Like hounds just before they get the
fox, they looked, and the blue mist of evil in the room thick-
ened as he watched them. Then he saw what he'd been about
to do, and he wiped his forehead, as a man might who's just
escaped falling into a pit in the dark.

For it was him they'd come for, not only Jabez Stone. He
read it in the glitter of their eyes and in the way the stranger
hid his mouth with one hand. And if he fought them with
their own weapons, he'd fall into their power; he knew that,
though he couldn't have told you how. It was his own anger
and horror that burned in their eyes; and he'd have to wipe
that out or the case was lost. He stood there for a moment,
his black eyes burning like anthracite. And then he began to
speak.

He started off in a low voice, though you could hear every

word. They say he could call on the harps of the blessed
when he chose. And this was just as simple and easy as a
man could talk. But he didn't start out by condemning or
reviling. He was talking about the things that make a country a country and a man a man.

And he began with the simple things that everybody's
known and felt—the freshness of a fine morning when you're
young, and the taste of food when you're hungry, and the
new day that's every day when you're a child. He took them
up and he turned them in his hands. They were good things
for any man. But without freedom they sickened. And when
he talked of those enslaved, and the sorrows of slavery, his
voice got like a big bell. He talked of the early days of America and the men who had made those days. It wasn't a
spread-eagle speech, but he made you see it. He admitted
all the wrong that had ever been done. But he showed how,
out of the wrong and the right, the suffering and the starva-
tions, something new had come. And everybody had played a
part in it, even the traitors.

Then he turned to Jabez Stone and showed him as he
was—an ordinary man who'd had hard luck and wanted to
change it. And, because he'd wanted to change it, now he
was going to be punished for all eternity. And yet there was
good in Jabez Stone, and he showed that good. He was
hard and mean, in some ways, but he was a man. There was
sadness in being a man, but it was a proud thing too. And
he showed what the pride of it was till you couldn't help
feeling it. Yes, even in hell, if a man was a man, you'd know
it. And he wasn't pleading for any one person any more,
though his voice rang like an organ. He was telling the story
and the failures and the endless journey of mankind. They
got tricked and trapped and bamboozled, but it was a great
journey. And no demon that was ever foaled could know the
inwardness of it—it took a man to do that.

The fire began to die on the hearth and the wind before
morning to blow. The light was getting gray in the room
when Dan'l Webster finished. And his words came back at
the end to New Hampshire ground, and the one spot of
land that each man loves and clings to. He painted a picture
of that, and to each one of that jury he spoke of things

long forgotten. For his voice could search the heart, and that
was his gift and his strength. And to one his voice was like
the forest and its secrecy, and to another like the sea and
the storms of the sea; and one heard the cry of his lost
nation in it, and another saw a little harmless scene he hadn't
remembered for years. But each saw something. And when
Dan'l Webster finished he didn't know whether or not he'd
saved Jabez Stone. But he knew he'd done a miracle. For
the glitter was gone from the eyes of judge and jury, and,
for the moment, they were men again, and knew they were
men.

"The defense rests," said Dan'l Webster and stood there
like a mountain. His ears were still ringing with his speech,
and he didn't hear anything else till he heard Judge Hathorne
say, "The jury will retire to consider its verdict."

Walter Butler rose in his place and his face had a dark,
gay pride on it. "The jury has considered its verdict," he said
and looked the stranger full in the eye. "We find for the
defendant, Jabez Stone."

With that, the smile left the stranger's face, but Walter
Butler did not flinch. "Perhaps 'tis not strictly in accordance
with the evidence," he said, "but even the damned may
salute the eloquence of Mr. Webster."

With that, the long crow of a rooster split the gray morning sky, and judge and jury were gone from the room like
a puff of smoke and as if they had never been there. The
stranger returned to Dan'l Webster, smiling wryly.

"Major Butler was always a bold man," he said. "I had
not thought him quite so bold. Nevertheless, my congratula-
tions, as between two gentlemen."

"I'll have that paper first, if you please," said Dan'l Webster, and he took it and tore it into four pieces. It was queerly
warm to the touch. "And now," he said, "I'll have you!" and
his hand came down like a bear trap on the stranger's arm.
For he knew that once you bested anybody like Mr. Scratch
in fair fight, his power on you was gone. And he could see
that Mr. Scratch knew it too.

The stranger twisted and wriggled, but he couldn't get out
of that grip. "Come, come, Mr. Webster," he said, smiling
palely. "This sort of thing is ridic—ouch!—is ridiculous. If

you're worried about the costs of the case, naturally, I'd be glad to pay——"

"And so you shall!" said Dan'l Webster, shaking him till his teeth rattled. "For you'll sit right down at that table and draw up a document, promising never to bother Jabez Stone nor his heirs or assigns nor any other New Hampshireman till doomsday! For any hades we want to raise in this state, we can raise ourselves, without assistance from strangers."

"Ouch!" said the stranger. "Ouch! Well, they never did run very big to the barrel, but—ouch!—I agree!"

So he sat down and drew up the document. But Dan'l Webster kept his hand on his coat collar all the time.

"And now may I go?" said the stranger, quite humble, when Dan'l'd seen the documents in proper and legal form.

"Go?" said Dan'l, giving him another shake. "I'm still trying to figure out what I'll do with you. For you've settled the costs of the case, but you haven't settled with me. I think I'll take you back to Marshfield," he said, kind of reflective. "I've got a ram there named Goliath that can butt through an iron door. I'd kind of like to turn you loose in his field and see what he'd do."

Well, with that the stranger began to beg and to plead. And he begged and he pled so humble that finally Dan'l, who was naturally kindhearted, agreed to let him go. The stranger seemed terrible grateful for that and said, just to show they were friends, he'd tell Dan'l's fortune before leaving. So Dan'l agreed to that, though he didn't take much stock in fortune-tellers ordinarily. But, naturally, the stranger was a little different.

Well, he pried and he peered at the lines in Dan'l's hands. And he told him one thing and another that was quite remarkable. But they were all in the past.

"Yes, all that's true, and it happened," said Dan'l Webster. "But what's to come in the future?"

The stranger grinned, kind of happily, and shook his head.

"The future's not as you think it," he said. "It's dark. You have a great ambition, Mr. Webster."

"I have," said Dan'l firmly, for everybody knew he wanted to be President.

"It seems almost within your grasp," said the stranger,

"but you will not attain it. Lesser men will be made President and you will be passed over."

"And, if I am, I'll still be Daniel Webster," said Dan'l. "Say on."

"You have two strong sons," said the stranger, shaking his head. "You look to found a line. But each will die in war and neither reach greatness."

"Live or die, they are still my sons," said Dan'l Webster. "Say on."

"You have made great speeches," said the stranger. "You will make more."

"Ah," said Dan'l Webster.

"But the last great speech you make will turn many of your own against you," said the stranger. "They will call you Ichabod; they will call you by other names. Even in New England some will say you have turned your coat and sold your country, and their voices will be loud against you till you die."

"So it is an honest speech, it does not matter what men say," said Dan'l Webster. Then he looked at the stranger and their glances locked.

"One question," he said. "I have fought for the Union all my life. Will I see that fight won against those who would tear it apart?"

"Not while you live," said the stranger grimly, "but it will be won. And after you are dead, there are thousands who will fight for your cause, because of words that you spoke."

"Why, then, you long-barreled, slab-sided, lantern-jawed, fortune-telling note shaver," said Dan'l Webster with a great roar of laughter, "be off with you to your own place before I put my mark on you! For, by the thirteen original colonies, I'd go to the Pit itself to save the Union!"

And with that he drew back his foot for a kick that would have stunned a horse. It was only the tip of his shoe that caught the stranger, but he went flying out of the door with his collecting box under his arm.

"And now," said Dan'l Webster, seeing Jabez Stone beginning to rouse from his swoon, "let's see what's left in the jug, for it's dry work talking all night. I hope there's pie for breakfast, Neighbor Stone."

But they say that whenever the devil comes near Marshfield, even now, he gives it a wide berth. And he hasn't been seen in the state of New Hampshire from that day to this. I'm not talking about Massachusetts or Vermont.

DOROTHY PARKER *(1893–1967)*

BIG BLONDE

HAZEL MORSE was a large, fair woman of the type that incites some men when they use the word "blonde" to click their tongues and wag their heads roguishly. She prided herself upon her small feet and suffered for her vanity, boxing them in snub-toed, high-heeled slippers of the shortest bearable size. The curious things about her were her hands, strange terminations to the flabby white arms splattered with pale tan spots—long, quivering hands with deep and convex nails. She should not have disfigured them with little jewels.

She was not a woman given to recollections. At her middle thirties, her old days were a blurred and flickering sequence, an imperfect film, dealing with the actions of strangers.

In her twenties, after the deferred death of a hazy widowed mother, she had been employed as a model in a wholesale dress establishment—it was still the day of the big woman, and she was then prettily colored and erect and high-breasted. Her job was not onerous, and she met numbers of men and spent numbers of evenings with them, laughing at their jokes and telling them she loved their neckties. Men liked her, and she took it for granted that the liking of many men was a desirable thing. Popularity seemed to her to be worth all the work that had to be put into its achievement. Men liked you because you were fun, and when they liked you they took you out, and there you were. So, and successfully, she was fun. She was a good sport. Men like a good sport.

No other form of diversion, simpler or more complicated,

drew her attention. She never pondered if she might not be better occupied doing something else. Her ideas, or, better, her acceptances, ran right along with those of the other substantially built blondes in whom she found her friends.

When she had been working in the dress establishment some years she met Herbie Morse. He was thin, quick, attractive, with shifting lines about his shiny, brown eyes and a habit of fiercely biting at the skin around his finger nails. He drank largely; she found that entertaining. Her habitual greeting to him was an allusion to his state of the previous night.

"Oh, what a peach you had," she used to say, through her easy laugh. "I thought I'd die, the way you kept asking the waiter to dance with you."

She liked him immediately upon their meeting. She was enormously amused at his fast, slurred sentences, his interpolations of apt phrases from vaudeville acts and comic strips; she thrilled at the feel of his lean arm tucked firm beneath the sleeve of her coat; she wanted to touch the wet, flat surface of his hair. He was as promptly drawn to her. They were married six weeks after they had met.

She was delighted at the idea of being a bride; coquetted with it, played upon it. Other offers of marriage she had had, and not a few of them, but it happened that they were all from stout, serious men who had visited the dress establishment as buyers; men from Des Moines and Houston and Chicago and, in her phrase, even funnier places. There was always something immensely comic to her in the thought of living elsewhere than New York. She could not regard as serious proposals that she share a Western residence.

She wanted to be married. She was nearing thirty now, and she did not take the years well. She spread and softened, and her darkening hair turned her to inexpert dabblings with peroxide. There were times when she had little flashes of fear about her job. And she had had a couple of thousand evenings of being a good sport among her male acquaintances. She had come to be more conscientious than spontaneous about it.

Herbie earned enough, and they took a little apartment far uptown. There was a Mission-furnished dining room with a hanging central light globed in liver-colored glass; in the living room were an "overstuffed suite," a Boston fern, and a reproduction of the Henner *Magdalene* with the red hair and the blue draperies; the bedroom was in gray enamel and old rose, with Herbie's photograph on Hazel's dressing table and Hazel's likeness on Herbie's chest of drawers.

She cooked—and she was a good cook—and marketed and chatted with the delivery boys and the colored laundress. She loved the flat, she loved her life, she loved Herbie. In the first months of their marriage she gave him all the passion she was ever to know.

She had not realized how tired she was. It was a delight, a new game, a holiday, to give up being a good sport. If her head ached or her arches throbbed, she complained piteously, babyishly. If her mood was quiet, she did not talk. If tears came to her eyes, she let them fall.

She fell readily into the habit of tears during the first year of her marriage. Even in her good sport days she had been known to weep lavishly and disinterestedly on occasion. Her behavior at the theater was a standing joke. She could weep at anything in a play—tiny garments, love both unrequited and mutual, seduction, purity, faithful servitors, wedlock, the triangle.

"There goes Haze," her friends would say, watching her. "She's off again."

Wedded and relaxed, she poured her tears freely. To her who had laughed so much, crying was delicious. All sorrows became her sorrows; she was Tenderness. She would cry long and softly over newspaper accounts of kidnaped babies, deserted wives, unemployed men, strayed cats, heroic dogs. Even when the paper was no longer before her, her mind revolved upon these things and the drops slipped rhythmically over her plump cheeks.

"Honestly," she would say to Herbie, "all the sadness there is in the world when you stop to think about it!"

"Yeah," Herbie would say.

She missed nobody. The old crowd, the people who had brought her and Herbie together, dropped from their lives, lingeringly at first. When she thought of this at all it was only to consider it fitting. This was marriage. This was peace.

But the thing was that Herbie was not amused.

For a time he had enjoyed being alone with her. He found the voluntary isolation novel and sweet. Then it palled with a ferocious suddenness. It was as if one night, sitting with her in the steam-heated living room, he would ask no more; and the next night he was through and done with the whole thing.

He became annoyed by her misty melancholies. At first, when he came home to find her softly tired and moody, he kissed her neck and patted her shoulder and begged her to tell her Herbie what was wrong. She loved that. But time slid by, and he found that there was never anything really, personally, the matter.

"Ah, for God's sake," he would say. "Crabbing again. All right, sit here and crab your head off. I'm going out." And he would slam out of the flat and come back late and drunk.

She was completely bewildered by what happened to their Marriage. First they were lovers; and then, it seemed without transition, they were enemies. She never understood it.

There were longer and longer intervals between his leaving his office and his arrival at the apartment. She went through agonies of picturing him run over and bleeding, dead and covered with a sheet. Then she lost her fears for his safety and grew sullen and wounded. When a person wanted to be with a person he came as soon as possible. She desperately wanted him to want to be with her; her own hours only marked the time till he would come. It was often nearly nine o'clock before he came home to dinner. Always he had had many drinks, and their effect would die in him, leaving him loud and querulous and bristling for affronts.

He was too nervous, he said, to sit and do nothing for an evening. He boasted, probably not in all truth, that he had never read a book in his life. "What am I expected to do—sit around this dump on my tail all night?" he would ask rhetorically. And again he would slam out.

She did not know what to do. She could not manage him. She could not meet him.

She fought him furiously. A terrific domesticity had come upon her, and she would bite and scratch to guard it. She wanted what she called "a nice home." She wanted a sober,

tender husband, prompt at dinner, punctual at work. She
wanted sweet, comforting evenings. The idea of intimacy
with other men was terrible to her; the thought that Herbie
might be seeking entertainment in other women set her
frantic.

It seemed to her that almost everything she read—novels
from the drugstore lending library, magazine stories, wom-
en's pages in the papers—dealt with wives who lost their
husbands' love. She could bear those, at that, better than
accounts of neat, companionable marriage and living happily
ever after.

She was frightened. Several times when Herbie came home
in the evening he found her determinedly dressed—she had
had to alter those of her clothes that were not new, to make
them fasten—and rouged.

"Let's go wild to-night, what do you say?" she would hail
him. "A person's got lots of time to hang around and do
nothing when they're dead."

So they would go out, to chop houses and the less expensive cabarets. But it turned out badly. She could no longer
find amusement in watching Herbie drink. She could not
laugh at his whimsicalities, she was so tensely counting his
indulgences. And she was unable to keep back her remon-
strances— "Ah, come on, Herb, you've had enough, haven't
you? You'll feel something terrible in the morning."

He would be immediately enraged. All right, crab; crab,
crab, crab, that was all she ever did. What a lousy sport *she*
was! There would be scenes, and one or the other of them
would rise and stalk out in fury.

She could not recall the definite day that she started drinking, herself. There was nothing separate about her days. Like
drops upon a window-pane, they ran together and trickled
away. She had been married six months; then a year; then
three years.

She had never needed to drink, formerly. She could sit for
most of a night at a table where the others were imbibing
earnestly and never droop in looks or spirits, nor be bored
by the doings of those about her. If she took a cocktail, it
was so unusual as to cause twenty minutes or so of jocular
comment. But now anguish was in her. Frequently, after a

quarrel, Herbie would stay out for the night, and she could not learn from him where the time had been spent. Her heart felt tight and sore in her breast, and her mind turned like an electric fan.

She hated the taste of liquor. Gin, plain or in mixtures, made her promptly sick. After experiment, she found that Scotch whisky was best for her. She took it without water, because that was the quickest way to its effect.

Herbie pressed it on her. He was glad to see her drink. They both felt it might restore her high spirits, and their good times together might again be possible. " 'Atta girl," he would approve her. "Let's see you get boiled, baby."

But it brought them no nearer. When she drank with him there would be a little while of gayety and then, strangely without beginning, they would be in a wild quarrel. They would wake in the morning not sure what it had all been about, foggy as to what had been said and done, but each deeply injured and bitterly resentful. There would be days of vengeful silence.

There had been a time when they had made up their quarrels, usually in bed. There would be kisses and little names and assurances of fresh starts . . . "Oh, it's going to be great now, Herb. We'll have swell times. I was a crab. I guess I might have been tired. But everything's going to be swell. You'll see."

Now there were no gentle reconciliations. They resumed friendly relations only in the brief magnanimity caused by liquor, before more liquor drew them into new battles. The scenes became more violent. There were shouted invectives and pushes, and sometimes sharp slaps. Once she had a black eye. Herbie was horrified next day at sight of it. He did not go to work; he followed her about, suggesting remedies and heaping dark blame on himself. But after they had had a few drinks—"to pull themselves together"—she made so many wistful references to her bruise that he shouted at her, and rushed out, and was gone for two days.

Each time he left the place in rage he threatened never to come back. She did not believe him, nor did she consider separation. Somewhere in her head or her heart was the lazy, nebulous hope that things would change and she and Herbie

settle suddenly into soothing married life. Here were her
home, her furniture, her husband, her station. She summoned
no alternatives.

She could no longer bustle and potter. She had no more
vicarious tears; the hot drops she shed were for herself. She
walked ceaselessly about the rooms, her thoughts running
mechanically round and round Herbie. In those days began
the hatred of being alone that she was never to overcome.
You could be by yourself when things were all right, but
when you were blue you got the howling horrors.

She commenced drinking alone, little, short drinks all
through the day. It was only with Herbie that alcohol made
her nervous and quick in offense. Alone, it blurred sharp
things for her. She lived in a haze of it. Her life took on a
dream-like quality. Nothing was astonishing.

A Mrs. Martin moved into the flat across the hall. She
was a great blonde woman of forty, a promise in looks of
what Mrs. Morse was to be. They made acquaintance,
quickly became inseparable. Mrs. Morse spent her days in
the opposite apartment. They drank together, to brace themselves after the drinks of the nights before.

She never confided her troubles about Herbie to Mrs.
Martin. The subject was too bewildering to her to find comfort in talk. She let it be assumed that her husband's business kept him much away. It was not regarded as important;
husbands, as such, played but shadowy parts in Mrs. Martin's circle.

Mrs. Martin had no visible spouse; you were left to decide
for yourself whether he was or was not dead. She had an
admirer, Joe, who came to see her almost nightly. Often he
brought several friends with him—"The Boys," they were
called. The Boys were big, red, good-humored men, perhaps
forty-five, perhaps fifty. Mrs. Morse was glad of invitations
to join the parties—Herbie was scarcely ever at home at
night now. If he did come home, she did not visit Mrs. Martin. An evening alone with Herbie meant inevitably a quarrel, yet she would stay with him. There was always her thin
and wordless idea that, maybe, this night, things would begin
to be all right.

The boys brought plenty of liquor along with them whenever they came to Mrs. Martin's. Drinking with them, Mrs. Morse became lively and good-natured and audacious. She was quickly popular. When she had drunk enough to cloud her most recent battle with Herbie, she was excited by their approbation. Crab, was she? Rotten sport, was she? Well, there were some that thought different.

Ed was one of The Boys. He lived in Utica—had "his own business" there, was the awed report—but he came to New York almost every week. He was married. He showed Mrs. Morse the then current photographs of Junior and Sister, and she praised them abundantly and sincerely. Soon it was accepted by the others that Ed was her particular friend.

He staked her when they all played poker; sat next to her and occasionally rubbed his knee against hers during the game. She was rather lucky. Frequently she went home with a twenty-dollar bill or a ten-dollar bill or a handful of crumpled dollars. She was glad of them. Herbie was getting, in her words, something awful about money. To ask him for it brought an instant row.

"What the hell do you do with it?" he would say. "Shoot it all on Scotch?"

"I try to run this house halfway decent," she would retort. "Never thought of that, did you? Oh, no, his lordship couldn't be bothered with that."

Again, she could not find a definite day to fix the beginning of Ed's proprietorship. It became his custom to kiss her on the mouth when he came in, as well as for farewell, and he gave her little quick kisses of approval all through the evening. She liked this rather more than she disliked it. She never thought of his kisses when she was not with him.

He would run his hand lingeringly over her back and shoulders.

"Some dizzy blonde, eh?" he would say. "Some doll."

One afternoon she came home from Mrs. Martin's to find Herbie in the bedroom. He had been away for several nights, evidently on a prolonged drinking bout. His face was gray, his hands jerked as if they were on wires. On the bed were two old suitcases, packed high. Only her photograph remained on his bureau, and the wide doors of his closet disclosed nothing but coat hangers.

"I'm blowing," he said. "I'm through with the whole works. I got a job in Detroit."

She sat down on the edge of the bed. She had drunk much the night before, and the four Scotches she had had with Mrs. Martin had only increased her fogginess.

"Good job?" she said.

"Oh, yeah," he said. "Looks all right."

He closed a suitcase with difficulty, swearing at it in whispers.

"There's some dough in the bank," he said. "The bank book's in your top drawer. You can have the furniture and stuff." He looked at her, and his forehead twitched.

"God damn it, I'm through, I'm telling you," he cried. "I'm through."

"All right, all right," she said. "I heard you, didn't I?"

She saw him as if he were at one end of a cañon and she at the other. Her head was beginning to ache bumpingly, and her voice had a dreary, tiresome tone. She could not have raised it. "Like a drink before you go?" she asked.

Again he looked at her, and a corner of his mouth jerked up.

"Cockeyed again for a change, aren't you?" he said. "That's nice. Sure, get a couple of shots, will you?"

She went to the pantry, mixed him a stiff highball, poured herself a couple of inches of whisky, and drank it. Then she gave herself another portion and brought the glasses into the bedroom. He had strapped both suitcases and had put on his hat and overcoat. He took his highball.

"Well," he said, and he gave a sudden, uncertain laugh. "Here's mud in your eye."

"Mud in your eye," she said.

They drank. He put down his glass and took up the heavy suitcases. "Got to get a train around six," he said.

She followed him down the hall. There was a song, a song that Mrs. Martin played doggedly on the phonograph, running loudly through her mind. She had never liked the thing.

> Night and daytime,
> Always playtime.
> Ain't we got fun?

At the door he put down the bags and faced her.

"Well," he said. "Well, take care of yourself. You'll be all right, will you?"

"Oh, sure," she said.

He opened the door, then came back to her, holding out his hand.

" 'Bye, Haze," he said. "Good luck to you."

She took his hand and shook it.

"Pardon my wet glove," she said.

When the door had closed behind him she went back to the pantry.

She was flushed and lively when she went in to Mrs. Martin's that evening. The Boys were there, Ed among them. He was glad to be in town, frisky and loud and full of jokes. But she spoke quietly to him for a minute.

"Herbie blew to-day," she said. "Going to live out West."

"That so?" he said. He looked at her and played with the fountain pen clipped to his waistcoat pocket.

"Think he's gone for good, do you?" he asked.

"Yeah," she said. "I know he is. I know. Yeah."

"You going to live on across the hall just the same?" he said. "Know what you're going to do?"

"Gee, I don't know," she said. "I don't give much of a damn."

"Oh, come on, that's no way to talk," he told her. "What you need—you need a little snifter. How about it?"

"Yeah," she said. "Just straight."

She won forty-three dollars at poker. When the game broke up Ed took her back to her apartment.

"Got a little kiss for me?" he asked.

He wrapped her in his big arms and kissed her violently. She was entirely passive. He held her away and looked at her.

"Little tight, honey?" he asked anxiously. "Not going to be sick, are you?"

"Me?" she said. "I'm swell."

II

When Ed left in the morning he took her photograph with him. He said he wanted her picture to look at, up in Utica. "You can have that one on the bureau," she said.

She put Herbie's picture in a drawer, out of her sight. When she could look at it she meant to tear it up. She was fairly successful in keeping her mind from racing around him. Whisky slowed it for her. She was almost peaceful, in her mist.

She accepted her relationship with Ed without question or enthusiasm. When he was away she seldom thought definitely of him. He was good to her; he gave her frequent presents and a regular allowance. She was even able to save. She did not plan ahead of any day, but her wants were few, and you might as well put money in the bank as have it lying around.

When the lease of her apartment neared its end it was Ed who suggested moving. His friendship with Mrs. Martin and Joe had become strained over a dispute at poker; a feud was impending.

"Let's get the hell out of here," Ed said. "What I want you to have is a place near the Grand Central. Make it easier for me." So she took a little flat in the Forties. A colored maid came in every day to clean and to make coffee for her —she was "through with that housekeeping stuff," she said, and Ed, twenty years married to a passionately domestic woman, admired this romantic uselessness and felt doubly a man of the world in abetting it.

The coffee was all she had until she went out to dinner, but alcohol kept her fat. Prohibition she regarded only as a basis for jokes. You could always get all you wanted. She was never noticeably drunk and seldom nearly sober. It required a larger daily allowance to keep her misty-minded. Too little, and she was achingly melancholy.

Ed brought her to Jimmy's. He was proud, with the pride of the transient who would be mistaken for a native, in his knowledge of small, recent restaurants occupying the lower floors of shabby brownstone houses; places where, upon mentioning the name of an habitué friend, might be obtained strange whisky and fresh gin in many of their ramifications. Jimmy's place was the favorite of his acquaintances.

There, through Ed, Mrs. Morse met many men and women, formed quick friendships. The men often took her out when Ed was in Utica. He was proud of her popularity.

She fell into the habit of going to Jimmy's alone when she had no engagement. She was certain to meet some people she knew, and join them. It was a club for her friends, both men and women.

The women at Jimmy's looked remarkably alike, and this was curious, for, through feuds, removals and opportunities of more profitable contacts, the personnel of the group changed constantly. Yet always the newcomers resembled those whom they replaced. They were all big women and stout, broad of shoulder and abundantly breasted, with faces thickly clothed in soft, high-colored flesh. They laughed loud and often, showing opaque and lusterless teeth like squares of crockery. There was about them the health of the big, yet a slight, unwholesome suggestion of stubborn preservation. They might have been thirty-six or forty-five or anywhere between.

They composed their titles of their own first names with their husbands' surnames—Mrs. Florence Miller, Mrs. Vera Riley, Mrs. Lilian Block. This gave at the same time the solidity of marriage and the glamour of freedom. Yet only one or two were actually divorced. Most of them never referred to their dimmed spouses; some, a shorter time separate, described them in terms of great biological interest.

Several were mothers, each of an only child—a boy at school somewhere, or a girl being cared for by a grandmother. Often, well on toward morning, there would be displays of kodak portraits and of tears.

They were comfortable women, cordial and friendly and irrepressibly matronly. Theirs was the quality of ease. Become fatalistic, especially about money matters, they were unworried. Whenever their funds dropped alarmingly, a new donor appeared; this had always happened. The aim of each was to have one man, permanently, to pay all her bills, in return for which she would have immediately given up other

admirers and probably would have become exceedingly fond
of him; for the affections of all of them were, by now, unex-
acting, tranquil, and easily arranged. This end, however,
grew increasingly difficult yearly. Mrs. Morse was regarded
as fortunate.

Ed had a good year, increased her allowance and gave
her a sealskin coat. But she had to be careful of her moods
with him. He insisted upon gayety. He would not listen to
admissions of aches or weariness.

"Hey, listen," he would say, "I got worries of my own,
and plenty. Nobody wants to hear other people's troubles,
sweetie. What you got to do, you got to be a sport and forget
it. See? Well, slip us a little smile, then. That's my girl."

She never had enough interest to quarrel with him as she
had with Herbie, but she wanted the privilege of occasional
admitted sadness. It was strange. The other women she saw
did not have to fight their moods. There was Mrs. Florence
Miller who got regular crying jags, and the men sought only
to cheer and comfort her. The others spent whole evenings
in grieved recitals of worries and ills; their escorts paid them
deep sympathy. But she was instantly undesirable when she
was in low spirits. Once, at Jimmy's, when she could not
make herself lively, Ed had walked out and left her.

"Why the hell don't you stay home and not go spoiling
everybody's evening?" he had roared.

Even her slightest acquaintance seemed irritated if she
were not conspicuously light-hearted.

"What's the matter with you, anyway?" they would say.
"Be your age, why don't you? Have a little drink and snap
out of it."

When her relationship with Ed had continued nearly three
years he moved to Florida to live. He hated leaving her; he
gave her a large check and some shares of a sound stock, and
his pale eyes were wet when he said good-bye. She did not
miss him. He came to New York infrequently, perhaps two
or three times a year, and hurried directly from the train to
see her. She was always pleased to have him come and never
sorry to see him go.

Charley, an acquaintance of Ed's that she had met at
Jimmy's, had long admired her. He had always made oppor-

tunities of touching her and leaning close to talk to her. He asked repeatedly of all their friends if they had ever heard such a fine laugh as she had. After Ed left Charley became the main figure in her life. She classified him and spoke of him as "not so bad." There was nearly a year of Charley; then she divided her time between him and Sydney, another frequenter of Jimmy's; then Charley slipped away altogether.

Sydney was a little, brightly dressed, clever Jew. She was perhaps nearest contentment with him. He amused her always; her laughter was not forced.

He admired her completely. Her softness and size delighted him. And he thought she was great, he often told her, because she kept gay and lively when she was drunk.

"Once I had a gal," he said, "used to try to throw herself out of the window every time she got a can on, Jee-*zuss*," he added feelingly.

Then Sydney married a rich and watchful bride, and then there was Billy. No—after Sydney came Fred, then Billy. In her haze she never recalled how men entered her life and left it. There were no surprises. She had no thrill at their advent nor woe at their departure. She seemed to be always able to attract men. There was never another as rich as Ed, but they were all generous to her, in their means.

Once she had news of Herbie. She met Mrs. Martin dining at Jimmy's, and the old friendship was vigorously renewed. The still admiring Joe, while on a business trip, had seen Herbie. He had settled in Chicago, he looked fine, he was living with some woman—seemed to be crazy about her. Mrs. Morse had been drinking vastly that day. She took the news with mild interest, as one hearing of the sex peccadilloes of somebody whose name is, after a moment's groping, familiar.

"Must be damn near seven years since I saw him," she commented. "Gee, seven years."

More and more her days lost their individuality. She never knew dates, nor was sure of the day of the week.

"My God, was that a year ago!" she would exclaim, when an event was recalled in conversation.

She was tired so much of the time. Tired and blue. Almost everything could give her the blues. Those old horses she saw on Sixth Avenue—struggling and slipping along the car tracks, or standing at the curb, their heads dropped level with their worn knees. The tightly stored tears would squeeze from her eyes as she teetered past on her aching feet in the stubby, champagne-colored slippers.

The thought of death came and stayed with her and lent her a sort of drowsy cheer. It would be nice, nice and restful, to be dead.

There was no settled, shocked moment when she first thought of killing herself; it seemed to her as if the idea had always been with her. She pounced upon all the accounts of suicides in the newspapers. There was an epidemic of self-killings—or maybe it was just that she searched for the stories of them so eagerly that she found many. To read of them roused reassurance in her; she felt cozy solidarity with the big company of the voluntary dead.

She slept, aided by whisky, till deep into the afternoons, then lay abed, a bottle and glass at her hand, until it was time to dress to go out for dinner. She was beginning to feel toward alcohol a little puzzled distrust, as toward an old friend who has refused a simple favor. Whisky could still soothe her for most of the time, but there were sudden, inexplicable moments when the cloud fell treacherously away from her, and she was sawn by the sorrow and bewilderment and nuisance of all living. She played voluptuously with the thought of cool, sleepy retreat. She had never been troubled by religious belief, and no vision of an after-life intimidated her. She dreamed by day of never again putting on tight shoes, of never having to laugh and listen and admire, of never more being a good sport. Never.

But how would you do it? It made her sick to think of jumping from heights. She could not stand a gun. At the theater, if one of the actors drew a revolver, she crammed her fingers into her ears and could not even look at the stage until after the shot had been fired. There was no gas in her flat. She looked long at the bright blue veins in her slim wrists—a cut with a razor blade, and there you'd be. But it would hurt, hurt like hell, and there would be blood to see. Poison—something tasteless and quick and painless—was the thing. But they wouldn't sell it to you in the drug stores, because of the law. She had few other thoughts.

There was a new man now—Art. He was short and fat and exacting and hard on her patience when he was drunk. But there had been only occasionals for some time before him, and she was glad of a little stability. Too, Art must be away for weeks at a stretch, selling silks, and that was restful. She was convincingly gay with him, though the effort shook her viciously.

"The best sport in the world," he would murmur, deep in her neck. "The best sport in the world."

One night, when he had taken her to Jimmy's, she went into the dressing room with Mrs. Florence Miller. There, while designing curly mouths on their faces with lip rouge, they compared experiences of insomnia.

"Honestly," Mrs. Morse said, "I wouldn't close an eye if I didn't go to bed full of Scotch. I lie there and toss and turn and toss and turn. Blue! Does a person get blue lying awake that way!"

"Say, listen, Hazel," Mrs. Miller said impressively, "I'm telling you I'd be awake for a year if I didn't take veronal. That stuff makes you sleep like a fool."

"Isn't it poison or something?" Mrs. Morse asked.

"Oh, you take too much and you're out for the count," said Mrs. Miller. "I just take five grains—they come in tablets. I'd be scared to fool around with it. But five grains and you cork off pretty."

"Can you get it anywhere?" Mrs. Morse felt superbly Machiavellian.

"Get all you want in Jersey," said Mrs. Miller. "They won't give it to you here without you have a doctor's prescription. Finished? We'd better go back and see what the boys are doing."

That night Art left Mrs. Morse at the door of her apartment; his mother was in town. Mrs. Morse was still sober, and it happened that there was no whisky left in her cupboard. She lay in bed, looking up at the black ceiling.

She rose early, for her, and went to New Jersey. She had never taken the tube, and did not understand it. So she went to the Pennsylvania Station and bought a railroad ticket to Newark. She thought of nothing in particular on the trip out. She looked at the uninspired hats of the women about her and gazed through the smeared window at the flat, gritty scene.

In Newark, in the first drug store she came to, she asked for a tin of talcum powder, a nail brush, and a box of veronal tablets. The powder and the brush were to make the hypnotic seem also a casual need. The clerk was entirely unconcerned. "We only keep them in bottles," he said, and wrapped up for her a little glass vial containing ten white tablets, stacked one on another.

She went to another drug store and bought a face cloth, an orangewood stick and a bottle of veronal tablets. The clerk was also uninterested.

"Well, I guess I got enough to kill an ox," she thought, and went back to the station.

At home, she put the little vials in the drawer of her dressing table and stood looking at them with a dreamy tenderness.

"There they are, God bless them," she said, and she kissed her finger tip and touched each bottle.

The colored maid was busy in the living room.

"Hey, Nettie," Mrs. Morse called. "Be an angel, will you? Run around to Jimmy's and get me a quart of Scotch."

She hummed while she awaited the girl's return.

During the next few days, whisky ministered to her as tenderly as it had done when she first turned to its aid. Alone, she was soothed and vague, at Jimmy's she was the gayest of the group. Art was delighted with her.

Then, one night, she had an appointment to meet Art at Jimmy's for an early dinner. He was to leave afterward on a business excursion, to be away for a week. Mrs. Morse had been drinking all the afternoon; while she dressed to go out she felt herself rising pleasurably from drowsiness to high spirits. But as she came out into the street the effects of the whisky deserted her completely, and she was filled with a slow, grinding wretchedness so horrible that she stood swaying on the pavement, unable for a moment to move forward. It was a gray night with spurts of mean, thin snow, and the streets shone with dark ice. As she slowly crossed Sixth Avenue consciously dragging one foot past the other, a big, scarred horse pulling a rickety express wagon crashed to his

knees before her. The driver swore and screamed and lashed
the beast insanely, bringing the whip back over his shoulder
for every blow, while the horse struggled to get a footing
on the slippery asphalt. A group gathered and watched with
interest.

Art was waiting, when Mrs. Morse reached Jimmy's.

"What's the matter with you, for God's sake?" was his
greeting to her.

"I saw a horse," she said. "Gee, I—a person feels sorry for
horses. I—it isn't just horses. Everything's kind of terrible,
isn't it? I can't help getting sunk."

"Ah, sunk, me eye," he said. "What's the idea of all the
bellyaching? What have you got to be sunk about?"

"I can't help it," she said.

"Ah, help it, me eye," he said. "Pull yourself together, will
you? Come on and sit down, and take that face off you."

She drank industriously and she tried hard, but she could
not overcome her melancholy. Others joined them and commented on her gloom, and she could do no more for them
than smile weakly. She made little dabs at her eyes with
her handkerchief, trying to time her movements so they
would be unnoticed, but several times Art caught her and
scowled and shifted impatiently in his chair.

When it was time for him to go to his train she said she
would leave, too, and go home.

"And not a bad idea, either," he said. "See if you can't
sleep yourself out of it. I'll see you Thursday. For God's
sake, try and cheer up by then, will you?"

"Yeah," she said. "I will."

In her bedroom she undressed with a tense speed wholly
unlike her usually slow uncertainty. She put on her nightgown,
took off her hair net, and passed the comb quickly through
her dry, varicolored hair. Then she took the two little vials
from the drawer and carried them into the bathroom. The
splintering misery had gone from her, and she felt the quick
excitement of one who is about to receive an anticipated gift.

She uncorked the vials, filled a glass with water, and stood
before the mirror, a tablet between her fingers. Suddenly she
bowed graciously to her reflection and raised the glass to it.

"Well, here's mud in your eye," she said.

The tablets were unpleasant to take, dry and powdery and sticking obstinately halfway down her throat. It took her a long time to swallow all twenty of them. She stood watching her reflection with deep, impersonal interest, studying the movements of the gulping throat. Once more she spoke aloud to it.

"For God's sake, try and cheer up by Thursday, will you?" she said. "Well, you know what he can do. He and the whole lot of them."

She had no idea how quickly to expect effect from the veronal. When she had taken the last tablet she stood uncertainly, wondering, still with a courteous, vicarious interest, if death would strike her down then and there. She felt in no way strange, save for a slight stirring of sickness from the effort of swallowing the tablets, nor did her reflected face look at all different. It would not be immediate, then; it might even take an hour or so.

She stretched her arms high and gave a vast yawn.

"Guess I'll go to bed," she said. "Gee, I'm nearly dead."

That struck her as comic, and she turned out the bathroom light and went in and laid herself down in her bed, chuckling softly all the time.

"Gee, I'm nearly dead," she quoted. "That's a hot one!"

III

Nettie, the colored maid, came in late the next afternoon to clean the apartment and found Mrs. Morse in her bed. But then, that was not unusual. Usually, though, the sounds of cleaning waked her, and she did not like to wake up. Nettie, an agreeable girl, had learned to move softly about her work.

But when she had done the living room and stolen in to tidy the little square bedroom, she could not avoid a tiny clatter as she arranged the objects on the dressing table. Instinctively she glanced over her shoulder at the sleeper, and without warning a sickly uneasiness crept over her. She came to the bed and stared down at the woman lying there.

Mrs. Morse lay on her back, one flabby white arm flung up, the wrist against her forehead. Her stiff hair hung untenderly along her face. The bed covers were pushed down, exposing a deep square of soft neck and a pink nightgown, its fabric uneven by many launderings, her great breasts, freed from their tight confiner, sagged beneath her armpits. Now and then she made knotted, snoring sounds, and from the corner of her opened mouth to the blurred turn of her jaw ran a lane of crusted spittle.

"Mis' Morse," Nettie called. "Oh, Mis' Morse! It's terrible late." Mrs. Morse made no move.

"Mis' Morse," said Nettie. "Look, Mis' Morse. How'm I goin' get this bed made?" Panic sprang upon the girl. She shook the woman's hot shoulder.

"Ah, wake up, will yuh?" she whined. "Ah, please wake up."

Suddenly the girl turned and ran out in the hall to the elevator door, keeping her thumb firm on the black, shiny button until the elderly car and its Negro attendant stood before her. She poured a jumble of words over the boy and led him back to the apartment. He tiptoed creakingly in to the bedside; first gingerly, then so lustily that he left marks in the soft flesh, he prodded the unconscious woman.

"Hey, there!" he cried, and listened intently, as for an echo.

"Jeez. Out like a light," he commented.

At his interest in the spectacle, Nettie's panic left her. Importance was big in both of them. They talked in quick, unfinished whispers, and it was the boy's suggestion that he fetch the young doctor who lived on the ground floor. Nettie hurried along with him. They looked forward to the limelit moment of breaking their news of something untoward, something pleasurably unpleasant. Mrs. Morse had become the medium of drama. With no ill wish to her, they hoped that her state was serious, that she would not let them down by being awake and normal on their return. A little fear of this determined them to make the most, to the doctor, of her present condition. "Matter of life and death" returned to Nettie from her thin store of reading. She considered startling the doctor with the phrase.

The doctor was in and none too pleased at the interruption. He wore a yellow and blue striped dressing gown, and he

was lying on his sofa, laughing, with a dark girl, her face
scaly with inexpensive powder, who perched on the arm.
Half-emptied highball glasses stood beside them, and her
coat and hat were neatly hung up with the comfortable implication of a long stay.

Always something, the doctor grumbled. Couldn't let anybody alone after a hard day. But he put some bottles and
instruments into a case, changed his dressing gown for his
coat, and started out with the Negroes.

"Snap it up there, big boy," the girl called after him.
"Don't be all night."

The doctor strode loudly into Mrs. Morse's flat and on to
the bedroom, Nettie and the boy right behind him. Mrs.
Morse had not moved; her sleep was as deep, but soundless,
now. The doctor looked sharply at her, then plunged his
thumbs into the lidded pits above her eyeballs and threw his
weight upon them. A high, sickened cry broke from Nettie.

"Look like he tryin' to push her right on th'ough the bed,"
said the boy. He chuckled. Mrs. Morse gave no sign under
the pressure. Abruptly the doctor abandoned it, and with
one quick movement swept the covers down to the foot of
the bed. With another he flung her nightgown back and
lifted the thick, white legs, crosshatched with blocks of tiny,
iris-colored veins. He pinched them repeatedly, with long,
cruel nips, back of the knees. She did not awaken.

"What's she been drinking?" he asked Nettie, over his
shoulder.

With the certain celerity of one who knows just where to
lay hands on a thing, Nettie went into the bathroom, bound
for the cupboard where Mrs. Morse kept her whisky. But
she stopped at the sight of the two vials, with their red and
white labels, lying before the mirror. She brought them to
the doctor.

"Oh, for the Lord Almighty's sweet sake!" he said. He
dropped Mrs. Morse's limp legs and pushed them impatiently
across the bed. "What did she want to go taking that tripe
for? Rotten yellow trick, that's what a thing like that is. Now
we'll have to pump her out, and all that stuff. Nuisance, a
thing like that is; that's what it amounts to. Here, George,

take me down in the elevator. You wait here, maid. She won't do anything."

"She won't die on me, will she?" cried Nettie.

"No," said the doctor. "God, no. You couldn't kill her with an ax."

IV

After two days, Mrs. Morse came back to consciousness, dazed at first, then with a comprehension that brought with it the slow, saturating wretchedness.

"Oh, Lord, oh, Lord," she moaned, and tears for herself and for life striped her cheeks.

Nettie came in at the sound. For two days she had done the ugly, incessant tasks in the nursing of the unconscious, for two nights she had caught broken bits of sleep on the living room couch. She looked coldly at the big, blown woman in the bed.

"What you been tryin' to do, Mis' Morse?" she said. "What kine o' work is that, takin' all that stuff?"

"Oh, Lord," moaned Mrs. Morse again, and she tried to cover her eyes with her arms. But the joints felt stiff and brittle, and she cried out at their ache.

"That's no way to ack, takin' them pills," said Nettie. "You can thank you' stars you heah at all. How you feel now?"

"Oh, I feel great," said Mrs. Morse. "Swell, I feel."

Her hot, painful tears fell as if they would never stop.

"Tha's no way to take on, cryin' like that," Nettie said. "After what you done. The doctor, he says he could have you arrested, doin' a thing like that. He was fit to be tied, here."

"Why couldn't he let me alone?" wailed Mrs. Morse. "Why the hell couldn't he have?"

"That's terr'ble, Mis' Morse, swearin' an' talkin' like that," said Nettie, "after what people done for you. Here I ain' had no sleep at all, an' I had to give up goin' out to my other ladies!"

"Oh, I'm sorry, Nettie," she said. "You're a peach. I'm sorry I've given you so much trouble. I couldn't help it. I just got sunk. Didn't you ever feel like doing it? When everything looks just lousy to you?"

"I wouldn't think o' no such thing," declared Nettie. "You got to cheer up. Tha's what you got to do. Everybody's got their troubles."

"Yeah," said Mrs. Morse. "I know."

"Come a pretty picture card for you," Nettie said. "Maybe that will cheer you up."

She handed Mrs. Morse a post card. Mrs. Morse had to cover one eye with her hand, in order to read the message; her eyes were not yet focusing correctly.

It was from Art. On the back of a view of the Detroit Athletic Club he had written: *Greetings and salutations. Hope you have lost that gloom. Cheer up and don't take any rubber nickels. See you on Thursday.* She dropped the card to the floor. Misery crushed her as if she were between great smooth stones. There passed before her a slow, slow pageant of days spent lying in her flat, of evenings at Jimmy's being a good sport, making herself laugh and coo at Art and other Arts; she saw a long parade of weary horses and shivering beggars and all beaten, driven, stumbling things. Her feet throbbed as if she had crammed them into the stubby champagne-colored slippers. Her heart seemed to swell and fester.

"Nettie," she cried, "for heaven's sake, pour me a drink, will you?"

The maid looked doubtful.

"Now you know, Mis' Morse," she said, "you been near daid. I don' know if the doctor he let you drink nothin' yet."

"Oh, never mind him," she said. "You get me one and bring in the bottle. Take one yourself."

"Well," said Nettie.

She poured them each a drink, deferentially leaving hers in the bathroom to be taken in solitude, and brought Mrs. Morse's glass in to her.

Mrs. Morse looked into the liquor and shuddered back from its odor. Maybe it would help. Maybe, when you had been knocked cold for a few days, your very first drink would give you a lift. Maybe whisky would be her friend again. She prayed without addressing God, without knowing a God. Oh, please, please, let her be able to get drunk, please keep her always drunk. She lifted the glass.

"Thanks, Nettie," she said. "Here's mud in your eye."

The maid giggled. "Tha's the way, Mis' Morse," she said. "You cheer up, now."

"Yeah," said Mrs. Morse. "Sure."

WILLA CATHER *(1876–1947)*

PAUL'S CASE

IT WAS Paul's afternoon to appear before the faculty of the Pittsburgh High School to account for his various misdemeanors. He had been suspended a week ago, and his father had called at the Principal's office and confessed his perplexity about his son. Paul entered the faculty room suave and smiling. His clothes were a trifle outgrown, and the tan velvet on the collar of his open overcoat was frayed and worn; but for all that there was something of the dandy about him, and he wore an opal pin in his neatly knotted black four-in-hand, and a red carnation in his buttonhole. This latter adornment the faculty somehow felt was not properly significant of the contrite spirit befitting a boy under the ban of suspension.

Paul was tall for his age and very thin, with high, cramped shoulders and a narrow chest. His eyes were remarkable for a certain hysterical brilliancy, and he continually used them in a conscious, theatrical sort of way, peculiarly offensive in a boy. The pupils were abnormally large, as though he were addicted to belladonna, but there was a glassy glitter about them which that drug does not produce.

When questioned by the Principal as to why he was there, Paul stated, politely enough, that he wanted to come back to school. This was a lie, but Paul was quite accustomed to lying; found it, indeed, indispensable for overcoming friction. His teachers were asked to state their respective charges against him, which they did with such a rancor and aggrievedness as evinced that this was not a usual case. Disorder and impertinence were among the offenses named, yet each of his instructors felt that it was scarcely possible to put into words the real cause of the trouble, which lay in a sort of hysterically defiant manner of the boy's; in the contempt which they all knew he felt for them, and which he seemingly made not the least effort to conceal. Once, when he had been making a synopsis of a paragraph at the blackboard, his English teacher had stepped to his side and attempted to guide his hand. Paul had started back with a shudder and thrust his hands violently behind him. The astonished woman could scarcely have been more hurt and embarrassed had he struck at her. The insult was so involuntary and definitely personal as to be unforgettable. In one way and another, he had made all his teachers, men and women alike, conscious of the same feeling of physical aversion. In one class he habitually sat with his hand shading his eyes; in another he always looked out of the window during the recitation; in another he made a running commentary on the lecture, with humorous intent.

His teachers felt this afternoon that his whole attitude was symbolized by his shrug and his flippantly red carnation flower, and they fell upon him without mercy, his English teacher leading the pack. He stood through it smiling, his pale lips parted over his white teeth. (His lips were continually twitching, and he had a habit of raising his eyebrows that was contemptuous and irritating to the last degree.) Older boys than Paul had broken down and shed tears under the ordeal, but his set smile did not once desert him, and his only sign of discomfort was the nervous trembling of the fingers that toyed with the buttons of his overcoat, and an occasional jerking of the other hand which held his hat. Paul was always smiling, always glancing about him, seeming to feel that people might be watching him and trying to detect something. This conscious expression, since it was as far as possible from boyish mirthfulness, was usually attributed to insolence or "smartness."

As the inquisition proceeded, one of his instructors repeated an impertinent remark of the boy's, and the Principal asked him whether he thought that a courteous speech to make to a woman. Paul shrugged his shoulder slightly and his eyebrows twitched.

"I don't know," he replied. "I didn't mean to be polite or impolite, either. I guess it's a sort of way I have, of saying things regardless."

The Principal asked him whether he didn't think that a way it would be well to get rid of. Paul grinned and said he guessed so. When he was told that he could go, he bowed gracefully and went out. His bow was like a repetition of the scandalous red carnation.

His teachers were in despair, and his drawing master voiced the feeling of them all when he declared there was something about the boy which none of them understood. He added: "I don't really believe that smile of his comes altogether from insolence; there's something sort of haunted about it. The boy is not strong, for one thing. There is something wrong about the fellow."

The drawing master had come to realize that, in looking at Paul, one saw only his white teeth and the forced animation of his eyes. One warm afternoon the boy had gone to sleep at his drawing board, and his master had noted with amazement what a white, blue-veined face it was; drawn and wrinkled like an old man's about the eyes, the lips twitching even in his sleep.

His teachers left the building dissatisfied and unhappy; humiliated to have felt so vindictive toward a mere boy, to have uttered this feeling in cutting terms, and to have set each other on, as it were, in the gruesome game of intemperate reproach. One of them remembered having seen a miserable street cat set at bay by a ring of tormentors.

As for Paul, he ran down the hill whistling the Soldiers' Chorus from *Faust*, looking wildly behind him now and then to see whether some of his teachers were not there to witness his light-heartedness. As it was now late in the afternoon and Paul was on duty that evening as usher at Carnegie Hall, he decided that he would not go home to supper.

When he reached the concert hall the doors were not yet open. It was chilly outside, and he decided to go up into the picture gallery—always deserted at this hour—where there were some of Raffelli's gay studies of Paris streets and an airy blue Venetian scene or two that always exhilarated him. He was delighted to find no one in the gallery but the old guard, who sat in the corner, a newspaper on his knee, a black patch over one eye and the other closed. Paul possessed himself of the place and walked confidently up and down, whistling under his breath. After a while he sat down before a blue Rico and lost himself. When he bethought him to look at his watch, it was after seven o'clock, and he rose with a start and ran downstairs, making a face at Augustus Cæsar, peering out from the cast-room, and an evil gesture at the Venus of Milo as he passed her on the stairway.

When Paul reached the ushers' dressing-room half a dozen boys were there already, and he began excitedly to tumble into his uniform. It was one of the few that at all approached fitting, and Paul thought it very becoming—though he knew the tight, straight coat accentuated his narrow chest, about which he was exceedingly sensitive. He was always excited while he dressed, twangling all over to the tuning of the strings and the preliminary flourishes of the horns in the music-room; but tonight he seemed quite beside himself, and he teased and plagued the boys until, telling him that he was crazy, they put him down on the floor and sat on him.

Somewhat calmed by his suppression, Paul dashed out to the front of the house to seat the early comers. He was a model usher. Gracious and smiling he ran up and down the aisles. Nothing was too much trouble for him; he carried messages and brought programs as though it were his greatest pleasure in life, and all the people in his section thought him a charming boy, feeling that he remembered and admired them. As the house filled, he grew more and more vivacious and animated, and the color came to his cheeks and lips. It was very much as though this were a great reception and Paul were the host. Just as the musicians came out to take their places, his English teacher arrived with checks for the seats which a prominent manufacturer had taken for the season. She betrayed some embarrassment when she handed Paul the tickets, and a *hauteur* which subsequently made her feel very foolish. Paul was startled for a moment, and had the feeling of wanting to put her out;

what business had she here among all these fine people and
gay colors? He looked her over and decided that she was
not appropriately dressed and must be a fool to sit downstairs in such togs. The tickets had probably been sent her
out of kindness, he reflected, as he put down a seat for her,
and she had about as much right to sit there as he had.

When the symphony began Paul sank into one of the rear
seats with a long sigh of relief, and lost himself as he had
done before the Rico. It was not that symphonies, as such,
meant anything in particular to Paul, but the first sigh of the
instruments seemed to free some hilarious spirit within him;
something that struggled there like the Genius in the bottle
found by the Arab fisherman. He felt a sudden zest of life;
the lights danced before his eyes and the concert hall blazed
into unimaginable splendor. When the soprano soloist came
on, Paul forgot even the nastiness of his teacher's being
there, and gave himself up to the peculiar intoxication such
personages always had for him. The soloist chanced to be a
German woman, by no means in her first youth, and the
mother of many children; but she wore a satin gown and a
tiara, and she had that indefinable air of achievement, that
world-shine upon her, which always blinded Paul to any possible defects.

After a concert was over, Paul was often irritable and
wretched until he got to sleep—and tonight he was even
more than usually restless. He had the feeling of not being
able to let down; of its being impossible to give up this delicious excitement which was the only thing that could be
called living at all. During the last number he withdrew
and, after hastily changing his clothes in the dressing-room,
slipped out to the side door where the singer's carriage stood.
Here he began pacing rapidly up and down the walk, waiting to see her come out.

Over yonder the Schenley, in its vacant stretch, loomed
big and square through the fine rain, the windows of its
twelve stories glowing like those of a lighted cardboard house
under a Christmas tree. All the actors and singers of any
importance stayed there when they were in the city, and a
number of the big manufacturers of the place lived there in
the winter. Paul had often hung about the hotel, watching

the people go in and out, longing to enter and leave school-masters and dull care behind him forever.

At last the singer came out, accompanied by the conductor, who helped her into her carriage and closed the door with a cordial *auf wiedersehen*—which set Paul to wondering whether she were not an old sweetheart of his. Paul followed the carriage over to the hotel, walking so rapidly as not to be far from the entrance when the singer alighted and disappeared behind the swinging glass doors which were opened by a Negro in a tall hat and a long coat. In the moment that the door was ajar, it seemed to Paul that he, too, entered. He seemed to feel himself go after her up the steps, into the warm, lighted building, into an exotic, a tropical world of shiny, glistening surfaces and basking ease. He reflected upon the mysterious dishes that were brought into the dining room, the green bottles in buckets of ice, as he had seen them in the supper party pictures of the Sunday supplement. A quick gust of wind brought the rain down with sudden vehemence, and Paul was startled to find that he was still outside in the slush of the gravel driveway; that his boots were letting in the water and his scanty overcoat was clinging wet about him; that the lights in front of the concert hall were out, and that the rain was driving in sheets between him and the orange glow of the windows above him. There it was, what he wanted—tangibly before him, like the fairy world of a Christmas pantomime; as the rain beat in his face, Paul wondered whether he were destined always to shiver in the black night outside, looking up at it.

He turned and walked reluctantly toward the car tracks. The end had to come some time; his father in his night-clothes at the top of the stairs, explanations that did not explain, hastily improvised fictions that were forever tripping him up, his upstairs room and its horrible yellow wallpaper, the creaking bureau with the greasy plush collarbox, and over his painted wooden bed the pictures of George Washington and John Calvin, and the framed motto, "Feed my Lambs," which had been worked in red worsted by his mother, whom Paul could not remember.

Half an hour later, Paul alighted from the Negley Avenue car and went slowly down one of the side streets off the

main thoroughfare. It was a highly respectable street, where
all the houses were exactly alike, and where business men of
moderate means begot and reared large families of children,
all of whom went to Sabbath-school and learned the shorter
catechism, and were interested in arithmetic; all of whom
were as exactly alike as their homes, and of a piece with the
monotony in which they lived. Paul never went up Cordelia
Street without a shudder of loathing. His home was next to the
house of the Cumberland minister. He approached it tonight with the nerveless sense of defeat, the hopeless feeling of sinking back forever into ugliness and commonness
that he had always had when he came home. The moment
he turned into Cordelia Street he felt the waters close above
his head. After each of these orgies of living, he experienced
all the physical depression which follows a debauch; the
loathing of respectable beds, of common food, of a house
permeated by kitchen odors; a shuddering repulsion for the
flavorless, colorless mass of everyday existence; a morbid desire for cool things and soft lights and fresh flowers.

The nearer he approached the house, the more absolutely
unequal Paul felt to the sight of it all; his ugly sleeping
chamber; the cold bathroom with the grimy zinc tub, the
cracked mirror, the dripping spigots; his father, at the top
of the stairs, his hairy legs sticking out from his nightshirt,
his feet thrust into carpet slippers. He was so much later
than usual that there would certainly be inquiries and re-
proaches. Paul stopped short before the door. He felt that he
could not be accosted by his father tonight; that he could
not toss again on that miserable bed. He would not go in.
He would tell his father that he had no carfare, and it was
raining so hard he had gone home with one of the boys and
stayed all night.

Meanwhile, he was wet and cold. He went around to the
back of the house and tried one of the basement windows,
found it open, raised it cautiously, and scrambled down the
cellar wall to the floor. There he stood, holding his breath,
terrified by the noise he had made; but the floor above him
was silent, and there was no creak on the stairs. He found
a soap-box, and carried it over to the soft ring of light that
streamed from the furnace door, and sat down. He was hor-

ribly afraid of rats, so he did not try to sleep, but sat looking distrustfully at the dark, still terrified lest he might have awakened his father. In such reactions, after one of the experiences which made days and nights out of the dreary blanks of the calendar, when his senses were deadened, Paul's head was always singularly clear. Suppose his father had heard him getting in at the window and had come down and shot him for a burglar? Then, again, suppose his father had come down, pistol in hand, and he had cried out in time to save himself, and his father had been horrified to think how nearly he had killed him? Then, again, suppose a day should come when his father would remember that night, and wish there had been no warning cry to stay his hand? With this last supposition Paul entertained himself until daybreak.

The following Sunday was fine; the sodden November chill was broken by the last flash of autumnal summer. In the morning Paul had to go to church and Sabbath-school, as always. On seasonable Sunday afternoons the burghers of Cordelia Street usually sat out on their front "stoops," and talked to their neighbors on the next stoop, or called to those across the street in neighborly fashion. The men sat placidly on gay cushions placed upon the steps that led down to the sidewalk, while the women, in their Sunday "waists," sat in rockers on the cramped porches, pretending to be greatly at their ease. The children played in the streets; there were so many of them that the place resembled the recreation grounds of a kindergarten. The men on the steps—all in their shirt sleeves, their vests unbuttoned—sat with their legs well apart, their stomachs comfortably protruding, and talked of the prices of things, or told anecdotes of the sagacity of their various chiefs and overlords. They occasionally looked over the multitude of squabbling children, listened affectionately to their high-pitched, nasal voices, smiling to see their own proclivities reproduced in their offspring, and interspersed their legends of the iron kings with remarks about their sons' progress at school, their grades in arithmetic, and the amounts they had saved in their toy banks. On this last Sunday of November, Paul sat all the afternoon on the lowest step of his "stoop," staring into the street, while his sisters, in their rockers, were talking to the minister's daughters next door about how many shirtwaists they had made in the last week, and how many waffles someone had eaten at the last church supper. When the weather was warm, and his father was in a particularly jovial frame of mind, the girls made lemonade, which was always brought out in a red-glass pitcher, ornamented with forget-me-nots in blue enamel. This the girls thought very fine, and the neighbors joked about the suspicious color of the pitcher.

Today Paul's father, on the top step, was talking to a young man who shifted a restless baby from knee to knee. He happened to be the young man who was daily held up to Paul as a model, and after whom it was his father's dearest hope that he would pattern. This young man was of a ruddy complexion, with a compressed, red mouth, and faded near-sighted eyes, over which he wore thick spectacles, with gold bows that curved about his ears. He was clerk to one of the magnates of a great steel corporation, and was looked upon in Cordelia Street as a young man with a future. There was a story that, some five years ago—he was now barely twenty-six—he had been a trifle "dissipated," but in order to curb his appetites and save the loss of time and strength that a sowing of wild oats might have entailed, he had taken his chief's advice, oft reiterated to his employees, and at twenty-one had married the first woman whom he could persuade to share his fortunes. She happened to be an angular school mistress, much older than he, who also wore thick glasses, and who had now borne him four children, all near-sighted, like herself.

The young man was relating how his chief, now cruising in the Mediterranean, kept in touch with all the details of the business, arranging his office hours on his yacht just as though he were at home, and "knocking off work enough to keep two stenographers busy." His father told, in turn, the plan his corporation was considering, of putting in an electric railway plant at Cairo. Paul snapped his teeth; he had an awful apprehension that they might spoil it all before he got there. Yet he rather liked to hear these legends of the iron kings, that were told and retold on Sundays and holidays; these stories of palaces in Venice, yachts on the Mediterranean, and high play at Monte Carlo appealed to his fancy, and he was interested in the triumphs of cash boys who had become famous, though he had no mind for the cash-boy stage.

After supper was over, and he had helped to dry the dishes, Paul nervously asked his father whether he could go to George's to get some help in his geometry, and still more nervously asked for carfare. This latter request he had to repeat, as his father, on principle, did not like to hear requests for money, whether much or little. He asked Paul whether he could not go to some boy who lived nearer, and told him that he ought not to leave his school work until Sunday; but he gave him the dime. He was not a poor man, but he had a worthy ambition to come up in the world. His only reason for allowing Paul to usher was that he thought a boy ought to be earning a little.

Paul bounded upstairs, scrubbed the greasy odor of the dishwater from his hands with the ill-smelling soap he hated, and then shook over his fingers a few drops of violet water from the bottle he kept hidden in his drawer. He left the house with his geometry conspicuously under his arm, and the moment he got out of Cordelia Street and boarded a downtown car, he shook off the lethargy of two deadening days, and began to live again.

The leading juvenile of the permanent stock company which played at one of the downtown theaters was an acquaintance of Paul's, and the boy had been invited to drop in at the Sunday night rehearsals whenever he could. For more than a year Paul had spent every available moment loitering about Charley Edwards's dressing-room. He had won a place among Edwards's following not only because the young actor, who could not afford to employ a dresser, often found him useful, but because he recognized in Paul something akin to what churchmen termed "vocation."

It was at the theater and at Carnegie Hall that Paul really lived; the rest was but a sleep and a forgetting. This was Paul's fairy tale, and it had for him all the allurement of a secret love. The moment he inhaled the gassy, painty, dusty odor behind the scenes, he breathed like a prisoner set free, and felt within him the possibility of doing or saving splen-

did, brilliant things. The moment the cracked orchestra beat
out the overture from *Martha,* or jerked at the serenade from
Rigoletto, all stupid and ugly things slid from him, and his
senses were deliciously, yet delicately fired.

Perhaps it was because, in Paul's world, the natural nearly
always wore the guise of ugliness, that a certain element of
artificiality seemed to him necessary in beauty. Perhaps it
was because his experience of life elsewhere was so full of
Sabbath-school picnics, petty economies, wholesome advice
as to how to succeed in life, and the unescapable odors of
cooking, that he found this existence so alluring, these
smartly-clad men and women so attractive, that he was so
moved by these starry apple orchards that bloomed peren-
nially under the limelight.

It would be difficult to put it strongly enough how convincingly the stage entrance of that theater was for Paul the
actual portal of Romance. Certainly none of the company
ever suspected it, least of all Charley Edwards. It was very
like the old stories that used to float about London of fabu-
lously rich Jews, who had subterranean halls, with palms,
and fountains, and soft lamps and richly apparelled women
who never saw the disenchanting light of London day. So, in
the midst of that smoke-palled city, enamored of figures and
grimy toil, Paul had his secret temple, his wishing-carpet, his
bit of blue-and-white Mediterranean shore bathed in perpetual sunshine.

Several of Paul's teachers had a theory that his imagination had been perverted by garish fiction; but the truth was,
he scarcely ever read at all. The books at home were not
such as would either tempt or corrupt a youthful mind, and
as for reading the novels that some of his friends urged upon
him—well, he got what he wanted much more quickly from
music; any sort of music, from an orchestra to a barrel organ.
He needed only the spark, the indescribable thrill that made
his imagination master of his senses, and he could make plots
and pictures enough of his own. It was equally true that he
was not stage-struck—not, at any rate, in the usual accepta-
tion of that expression. He had no desire to become an actor,
any more than he had to become a musician. He felt no
necessity to do any of these things; what he wanted was to

see, to be in the atmosphere, float on the wave of it, to be carried out, blue league after blue league, away from everything.

After a night behind the scenes, Paul found the schoolroom more than ever repulsive; the bare floors and naked walls; the prosy men who never wore frock coats, or violets in their buttonholes; the women with their dull gowns, shrill voices, and pitiful seriousness about prepositions that govern the dative. He could not bear to have the other pupils think, for a moment, that he took these people seriously; he must convey to them that he considered it all trivial, and was there only by way of a joke, anyway. He had autograph pictures of all the members of the stock company which he showed his classmates, telling them the most incredible stories of his familiarity with these people, of his acquaintance with the soloists who came to Carnegie Hall, his suppers with them and the flowers he sent them. When these stories lost their effect, and his audience grew listless, he would bid all the boys good-by, announcing that he was going to travel for a while; going to Naples, to California, to Egypt. Then, next Monday, he would slip back, conscious and nervously smiling, his sister was ill, and he would have to defer his voyage until spring.

Matters went steadily worse with Paul at school. In the itch to let his instructors know how heartily he despised them, and how thoroughly he was appreciated elsewhere, he mentioned once or twice that he had no time to fool with theorems; adding—with a twitch of the eyebrows and a touch of that nervous bravado which so perplexed them—that he was helping the people down at the stock company; they were old friends of his.

The upshot of the matter was that the Principal went to Paul's father, and Paul was taken out of school and put to work. The manager at Carnegie Hall was told to get another usher in his stead; the door-keeper at the theater was warned not to admit him to the house; and Charley Edwards remorsefully promised the boy's father not to see him again.

The members of the stock company were vastly amused when some of Paul's stories reached them—especially the women. They were hard-working women, most of them supporting indolent husbands or brothers, and they laughed rather bitterly at having stirred the boy to such fervid and florid inventions. They agreed with the faculty and with his father, that Paul's was a bad case.

The east-bound train was plowing through a January snowstorm; the dull dawn was beginning to show gray when the engine whistled a mile out of Newark. Paul started up from the seat where he had lain curled in uneasy slumber, rubbed the breath-misted window glass with his hand, and peered out. The snow was whirling in curling eddies above the white bottom lands, and the drifts lay already deep in the fields and along the fences, while here and there the long dead grass and dried weed stalks protruded black above it. Lights shone from the scattered houses, and a gang of laborers who stood beside the track waved their lanterns.

Paul had slept very little, and he felt grimy and uncomfortable. He had made the all-night journey in a day coach because he was afraid if he took a Pullman he might be seen by some Pittsburgh business man who had noticed him in Denny & Carson's office. When the whistle woke him, he clutched quickly at his breast pocket, glancing about him with an uncertain smile. But the little, clay-bespattered Italians were still sleeping, the slatternly women across the aisle were in open-mouthed oblivion, and even the crumby, crying babies were for the nonce stilled. Paul settled back to struggle with his impatience as best he could.

When he arrived at the Jersey City station, he hurried through his breakfast, manifestly ill at ease and keeping a sharp eye about him. After he reached the Twenty-third Street station, he consulted a cabman, and had himself driven to a men's furnishing establishment which was just opening for the day. He spent upward of two hours there, buying with endless reconsidering and great care. His new street suit he put on in the fitting-room; the frock coat and dress clothes he had bundled into the cab with his new shirts. Then he drove to a hatter's and a shoe house. His next errand was at Tiffany's, where he selected silver-mounted brushes and a scarf-pin. He would not wait to have his silver marked, he said. Lastly, he stopped at a trunk shop on Broadway, and had his purchases packed into various traveling bags.

It was a little after one o'clock when he drove up to the Waldorf, and, after settling with the cabman, went into the office. He registered from Washington; said his mother and father had been abroad, and that he had come down to await the arrival of their steamer. He told his story plausibly and had no trouble, since he offered to pay for them in advance, in engaging his rooms; a sleeping-room, sitting room and bath.

Not once, but a hundred times Paul had planned this entry into New York. He had gone over every detail of it with Charley Edwards, and in his scrap book at home there were pages of description about New York hotels, cut from the Sunday papers.

When he was shown to his sitting room on the eighth floor, he saw at a glance that everything was as it should be; there was but one detail in his mental picture that the place did not realize, so he rang for the bell boy and sent him down for flowers. He moved about nervously until the boy returned, putting away his new linen and fingering it delightedly as he did so. When the flowers came, he put them hastily into water, and then tumbled into a hot bath. Presently he came out of his white bathroom, resplendent in his new silk underwear, and playing with the tassels of his red robe. The snow was whirling so fiercely outside his windows that he could scarcely see across the street; but within, the air was deliciously soft and fragrant. He put the violets and jonquils on the tabouret beside the couch, and threw himself down with a long sigh, covering himself with a Roman blanket. He was thoroughly tired; he had been in such haste, he had stood up to such a strain, covered so much ground in the last twenty-four hours, that he wanted to think how it had all come about. Lulled by the sound of the wind, the warm air, and the cool fragrance of the flowers, he sank into deep, drowsy retrospection.

It had been wonderfully simple; when they had shut him out of the theater and concert hall, when they had taken away his bone, the whole thing was virtually determined. The rest was a mere matter of opportunity. The only thing that at all surprised him was his own courage—for he realized well enough that he had always been tormented by

fear, a sort of apprehensive dread that, of late years, as the
meshes of the lies he had told closed about him, had been
pulling the muscles of his body tighter and tighter. Until
now, he could not remember a time when he had not been
dreading something. Even when he was a little boy, it was
always there—behind him, or before, or on either side. There
had always been the shadowed corner, the dark place into
which he dared not look, but from which something seemed
always to be watching him—and Paul had done things that
were not pretty to watch, he knew.

But now he had a curious sense of relief, as though he had
at last thrown down the gauntlet to the thing in the corner.

Yet it was but a day since he had been sulking in the
traces; but yesterday afternoon that he had been sent to the
bank with Denny & Carson's deposit, as usual—but this time
he was instructed to leave the book to be balanced. There
was above two thousand dollars in checks, and nearly a
thousand in the bank notes which he had taken from the
book and quietly transferred to his pocket. At the bank he
had made out a new deposit slip. His nerves had been steady
enough to permit of his returning to the office, where he had
finished his work and asked for a full day's holiday tomorrow, Saturday, giving a perfectly reasonable pretext. The
bank book, he knew, would not be returned before Monday
or Tuesday, and his father would be out of town for the
next week. From the time he slipped the bank notes into
his pocket until he boarded the night train for New York, he
had not known a moment's hesitation.

How astonishingly easy it had all been; here he was, the
thing done; and this time there would be no awakening, no
figure at the top of the stairs. He watched the snowflakes
whirling by his window until he fell asleep.

When he awoke, it was four o'clock in the afternoon. He
bounded up with a start; one of his precious days gone already! He spent nearly an hour in dressing, watching every
stage of his toilet carefully in the mirror. Everything was
quite perfect; he was exactly the kind of boy he had always
wanted to be.

When he went downstairs, Paul took a carriage and drove
up Fifth Avenue toward the Park. The snow had somewhat

abated; carriages and tradesmen's wagons were hurrying soundlessly to and fro in the winter twilight; boys in woolen mufflers were shoveling off the doorsteps; the avenue stages made fine spots of color against the white street. Here and there on the corners whole flower gardens blooming behind glass windows, against which the snowflakes stuck and melted; violets, roses, carnations, lilies of the valley—somehow vastly more lovely and alluring that they blossomed thus unnaturally in the snow. The Park itself was a wonderful stage winter-piece.

When he returned, the pause of the twilight had ceased, and the tune of the streets had changed. The snow was falling faster, lights streamed from the hotels that reared their many stories fearlessly up into the storm, defying the raging Atlantic winds. A long, black stream of carriages poured down the avenue, intersected here and there by other streams, tending horizontally. There were a score of cabs about the entrance of his hotel, and his driver had to wait. Boys in livery were running in and out of the awning stretched across the sidewalk, up and down the red velvet carpet laid from the door to the street. Above, about, within it all, was the rumble and roar, the hurry and toss of thousands of human beings as hot for pleasure as himself, and on every side of him towered the glaring affirmation of the omnipotence of wealth.

The boy set his teeth and drew his shoulders together in a spasm of realization; the plot of all dramas, the text of all romances, the nerve-stuff of all sensations was whirling about him like the snowflakes. He burnt like a faggot in a tempest.

When Paul came down to dinner, the music of the orchestra floated up the elevator shaft to greet him. As he stepped into the thronged corridor, he sank back into one of the chairs against the wall to get his breath. The lights, the chatter, the perfumes, the bewildering medley of color—he had, for a moment, the feeling of not being able to stand it. But only for a moment; these were his own people, he told himself. He went slowly about the corridors, through the writing-rooms, smoking-rooms, reception-rooms, as though he were exploring the chambers of an enchanted palace, built and peopled for him alone.

When he reached the dining room he sat down at a table near a window. The flowers, the white linen, the many-colored wine glasses, the gay toilettes of the women, the low popping of corks, the undulating repetitions of the *Blue Danube* from the orchestra, all flooded Paul's dream with bewildering radiance. When the roseate tinge of his champagne was added—that cold, precious, bubbling stuff that creamed and foamed in his glass—Paul wondered that there were honest men in the world at all. This was what all the world was fighting for, he reflected; this was what all the struggle was about. He doubted the reality of his past. Had he ever known a place called Cordelia Street, a place where fagged-looking business men boarded the early car? Mere rivets in a machine they seemed to Paul—sickening men, with combings of children's hair always hanging to their coats, and the smell of cooking in their clothes. Cordelia Street—Ah, that belonged to another time and country! Had he not always been thus, had he not sat here night after night, from as far back as he could remember, looking pensively over just such shimmering textures, and slowly twirling the stem of a glass like this one between his thumb and middle finger? He rather thought he had.

He was not in the least abashed or lonely. He had no especial desire to meet or to know any of these people; all he demanded was the right to look on and conjecture, to watch the pageant. The mere stage properties were all he contended for. Nor was he lonely later in the evening, in his loge at the Opera. He was entirely rid of his nervous misgivings, of his forced aggressiveness, of the imperative desire to show himself different from his surroundings. He felt now that his surroundings explained him. Nobody questioned the purple; he had only to wear it passively. He had only to glance down at his dress coat to reassure himself that here it would be impossible for anyone to humiliate him.

He found it hard to leave his beautiful sitting room to go to bed that night, and sat long watching the raging storm from his turret window. When he went to sleep, it was with the lights turned on in his bedroom; partly because of his old timidity, and partly so that, if he should wake in the night, there would be no wretched moment of doubt, no

horrible suspicion of yellow wallpaper, or of Washington and
Calvin above his bed.

On Sunday morning the city was practically snow-bound.
Paul breakfasted late, and in the afternoon he fell in with a
wild San Francisco boy, a freshman at Yale, who said he had
run down for a "little flyer" over Sunday. The young man
offered to show Paul the night side of the town, and the two
boys went off together after dinner, not returning to the
hotel until seven o'clock the next morning. They had started
out in the confiding warmth of a champagne friendship, but
their parting in the elevator was singularly cool. The freshman pulled himself together to make his train, and Paul
went to bed. He awoke at two o'clock in the afternoon, very
thirsty and dizzy, and rang for ice water, coffee and the
Pittsburgh papers.

On the part of the hotel management, Paul excited no suspicion. There was this to be said for him, that he wore his
spoils with dignity and in no way made himself conspicuous.
His chief greediness lay in his ears and eyes, and his excesses
were not offensive ones. His dearest pleasures were the gray
winter twilights in his sitting room; his quiet enjoyment of
his flowers, his clothes, his wide divan, his cigarette and his
sense of power. He could not remember a time when he had
felt so at peace with himself. The mere release from the
necessity of petty lying, lying every day and every day, restored his self-respect. He had never lied for pleasure, even
at school; but to make himself noticed and admired, to assert his difference from other Cordelia Street boys; and he
felt a good deal more manly, more honest, even, now that
he had no need for boastful pretensions, now that he could,
as his actor friends used to say, "dress the part." It was characteristic that remorse did not occur to him. His golden days
went by without a shadow, and he made each as perfect as
he could.

On the eighth day after his arrival in New York, he found
the whole affair exploited in the Pittsburgh papers, exploited
with a wealth of detail which indicated that local news of a
sensational nature was at a low ebb. The firm of Denny &
Carson announced that the boy's father had refunded the
full amount of his theft, and that they had no intention of

prosecuting. The Cumberland minister had been interviewed, and expressed his hope of yet reclaiming the motherless lad, and Paul's Sabbath-school teacher declared that she would spare no effort to that end. The rumor had reached Pittsburgh that the boy had been seen in a New York hotel, and his father had gone East to find him and bring him home.

Paul had just come in to dress for dinner; he sank into a chair, weak in the knees, and clasped his head in his hands. It was to be worse than jail, even; the tepid waters of Cordelia Street were to close over him finally and forever. The gray monotony stretched before him in hopeless, unrelieved years; Sabbath-school, Young People's Meeting, the yellow-papered room, the damp dish-towels; it all rushed back upon him with sickening vividness. He had the old feeling that the orchestra had suddenly stopped, the sinking sensation that the play was over. The sweat broke out on his face, and he sprang to his feet, looked about him with his white, conscious smile, and winked at himself in the mirror. With something of the childish belief in miracles with which he had so often gone to class, all his lessons unlearned, Paul dressed and dashed whistling down the corridor to the elevator.

He had no sooner entered the dining room and caught the measure of the music, than his remembrance was lightened by his old elastic power of claiming the moment, mounting with it, and finding it all sufficient. The glare and glitter about him, the mere scenic accessories had again, and for the last time, their old potency. He would show himself that he was game, he would finish the thing splendidly. He doubted, more than ever, the existence of Cordelia Street, and for the first time he drank his wine recklessly. Was he not, after all, one of these fortunate beings? Was he not still himself, and in his own place? He drummed a nervous accompaniment to the music and looked about him, telling himself over and over that it had paid.

He reflected drowsily, to the swell of the violin and the chill sweetness of his wine, that he might have done it more wisely. He might have caught an outbound steamer and been well out of their clutches before now. But the other side of the world had seemed too far away and too uncertain then;

he could not have waited for it; his need had been too sharp. If he had to choose over again, he would do the same thing tomorrow. He looked affectionately about the dining room, now gilded with a soft mist. Ah, it had paid indeed!

Paul was awakened next morning by a painful throbbing in his head and feet. He had thrown himself across the bed without undressing, and had slept with his shoes on. His limbs and hands were lead heavy, and his tongue and throat were parched. There came upon him one of those fateful attacks of clear-headedness that never occurred except when he was physically exhausted and his nerves hung loose. He lay still and closed his eyes and let the tide of realities wash over him.

His father was in New York; "stopping at some joint or other," he told himself. The memory of successive summers on the front stoop fell upon him like a weight of black water. He had not a hundred dollars left; and he knew now, more than ever, that money was everything, the wall that stood between all he loathed and all he wanted. The thing was winding itself up; he had thought of that on his first glorious day in New York, and had even provided a way to snap the thread. It lay on his dressing-table now; he had got it out last night when he came blindly up from dinner—but the shiny metal hurt his eyes, and he disliked the look of it, anyway.

He rose and moved about with a painful effort, succumbing now and again to attacks of nausea. It was the old depression exaggerated; all the world had become Cordelia Street. Yet somehow he was not afraid of anything, was absolutely calm; perhaps because he had looked into the dark corner at last, and knew. It was bad enough, what he saw there; but somehow not so bad as his long fear of it had been. He saw everything clearly now. He had a feeling that he had made the best of it, that he had lived the sort of life he was meant to live, and for half an hour he sat staring at the revolver point. But he told himself that was not the way, so he went downstairs and took a cab to the ferry.

When Paul arrived at Newark, he got off the train and took another cab, directing the driver to follow the Pennsylvania tracks out of the town. The snow lay heavy on the roadways and had drifted deep in the open fields. Only here and there the dead grass or dried weed stalks projected, singularly black, above it. Once well into the country, Paul dismissed the carriage and walked, floundering along the tracks, his mind a medley of irrelevant things. He seemed to hold in his brain an actual picture of everything he had seen that morning. He remembered every feature of both his drivers, the toothless old woman from whom he had bought the red flowers in his coat, the agent from whom he had got his ticket, and all of his fellow-passengers on the ferry. His mind, unable to cope with vital matters near at hand, worked feverishly and deftly at sorting and grouping these images. They made for him a part of the ugliness of the world, of the ache in his head, and the bitter burning on his tongue. He stooped and put a handful of snow into his mouth as he walked, but that, too, seemed hot. When he reached a little hillside, where the tracks ran through a cut some twenty feet below him, he stopped and sat down.

The carnations in his coat were drooping with the cold, he noticed; all their red glory over. It occurred to him that all the flowers he had seen in the show windows that first night must have gone the same way, long before this. It was only one splendid breath they had, in spite of their brave mockery at the winter outside the glass. It was a losing game in the end, it seemed, this revolt against the homilies by which the world is run. Paul took one of the blossoms carefully from his coat and scooped a little hole in the snow, where he covered it up. Then he dozed a while, from his weak condition, seeming insensible to the cold.

The sound of an approaching train woke him, and he started to his feet, remembering only his resolution, and afraid lest he should be too late. He stood watching the approaching locomotive, his teeth chattering, his lips drawn away from them in a frightened smile; once or twice he glanced nervously sidewise, as though he were being watched. When the right moment came, he jumped. As he fell, the folly of his haste occurred to him with merciless clearness, the vastness of what he had left undone. There flashed through his brain, clearer than ever before, the blue of Adriatic water, the yellow of Algerian sands.

He felt something strike his chest—his body was being thrown swiftly through the air, on and on, immeasurably far and fast, while his limbs gently relaxed. Then, because the picture-making mechanism was crushed, the disturbing visions flashed into black, and Paul dropped back into the immense design of things.

SHERWOOD ANDERSON (1876–1941)

SEEDS

HE WAS a small man with a beard and was very nervous. I remember how the cords of his neck were drawn taut.

For years he had been trying to cure people of illness by the method called psychoanalysis. The idea was the passion of his life. "I came here because I am tired," he said dejectedly. "My body is not tired but something inside me is old and worn-out. I want joy. For a few days or weeks I would like to forget men and women and the influences that make them the sick things they are."

There is a note that comes into the human voice by which you may know real weariness. It comes when one has been trying with all his heart and soul to think his way along some difficult road of thought. Of a sudden he finds himself unable to go on. Something within him stops. A tiny explosion takes place. He bursts into words and talks, perhaps foolishly. Little side currents of his nature he didn't know were there run out and get themselves expressed. It is at such times that a man boasts, uses big words, makes a fool of himself in general.

And so it was the doctor became shrill. He jumped up from the steps where he had been sitting, talking, and walked about. "You come from the West. You have kept away from people. You have preserved yourself—damn you! I haven't——" His voice had indeed become shrill. "I have entered into lives. I have gone beneath the surface of the lives of men and women. Women especially I have studied—our own women, here in America."

"You have loved them?" I suggested.

"Yes," he said. "Yes—you are right there. I have done that. It is the only way I can get at things. I have to try to love. You see how that is? It's the only way. Love must be the beginning of things with me."

I began to sense the depths of his weariness. "We will go swim in the lake," I urged.

"I don't want to swim or do any damn plodding thing. I want to run and shout," he declared. "For a while, for a few hours, I want to be like a dead leaf blown by the winds over these hills. I have one desire and one only—to free myself."

We walked in a dusty country road. I wanted him to know that I thought I understood, so I put the case in my own way.

When he stopped and stared at me I talked. "You are no more and no better than myself," I declared. "You are a dog that has rolled in offal, and because you are not quite a dog you do not like the smell of your own hide."

In turn my voice became shrill. "You blind fool," I cried impatiently. "Men like you are fools. You cannot go along that road. It is given to no man to venture far along the road of lives." I became passionately in earnest. "The illness you pretend to cure is the universal illness," I said. "The thing you want to do cannot be done. Fool—do you expect love to be understood?"

We stood in the road and looked at each other. The suggestion of a sneer played about the corners of his mouth. He put a hand on my shoulder and shook me. "How smart we are—how aptly we put things!"

He spat the words out and then turned and walked a little away. "You think you understand, but you don't understand," he cried. "What you say can't be done can be done. You're a liar. You cannot be so definite without missing something vague and fine. You miss the whole point. The lives of people are like young trees in a forest. They are being choked by climbing vines. The vines are old thoughts and beliefs planted by dead men. I am myself covered by crawling creeping vines that choke me."

He laughed bitterly. "And that's why I want to run and play," he said. "I want to be a leaf blown by the wind over hills. I want to die and be born again, and I am only a tree covered with vines and slowly dying. I am, you see, weary and want to be made clean. I am an amateur venturing timidly into lives," he concluded. "I am weary and want to be made clean. I am covered by creeping crawling things."

A woman from Iowa came here to Chicago and took a room in a house on the west-side. She was about twenty-seven years old and ostensibly she came to the city to study advanced methods for teaching music.

A certain young man also lived in the west-side house. His room faced a long hall on the second floor of the house and the one taken by the woman was across the hall facing his room.

In regard to the young man—there is something very sweet in his nature. He is a painter but I have often wished he would decide to become a writer. He tells things with understanding and he does not paint brilliantly.

And so the woman from Iowa lived in the west-side house and came home from the city in the evening. She looked like a thousand other women one sees in the streets every day. The only thing that at all made her stand out among the women in the crowds was that she was a little lame. Her right foot was slightly deformed and she walked with a limp. For three months she lived in the house—where she was the only woman except the landlady—and then a feeling in regard to her began to grow up among the men of the house.

The men all said the same thing concerning her. When they met in the hallway at the front of the house, they stopped, laughed and whispered. "She wants a lover," they said and winked. "She may not know it but a lover is what she needs." One knowing Chicago and Chicago men would think that an easy want to be satisfied. I laughed when my friend—whose name is LeRoy—told me the story, but he did not laugh. He shook his head. "It wasn't so easy," he said. "There would be no story were the matter that simple."

LeRoy tried to explain. "Whenever a man approached her she became alarmed," he said. Men kept smiling and speaking to her. They invited her to dinner and to the theatre, but nothing would induce her to walk in the streets with a man. She never went into the streets at night. When a man stopped and tried to talk with her in the hallway she turned her eyes to the floor and then ran into her room. Once a young drygoods clerk who lived there induced her to sit with him on the steps before the house.

He was a sentimental fellow and took hold of her hand. When she began to cry he was alarmed and arose. He put a hand on her shoulder and tried to explain, but under the touch of his fingers her whole body shook with terror. "Don't touch me," she cried, "don't let your hands touch me!" She began to scream and people passing in the street stopped to listen. The drygoods clerk was alarmed and ran upstairs to his own room. He bolted the door and stood listening. "It is a trick," he declared in a trembling voice. "She is trying to make trouble. I did nothing to her. It was an accident and anyway what's the matter? I only touched her arm with my fingers."

Perhaps a dozen times LeRoy has spoken to me of the experience of the Iowa woman in the west-side house. The men there began to hate her. Although she would have nothing to do with them she would not let them alone. In a hundred ways she continually invited approaches that when made she repelled. When she stood naked in the bathroom facing the hallway where the men passed up and down she left the door slightly ajar. There was a couch in the living room downstairs, and when men were present she would sometimes enter and without saying a word throw herself down before them. On the couch she lay with lips drawn slightly apart. Her eyes stared at the ceiling. Her whole physical being seemed to be waiting for something. The sense of her filled the room. The men standing about pretended not to see. They talked loudly. Embarrassment took possession of them and one by one they crept quietly away.

One evening the woman was ordered to leave the house. Someone, perhaps the drygoods clerk, had talked to the landlady and she acted at once. "If you leave tonight I shall like it that much better," LeRoy heard the elder woman's voice saying. She stood in the hallway before the Iowa woman's room. The landlady's voice rang through the house.

LeRoy the painter is tall and lean and his life has been spent in devotion to ideas. The passions of his brain have consumed the passions of his body. His income is small and he has not married. Perhaps he has never had a sweetheart. He is not without physical desire but he is not primarily concerned with desire.

On the evening when the Iowa woman was ordered to leave the west-side house, she waited until she thought the landlady had gone downstairs, and then went into LeRoy's room. It was about eight o'clock and he sat by a window reading a book. The woman did not knock but opened the door. She said nothing but ran across the floor and knelt at his feet. LeRoy said that her twisted foot made her run like a wounded bird, that her eyes were burning and that her breath came in little gasps. "Take me," she said, putting her face down upon his knees and trembling violently. "Take me quickly. There must be a beginning to things. I can't stand the waiting. You must take me at once."

You may be quite sure LeRoy was perplexed by all this. From what he has said I gathered that until that evening he had hardly noticed the woman. I suppose that of all the men in the house he had been the most indifferent to her. In the room something happened. The landlady followed the woman when she ran to LeRoy, and the two women confronted him. The woman from Iowa knelt trembling and frightened at his feet. The landlady was indignant. LeRoy acted on impulse. An inspiration came to him. Putting his hand on the kneeling woman's shoulder he shook her violently. "Now behave yourself," he said quickly. "I will keep my promise." He turned to the landlady and smiled. "We have been engaged to be married," he said. "We have quarreled. She came here to be near me. She has been unwell and excited. I will take her away. Please don't let yourself be annoyed. I will take her away."

When the woman and LeRoy got out of the house she

stopped weeping and put her hand into his. Her fears had all gone away. He found a room for her in another house and then went with her into a park and sat on a bench.

Everything LeRoy has told me concerning this woman strengthens my belief in what I said to the man that day in the mountains. You cannot venture along the road of lives. On the bench he and the woman talked until midnight and he saw and talked with her many times later. Nothing came of it. She went back, I suppose, to her place in the West.

In the place from which she had come the woman had been a teacher of music. She was one of four sisters, all engaged in the same sort of work and, LeRoy says, all quiet capable women. Their father had died when the eldest girl was not yet ten, and five years later the mother died also. The girls had a house and a garden.

In the nature of things I cannot know what the lives of the women were like but of this one may be quite certain—they talked only of women's affairs, thought only of women's affairs. No one of them ever had a lover. For years no man came near the house.

Of them all only the youngest, the one who came to Chicago, was visibly affected by the utterly feminine quality of their lives. It did something to her. All day and every day she taught music to young girls and then went home to the women. When she was twenty-five she began to think and to dream of men. During the day and through the evening she talked with women of women's affairs, and all the time she wanted desperately to be loved by a man. She went to Chicago with that hope in mind. LeRoy explained her attitude in the matter and her strange behavior in the westside house by saying she had thought too much and acted too little. "The life force within her became decentralized," he declared. "What she wanted she could not achieve. The living force within could not find expression. When it could not get expressed in one way it took another. Sex spread itself out over her body. It permeated the very fibre of her being. At the last she was sex personified, sex become condensed and impersonal. Certain words, the touch of a man's hand, sometimes even the sight of a man passing in the street did something to her."

Yesterday I saw LeRoy and he talked to me again of the woman and her strange and terrible fate. We walked in the park by the lake. As we went along the figure of the woman kept coming into my mind. An idea came to me.

"You might have been her lover," I said. "That was possible. She was not afraid of you."

LeRoy stopped. Like the doctor who was so sure of his ability to walk into lives he grew angry and scolded. For a moment he stared at me and then a rather odd thing happened. Words said by the other man in the dusty road in the hills came to LeRoy's lips and were said over again. The suggestion of a sneer played about the corners of his mouth. "How smart we are. How aptly we put things," he said.

The voice of the young man who walked with me in the park by the lake in the city became shrill. I sensed the weariness in him. Then he laughed and said quietly and softly, "It isn't so simple. By being sure of yourself you are in danger of losing all of the romance of life. You miss the whole point. Nothing in life can be settled so definitely. The woman—you see—was like a young tree choked by a climbing vine. The thing that wrapped her about had shut out the light. She was a grotesque as many trees in the forest are grotesques. Her problem was such a difficult one that thinking of it has changed the whole current of my life. At first I was like you. I was quite sure. I thought I would be her lover and settle the matter."

LeRoy turned and walked a little away. Then he came back and took hold of my arm. A passionate earnestness took possession of him. His voice trembled. "She needed a lover, yes, the men in the house were quite right about that," he said. "She needed a lover and at the same time a lover was not what she needed. The need of a lover was, after all, a quite secondary thing. She needed to be loved, to be long and quietly and patiently loved. To be sure she is a grotesque, but then all the people in the world are grotesques. We all need to be loved. What would cure her would cure the rest of us also. The disease she had is, you see, universal.

We all want to be loved and the world has no plan for creating our lovers."

LeRoy's voice dropped and he walked beside me in silence. We turned away from the lake and walked under trees. I looked closely at him. The cords of his neck were drawn taut. "I have seen under the shell of life and I am afraid," he mused. "I am myself like the woman. I am covered with creeping crawling vine-like things. I cannot be a lover. I am not subtle or patient enough. I am paying old debts. Old thoughts and beliefs—seeds planted by dead men—spring up in my soul and choke me."

For a long time we walked and LeRoy talked, voicing the thoughts that came into his mind. I listened in silence. His mind struck upon the refrain voiced by the man in the mountains. "I would like to be a dead dry thing," he muttered looking at the leaves scattered over the grass. "I would like to be a leaf blown away by the wind." He looked up and his eyes turned to where among the trees we could see the lake in the distance. "I am weary and want to be made clean. I am a man covered by creeping crawling things. I would like to be dead and blown by the wind over limitless waters," he said. "I want more than anything else in the world to be clean."

KATHERINE MANSFIELD *(1888–1923)*

BLISS

ALTHOUGH Bertha Young was thirty she still had moments like this when she wanted to run instead of walk, to take dancing steps on and off the pavement, to bowl a hoop, to throw something up in the air and catch it again, or to stand still and laugh at—nothing—at nothing, simply.

What can you do if you are thirty and, turning the corner of your own street, you are overcome, suddenly, by a feeling of bliss—absolute bliss!—as though you'd suddenly swallowed a bright piece of that late afternoon sun and it burned in your bosom, sending out a little shower of sparks into every particle, into every finger and toe? . . .

Oh, is there no way you can express it without being "drunk and disorderly"? How idiotic civilization is! Why be given a body if you have to keep it shut up in a case like a rare, rare fiddle?

"No, that about the fiddle is not quite what I mean," she thought, running up the steps and feeling in her bag for the key—she'd forgotten it, as usual—and rattling the letterbox. "It's not what I mean, because—Thank you, Mary"—she went into the hall. "Is Nurse back?"

"Yes, M'm."

"And has the fruit come?"

"Yes, M'm. Everything's come."

"Bring the fruit up to the dining-room, will you? I'll arrange it before I go upstairs."

It was dusky in the dining-room and quite chilly. But all the same Bertha threw off her coat; she could not bear the tight clasp of it another moment, and the cold air fell on her arms.

But in her bosom there was still that bright glowing place

—that shower of little sparks coming from it. It was almost unbearable. She hardly dared to breathe for fear of fanning it higher, and yet she breathed deeply, deeply. She hardly dared to look into the cold mirror—but she did look, and it gave her back a woman, radiant, with smiling, trembling lips, with big, dark eyes and an air of listening, waiting for something . . . divine to happen . . . that she knew must happen . . . infallibly.

Mary brought in the fruit on a tray and with it a glass bowl, and a blue dish, very lovely, with a strange sheen on it as though it had been dipped in milk.

"Shall I turn on the light, M'm?"

"No, thank you. I can see quite well."

There were tangerines and apples stained with strawberry pink. Some yellow pears, smooth as silk, some white grapes covered with a silver bloom and a big cluster of purple ones. These last she had bought to tone in with the new dining-room carpet. Yes, that did sound rather far-fetched and absurd, but it was really why she had bought them. She had thought in the shop: "I must have some purple ones to bring the carpet up to the table." And it had seemed quite sensible at the time.

When she had finished with them and had made two pyramids of these bright round shapes, she stood away from the table to get the effect—and it really was most curious. For the dark table seemed to melt into the dusky light and the glass dish and the blue bowl to float in the air. This, of course in her present mood, was so incredibly beautiful. . . . She began to laugh.

"No, no. I'm getting hysterical." And she seized her bag and coat and ran upstairs to the nursery.

Nurse sat at a low table giving Little B her supper after her bath. The baby had on a white flannel gown and a blue woollen jacket, and her dark, fine hair was brushed up into a funny little peak. She looked up when she saw her mother and began to jump.

"Now, my lovey, eat it up like a good girl," said Nurse, setting her lips in a way that Bertha knew, and that meant she had come into the nursery at another wrong moment.

"Has she been good, Nanny?"

"She's been a little sweet all the afternoon," whispered Nanny. "We went to the park and I sat down on a chair and took her out of the pram and a big dog came along and put its head on my knee and she clutched its ear, tugged it. Oh, you should have seen her."

Bertha wanted to ask if it wasn't rather dangerous to let her clutch at a strange dog's ear. But she did not dare to. She stood watching them, her hands by her sides, like the poor little girl in front of the rich little girl with the doll.

The baby looked up at her again, stared, and then smiled so charmingly that Bertha couldn't help crying:

"Oh, Nanny, do let me finish giving her her supper while you put the bath things away."

"Well, M'm, she oughtn't to be changed hands while she's eating," said Nanny, still whispering. "It unsettles her; it's very likely to upset her."

How absurd it was. Why have a baby if it has to be kept —not in a case like a rare, rare fiddle—but in another woman's arms? "Oh, I must!" she said.

Very offended, Nanny handed her over.

"Now, don't excite her after her supper. You know you do, M'm. And I have such a time with her after!"

Thank heaven! Nanny went out of the room with the bath towels.

"Now I've got you to myself, my little precious," said Bertha, as the baby leaned against her.

She ate delightfully, holding up her lips for the spoon and then waving her hands. Sometimes she wouldn't let the spoon go; and sometimes, just as Bertha had filled it, she waved it away to the four winds.

When the soup was finished Bertha turned round to the fire.

"You're nice—you're very nice!" said she, kissing her warm baby. "I'm fond of you. I like you."

And, indeed, she loved Little B so much—her neck as she bent forward, her exquisite toes as they shone transparent in the firelight—that all her feeling of bliss came back again, and again she didn't know how to express it—what to do with it.

"You're wanted on the telephone," said Nanny, coming back in triumph and seizing *her* Little B.

Down she flew. It was Harry.

"Oh, is that you, Ber? Look here. I'll be late. I'll take a taxi and come along as quickly as I can, but get dinner put back ten minutes—will you? All right?"

"Yes, perfectly. Oh, Harry!"

"Yes?"

What had she to say? She'd nothing to say. She only wanted to get in touch with him for a moment. She couldn't absurdly cry: "Hasn't it been a divine day!"

"What is it?" rapped out the little voice.

"Nothing. *Entendu*," said Bertha, and hung up the receiver, thinking how more than idiotic civilization was.

They had people coming to dinner. The Norman Knights —a very sound couple—he was about to start a theatre, and she was awfully keen on interior decoration, a young man, Eddie Warren, who had just published a little book of poems and whom everybody was asking to dine, and a "find" of Bertha's called Pearl Fulton. What Miss Fulton did, Bertha didn't know. They had met at the club and Bertha had fallen in love with her, as she always did fall in love with beautiful women who had something strange about them.

The provoking thing was that, though they had been about together and met a number of times and really talked, Bertha couldn't yet make her out. Up to a certain point Miss Fulton was rarely, wonderfully frank, but the certain point was there, and beyond that she would not go.

Was there anything beyond it? Harry said, "No." Voted her dullish, and "cold like all blond women, with a touch, perhaps, of anæmia of the brain." But Bertha wouldn't agree with him; not yet, at any rate.

"No, the way she has of sitting with her head a little on one side, and smiling, has something behind it, Harry, and I must find out what that something is."

"Most likely it's a good stomach," answered Harry.

He made a point of catching Bertha's heels with replies of that kind . . . "liver frozen, my dear girl," or "pure flatu-

lence," or "kidney disease," . . . and so on. For some strange
reason Bertha liked this, and almost admired it in him very
much.

She went into the drawing-room and lighted the fire; then,
picking up the cushions, one by one, that Mary had disposed
so carefully, she threw them back on to the chairs and the
couches. That made all the difference; the room came alive
at once. As she was about to throw the last one she surprised
herself by suddenly hugging it to her, passionately, passionately. But it did not put out the fire in her bosom. Oh, on
the contrary!

The windows of the drawing-room opened on to a balcony
overlooking the garden. At the far end, against the wall,
there was a tall, slender pear tree in fullest, richest bloom; it
stood perfect, as though becalmed against the jade-green sky.
Bertha couldn't help feeling, even from this distance, that
it had not a single bud or a faded petal. Down below, in
the garden beds, the red and yellow tulips, heavy with flowers, seemed to lean upon the dusk. A grey cat, dragging its
belly, crept across the lawn, and a black one, its shadow,
trailed after. The sight of them, so intent and so quick, gave
Bertha a curious shiver.

"What creepy things cats are!" she stammered, and she
turned away from the window and began walking up and
down. . . .

How strong the jonquils smelled in the warm room. Too
strong? Oh, no. And yet, as though overcome, she flung down
on a couch and pressed her hands to her eyes.

"I'm too happy—too happy!" she murmured.

And she seemed to see on her eyelids the lovely pear tree
with its wide open blossoms as a symbol of her own life.

Really—really—she had everything. She was young. Harry
and she were as much in love as ever, and they got on
together splendidly and were really good pals. She had an
adorable baby. They didn't have to worry about money.
They had this absolutely satisfactory house and garden. And
friends—modern, thrilling friends, writers and painters and
poets or people keen on social questions—just the kind of
friends they wanted. And then there were books, and there
was music, and she had found a wonderful little dressmaker,

and they were going abroad in the summer, and their new cook made the most superb omelettes. . . .

"I'm absurd. Absurd!" She sat up; but she felt quite dizzy, quite drunk. It must have been the spring.

Yes, it was the spring. Now she was so tired she could not drag herself upstairs to dress.

A white dress, a string of jade beads, green shoes and stockings. It wasn't intentional. She had thought of this scheme hours before she stood at the drawing-room window.

Her petals rustled softly into the hall, and she kissed Mrs. Norman Knight, who was taking off the most amusing orange coat with a procession of black monkeys round the hem and up the fronts.

". . . Why! Why! Why is the middle-class so stodgy—so utterly without a sense of humour! My dear, it's only by a fluke that I am here at all—Norman being the protective fluke. For my darling monkeys so upset the train that it rose to a man and simply ate me with its eyes. Didn't laugh—wasn't amused—that I should have loved. No, just stared—and bored me through and through."

"But the cream of it was," said Norman, pressing a large tortoise-shell-rimmed monocle into his eye, "you don't mind me telling this, Face, do you?" (In their home and among their friends they called each other Face and Mug.) "The cream of it was when she, being full fed, turned to the woman beside her and said: 'Haven't you ever seen a monkey before?'"

"Oh, yes!" Mrs. Norman Knight joined in the laughter. "Wasn't that too absolutely creamy?"

And a funnier thing still was that now her coat was off she did look like a very intelligent monkey—who had even made that yellow silk dress out of scraped banana skins. And her amber ear-rings; they were like little dangling nuts.

"This is a sad, sad fall!" said Mug, pausing in front of Little B's perambulator. "When the perambulator comes into the hall—" and he waved the rest of the quotation away.

The bell rang. It was lean, pale Eddie Warren (as usual) in a state of acute distress.

"It *is* the right house, *isn't* it?" he pleaded.

"Oh, I think so—I hope so," said Bertha brightly.

"I have had such a *dreadful* experience with a taxi-man; he was *most* sinister. I couldn't get him to stop. The *more* I knocked and called the *faster* he went. And *in* the moonlight this *bizarre* figure with the *flattened* head *crouching* over the *lit-tle* wheel . . ."

He shuddered, taking off an immense white silk scarf. Bertha noticed that his socks were white, too—most charming.

"But how dreadful!" she cried.

"Yes, it really was," said Eddie, following her into the drawing-room. "I saw myself *driving* through Eternity in a *timeless* taxi."

He knew the Norman Knights. In fact, he was going to write a play for N.K. when the theatre scheme came off.

"Well, Warren, how's the play?" said Norman Knight, dropping his monocle and giving his eye a moment in which to rise to the surface before it was screwed down again.

And Mrs. Norman Knight: "Oh, Mr. Warren, what happy socks!"

"I *am* so glad you like them," said he, staring at his feet. "They seem to have got so *much* whiter since the moon rose." And he turned his lean sorrowful young face to Bertha. "There *is* a moon, you know."

She wanted to cry: "I am sure there is—often—often!"

He really was a most attractive person. But so was Face, crouched before the fire in her banana skins, and so was Mug, smoking a cigarette and saying as he flicked the ash: "Why doth the bridegroom tarry?"

"There he is, now."

Bang went the front door open and shut. Harry shouted: "Hullo, you people. Down in five minutes." And they heard him swarm up the stairs. Bertha couldn't help smiling; she knew how he loved doing things at high pressure. What, after all, did an extra five minutes matter? But he would pretend to himself that they mattered beyond measure. And then he would make a great point of coming into the drawing-room, extravagantly cool and collected.

Harry had such a zest for life. Oh, how she appreciated it in him. And his passion for fighting—for seeking in everything that came up against him another test of his power and of his courage—that, too, she understood. Even when it made

him just occasionally to other people, who didn't know him
well, a little ridiculous perhaps. . . . For there were moments when he rushed into battle where no battle was. . . .
She talked and laughed and positively forgot until he had
come in (just as she had imagined) that Pearl Fulton had
not turned up.

"I wonder if Miss Fulton has forgotten?"

"I expect so," said Harry. "Is she on the 'phone?"

"Ah! There's a taxi, now." And Bertha smiled with that
little air of proprietorship that she always assumed while her
women finds were new and mysterious. "She lives in taxis."

"She'll run to fat if she does," said Harry coolly, ringing
the bell for dinner. "Frightful danger for blond women."

"Harry—don't," warned Bertha, laughing up at him.

Came another tiny moment, while they waited, laughing
and talking, just a trifle too much at their ease, a trifle too
unaware. And then Miss Fulton, all in silver, with a silver
fillet binding her pale blond hair, came in smiling, her head
a little on one side. "Am I late?"

"No, not at all," said Bertha. "Come along." And she took
her arm and they moved into the dining-room.

What was there in the touch of that cool arm that could
fan—fan—start blazing—blazing—the fire of bliss that Bertha
did not know what to do with?

Miss Fulton did not look at her; but then she seldom did
look at people directly. Her heavy eyelids lay upon her eyes
and the strange half smile came and went upon her lips as
though she lived by listening rather than seeing. But Bertha
knew, suddenly, as if the longest, most intimate look had
passed between them—as if they had said to each other:
"You, too?"—that Pearl Fulton, stirring the beautiful red
soup in the grey plate, was feeling just what she was feeling.

And the others? Face and Mug, Eddie and Harry, their
spoons rising and falling—dabbing their lips with their nap-
kins, crumbling bread, fiddling with the forks and glasses and
talking.

"I met her at the Alpha show—the weirdest little person.
She'd not only cut off her hair, but she seemed to have taken
a dreadfully good snip off her legs and arms and her neck
and her poor little nose as well."

"Isn't she very *liée* with Michael Oat?"

"The man who wrote *Love in False Teeth?*"

"He wants to write a play for me. One act. One man. Decides to commit suicide. Gives all the reasons why he should and why he shouldn't. And just as he has made up his mind either to do it or not to do it—curtain. Not half a bad idea."

"What's he going to call it—'Stomach Trouble'?"

"I *think* I've come across the *same* idea in a lit-tle French review, *quite* unknown in England."

No, they didn't share it. They were dears—dears—and she loved having them there, at her table, and giving them delicious food and wine. In fact, she longed to tell them how delightful they were, and what a decorative group they made, how they seemed to set one another off and how they reminded her of a play by Chekhov!

Harry was enjoying his dinner. It was part of his—well, not his nature, exactly, and certainly not his pose—his—something or other—to talk about food and to glory in his "shameless passion for the white flesh of the lobster" and "the green of pistachio ices—green and cold like the eyelids of Egyptian dancers."

When he looked up at her and said: "Bertha, this is a very admirable *soufflée!*" she almost could have wept with childlike pleasure.

Oh, why did she feel so tender towards the whole world tonight? Everything was good—was right. All that happened seemed to fill again her brimming cup of bliss.

And still, in the back of her mind, there was the pear tree. It would be silver now, in the light of poor dear Eddie's moon, silver as Miss Fulton, who sat there turning a tangerine in her slender fingers that were so pale a light seemed to come from them.

What she simply couldn't make out—what was miraculous—was how she should have guessed Miss Fulton's mood so exactly and so instantly. For she never doubted for a moment that she was right, and yet what had she to go on? Less than nothing. "I believe this does happen very, very rarely between women. Never between men," thought Bertha. "But while I am making the coffee in the drawing-room perhaps she will 'give a sign.'"

What she meant by that she did not know, and what would happen after that she could not imagine.

While she thought like this she saw herself talking and laughing. She had to talk because of her desire to laugh.

"I must laugh or die."

But when she noticed Face's funny little habit of tucking something down the front of her bodice—as if she kept a tiny, secret hoard of nuts there, too—Bertha had to dig her nails into her hands—so as not to laugh too much.

It was over at last. And: "Come and see my new coffee machine," said Bertha.

"We only have a new coffee machine once a fortnight," said Harry. Face took her arm this time; Miss Fulton bent her head and followed after.

The fire had died down in the drawing-room to a red, flickering "nest of baby phœnixes," said Face.

"Don't turn up the light for a moment. It is so lovely." And down she crouched by the fire again. She was always cold . . . "without her little red flannel jacket, of course," thought Bertha.

At that moment Miss Fulton "gave the sign."

"Have you a garden?" said the cool, sleepy voice.

This was so exquisite on her part that all Bertha could do was to obey. She crossed the room, pulled the curtains apart, and opened those long windows. "There!" she breathed.

And the two women stood side by side looking at the slender, flowering tree. Although it was so still it seemed, like the flame of a candle, to stretch up, to point, to quiver in the bright air, to grow taller and taller as they gazed—almost to touch the rim of the round, silver moon.

How long did they stand there? Both, as it were, caught in that circle of unearthly light, understanding each other perfectly, creatures of another world, and wondering what they were to do in this one with all this blissful treasure that burned in their bosoms and dropped, in silver flowers, from their hair and hands?

For ever—for a moment? And did Miss Fulton murmur: "Yes. Just *that*." Or did Bertha dream it?

Then the light was snapped on and Face made the coffee and Harry said: "My dear Mrs. Knight, don't ask me about my baby. I never see her. I shan't feel the slightest interest in her until she has a lover," and Mug took his eye out of the conservatory for a moment and then put it under glass again and Eddie Warren drank his coffee and set down the cup with a face of anguish as though he had drunk and seen the spider.

"What I want to do is to give the young men a show. I believe London is simply teeming with first-chop, unwritten plays. What I want to say to 'em is: 'Here's the theatre. Fire ahead.'"

"You know, my dear, I am going to decorate a room for the Jacob Nathans. Oh, I am so tempted to do a fried-fish scheme, with the backs of the chairs shaped like frying pans and lovely chip potatoes embroidered all over the curtains."

"The trouble with our young writing men is that they are still too romantic. You can't put out to sea without being seasick and wanting a basin. Well, why won't they have the courage of those basins?"

"A *dreadful* poem about a *girl* who was *violated* by a beggar *without* a nose in a lit-tle wood. . . ."

Miss Fulton sank into the lowest, deepest chair and Harry handed round the cigarettes.

From the way he stood in front of her shaking the silver box and saying abruptly: "Egyptian? Turkish? Virginian? They're all mixed up," Bertha realized that she not only bored him; he really disliked her. And she decided from the way Miss Fulton said "No, thank you, I won't smoke," that she felt it, too, and was hurt.

"Oh, Harry, don't dislike her. You are quite wrong about her. She's wonderful, wonderful. And, besides, how can you feel so differently about someone who means so much to me. I shall try to tell you when we are in bed to-night what has been happening. What she and I have shared."

At those last words something strange and almost terrifying darted into Bertha's mind. And this something blind and smiling whispered to her: "Soon these people will go. The house will be quiet—quiet. The lights will be out. And you and he will be alone together in the dark room—the warm bed. . . ."

She jumped up from her chair and ran over to the piano.

"What a pity someone does not play!" she cried. "What a pity somebody does not play."

For the first time in her life Bertha Young desired her husband.

Oh, she loved him—she'd been in love with him, of course, in every other way, but just not in that way. And, equally, of course, she'd understood that he was different. They'd discussed it so often. It had worried her dreadfully at first to find that she was so cold, but after a time it had not seemed to matter. They were so frank with each other—such good pals. That was the best of being modern.

But now—ardently! ardently! The word ached in her ardent body! Was this what that feeling of bliss had been leading up to? But then—

"My dear," said Mrs. Norman Knight, "you know our shame. We are the victims of time and train. We live in Hampstead. It's been so nice."

"I'll come with you into the hall," said Bertha. "I loved having you. But you must not miss the last train. That's so awful, isn't it?"

"Have a whisky, Knight, before you go?" called Harry.

"No, thanks, old chap."

Bertha squeezed his hand for that as she shook it.

"Good night, good-bye," she cried from the top step, feeling that this self of hers was taking leave of them for ever.

When she got back into the drawing-room the others were on the move.

". . . Then you can come part of the way in my taxi."

"I shall be *so* thankful *not* to have to face *another* drive *alone* after my *dreadful* experience."

"You can get a taxi at the rank just at the end of the street. You won't have to walk more than a few yards."

"That's a comfort. I'll go and put on my coat."

Miss Fulton moved towards the hall and Bertha was following when Harry almost pushed past.

"Let me help you."

Bertha knew that he was repenting his rudeness—she let him go. What a boy he was in some ways—so impulsive—so —simple. And Eddie and she were left by the fire.

"I *wonder* if you have seen Bilks' *new* poem called *Table d'Hôte*," said Eddie softly. "It's *so* wonderful. In the last Anthology. Have you got a copy? I'd *so* like to *show* it to you. It begins with an *incredibly* beautiful line: 'Why Must it Always be Tomato Soup?' "

"Yes," said Bertha. And she moved noiselessly to a table opposite the drawing-room door and Eddie glided noiselessly after her. She picked up the little book and gave it to him; they had not made a sound.

While he looked it up she turned her head towards the hall. And she saw . . . Harry with Miss Fulton's coat in his arms and Miss Fulton with her back turned to him and her head bent. He tossed the coat away, put his hands on her shoulders and turned her violently to him. His lips said: "I adore you," and Miss Fulton laid her moonbeam fingers on his cheeks and smiled her sleepy smile. Harry's nostrils quivered; his lips curled back in a hideous grin while he whispered: "To-morrow," and with her eyelids Miss Fulton said: "Yes."

"Here it is," said Eddie. " 'Why Must it Always be Tomato Soup?' It's so *deeply* true, don't you feel? Tomato soup is so *dreadfully* eternal."

"If you prefer," said Harry's voice, very loud, from the hall, "I can phone you a cab to come to the door."

"Oh, no. It's not necessary," said Miss Fulton, and she came up to Bertha and gave her the slender fingers to hold.

"Good-bye. Thank you so much."

"Good-bye," said Bertha.

Miss Fulton held her hand a moment longer.

"Your lovely pear tree!" she murmured.

And then she was gone, with Eddie following, like the black cat following the grey cat.

"I'll shut up shop," said Harry, extravagantly cool and collected.

"Your lovely pear tree—pear tree—pear tree!"

Bertha simply ran over to the long windows.

"Oh, what is going to happen now?" she cried.

But the pear tree was as lovely as ever and as full of flower and as still.

Thomas Mann (1875–1955)

DISORDER AND EARLY SORROW

The principal dish at dinner had been croquettes made of turnip greens. So there follows a trifle, concocted out of one of those dessert powders we use nowadays, that taste like almond soap. Xaver, the youthful manservant, in his outgrown striped jacket, white woollen gloves, and yellow sandals, hands it round, and the "big folk" take this opportunity to remind their father, tactfully, that company is coming today.

The "big folk" are two, Ingrid and Bert. Ingrid is brown-eyed, eighteen, and perfectly delightful. She is on the eve of her exams, and will probably pass them, if only because she knows how to wind masters, and even headmasters, round her finger. She does not, however, mean to use her certificate once she gets it; having leanings towards the stage, on the ground of her ingratiating smile, her equally ingratiating voice, and a marked and irresistible talent for burlesque. Bert is blond and seventeen. He intends to get done with school somehow, anyhow, and fling himself into the arms of life. He will be a dancer, or a cabaret actor, possibly even a waiter—but not a waiter anywhere else save at the Cairo, the nightclub, whither he has once already taken flight, at five in the morning, and been brought back crestfallen. Bert bears a strong resemblance to the youthful manservant Xaver Kleinsgutl, of about the same age as himself; not because he looks common—in features he is strikingly like his father, Professor Cornelius—but by reason of an approximation of types, due in its turn to far-reaching compromises in matters of dress and bearing generally. Both lads wear their heavy hair very long on top, with a cursory parting in the middle, and give their heads the same characteristic toss to throw it off the forehead. When one of them leaves the

91

house, by the garden gate, bareheaded in all weathers, in a blouse rakishly girt with a leather strap, and sheers off bent well over with his head on one side; or else mounts his pushbike—Xaver makes free with his employers', of both sexes, or even, in acutely irresponsible mood, with the Professor's own —Dr. Cornelius from his bedroom window cannot, for the life of him, tell whether he is looking at his son or his servant. Both, he thinks, look like young moujiks. And both are impassioned cigarette-smokers, though Bert has not the means to compete with Xaver, who smokes as many as thirty a day, of a brand named after a popular cinema star. The big folk call their father and mother the "old folk"—not behind their backs, but as a form of address and in all affection: "Hullo, old folks," they will say; though Cornelius is only forty-seven years old and his wife eight years younger. And the Professor's parents, who lead in his household the humble and hesitant life of the really old, are on the big folk's lips the "ancients." As for the "little folk," Ellie and Snapper, who take their meals upstairs with blue-faced Ann—so-called because of her prevailing facial hue—Ellie and Snapper follow their mother's example and address their father by his first name, Abel. Unutterably comic it sounds, in its pert, confiding familiarity; particularly on the lips, in the sweet accents, of five-year-old Eleanor, who is the image of Frau Cornelius's baby pictures and whom the Professor loves above everything else in the world.

"Darling old thing," says Ingrid affably, laying her large but shapely hand on his, as he presides in proper middle-class style over the family table, with her on his left and the mother opposite: "Parent mine, may I ever so gently jog your memory, for you have probably forgotten: this is the afternoon we were to have our little jollification, our turkey-trot with eats to match. You haven't a thing to do but just bear up and not funk it; everything will be over by nine o'clock."

"Oh—ah!" says Cornelius, his face falling. "Good!" he goes on, and nods his head to show himself in harmony with the inevitable. "I only meant—is this really the day? Thursday, yes. How time flies! Well, what time are they coming?"

"Half past four they'll be dropping in, I should say," an-

swers Ingrid, to whom her brother leaves the major rôle in
all dealings with the father. Upstairs, while he is resting, he
will hear scarcely anything, and from seven to eight he takes
his walk. He can slip out by the terrace if he likes.

"Tut!" says Cornelius deprecatingly, as who should say:
"You exaggerate." But Bert puts in: "It's the one evening
in the week Wanja doesn't have to play. Any other night
he'd have to leave by half past six, which would be painful
for all concerned."

Wanja is Ivan Herzl, the celebrated young leading man at
the Stadttheater. Bert and Ingrid are on intimate terms with
him, they often visit him in his dressing-room and have tea.
He is an artist of the modern school, who stands on the stage
in strange and, to the Professor's mind, utterly affected dancing attitudes, and shrieks lamentably. To a professor of history, all highly repugnant; but Bert has entirely succumbed
to Herzl's influence, blackens the lower rim of his eyelids—
despite painful but fruitless scenes with the father—and with
youthful carelessness of the ancestral anguish declares that
not only will he take Herzl for his model if he becomes a
dancer, but in case he turns out to be a waiter at the Cairo
he means to walk precisely thus.

Cornelius slightly raises his brows and makes his son a
little bow—indicative of the unassumingness and self-abnega-
tion that befits his age. You could not call it a mocking bow
or suggestive in any special sense. Bert may refer it to himself or equally to his so talented friend.

"Who else is coming?" next inquires the master of the
house. They mention various people, names all more or less
familiar, from the city, from the suburban colony, from Ingrid's school. They still have some telephoning to do, they
say. They have to phone Max. This is Max Hergesell, an
engineering student; Ingrid utters his name in the nasal drawl
which according to her is the traditional intonation of all
the Hergesells. She goes on to parody it in the most aban-
donedly funny and lifelike way, and the parents laugh until
they nearly choke over the wretched trifle. For even in these
times when something funny happens people have to laugh.

From time to time the telephone bell rings in the Professor's study, and the big folk run across, knowing it is their

affair. Many people had to give up their telephones the last
time the price rose, but so far the Corneliuses have been able
to keep theirs, just as they have kept their villa, which was
built before the war, by dint of the salary Cornelius draws as
professor of history—a million marks, and more or less ade-
quate to the chances and changes of post-war life. The house
is comfortable, even elegant, though sadly in need of repairs
that cannot be made for lack of materials, and at present
disfigured by iron stoves with long pipes. Even so, it is still
the proper setting of the upper middle class, though they
themselves look odd enough in it, with their worn and turned
clothing and altered way of life. The children, of course,
know nothing else; to them it is normal and regular, they
belong by birth to the "villa proletariat." The problem of
clothing troubles them not at all. They and their like have
evolved a costume to fit the time, by poverty out of taste for
innovation: in summer it consists of scarcely more than a
belted linen smock and sandals. The middle-class parents
find things rather more difficult.

The big folk's table-napkins hang over their chair-backs,
they talk with their friends over the telephone. These friends
are the invited guests who have rung up to accept or decline
or arrange; and the conversation is carried on in the jargon
of the clan, full of slang and high spirits, of which the old
folk understand hardly a word. These consult together meantime about the hospitality to be offered to the impending
guests. The Professor displays a middle-class ambitiousness:
he wants to serve a sweet—or something that looks like a
sweet—after the Italian salad and brown-bread sandwiches.
But Frau Cornelius says that would be going too far. The
guests would not expect it, she is sure—and the big folk, returning once more to their trifle, agree with her.

The mother of the family is of the same general type as
Ingrid, though not so tall. She is languid; the fantastic difficulties of the housekeeping have broken and worn her. She
really ought to go and take a cure, but feels incapable; the
floor is always swaying under her feet, and everything seems
upside down. She speaks of what is uppermost in her mind:
the eggs, they simply must be bought to-day. Six thousand
marks apiece they are, and just so many are to be had on this

one day of the week at one single shop fifteen minutes' journey away. Whatever else they do, the big folk must go and
fetch them immediately after luncheon, with Danny, their
neighbor's son, who will soon be calling for them; and Xaver
Kleinsgutl will don civilian garb and attend his young master
and mistress. For no single household is allowed more than
five eggs a week; therefore the young people will enter the
shop singly, one after another, under assumed names, and
thus wring twenty eggs from the shopkeeper for the Cornelius
family. This enterprise is the sporting event of the week for
all participants, not excepting the moujik Kleinsgutl, and
most of all for Ingrid and Bert, who delight in misleading
and mystifying their fellowmen and would revel in the performance even if it did not achieve one single egg. They
adore impersonating fictitious characters; they love to sit in
a bus and carry on long lifelike conversations in a dialect
which they otherwise never speak, the most commonplace
dialogue about politics and people and the price of food,
while the whole bus listens open-mouthed to this incredibly
ordinary prattle, though with a dark suspicion all the while
that something is wrong somewhere. The conversation waxes
ever more shameless, it enters into revolting detail about
these people who do not exist. Ingrid can make her voice
sound ever so common and twittering and shrill as she im-
personates a shop-girl with an illegitimate child, said child
being a son with sadistic tendencies, who lately out in the
country treated a cow with such unnatural cruelty that no
Christian could have borne to see it. Bert nearly explodes at
her twittering, but restrains himself and displays a grisly
sympathy; he and the unhappy shop-girl entering into a
long, stupid, depraved, and shuddery conversation over the
particular morbid cruelty involved; until an old gentleman
opposite, sitting with his ticket folded between his index
finger and his seal ring, can bear it no more and makes
public protest against the nature of the themes these young
folk are discussing with such particularity. He uses the Greek
plural: "themata." Whereat Ingrid pretends to be dissolv-
ing in tears, and Bert behaves as though his wrath against
the old gentleman was with difficulty being held in check
and would probably burst out before long. He clenches his

fists, he gnashes his teeth, he shakes from head to foot; and the unhappy old gentleman, whose intentions had been of the best, hastily leaves the bus at the next stop.

Such are the diversions of the big folk. The telephone plays a prominent part in them: they ring up any and everybody—members of government, opera singers, dignitaries of the Church—in the character of shop assistants, or perhaps as Lord or Lady Doolittle. They are only with difficulty persuaded that they have the wrong number. Once they emptied their parents' card-tray and distributed its contents among the neighbors' letter-boxes, wantonly, yet not without impish sense of the fitness of things to make it highly upsetting. God only knowing why certain people should have called where they did.

Xaver comes to clear away, tossing the hair out of his eyes. Now that he has taken off his gloves you can see the yellow chain-ring on his left hand. And as the Professor finishes his watery eight-thousand-mark beer and lights a cigarette, the little folk can be heard scrambling down the stair, coming, by established custom, for their after-dinner call on Father and Mother. They storm the dining-room, after a struggle with the latch, clutched by both pairs of little hands at once; their clumsy small feet twinkle over the carpet, in red felt slippers with the socks falling down on them. With prattle and shoutings each makes for his own place: Snapper to Mother, to climb on her lap, boast of all he has eaten, and thump his fat little tum; Ellie to her Abel, so much hers because she is so very much his; because she consciously luxuriates in the deep tenderness—like all deep feeling, concealing a melancholy strain—with which he holds her small form embraced; in the love in his eyes as he kisses her little fairy hand or the sweet brow with its delicate tracery of tiny blue veins.

The little folk look like each other, with the strong undefined likeness of brother and sister. In clothing and haircut they are twins. Yet they are sharply distinguished after all, and quite on sex lines. It is a little Adam and a little Eve. Not only is Snapper the sturdier and more compact, he appears consciously to emphasize his four-year-old masculinity in speech, manner, and carriage, lifting his shoulders and letting the little arms hang down quite like a young American athlete, drawing down his mouth when he talks and seeking to give his voice a gruff and forthright ring. But all this masculinity is the result of effort rather than natively his. Born and brought up in these desolate, distracted times, he has been endowed by them with an unstable and hypersensitive nervous system and suffers greatly under life's disharmonies. He is prone to sudden anger and outbursts of bitter tears, stamping his feet at every trifle; for this reason he is his mother's special nursling and care. His round, round eyes are chestnut brown and already inclined to squint, so that he will need glasses in the near future. His little nose is long, the mouth small—the father's nose and mouth they are, more plainly than ever since the Professor shaved his pointed beard and goes smooth-faced. The pointed beard had become impossible—even professors must make some concession to the changing times.

But the little daughter sits on her father's knee, his Eleonorchen, his little Eve, so much more gracious a little being, so much sweeter-faced than her brother—and he holds his cigarette away from her while she fingers his glasses with her dainty wee hands. The lenses are divided for reading and distance, and each day they tease her curiosity afresh.

At bottom he suspects that his wife's partiality may have a firmer basis than his own; that Snapper's refractory masculinity perhaps is solider stuff than his own little girl's more explicit charm and grace. But the heart will not be commanded, that he knows; and once and for all his heart belongs to the little one, as it has since the day she came, since the first time he saw her. Almost always when he holds her in his arms he remembers that first time: remembers the sunny room in the Women's Hospital, where Ellie first saw the light, twelve years after Bert was born. He remembers how he drew near, the mother smiling the while, and cautiously put aside the canopy of the diminutive bed that stood beside the large one. There lay the little miracle among the pillows: so well formed, so encompassed, as it were, with the harmony of sweet proportions, with little hands that even then, though so much tinier, were beautiful as now; with wide-open eyes blue as the sky and brighter than the sunshine—and almost in that very second he felt himself captured and held fast. This was love at first sight, love everlasting: a feeling unknown, unhoped for, unexpected—in so far as it could be a matter of conscious awareness; it took entire possession of him, and he understood, with joyous amazement, that this was for life.

But he understood more. He knows, does Dr. Cornelius, that there is something not quite right about this feeling, so unaware, so undreamed of, so involuntary. He has a shrewd suspicion that it is not by accident it has so utterly mastered him and bound itself up with his existence; that he had— even subconsciously—been preparing for it, or, more precisely, been prepared for it. There is, in short, something in him which at a given moment was ready to issue in such a feeling; and this something, highly extraordinary to relate, is his essence and quality as a professor of history. Dr. Cornelius, however, does not actually say this, even to himself; he merely realizes it, at odd times, and smiles a private smile. He knows that history professors do not love history because it is something that comes to pass, but only because it is something that *has* come to pass; that they hate a revolution like the present one because they feel it is lawless, incoherent, irrelevant—in a word, unhistoric; that their hearts belong to the coherent, disciplined, historic past. For the temper of timelessness, the temper of eternity—thus the scholar communes with himself when he takes his walk by the river before supper—that temper broods over the past; and it is a temper much better suited to the nervous system of a history professor than are the excesses of the present. The past is immortalized; that is to say, it is dead; and death is the root of all godliness and all abiding significance. Dr. Cornelius, walking alone in the dark, has a profound insight into this truth. It is this conservative instinct of his, his sense of the eternal, that has found in his love for his little daughter a way to save itself from the wounding inflicted by the times. For father love, and a little child on its mother's breast—are not these timeless, and thus very, very holy and beautiful? Yet Cornelius, pondering there in the dark, descries something not perfectly right and good in his love. Theoretically, in the interests of science, he admits it to himself. There is something ulterior about it, in the nature of it; that something is hostility, hostility against the history of to-day, which is still in the making, and thus not history at all, in behalf of the genuine history that has already happened—that is to say, death. Yes, passing strange though all this is, yet it is true; true in a sense, that is. His devotion to this priceless little morsel of life and new growth has something to do with death, it clings to death as against life; and that is neither right nor beautiful—in a sense. Though only the most fanatical asceticism could be capable, on no other ground than such casual scientific perception, of tearing this purest and most precious of feelings out of his heart.

He holds his darling on his lap and her slim rosy legs hang down. He raises his brows as he talks to her, tenderly, with a half-teasing note of respect, and listens enchanted to her high, sweet little voice calling him Abel. He exchanges a look with the mother, who is caressing her Snapper and reading him a gentle lecture. He must be more reasonable, he must learn self-control; to-day again, under the manifold exasperations of life, he has given way to rage and behaved like a howling dervish. Cornelius casts a mistrustful glance at the big folk now and then, too; he thinks it not unlikely they are not unaware of those scientific preoccupations of his evening walks. If such be the case they do not show it. They stand there leaning their arms on their chairbacks and with a benevolence not untinctured with irony look on at the parental happiness.

The children's frocks are of heavy, brick-red stuff, embroidered in modern "arty" style. They once belonged to Ingrid and Bert and are precisely alike, save that little knickers come out beneath Snapper's smock. And both have their hair bobbed. Snapper's is a streaky blond, inclined to turn dark. It is bristly and sticky and looks for all the world like a droll, badly fitting wig. But Ellie's is chestnut brown, glossy and fine as silk, as pleasing as her whole little personality. It covers her ears—and these ears are not a pair, one of them being the right size, the other distinctly too large. Her father will sometimes uncover this little abnormality and exclaim over it as though he had never noticed it before, which both makes Ellie giggle and covers her with shame. Her eyes are now golden brown, set far apart and with sweet gleams in them—such a clear and lovely look! The brows above are blond; the nose still unformed, with thick nostrils and almost circular holes; the mouth large and expressive, with a beautifully arching and mobile upper lip. When she laughs, dimples come in her cheeks and she shows her teeth like loosely strung pearls. So far she has lost but one tooth, which her father gently twisted out with his handkerchief after it had grown very wobbling. During this small operation she had paled and trembled very much. Her cheeks have the softness proper to her years, but they are not chubby; indeed, they are rather concave, due to her facial structure, with its somewhat prominent jaw. On one, close to the soft fall of her hair, is a downy freckle.

Ellie is not too well pleased with her looks—a sign that already she troubles about such things. Sadly she thinks it is best to admit it once for all, her face is "homely"; though the rest of her, "on the other hand," is not bad at all. She loves expressions like "on the other hand"; they sound choice and grown-up to her, and she likes to string them together, one after the other: "very likely," "probably," "after all." Snapper is self-critical too, though more in the moral sphere: he suffers from remorse for his attacks of rage and considers himself a tremendous sinner. He is quite certain that heaven is not for such as he; he is sure to go to "the bad place" when he dies, and no persuasions will convince him to the contrary —as that God sees the heart and gladly makes allowances. Obstinately he shakes his head, with the comic, crooked little peruke, and vows there is no place for him in heaven. When he has a cold he is immediately quite choked with mucus; rattles and rumbles from top to toe if you even look at him; his temperature flies up at once and he simply puffs. Nursy is pessimistic on the score of his constitution: such fat-blooded children as he might get a stroke any minute. Once she even thought she saw the moment at hand: Snapper had been in one of his berserker rages, and in the ensuing fit of penitence stood himself in the corner with his back to the room. Suddenly Nursy noticed that his face had gone all blue, far bluer, even, than her own. She raised the alarm, crying out that the child's all too rich blood had at length brought him to his final hour; and Snapper, to his vast astonishment, found himself, so far from being rebuked for evil-doing, encompassed in tenderness and anxiety—until it turned out that his color was not caused by apoplexy but by the distempering on the nursery wall, which had come off on his tear-wet face.

Nursy had come downstairs too, and stands by the door, sleek-haired, owl-eyed, with her hands folded over her white apron, and a severely dignified manner born of her limited intelligence. She is very proud of the care and training she gives her nurslings and declares that they are "enveloping wonderfully." She has had seventeen suppurated teeth lately removed from her jaws and been measured for a set of symmetrical yellow ones in dark rubber gums; these now embellish her peasant face. She is obsessed with the strange conviction that these teeth of hers are the subject of general conversation, that, as it were, the sparrows on the housetops chatter of them. "Everybody knows I've had a false set put in," she will say; "there has been a great deal of foolish talk about them." She is much given to dark hints and veiled innuendo: speaks, for instance, of a certain Dr. Bleifuss, whom every child knows, and "there are even some in the house who pretend to be him." All one can do with talk like this is charitably to pass it over in silence. But she teaches the children nursery rhymes: gems like:

> *Puff, puff, here comes the train!*
> *Puff, puff, toot, toot,*
> *Away it goes again.*

Or that gastronomical jingle, so suited, in its sparseness, to the times, and yet seemingly with a blitheness of its own:

> *Monday we begin the week,*
> *Tuesday there's a bone to pick.*
> *Wednesday we're half way through,*
> *Thursday what a great to-do!*
> *Friday we eat what fish we're able,*
> *Saturday we dance round the table.*
> *Sunday brings us pork and greens—*
> *Here's a feast for kings and queens!*

Also a certain four-line stanza with a romantic appeal, unutterable and unuttered:

Open the gate, open the gate
And let the carriage drive in.
Who is it in the carriage sits?
A lordly sir with golden hair.

Or, finally that ballad about golden-haired Marianne who sat on a, sat on a, sat on a stone, and combed out her, combed out her, combed out her hair; and about blood-thirsty Rudolph, who pulled out a, pulled out a, pulled out a knife—and his ensuing direful end. Ellie enunciates all the ballads charmingly, with her mobile little lips, and sings them in her sweet little voice—much better than Snapper. She does everything better than he does, and he pays her honest admiration and homage and obeys her in all things except when visited by one of his attacks. Sometimes she teaches him, instructs him upon the birds in the picture-book and tells him their proper names: "This is a chaffinch, Buddy, this is a bullfinch, this is a cowfinch." He has to repeat them after her. She gives him medical instruction too, teaches him the names of diseases, such as inflammation of the lungs, inflammation of the blood, inflammation of the air. If he does not pay attention and cannot say the words after her, she stands him in the corner. Once she even boxed his ears, but was so ashamed that she stood herself in the corner for a long time. Yes, they are fast friends, two souls with but a single thought, and have all their adventures in common. They come home from a walk and relate as with one voice that they have seen two moollies and a teenty-weenty baby calf. They are on familiar terms with the kitchen, which consists of Xaver and the ladies Hinterhofer, two sisters once of the lower middle class who, in these evil days, are reduced to living *"au pair"* as the phrase goes and officiating as cook and housemaid for their board and keep. The little ones have a feeling that Xaver and the Hinterhofers are on much the same footing with their father and mother as they are themselves. At least sometimes, when they have been scolded, they go downstairs and announce that the master and mistress are cross. But playing with the servants lacks charm compared with the joys of playing upstairs. The kitchen could never rise to the height of the games their father can invent. For instance, there is "four gentlemen taking a walk." When they play it Abel will crook his knees until he is the same height with themselves and go walking with them, hand in hand. They never get enough of this sport; they could walk round and round the dining-room a whole day on end, five gentlemen in all, counting the diminished Abel.

Then there is the thrilling cushion game. One of the children, usually Ellie, seats herself, unbeknownst to Abel, in his seat at table. Still as a mouse she awaits his coming. He draws near with his head in the air, descanting in loud, clear tones upon the surpassing comfort of his chair; and sits down on top of Ellie. "What's this, what's this?" says he. And bounces about, deaf to the smothered giggles exploding behind him. "Why have they put a cushion in my chair? And what a queer, hard, awkward-shaped cushion it is!" he goes on. "Frightfully uncomfortable to sit on!" And keeps pushing and bouncing about more and more on the astonishing cushion and clutching behind him into the rapturous giggling and squeaking, until at last he turns round, and the game ends with a magnificent climax of discovery and recognition. They might go through all this a hundred times without diminishing by an iota its power to thrill.

To-day is no time for such joys. The imminent festivity disturbs the atmosphere, and besides there is work to be done, and, above all, the eggs to be got. Ellie has just time to recite "Puff, puff," and Cornelius to discover that her ears are not mates, when they are interrupted by the arrival of Danny, come to fetch Bert and Ingrid. Xaver, meantime, has exchanged his striped livery for an ordinary coat, in which he looks rather rough-and-ready, though as brisk and attractive as ever. So then Nursy and the children ascend to the upper regions, the Professor withdraws to his study to read, as always after dinner, and his wife bends her energies upon the sandwiches and salad that must be prepared. And she has another errand as well. Before the young people arrive she has to take her shopping-basket and dash into town on her bicycle, to turn into provisions a sum of money she has in hand, which she dares not keep lest it lose all value.

Cornelius reads, leaning back in his chair, with his cigar between his middle and index fingers. First he reads Macaulay on the origin of the English public debt at the end of the seventeenth century; then an article in a French periodical on the rapid increase in the Spanish debt towards the end of the sixteenth. Both these for his lecture on the morrow. He intends to compare the astonishing prosperity which accompanied the phenomenon in England with its fatal effects a hundred years earlier in Spain, and to analyze the ethical and psychological grounds of the difference in results. For that will give him a chance to refer back from the England of William III, which is the actual subject in hand, to the time of Philip II and the Counter-Reformation, which is his own special field. He has already written a valuable work on this period; it is much cited and got him his professorship. While his cigar burns down and gets strong, he excogitates a few pensive sentences in a key of gentle melancholy, to be delivered before his class next day: about the practically hopeless struggle carried on by the belated Philip against the whole trend of history: against the new, the kingdom-disrupting power of the Germanic ideal of freedom and individual liberty. And about the persistent, futile struggle of the aristocracy, condemned by God and rejected of man, against the forces of progress and change. He savors his sentences; keeps on polishing them while he puts back the books he has been using; then goes upstairs for the usual pause in his day's work, the hour with drawn blinds and closed eyes, which he so imperatively needs. But to-day, he recalls, he will rest under disturbed conditions, amid the bustle of preparations for the feast. He smiles to find his heart giving a mild flutter at the thought. Disjointed phrases on the theme of black-clad Philip and his times mingle with a confused consciousness that they will soon be dancing down below. For five minutes or so he falls asleep.

As he lies and rests he can hear the sound of the garden gate and the repeated ringing at the bell. Each time a little pang goes through him, of excitement and suspense, at the thought that the young people have begun to fill the floor below. And each time he smiles at himself again—though even his smile is slightly nervous, is tinged with the pleasurable anticipations people always feel before a party. At half past four—it is already dark—he gets up and washes at the wash-

stand. The basin has been out of repair for two years. It is
supposed to tip, but has broken away from its socket on one
side and cannot be mended because there is nobody to mend
it; neither replaced because no shop can supply another. So
it has to be hung up above the vent and emptied by lifting
in both hands and pouring out the water. Cornelius shakes
his head over this basin, as he does several times a day—
whenever, in fact, he has occasion to use it. He finishes his
toilet with care, standing under the ceiling light to polish
his glasses till they shine. Then he goes downstairs.

On his way to the dining-room he hears the gramophone
already going, and the sound of voices. He puts on a polite,
society air; at his tongue's end is the phrase he means to
utter: "Pray don't let me disturb you," as he passes directly
into the dining-room for his tea. "Pray don't let me disturb
you"—it seems to him precisely the *mot juste;* towards the
guests cordial and considerate, for himself a very bulwark.

The lower floor is lighted up, all the bulbs in the chandelier
are burning save one that has burned out. Cornelius pauses
on a lower step and surveys the entrance hall. It looks pleasant and cosy in the bright light, with its copy of Marées over
the brick chimney-piece, its wainscoted walls—wainscoted in
soft wood—and red-carpeted floor, where the guests stand in
groups, chatting, each with his tea-cup and slice of bread-
and-butter spread with anchovy paste. There is a festal haze,
faint scents of hair and clothing and human breath come to
him across the room, it is all characteristic and familiar and
highly evocative. The door into the dressing-room is open,
guests are still arriving.

A large group of people is rather bewildering at first sight.
The Professor takes in only the general scene. He does not
see Ingrid, who is standing just at the foot of the steps, in a
dark silk frock with a pleated collar falling softly over the
shoulders, and bare arms. She smiles up at him, nodding and
showing her lovely teeth.

"Rested?" she asks, for his private ear. With a quite un-
warranted start he recognizes her, and she presents some of
her friends. "May I introduce Herr Zuber?" she says. "And
this is Fräulein Plaichinger."

Herr Zuber is insignificant. But Fräulein Plaichinger is a

perfect Germania, blond and voluptuous, arrayed in floating draperies. She has a snub nose, and answers the Professor's salutation in the high, shrill pipe so many stout women have.

"Delighted to meet you," he says. "How nice of you to come! A classmate of Ingrid's I suppose?"

And Herr Zuber is a golfing partner of Ingrid's. He is in business; he works in his uncle's brewery. Cornelius makes a few jokes about the thinness of the beer and professes to believe that Herr Zuber could easily do something about the quality if he would. "But pray don't let me disturb you," he goes on, and turns towards the dining-room.

"There comes Max," says Ingrid. "Max, you sweep, what do you mean by rolling up at this time of day?" For such is the way they talk to each other, offensively to an older ear; of social forms, of hospitable warmth, there is no faintest trace. They all call each other by their first names.

A young man comes up to them out of the dressing-room and makes his bow; he has an expanse of white shirt-front and a little black string tie. He is as pretty as a picture, dark, with rosy cheeks, clean-shaven of course, but with just a sketch of side-whisker. Not a ridiculous or flashy beauty, not like a gypsy fiddler, but just charming to look at, in a winning, well-bred way, with kind dark eyes. He even wears his dinner-jacket a little awkwardly.

"Please don't scold me, Cornelia," he says; "it's the idiotic lectures." And Ingrid presents him to her father as Herr Hergesell.

Well, and so this is Herr Hergesell. He knows his manners, does Herr Hergesell, and thanks the master of the house quite ingratiatingly for his invitation as they shake hands. "I certainly seem to have missed the bus," says he jocosely. "Of course I have lectures to-day up to four o'clock; I would have; and after that I had to go home to change." Then he talks about his pumps, with which he has just been struggling in the dressing-room.

"I brought them with me in a bag," he goes on. "Mustn't tramp all over the carpet in our brogues—it's not done. Well, I was ass enough not to fetch along a shoe-horn, and I find I simply can't get in! What a sell! They are the tightest I've ever had, the numbers don't tell you a thing, and all the leather to-day is just cast iron. It's not leather at all. My poor finger"—he confidingly displays a reddened digit and once more characterizes the whole thing as a "sell," and a putrid sell into the bargain. He really does talk just as Ingrid said he did, with a peculiar nasal drawl, not affectedly in the least, but merely because that is the way of all the Hergesells.

Dr. Cornelius says it is very careless of them not to keep a shoe-horn in the cloak-room and displays proper sympathy with the mangled finger. "But now you *really* must not let me disturb you any longer," he goes on. "*Auf wiedersehen!*" And he crosses the hall into the dining-room.

There are guests there too, drinking tea; the family table is pulled out. But the Professor goes at once to his own little upholstered corner with the electric light bulb above it—the nook where he usually drinks his tea. His wife is sitting there talking with Bert and two other young men, one of them Herzl, whom Cornelius knows and greets; the other a typical "Wandervogel" named Möller, a youth who obviously neither owns nor cares to own the correct evening dress of the middle classes (in fact, there is no such thing any more), nor to ape the manners of a gentleman (and, in fact, there is no such thing any more either). He has a wilderness of hair, horn spectacles, and a long neck, and wears golf stockings and a belted blouse. His regular occupation, the Professor learns, is banking, but he is by way of being an amateur folk-lorist and collects folk-songs from all localities and in all languages. He sings them, too, and at Ingrid's command has brought his guitar; it is hanging in the dressing-room in an oilcloth case. Herzl, the actor, is small and slight, but he has a strong growth of black beard, as you can tell by the thick coat of powder on his cheeks. His eyes are larger than life, with a deep and melancholy glow. He has put on rouge besides the powder—those dull carmine high-lights on the cheeks can be nothing but a cosmetic. "Queer," thinks the Professor. "You would think a man would be one thing or the other—not melancholic and use face paint at the same time. It's a psychological contradiction. How can a melancholy man rouge? But here we have a perfect illustration of the abnormality of the artist soul-form. It can make possible a contradiction like this—perhaps it even consists in the con-

tradiction. All very interesting—and no reason whatever for
not being polite to him. Politeness is a primitive convention
—and legitimate. . . . Do take some lemon, Herr Hof-
schauspieler!"

Court actors and court theatres—there are no such things
any more, really. But Herzl relishes the sound of the title,
notwithstanding he is a revolutionary artist. This must be
another contradiction inherent in his soul-form; so, at least,
the Professor assumes, and he is probably right. The flattery
he is guilty of is a sort of atonement for his previous hard
thoughts about the rouge.

"Thank you so much—it's really too good of you, sir,"
says Herzl, quite embarrassed. He is so overcome that he
almost stammers; only his perfect enunciation saves him.
His whole bearing towards his hostess and the master of the
house is exaggeratedly polite. It is almost as though he had a
bad conscience in respect of his rouge; as though an inward
compulsion had driven him to put it on, but now, seeing it
through the Professor's eyes, he disapproves of it himself,
and thinks, by an air of humility toward the whole of un-
rouged society, to mitigate its effect.

They drink their tea and chat: about Möller's folk-songs,
about Basque folk-songs and Spanish folk-songs; from which
they pass to the new production of *Don Carlos* at the Stadttheater, in which Herzl plays the title-rôle. He talks about his
own rendering of the part and says he hopes his conception
of the character has unity. They go on to criticize the rest of
the cast, the setting, and the production as a whole; and
Cornelius is struck, rather painfully, to find the conversation
trending towards his own special province, back to Spain and
the Counter-Reformation. He has done nothing at all to give
it this turn, he is perfectly innocent, and hopes it does not
look as though he had sought an occasion to play the professor. He wonders, and falls silent, feeling relieved when the
little folk come up to the table. Ellie and Snapper have on
their blue velvet Sunday frocks; they are permitted to par-
take in the festivities up to bedtime. They look shy and large-
eyed as they say how-do-you-do to the strangers and, under
pressure, repeat their names and ages. Herr Möller does nothing but gaze at them solemnly, but Herzl is simply ravished.

He rolls his eyes up to heaven and puts his hands over his mouth; he positively blesses them. It all, no doubt, comes from his heart, but he is so addicted to theatrical methods of making an impression and getting an effect that both words and behavior ring frightfully false. And even his enthusiasm for the little folk looks too much like part of his general craving to make up for the rouge on his cheeks.

The tea-table has meanwhile emptied of guests, and dancing is going on in the hall. The children run off, the Professor prepares to retire. "Go and enjoy yourselves," he says to Möller and Herzl, who have sprung from their chairs as he rises from his. They shake hands and he withdraws into his study, his peaceful kingdom, where he lets down the blinds, turns on the desk lamp, and sits down to work.

It is work which can be done, if necessary, under disturbed conditions: nothing but a few letters and a few notes. Of course, Cornelius's mind wanders. Vague impressions float through it: Herr Hergesell's refractory pumps, the high pipe in that plump body of the Plaichinger female. As he writes, or leans back in his chair and stares into space, his thoughts go back to Herr Möller's collection of Basque folksongs, to Herzl's posings and humility, to "his" Carlos and the court of Philip II. There is something strange, he thinks, about conversations. They are so ductile, they will flow of their own accord in the direction of one's dominating interest. Often and often he has seen this happen. And while he is thinking, he is listening to the sounds next door—rather subdued, he finds them. He hears only voices, no sound of footsteps. The dancers do not glide or circle round the room; they merely walk about over the carpet, which does not hamper their movements in the least. Their way of holding each other is quite different and strange, and they move to the strains of the gramophone, to the weird music of the new world. He concentrates on the music and makes out that it is a jazz-band record, with various percussion instruments and the clack and clatter of castanets, which, however, are not even faintly suggestive of Spain, but merely jazz like the rest. No, not Spain. . . . His thoughts are back at the old round.

Half an hour goes by. It occurs to him it would be no more

than friendly to go and contribute a box of cigarettes to the festivities next door. Too bad to ask the young people to smoke their own—though they have probably never thought of it. He goes into the empty dining-room and takes a box from his supply in the cupboard: not the best ones, nor yet the brand he himself prefers, but a certain long, thin kind he is not averse to getting rid of—after all, they are nothing but youngsters. He takes the box into the hall, holds it up with a smile, and deposits it on the mantel-shelf. After which he gives a look round and returns to his own room.

There comes a lull in dance and music. The guests stand about the room in groups or round the table at the window or are seated in a circle by the fireplace. Even the built-in stairs, with their worn velvet carpet, are crowded with young folk as in an amphitheatre: Max Hergesell is there, leaning back with one elbow on the step above and gesticulating with his free hand as he talks to the shrill, voluptuous Plaichinger. The floor of the hall is nearly empty, save just in the centre: there, directly beneath the chandelier, the two little ones in their blue velvet frocks clutch each other in an awkward embrace and twirl silently round and round, oblivious of all else. Cornelius, as he passes, strokes their hair, with a friendly word; it does not distract them from their small solemn preoccupation. But at his own door he turns to glance round and sees young Hergesell push himself off the stair by his elbow —probably because he noticed the Professor. He comes down into the arena, takes Ellie out of her brother's arms, and dances with her himself. It looks very comic, without the music, and he crouches down just as Cornelius does when he goes walking with the four gentlemen, holding the fluttered Ellie as though she were grown up and taking little "shimmying" steps. Everybody watches with huge enjoyment, the gramophone is put on again, dancing becomes general. The Professor stands and looks, with his hand on the door-knob. He nods and laughs; when he finally shuts himself into his study the mechanical smile still lingers on his lips.

Again he turns over pages by his desk lamp, takes notes, attends to a few simple matters. After a while he notices that the guests have forsaken the entrance hall for his wife's drawing-room, into which there is a door from his own study as well. He hears their voices and the sounds of a guitar being tuned. Herr Möller, it seems, is to sing—and does so. He twangs the strings of his instrument and sings in a powerful bass a ballad in a strange tongue, possibly Swedish. The Professor does not succeed in identifying it, though he listens attentively to the end, after which there is great applause. The sound is deadened by the portière that hangs over the dividing door. The young bank-clerk begins another song. Cornelius goes softly in.

It is half-dark in the drawing-room; the only light is from the shaded standard lamp, beneath which Möller sits, on the divan, with his legs crossed, picking his strings. His audience is grouped easily about; as there are not enough seats, some stand, and more, among them many young ladies, are simply sitting on the floor with their hands clasped round their knees or even with their legs stretched out before them. Hergesell sits thus, in his dinner jacket, next the piano, with Fräulein Plaichinger beside him. Frau Cornelius is holding both children on her lap as she sits in her easy-chair opposite the singer. Snapper, the Bœotian, begins to talk loud and clear in the middle of the song and has to be intimidated with hushings and finger-shakings. Never, never would Ellie allow herself to be guilty of such conduct. She sits there daintily erect and still on her mother's knee. The Professor tries to catch her eye and exchange a private signal with his little girl; but she does not see him. Neither does she seem to be looking at the singer. Her gaze is directed lower down.

Möller sings the "joli tambour":
> "*Sire, mon roi, donnez-moi votre fille—*"
They are all enchanted. "How good!" Hergesell is heard to say, in the odd, nasally condescending Hergesell tone. The next one is a beggar ballad, to a tune composed by young Möller himself; it elicits a storm of applause:
> *Gypsy lassie a-goin' to the fair,*
> *Huzza!*
> *Gypsy laddie a-goin' to be there—*
> *Huzza, diddlety umpty dido!*

Laughter and high spirits, sheer reckless hilarity, reigns after this jovial ballad. "Frightfully good!" Hergesell comments again, as before. Follows another popular song, this

time a Hungarian one; Möller sings it in its own outlandish
tongue, and most effectively. The Professor applauds with
ostentation. It warms his heart and does him good, this out-
cropping of artistic, historic, and cultural elements all
amongst the shimmying. He goes up to young Möller and
congratulates him, talks about the songs and their sources,
and Möller promises to lend him a certain annotated book
of folk-songs. Cornelius is the more cordial because all the
time, as fathers do, he has been comparing the parts and
achievements of this young stranger with those of his own
son, and being gnawed by envy and chagrin. This young
Möller, he is thinking, is a capable bank-clerk (though about
Möller's capacity he knows nothing whatever) and has this
special gift besides, which must have taken talent and energy
to cultivate. "And here is my poor Bert, who knows nothing
and can do nothing and thinks of nothing except playing the
clown, without even talent for that!" He tries to be just; he
tells himself that, after all, Bert has innate refinement; that
probably there is a good deal more to him than there is to the
successful Möller; that perhaps he has even something of the
poet in him, and his dancing and table-waiting are due to
mere boyish folly and the distraught times. But paternal
envy and pessimism win the upper hand; when Möller begins
another song, Dr. Cornelius goes back to his room.

He works as before, with divided attention, at this and
that, while it gets on for seven o'clock. Then he remembers a
letter he may just as well write, a short letter and not very
important, but letter-writing is wonderful for the way it takes
up the time, and it is almost half past when he has finished.
At half past eight the Italian salad will be served; so now is
the prescribed moment for the Professor to go out into the
wintry darkness to post his letters and take his daily quan-
tum of fresh air and exercise. They are dancing again, and he
will have to pass through the hall to get his hat and coat;
but they are used to him now, he need not stop and beg them
not to be disturbed. He lays away his papers, takes up the
letters he has written, and goes out. But he sees his wife
sitting near the door of his room and pauses a little by her
easy-chair.

She is watching the dancing. Now and then the big folk or

some of their guests stop to speak to her; the party is at its height, and there are more onlookers than these two: blue-faced Ann is standing at the bottom of the stairs, in all the dignity of her limitations. She is waiting for the children, who simply cannot get their fill of these unwonted festivities, and watching over Snapper, lest his all too rich blood be churned to the danger-point by too much twirling round. And not only the nursery but the kitchen takes an interest: Xaver and the two ladies Hinterhofer are standing by the pantry door looking on with relish. Fräulein Walburga, the elder of the two sunken sisters (the culinary section—she objects to being called a cook), is a whimsical, good-natured sort, brown-eyed, wearing glasses with thick circular lenses; the nose-piece is wound with a bit of rag to keep it from pressing on her nose. Fräulein Cecilia is younger, though not so precisely young either. Her bearing is as self-assertive as usual, this being her way of sustaining her dignity as a former member of the middle class. For Fräulein Cecilia feels acutely her descent into the ranks of domestic service. She positively declines to wear a cap or other badge of servitude, and her hardest trial is on the Wednesday evening when she has to serve dinner while Xaver has his afternoon out. She hands the dishes with averted face and elevated nose—a fallen queen; and so distressing is it to behold her degradation that one evening when the little folk happened to be at table and saw her they both with one accord burst into tears. Such anguish is unknown to young Xaver. He enjoys serving and does it with an ease born of practice as well as talent, for he was once a "piccolo." But otherwise he is a thorough-paced good-for-nothing and windbag—with quite distinct traits of character of his own, as his long-suffering employers are always ready to concede, but perfectly impossible and a bag of wind for all that. One must just take him as he is, they think, and not expect figs from thistles. He is the child and product of the disrupted times, a perfect specimen of his generation, follower of the revolution, Bolshevist sympathizer. The Professor's name for him is the "minute-man," because he is always to be counted on in any sudden crisis, if only it address his sense of humour or love of novelty, and will display therein amazing readiness and re-

source. But he utterly lacks a sense of duty and can as little
be trained to the performance of the daily round and common task as some kinds of dog can be taught to jump over a
stick. It goes so plainly against the grain that criticism is dis-
armed. One becomes resigned. On grounds that appealed to
him as unusual and amusing he would be ready to turn out
of his bed at any hour of the night. But he simply cannot get
up before eight in the morning, he cannot do it, he will not
jump over the stick. Yet all day long the evidence of this
free and untrammelled existence, the sound of his mouth-
organ, his joyous whistle, or his raucous but expressive voice
lifted in song, rises to the hearing of the world above-stairs;
and the smoke of his cigarettes fills the pantry. While the
Hinterhofer ladies work he stands and looks on. Of a morning while the Professor is breakfasting, he tears the leaf off
the study calendar—but does not lift a finger to dust the
room. Dr. Cornelius has often told him to leave the calendar
alone, for he tends to tear off two leaves at a time and thus
to add to the general confusion. But young Xaver appears to
find joy in this activity, and will not be deprived of it.

Again, he is fond of children, a winning trait. He will throw
himself into games with the little folk in the garden, make and
mend their toys with great ingenuity, even read aloud from
their books—and very droll it sounds in his thick-lipped pro-
nunciation. With his whole soul he loves the cinema; after an
evening spent there he inclines to melancholy and yearning
and talking to himself. Vague hopes stir in him that some day
he may make his fortune in that gay world and belong to it
by rights—hopes based on his shock of hair and his physical agility and daring. He likes to climb the ash tree in the
front garden, mounting branch by branch to the very top
and frightening everybody to death who sees him. Once there
he lights a cigarette and smokes it as he sways to and fro,
keeping a look-out for a cinema director who might chance
to come along and engage him.

If he changed his striped jacket for mufti, he might easily
dance with the others and no one would notice the difference.
For the big folk's friends are rather anomalous in their clothing: evening dress is worn by a few, but it is by no means the
rule. There is quite a sprinkling of guests, both male and fe-

male, in the same general style as Möller the ballad-singer. The Professor is familiar with the circumstances of most of this young generation he is watching as he stands beside his wife's chair; he has heard them spoken of by name. They are students at the high school or at the School of Applied Art; they lead, at least the masculine portion, that precarious and scrambling existence which is purely the product of the time. There is a tall, pale, spindling youth, the son of a dentist, who lives by speculation. From all the Professor hears, he is a perfect Aladdin. He keeps a car, treats his friends to champagne suppers, and showers presents upon them on every occasion, costly little trifles in mother-of-pearl and gold. So today he has brought gifts to the young givers of the feast: for Bert a gold lead-pencil, and for Ingrid a pair of ear-rings of barbaric size, great gold circles that fortunately do not have to go through the little ear-lobe, but are fastened over it by means of a clip. The big folk come laughing to their parents to display these trophies; and the parents shake their heads even while they admire—Aladdin bowing over and over from afar.

The young people appear to be absorbed in their dancing —if the performance they are carrying out with so much still concentration can be called dancing. They stride across the carpet, slowly, according to some unfathomable prescript, strangely embraced; in the newest attitude, tummy advanced and shoulders high, waggling the hips. They do not get tired, because nobody could. There is no such thing as heightened colour or heaving bosoms. Two girls may dance together or two young men—it is all the same. They move to the exotic strains of the gramophone, played with the loudest needles to procure the maximum of sound: shimmies, foxtrots, one-steps, double foxes, African shimmies, Java dances, and Creole polkas, the wild musky melodies follow one another, now furious, now languishing, a monotonous Negro programme in unfamiliar rhythm, to a clacking, clashing, and strumming orchestral accompaniment.

"What is that record?" Cornelius inquires of Ingrid, as she passes him by in the arms of the pale young speculator, with reference to the piece then playing, whose alternate languors

and furies he finds comparatively pleasing and showing a
certain resourcefulness in detail.

"Prince of Pappenheim: 'Console thee, dearest child,' "
she answers, and smiles pleasantly back at him with her
white teeth.

The cigarette smoke wreathes beneath the chandelier. The
air is blue with a festal haze compact of sweet and thrilling
ingredients that stir the blood with memories of green-sick
pains and are particularly poignant to those whose youth
—like the Professor's own—has been over-sensitive. . . . The
little folk are still on the floor. They are allowed to stop
up until eight, so great is their delight in the party. The
guests have got used to their presence; in their own way,
they have their place in the doings of the evening. They have
separated, anyhow: Snapper revolves all alone in the middle
of the carpet, in his little blue velvet smock, while Ellie is
running after one of the dancing couples, trying to hold the
man fast by his coat. It is Max Hergesell and Fräulein
Plaichinger. They dance well, it is a pleasure to watch them.
One has to admit that these mad modern dances, when the
right people dance them, are not so bad after all—they have
something quite taking. Young Hergesell is a capital leader,
dances according to rule, yet with individuality. So it looks.
With what aplomb can he walk backwards—when space
permits! And he knows how to be graceful standing still in
a crowd. And his partner supports him well, being unsus-
pectedly lithe and buoyant, as fat people often are. They
look at each other, they are talking, paying no heed to
Ellie, though others are smiling to see the child's persistence. Dr. Cornelius tries to catch up his little sweetheart as
she passes and draw her to him. But Ellie eludes him, almost
peevishly; her dear Abel is nothing to her now. She braces
her little arms against his chest and turns her face away
with a persecuted look. Then escapes to follow her fancy
once more.

The Professor feels an involuntary twinge. Uppermost in
his heart is hatred for this party, with its power to intoxicate
and estrange his darling child. His love for her—that not
quite disinterested, not quite unexceptionable love of his—is
easily wounded. He wears a mechanical smile, but his eyes

have clouded, and he stares fixedly at a point in the carpet, between the dancers' feet.

"The children ought to go to bed," he tells his wife. But she pleads for another quarter of an hour; she has promised already, and they do love it so! He smiles again and shakes his head, stands so a moment and then goes across to the cloak-room, which is full of coats and hats and scarves and overshoes. He has trouble in rummaging out his own coat, and Max Hergesell comes out of the hall, wiping his brow.

"Going out, sir?" he asks, in Hergesellian accents, dutifully helping the older man on with his coat. "Silly business this, with my pumps," he says. "They pinch like hell. The brutes are simply too tight for me, quite apart from the bad leather. They press just here on the ball of my great toe"— he stands on one foot and holds the other in his hand—"it's simply unbearable. There's nothing for it but to take them off; my brogues will have to do the business. . . . Oh, let me help you, sir."

"Thanks," says Cornelius. "Don't trouble. Get rid of your own tormentors. . . . Oh, thanks very much!" For Hergesell has gone on one knee to snap the fasteners of his snowboots.

Once more the Professor expresses his gratitude; he is pleased and touched by so much sincere respect and youthful readiness to serve. "Go and enjoy yourself," he counsels. "Change your shoes and make up for what you have been suffering. Nobody can dance in shoes that pinch. Good-bye, I must be off to get a breath of fresh air."

"I'm going to dance with Ellie now," calls Hergesell after him. "She'll be a first-rate dancer when she grows up, and that I'll swear to."

"Think so?" Cornelius answers, already half out. "Well, you are a connoisseur, I'm sure. Don't get curvature of the spine with stooping."

He nods again and goes. "Fine lad," he thinks as he shuts the door. "Student of engineering. Knows what he's bound for, got a good clear head, and so well set up and pleasant too." And again paternal envy rises as he compares his poor Bert's status with this young man's, which he puts in the rosiest light that his son's may look the darker. Thus he sets out on his evening walk.

He goes up the avenue, crosses the bridge, and walks along the bank on the other side as far as the next bridge but one. The air is wet and cold, with a little snow now and then. He turns up his coat-collar and slips the crook of his cane over the arm behind his back. Now and then he ventilates his lungs with a long deep breath of the night air. As usual when he walks, his mind reverts to his professional preoccupations, he thinks about his lectures and the things he means to say tomorrow about Philip's struggle against the Germanic revolution, things steeped in melancholy and penetratingly just. Above all just, he thinks. For in one's dealings with the young it behooves one to display the scientific spirit, to exhibit the principles of enlightenment—not only for purposes of mental discipline, but on the human and individual side, in order not to wound them or indirectly offend their political sensibilities; particularly in these days, when there is so much tinder in the air, opinions are so frightfully split up and chaotic, and you may so easily incur attacks from one party or the other, or even give rise to scandal, by taking sides on a point of history. "And taking sides is unhistoric anyhow," so he muses. "Only justice, only impartiality is historic." And could not, properly considered, be otherwise. . . . For justice can have nothing of youthful fire and blithe, fresh, loyal conviction. It is by nature melancholy. And, being so, has secret affinity with the lost cause and the forlorn hope rather than with the fresh and blithe and loyal—perhaps this affinity is its very essence and without it it would not exist at all! . . . "And is there then no such thing as justice?" the Professor asks himself, and ponders the question so deeply that he absently posts his letters in the next box and turns round to go home. This thought of his is unsettling and disturbing to the scientific mind—but is it not after all itself scientific, psychological, conscientious, and therefore to be accepted without prejudice, no matter how upsetting? In the midst of which musings Dr. Cornelius finds himself back at his own door.

On the outer threshold stands Xaver, and seems to be looking for him.

"Herr Professor," says Xaver, tossing back his hair, "go upstairs to Ellie straight off. She's in a bad way."

"What's the matter?" asks Cornelius in alarm. "Is she ill?"

"No-o, not to say ill," answers Xaver. "She's just in a bad way and crying fit to bust her little heart. It's along o' that chap with the shirt-front that danced with her—Herr Hergesell. She couldn't be got to go upstairs peaceably, not at no price at all, and she's b'en crying bucketfuls."

"Nonsense," says the Professor, who has entered and is tossing off his things in the cloak-room. He says no more; opens the glass door and without a glance at the guests turns swiftly to the stairs. Takes them two at a time, crosses the upper hall and the small room leading into the nursery. Xaver follows at his heels, but stops at the nursery door.

A bright light still burns within, showing the gay frieze that runs all round the room, the large row of shelves heaped with a confusion of toys, the rocking-horse on his swaying platform, with red-varnished nostrils and raised hoofs. On the linoleum lie other toys—building blocks, railway trains, a little trumpet. The two white cribs stand not far apart, Ellie's in the window corner, Snapper's out in the room.

Snapper is asleep. He has said his prayers in loud, ringing tones, prompted by Nurse, and gone off at once into vehement, profound, and rosy slumber—from which a cannonball fired at close range could not rouse him. He lies with both fists flung back on the pillows on either side of the tousled head with its funny crooked little slumber-tossed wig.

A circle of females surrounds Ellie's bed: not only blue-faced Ann is there, but the Hinterhofer ladies too, talking to each other and to her. They make way as the Professor comes up and reveal the child sitting all pale among her pillows, sobbing and weeping more bitterly than he has ever seen her sob and weep in her life. Her lovely little hands lie on the coverlet in front of her, the nightgown with its narrow lace border has slipped down from her shoulder—such a thin, bird-like little shoulder—and the sweet head Cornelius loves so well, set on the neck like a flower on its stalk, her head is on one side, with the eyes rolled up to the corner between wall and ceiling above her head. For there she seems to envisage the anguish of her heart and even to nod to it— either on purpose or because her head wobbles as her body is shaken with the violence of her sobs. Her eyes rain down tears. The bow-shaped lips are parted, like a little *mater dolorosa's,* and from them issue long, low wails that in nothing resemble the unnecessary and exasperating shrieks of a naughty child, but rise from the deep extremity of her heart and wake in the Professor's own a sympathy that is wellnigh intolerable. He has never seen his darling so before. His feelings find immediate vent in an attack on the ladies Hinterhofer.

"What about the supper?" he asks sharply. "There must be a great deal to do. Is my wife being left to do it alone?"

For the acute sensibilities of the former middle class this is quite enough. The ladies withdraw in righteous indignation, and Xaver Kleinsgutl jeers at them as they pass out. Having been born to low life instead of achieving it, he never loses a chance to mock at their fallen state.

"Childie, childie," murmurs Cornelius, and sitting down by the crib enfolds the anguished Ellie in his arms. "What is the trouble with my darling?"

She bedews his face with her tears.

"Abel . . . Abel . . ." she stammers between sobs. "Why —isn't Max—my brother? Max ought to be—my brother!"

Alas, alas! What mischance is this? Is this what the party has wrought, with its fatal atmosphere? Cornelius glances helplessly up at blue-faced Ann standing there in all the dignity of her limitations with her hands before her on her apron. She purses up her mouth and makes a long face. "It's pretty young," she says, "for the female instincts to be showing up."

"Hold your tongue," snaps Cornelius, in his agony. He has this much to be thankful for, that Ellie does not turn from him now; she does not push him away as she did downstairs, but clings to him in her need, while she reiterates her absurd, bewildered prayer that Max might be her brother, or with a fresh burst of desire demands to be taken downstairs so that he can dance with her again. But Max, of course, is dancing with Fräulein Plaichinger, that behemoth who is his rightful partner and has every claim upon him; whereas Ellie—never, thinks the Professor, his heart torn with the violence of his pity, never has she looked so tiny and birdlike as now, when she nestles to him shaken with sobs and all

unaware of what is happening in her little soul. No, she does
not know. She does not comprehend that her suffering is on
account of Fräulein Plaichinger, fat, overgrown, and utterly
within her rights in dancing with Max Hergesell, whereas
Ellie may only do it once, by way of a joke, although she is
incomparably the more charming of the two. Yet it would be
quite mad to reproach young Hergesell with the state of
affairs or to make fantastic demands upon him. No, Ellie's
suffering is without help or healing and must be covered up.
Yet just as it is without understanding, so it is also without
restraint—and that is what makes it so horribly painful. Xaver
and blue-faced Ann do not feel this pain, it does not affect
them—either because of native callousness or because they
accept it as the way of nature. But the Professor's fatherly
heart is quite torn by it, and by a distressful horror of this
passion, so hopeless and so absurd.

Of no avail to hold forth to poor Ellie on the subject of
the perfectly good little brother she already has. She only
casts a distraught and scornful glance over at the other crib,
where Snapper lies vehemently slumbering, and with fresh
tears calls again for Max. Of no avail either the promise of
a long, long walk tomorrow, all five gentlemen, round and
round the dining-room table; or a dramatic description of
the thrilling cushion games they will play. No, she will listen
to none of all this, nor to lying down and going to sleep. She
will not sleep, she will sit bolt upright and suffer. . . . But
on a sudden they stop and listen, Abel and Ellie; listen to
something miraculous that is coming to pass, that is approaching by strides, two strides, to the nursery door, that
now overwhelmingly appears. . . .

It is Xaver's work, not a doubt of that. He has not remained by the door where he stood to gloat over the ejection
of the Hinterhofers. No, he has bestirred himself, taken a
notion; likewise steps to carry it out. Downstairs he has
gone, twitched Herr Hergesell's sleeve, and made a thick-
lipped request. So here they both are. Xaver, having done his
part, remains by the door; but Max Hergesell comes up to
Ellie's crib; in his dinner-jacket, with his sketchy side-
whisker and charming black eyes; obviously quite pleased
with his rôle of swan knight and fairy prince, as one who

should say: "See, here am I, now all losses are restored and
sorrows end."

Cornelius is almost as much overcome as Ellie herself.

"Just look," he says feebly, "look who's here. This is un-
commonly good of you, Herr Hergesell."

"Not a bit of it," says Hergesell. "Why shouldn't I come
to say good-night to my fair partner?"

And he approaches the bars of the crib, behind which Ellie
sits struck mute. She smiles blissfully through her tears. A
funny, high little note that is half a sigh of relief comes from
her lips, then she looks dumbly up at her swan knight with
her golden-brown eyes—tear-swollen though they are, so
much more beautiful than the fat Plaichinger's. She does not
put up her arms. Her joy, like her grief, is without understanding; but she does not do that. The lovely little hands lie
quiet on the coverlet, and Max Hergesell stands with his
arms leaning over the rail as on a balcony.

"And now," he says smartly, "she need not 'sit the live-
long night and weep upon her bed'!" He looks at the Professor to make sure he is receiving due credit for the quotation. "Ha ha!" he laughs, "she's beginning young. 'Console
thee, dearest child!' Never mind, you're all right! Just as
you are you'll be wonderful! You've only got to grow up.
. . . And you'll lie down and go to sleep like a good girl,
now I've come to say good-night? And not cry any more,
little Lorelei?"

Ellie looks up at him, transfigured. One birdlike shoulder
is bare; the Professor draws the lace-trimmed nightie over
it. There comes into his mind a sentimental story he once
read about a dying child who longs to see a clown he had
once, with unforgettable ecstasy, beheld in a circus. And they
bring the clown to the bedside marvellously arrayed, embroidered before and behind with silver butterflies; and the
child dies happy. Max Hergesell is not embroidered, and
Ellie, thank God, is not going to die, she has only "been in a
bad way." But, after all, the effect is the same. Young
Hergesell leans over the bars of the crib and rattles on, more
for the father's ear than the child's, but Ellie does not know
that—and the father's feelings towards him are the most
singular mixture of thankfulness, embarrassment, and hatred.

"Good night, little Lorelei," says Hergesell, and gives her his hand through the bars. Her pretty, soft, white little hand is swallowed up in the grasp of his big, strong, red one. "Sleep well," he says, "and sweet dreams! But don't dream about me—God forbid! Not at your age—ha ha!" And then the fairy clown's visit is at an end. Cornelius accompanies him to the door. "No, no, positively, no thanks called for, don't mention it," he large-heartedly protests; and Xaver goes downstairs with him, to help serve the Italian salad.

But Dr. Cornelius returns to Ellie, who is now lying down, with her cheek pressed into her flat little pillow.

"Well, wasn't that lovely?" he says as he smooths the covers. She nods, with one last little sob. For a quarter of an hour he sits beside her and watches while she falls asleep in her turn, beside the little brother who found the right way so much earlier than she. Her silky brown hair takes the enchanting fall it always does when she sleeps; deep, deep lie the lashes over the eyes that late so abundantly poured forth their sorrow; the angelic mouth with its bowed upper lip is peacefully relaxed and a little open. Only now and then comes a belated catch in her slow breathing.

And her small hands, like pink and white flowers, lie so quietly, one on the coverlet, the other on the pillow by her face—Dr. Cornelius, gazing, feels his heart melt with tenderness as with strong wine.

"How good," he thinks, "that she breathes in oblivion with every breath she draws! That in childhood each night is a deep, wide gulf between one day and the next. Tomorrow, beyond all doubt, young Hergesell will be a pale shadow, powerless to darken her little heart. Tomorrow, forgetful of all but present joy, she will walk with Abel and Snapper, all five gentlemen, round and round the table, will play the ever-thrilling cushion game."

Heaven be praised for that!

W. Somerset Maugham (1874–1965)
RAIN

It was nearly bed-time and when they awoke next morning land would be in sight. Dr. Macphail lit his pipe and,
leaning over the rail, searched the heavens for the Southern
Cross. After two years at the front and a wound that had
taken longer to heal than it should, he was glad to settle
down quietly at Apia for twelve months at least, and he felt
already better for the journey. Since some of the passengers
were leaving the ship next day at Pago-Pago they had had a
little dance that evening and in his ears hammered still the
harsh notes of the mechanical piano. But the deck was quiet
at last. A little way off he saw his wife in a long chair talking with the Davidsons, and he strolled over to her. When
he sat down under the light and took off his hat you saw
that he had very red hair, with a bald patch on the crown,
and the red, freckled skin which accompanies red hair; he
was a man of forty, thin, with a pinched face, precise and
rather pedantic; and he spoke with a Scots accent in a very
low, quiet voice.

Between the Macphails and the Davidsons, who were
missionaries, there had arisen the intimacy of shipboard,
which is due to propinquity rather than to any community
of taste. Their chief tie was the disapproval they shared of
the men who spent their days and nights in the smoking-
room playing poker or bridge and drinking. Mrs. Macphail
was not a little flattered to think that she and her husband
were the only people on board with whom the Davidsons
were willing to associate, and even the doctor, shy but no
fool, half unconsciously acknowledged the compliment. It
was only because he was of an argumentative mind that in
their cabin at night he permitted himself to carp.

"Mrs. Davidson was saying she didn't know how they'd

have got through the journey if it hadn't been for us," said Mrs. Macphail, as she neatly brushed out her transformation. "She said we were really the only people on the ship they cared to know."

"I shouldn't have thought a missionary was such a big bug that he could afford to put on frills."

"It's not frills. I quite understand what she means. It wouldn't have been very nice for the Davidsons to have to mix with all that rough lot in the smoking-room."

"The founder of their religion wasn't so exclusive," said Dr. Macphail with a chuckle.

"I've asked you over and over again not to joke about religion," answered his wife. "I shouldn't like to have a nature like yours, Alec. You never look for the best in people."

He gave her a sidelong glance with his pale, blue eyes, but did not reply. After many years of married life he had learned that it was more conducive to peace to leave his wife with the last word. He was undressed before she was, and climbing into the upper bunk he settled down to read himself to sleep.

When he came on deck next morning they were close to land. He looked at it with greedy eyes. There was a thin strip of silver beach rising quickly to hills covered to the top with luxuriant vegetation. The coconut trees, thick and green, came nearly to the water's edge, and among them you saw the grass houses of the Samoans; and here and there, gleaming white, a little church. Mrs. Davidson came and stood beside him. She was dressed in black and wore round her neck a gold chain, from which dangled a small cross. She was a little woman, with brown, dull hair very elaborately arranged, and she had prominent blue eyes behind invisible *pince-nez*. Her face was long, like a sheep's, but she gave no impression of foolishness, rather of extreme alertness; she had the quick movements of a bird. The most remarkable thing about her was her voice, high, metallic, and without inflection; it fell on the ear with a hard monotony, irritating to the nerves like the pitiless clamour of the pneumatic drill.

"This must seem like home to you," said Dr. Macphail, with his thin, difficult smile.

"Ours are low islands, you know, not like these. Coral. These are volcanic. We've got another ten days' journey to reach them."

"In these parts that's almost like being in the next street at home," said Dr. Macphail facetiously.

"Well, that's rather an exaggerated way of putting it, but one does look at distances differently in the South Seas. So far you're right." Dr. Macphail sighed faintly.

"I'm glad we're not stationed here," she went on. "They say this is a terribly difficult place to work in. The steamers' touching makes the people unsettled; and then there's the naval station; that's bad for the natives. In our district we don't have difficulties like that to contend with. There are one or two traders, of course, but we take care to make them behave, and if they don't we make the place so hot for them they're glad to go." Fixing the glasses on her nose she looked at the green island with a ruthless stare.

"It's almost a hopeless task for the missionaries here. I can never be sufficiently thankful to God that we are at least spared that."

Davidson's district consisted of a group of islands to the north of Samoa; they were widely separated and he had frequently to go long distances by canoe. At these times his wife remained at their headquarters and managed the mission. Dr. Macphail felt his heart sink when he considered the efficiency with which she certainly managed it. She spoke of the depravity of the natives in a voice which nothing could hush, but with a vehemently unctuous horror. Her sense of delicacy was singular. Early in their acquaintance she had said to him:

"You know, their marriage customs when we first settled in the islands were so shocking that I couldn't possibly describe them to you. But I'll tell Mrs. Macphail and she'll tell you."

Then he had seen his wife and Mrs. Davidson, their deck-chairs close together, in earnest conversation for about two hours. As he walked past them backwards and forwards for the sake of exercise, he had heard Mrs. Davidson's agitated whisper, like the distant flow of a mountain torrent, and he saw by his wife's open mouth and pale face that she was enjoying an alarming experience. At night in their cabin she repeated to him with bated breath all she had heard.

"Well what did I say to you?" cried Mrs. Davidson, exultant, next morning. "Did you ever hear anything more dreadful? You don't wonder that I couldn't tell you myself, do you? Even though you are a doctor."

Mrs. Davidson scanned his face. She had a dramatic eagerness to see that she had achieved the desired effect.

"Can you wonder that when we first went there our hearts sank? You'll hardly believe me when I tell you it was impossible to find a single good girl in any of the villages."

She used the word *good* in a severely technical manner.

"Mr. Davidson and I talked it over, and we made up our minds the first thing to do was to put down the dancing. The natives were crazy about dancing."

"I was not averse to it myself when I was a young man," said Dr. Macphail.

"I guessed as much when I heard you ask Mrs. Macphail to have a turn with you last night. I don't think there's any real harm if a man dances with his wife, but I was relieved that she wouldn't. Under the circumstances I thought it better that we should keep ourselves to ourselves."

"Under what circumstances?"

Mrs. Davidson gave him a quick look through her *pince-nez*, but did not answer his question.

"But among white people it's not quite the same," she went on, "though I must say I agree with Mr. Davidson, who says he can't understand how a husband can stand by and see his wife in another man's arms, and as far as I'm concerned I've never danced a step since I married. But the native dancing is quite another matter. It's not only immoral in itself, but it distinctly leads to immorality. However, I'm thankful to God that we stamped it out, and I don't think I'm wrong in saying that no one has danced in our district for eight years."

But now they came to the mouth of the harbour and Mrs. Macphail joined them. The ship turned sharply and steamed slowly in. It was a great landlocked harbour big enough to hold a fleet of battleships; and all around it rose, high and steep, the green hills. Near the entrance, getting such breeze

as blew from the sea, stood the governor's house in a garden.
The Stars and Stripes dangled languidly from a flagstaff.
They passed two or three trim bungalows, and a tennis court,
and then they came to the quay with its warehouses. Mrs.
Davidson pointed out the schooner, moored two or three
hundred yards from the side, which was to take them to Apia.
There was a crowd of eager, noisy, and good-humoured natives come from all parts of the island, some from curiosity,
others to barter with the travellers on their way to Sydney;
and they brought pineapples and huge bunches of bananas,
tapa cloths, necklaces of shells or sharks' teeth, *kava*-bowls,
and models of war canoes. American sailors, neat and trim,
clean-shaven and frank of face, sauntered among them, and
there was a little group of officials. While their luggage was
being landed the Macphails and Mrs. Davidson watched the
crowd. Dr. Macphail looked at the yaws from which most of
the children and the young boys seemed to suffer, disfiguring
sores like torpid ulcers, and his professional eyes glistened
when he saw for the first time in his experience cases of ele-
phantiasis, men going about with a huge, heavy arm or
dragging along a grossly disfigured leg. Men and women
wore the *lava-lava.*

"It's a very indecent costume," said Mrs. Davidson. "Mr.
Davidson thinks it should be prohibited by law. How can
you expect people to be moral when they wear nothing but
a strip of red cotton round their loins?"

"It's suitable enough to the climate," said the doctor, wiping the sweat off his head.

Now that they were on land the heat, though it was so
early in the morning, was already oppressive. Closed in by
its hills, not a breath of air came in to Pago-Pago.

"In our islands," Mrs. Davidson went on in her high-
pitched tones, "we've practically eradicated the *lava-lava.*
A few old men still continue to wear it, but that's all. The
women have all taken to the Mother Hubbard, and the men
wear trousers and singlets. At the very beginning of our stay
Mr. Davidson said in one of his reports: the inhabitants of
these islands will never be thoroughly Christianised till every
boy of more than ten years is made to wear a pair of trousers."

But Mrs. Davidson had given two or three of her bird-like glances at heavy grey clouds that came floating over the mouth of the harbour. A few drops began to fall.

"We'd better take shelter," she said.

They made their way with all the crowd to the great shed of corrugated iron, and the rain began to fall in torrents. They stood there for some time and then were joined by Mr. Davidson. He had been polite enough to the Macphails during the journey, but he had not his wife's sociability, and had spent much of his time reading. He was a silent, rather sullen man, and you felt that his affability was a duty that he imposed upon himself Christianly; he was by nature reserved and even morose. His appearance was singular. He was very tall and thin, with long limbs loosely jointed; hollow cheeks and curiously high cheek-bones; he had so cadaverous an air that it surprised you to notice how full and sensual were his lips. He wore his hair very long. His dark eyes, set deep in their sockets, were large and tragic; and his hands with their big, long fingers, were finely shaped; they gave him a look of great strength. But the most striking thing about him was the feeling he gave you of suppressed fire. It was impressive and vaguely troubling. He was not a man with whom any intimacy was possible.

He brought now unwelcome news. There was an epidemic of measles, a serious and often fatal disease among the Kanakas, on the island, and a case had developed among the crew of the schooner which was to take them on their journey. The sick man had been brought ashore and put in hospital on the quarantine station, but telegraphic instructions had been sent from Apia to say that the schooner would not be allowed to enter the harbour till it was certain no other member of the crew was affected.

"It means we shall have to stay here for ten days at least."

"But I'm urgently needed at Apia," said Dr. Macphail.

"That can't be helped. If no more cases develop on board, the schooner will be allowed to sail with white passengers, but all native traffic is prohibited for three months."

"Is there a hotel here?" asked Mrs. Macphail.

Davidson gave a low chuckle. "There's not."

"What shall we do then?"

"I've been talking to the governor. There's a trader along the front who has rooms that he rents, and my proposition is that as soon as the rain lets up we should go along there and see what we can do. Don't expect comfort. You've just got to be thankful if we get a bed to sleep on and a roof over our heads."

But the rain showed no sign of stopping, and at length with umbrellas and waterproofs they set out. There was no town, but merely a group of official buildings, a store or two, and at the back, among the coconut trees and plantains, a few native dwellings. The house they sought was about five minutes' walk from the wharf. It was a frame house of two storeys, with broad verandahs on both floors and a roof of corrugated iron. The owner was a half-caste named Horn, with a native wife surrounded by little brown children, and on the ground-floor he had a store where he sold canned goods and cottons. The rooms he showed them were almost bare of furniture. In the Macphails' there was nothing but a poor, worn bed with a ragged mosquito net, a rickety chair, and a washstand. They looked round with dismay. The rain poured down without ceasing.

"I'm not going to unpack more than we actually need," said Mrs. Macphail.

Mrs. Davidson came into the room as she was unlocking a portmanteau. She was very brisk and alert. The cheerless surroundings had no effect on her.

"If you'll take my advice you'll get a needle and cotton and start right in to mend the mosquito net," she said, "or you'll not be able to get a wink of sleep to-night."

"Will they be very bad?" asked Dr. Macphail.

"This is the season for them. When you're asked to a party at Government House at Apia you'll notice that all the ladies are given a pillowslip to put their—their lower extremities in."

"I wish the rain would stop for a moment," said Mrs. Macphail. "I could try to make the place comfortable with more heart if the sun were shining."

"Oh, if you wait for that, you'll wait a long time; Pago-Pago is about the rainiest place in the Pacific. You see, the hills, and that bay, they attract the water, and one expects rain at this time of year anyway."

She looked from Macphail to his wife, standing helplessly in different parts of the room, like lost souls, and she pursed her lips. She saw that she must take them in hand. Feckless people like that made her impatient, but her hands itched to put everything in the order which came so naturally to her.

"Here, you give me a needle and cotton and I'll mend that net of yours, while you go on with your unpacking. Dinner's at one. Dr. Macphail, you'd better go down to the wharf and see that your heavy luggage has been put in a dry place. You know what these natives are, they're quite capable of storing it where the rain will beat in on it all the time."

The doctor put on his waterproof again and went downstairs. At the door Mr. Horn was standing in conversation with the quartermaster of the ship they had just arrived in and a second-class passenger whom Dr. Macphail had seen several times on board. The quartermaster, a little, shrivelled man, extremely dirty, nodded to him as he passed.

"This is a bad job about the measles, doc," he said. "I see you've fixed yourself up already."

Dr. Macphail thought he was rather familiar, but he was a timid man and he did not take offence easily.

"Yes, we've got a room upstairs."

"Miss Thompson was sailing with you to Apia, so I've brought her along here."

The quartermaster pointed with his thumb to the woman standing by his side. She was twenty-seven perhaps, plump, and in a coarse fashion pretty. She wore a white dress and a large white hat. Her fat calves in white cotton stockings bulged over the tops of long white boots in glacé kid. She gave Macphail an ingratiating smile.

"The feller's tryin' to soak me a dollar and a half a day for the meanest sized room," she said in a hoarse voice.

"I tell you she's a friend of mine, Jo," said the quartermaster. "She can't pay more than a dollar, and you've sure got to take her for that."

The trader was fat and smooth and quietly smiling.

"Well, if you put it like that, Mr. Swan, I'll see what I can do about it. I'll talk to Mrs. Horn and if we think we can make a reduction we will."

"Don't try to pull that stuff with me," said Miss Thompson. "We'll settle this right now. You get a dollar a day for the room and not one bean more."

Dr. Macphail smiled. He admired the effrontery with which she bargained. He was the sort of man who always paid what he was asked. He preferred to be over-charged than to haggle. The trader sighed.

"Well, to oblige Mr. Swan I'll take it."

"That's the goods," said Miss Thompson. "Come right in and have a shot of hooch. I've got some real good rye in that grip if you'll bring it along, Mr. Swan. You come along too, doctor."

"Oh, I don't think I will, thank you," he answered. "I'm just going down to see that our luggage is all right."

He stepped out into the rain. It swept in from the opening of the harbour in sheets and the opposite shore was all blurred. He passed two or three natives clad in nothing but the *lava-lava*, with huge umbrellas over them. They walked finely, with leisurely movements, very upright; and they smiled and greeted him in a strange tongue as they went by.

It was nearly dinner-time when he got back, and their meal was laid in the trader's parlour. It was a room designed not to live in but for purposes of prestige, and it had a musty, melancholy air. A suite of stamped plush was arranged neatly round the walls, and from the middle of the ceiling, protected from the flies by yellow tissue paper, hung a gilt chandelier. Davidson did not come.

"I know he went to call on the governor," said Mrs. Davidson, "and I guess he's kept him to dinner."

A little native girl brought them a dish of hamburger steak, and after a while the trader came up to see that they had everything they wanted.

"I see we have a fellow lodger, Mr. Horn," said Dr. Macphail.

"She's taken a room, that's all," answered the trader. "She's getting her own board."

He looked at the two ladies with an obsequious air.

"I put her downstairs so she shouldn't be in the way. She won't be any trouble to you."

"Is it someone who was on the boat?" asked Mrs. Macphail.

"Yes, ma'am, she was in the second cabin. She was going to Apia. She has a position as cashier waiting for her."

"Oh!"

When the trader was gone Macphail said:

"I shouldn't think she'd find it exactly cheerful having her meals in her room."

"If she was in the second cabin I guess she'd rather," answered Mrs. Davidson. "I don't exactly know who it can be."

"I happened to be there when the quartermaster brought her along. Her name's Thompson."

"It's not the woman who was dancing with the quartermaster last night?" asked Mrs. Davidson.

"That's who it must be," said Mrs. Macphail. "I wondered at the time what she was. She looked rather fast to me."

"Not good style at all," said Mrs. Davidson.

They began to talk of other things, and after dinner, tired with their early rise, they separated and slept. When they awoke, though the sky was still grey and the clouds hung low, it was not raining and they went for a walk on the high road which the Americans had built along the bay.

On their return they found that Davidson had just come in.

"We may be here for a fortnight," he said irritably. "I've argued it out with the governor, but he says there is nothing to be done."

"Mr. Davidson's just longing to get back to his work," said his wife, with an anxious glance at him.

"We've been away for a year," he said, walking up and down the verandah. "The mission has been in charge of native missionaries and I'm terribly nervous that they've let things slide. They're good men, I'm not saying a word against them, God-fearing, devout, and truly Christian men—their Christianity would put many so-called Christians at home to the blush—but they're pitifully lacking in energy. They can make a stand once, they can make a stand twice, but they can't make a stand all the time. If you leave a mission in charge of a native missionary, no matter how trustworthy he seems, in course of time you'll find he's let abuses creep in."

Mr. Davidson stood still. With his tall, spare form, and his great eyes flashing out of his pale face, he was an impressive figure. His sincerity was obvious in the fire of his gestures and in his deep, ringing voice.

"I expect to have my work cut out for me. I shall act and I shall act promptly. If the tree is rotten it shall be cut down and cast into the flames."

And in the evening after the high tea which was their last meal, while they sat in the stiff parlour, the ladies working and Dr. Macphail smoking his pipe, the missionary told them of his work in the islands.

"When we went there they had no sense of sin at all," he said. "They broke the commandments one after the other and never knew they were doing wrong. And I think that was the most difficult part of my work, to instil into the natives the sense of sin."

The Macphails knew already that Davidson had worked in the Solomons for five years before he met his wife. She had been a missionary in China, and they had become acquainted in Boston, where they were both spending part of their leave to attend a missionary congress. On their marriage they had been appointed to the islands in which they had laboured ever since.

In the course of all the conversations they had had with Mr. Davidson one thing had shone out clearly and that was the man's unflinching courage. He was a medical missionary, and he was liable to be called at any time to one or other of the islands in the group. Even the whaleboat is not so very safe a conveyance in the stormy Pacific of the wet season, but often he would be sent for in a canoe, and then the danger was great. In cases of illness or accident he never hesitated. A dozen times he had spent the whole night bailing for his life, and more than once Mrs. Davidson had given him up for lost.

"I'd beg him not to go sometimes," she said, "or at least to wait till the weather was more settled, but he'd never listen. He's obstinate, and when he's once made up his mind, nothing can move him."

"How can I ask the natives to put their trust in the Lord if I am afraid to do so myself?" cried Davidson. "And I'm not, I'm not. They know that if they send for me in their trouble I'll come if it's humanly possible. And do you think the Lord is going to abandon me when I am on his business? The wind blows at his bidding and the waves toss and rage at his word."

Dr. Macphail was a timid man. He had never been able to get used to the hurtling of the shells over the trenches, and when he was operating in an advanced dressing-station the sweat poured from his brow and dimmed his spectacles in the effort he made to control his unsteady hand. He shuddered a little as he looked at the missionary.

"I wish I could say that I've never been afraid," he said.

"I wish you could say that you believed in God," retorted the other.

But for some reason, that evening the missionary's thoughts travelled back to the early days he and his wife had spent on the islands.

"Sometimes Mrs. Davidson and I would look at one another and the tears would stream down our cheeks. We worked without ceasing, day and night, and we seemed to make no progress. I don't know what I should have done without her then. When I felt my heart sink, when I was very near despair, she gave me courage and hope."

Mrs. Davidson looked down at her work, and a slight colour rose to her thin cheeks. Her hands trembled a little. She did not trust herself to speak.

"We had no one to help us. We were alone, thousands of miles from any of our own people, surrounded by darkness. When I was broken and weary she would put her work aside and take the Bible and read to me till peace came and settled upon me like sleep upon the eyelids of a child, and when at last she closed the book she'd say: 'We'll save them in spite of themselves.' And I felt strong again in the Lord, and I answered: 'Yes, with God's help I'll save them. I must save them.'" He came over to the table and stood in front of it as though it were a lectern.

"You see, they were so naturally depraved that they couldn't be brought to see their wickedness. We had to make sins out of what they thought were natural actions. We had to make it a sin, not only to commit adultery and to lie and thieve, but to expose their bodies, and to dance and not to come to church. I made it a sin for a girl to show her bosom and a sin for a man not to wear trousers."

"How?" asked Dr. Macphail, not without surprise.

"I instituted fines. Obviously the only way to make people realise that an action is sinful is to punish them if they commit it. I fined them if they didn't come to church, and I fined them if they danced. I fined them if they were improperly dressed. I had a tariff, and every sin had to be paid for either in money or work. And at last I made them understand."

"But did they never refuse to pay?"

"How could they?" asked the missionary.

"It would be a brave man who tried to stand up against Mr. Davidson," said his wife, tightening her lips.

Dr. Macphail looked at Davidson with troubled eyes. What he heard shocked him, but he hesitated to express his disapproval.

"You must remember that in the last resort I could expel them from their church membership."

"Did they mind that?"

Davidson smiled a little and gently rubbed his hands.

"They couldn't sell their copra. When the men fished they got no share of the catch. It meant something very like starvation. Yes, they minded quite a lot."

"Tell him about Fred Ohlson," said Mrs. Davidson.

The missionary fixed his fiery eyes on Dr. Macphail.

"Fred Ohlson was a Danish trader who had been in the islands a good many years. He was a pretty rich man as traders go and he wasn't very pleased when we came. You see, he'd had things very much his own way. He paid the natives what he liked for their copra, and he paid in goods and whiskey. He had a native wife, but he was flagrantly unfaithful to her. He was a drunkard. I gave him a chance to mend his ways, but he wouldn't take it. He laughed at me."

Davidson's voice fell to a deep bass as he said the last

words, and he was silent for a minute or two. The silence was heavy with menace.

"In two years he was a ruined man. He'd lost everything he'd saved in a quarter of a century. I broke him, and at last he was forced to come to me like a beggar and beseech me to give him a passage back to Sydney."

"I wish you could have seen him when he came to see Mr. Davidson," said the missionary's wife. "He had been a fine, powerful man, with a lot of fat on him, and he had a great big voice, but now he was half the size, and he was shaking all over. He'd suddenly become an old man."

With abstracted gaze Davidson looked out into the night. The rain was falling again.

Suddenly from below came a sound, and Davidson turned and looked questioningly at his wife. It was the sound of a gramophone, harsh and loud, wheezing out a syncopated tune. "What's that?" he asked.

Mrs. Davidson fixed her *pince-nez* more firmly on her nose.

"One of the second-class passengers has a room in the house. I guess it comes from there."

They listened in silence, and presently they heard the sound of dancing. Then the music stopped, and they heard the popping of corks and voices raised in animated conversation.

"I daresay she's giving a farewell party to her friends on board," said Dr. Macphail. "The ship sails at twelve, doesn't it?"

Davidson made no remark, but he looked at his watch.

"Are you ready?" he asked his wife.

She got up and folded her work.

"Yes, I guess I am," she answered.

"It's early to go to bed yet, isn't it?" said the doctor.

"We have a good deal of reading to do," explained Mrs. Davidson. "Wherever we are, we read a chapter of the Bible before retiring for the night and we study it with the commentaries, you know, and discuss it thoroughly. It's a wonderful training for the mind."

The two couples bade one another good night. Dr. and Mrs. Macphail were left alone. For two or three minutes they did not speak.

"I think I'll go and fetch the cards," the doctor said at last.

Mrs. Macphail looked at him doubtfully. Her conversation with the Davidsons had left her a little uneasy, but she did not like to say that she thought they had better not play cards when the Davidsons might come in at any moment. Dr. Macphail brought them and she watched him, though with a vague sense of guilt, while he laid out his patience. Below the sound of revelry continued.

It was fine enough next day, and the Macphails, condemned to spend a fortnight of idleness at Pago-Pago, set about making the best of things. They went down to the quay and got out of their boxes a number of books. The doctor called on the chief surgeon of the naval hospital and went round the beds with him. They left cards on the governor. They passed Miss Thompson on the road. The doctor took off his hat, and she gave him a "Good morning, doc," in a loud, cheerful voice. She was dressed as on the day before, in a white frock, and her shiny white boots with their high heels, her fat legs bulging over the tops of them, were strange things on that exotic scene.

"I don't think she's very suitably dressed, I must say," said Mrs. Macphail. "She looks extremely common to me."

When they got back to their house, she was on the verandah playing with one of the trader's dark children.

"Say a word to her," Dr. Macphail whispered to his wife. "She's all alone here, and it seems rather unkind to ignore her."

Mrs. Macphail was shy, but she was in the habit of doing what her husband bade her. "I think we're fellow lodgers here," she said, rather foolishly.

"Terrible, ain't it, bein' cooped up in a one-horse burg like this?" answered Miss Thompson. "And they tell me I'm lucky to have gotten a room. I don't see myself livin' in a native house, and that's what some have to do. I don't know why they don't have a hotel."

They exchanged a few more words. Miss Thompson, loud-voiced and garrulous, was evidently quite willing to gossip, but Mrs. Macphail had a poor stock of small talk and presently she said: "Well, I think we must go upstairs."

In the evening when they sat down to their high-tea Davidson on coming in said:

"I see that woman downstairs has a couple of sailors sitting there. I wonder how she's gotten acquainted with them."

"She can't be very particular," said Mrs. Davidson.

They were all rather tired after the idle, aimless day.

"If there's going to be a fortnight of this I don't know what we shall feel like at the end of it," said Dr. Macphail.

"The only thing to do is to portion out the day to different activities," answered the missionary. "I shall set aside a certain number of hours to study and a certain number to exercise, rain or shine—in the wet season you can't afford to pay any attention to the rain—and a certain number to recreation."

Dr. Macphail looked at his companion with misgiving. Davidson's programme oppressed him. They were eating Hamburger steak again. It seemed the only dish the cook knew how to make. Then below the gramophone began. Davidson started nervously when he heard it, but said nothing. Men's voices floated up. Miss Thompson's guests were joining in a well-known song and presently they heard her voice too, hoarse and loud. There was a good deal of shouting and laughing. The four people upstairs, trying to make conversation, listened despite themselves to the clink of glasses and the scrape of chairs. More people had evidently come. Miss Thompson was giving a party.

"I wonder how she gets them all in," said Mrs. Macphail, suddenly breaking into a medical conversation between the missionary and her husband.

It showed whither her thoughts were wandering. The twitch of Davidson's face proved that, though he spoke of scientific things, his mind was busy in the same direction. Suddenly, while the doctor was giving some experience of practice on the Flanders front, rather prosily, he sprang to his feet with a cry.

"What's the matter, Alfred?" asked Mrs. Davidson.

"Of course! It never occurred to me. She's out of Iwelei."

"She can't be."

"She came on board at Honolulu. It's obvious. And she's carrying on her trade here. Here."

He uttered the last word with a passion of indignation.

"What's Iwelei?" asked Mrs. Macphail.

He turned his gloomy eyes on her and his voice trembled with horror.

"The plague spot of Honolulu. The Red Light district. It was a blot on our civilisation."

Iwelei was on the edge of the city. You went down side streets by the harbour, in the darkness, across a rickety bridge, till you came to a deserted road, all ruts and holes, and then suddenly you came out into the light. There was parking room for motors on each side of the road, and there were saloons, tawdry and bright, each one noisy with its mechanical piano, and there were barbers' shops and tobacconists. There was a stir in the air and a sense of expectant gaiety. You turned down a narrow alley, either to the right or to the left, for the road divided Iwelei into two parts, and you found yourself in the district. There were rows of little bungalows, trim and neatly painted in green, and the pathway between them was broad and straight. It was laid out like a garden-city. In its respectable regularity, its order and spruceness, it gave an impression of sardonic horror; for never can the search for love have been so systematised and ordered. The pathways were lit by a rare lamp, but they would have been dark except for the lights that came from the open windows of the bungalows. Men wandered about, looking at the women who sat at their windows, reading or sewing, for the most part taking no notice of the passersby; and like the women they were of all nationalities. There were Americans, sailors from the ships in port, enlisted men off the gunboats, sombrely drunk, and soldiers from the regiments, white and black, quartered on the island; there were Japanese, walking in twos and threes; Hawaiians, Chinese in long robes, and Filipinos in preposterous hats. They were silent and as it were oppressed. Desire is sad.

"It was the most crying scandal of the Pacific," exclaimed Davidson vehemently. "The missionaries had been agitating against it for years, and at last the local press took it up. The police refused to stir. You know their argument. They say that vice is inevitable and consequently the best thing is to localise and control it. The truth is, they were paid. Paid.

They were paid by the saloon-keepers, paid by the bullies, paid by the women themselves. At last they were forced to move."

"I read about it in the papers that came on board in Honolulu," said Dr. Macphail.

"Iwelei, with its sin and shame, ceased to exist on the very day we arrived. The whole population was brought before the justices. I don't know why I didn't understand at once what that woman was."

"Now you come to speak of it," said Mrs. Macphail, "I remember seeing her come on board only a few minutes before the boat sailed. I remember thinking at the time she was cutting it rather fine."

"How dare she come here!" cried Davidson indignantly. "I'm not going to allow it." He strode towards the door.

"What are you going to do?" asked Macphail.

"What do you expect me to do? I'm going to stop it. I'm not going to have this house turned into—into . . ."

He sought for a word that would not offend the ladies' ears. His eyes were flashing and his pale face was paler still in his emotion.

"It sounds as though there were three or four men down there," said the doctor. "Don't you think it's rather rash to go in just now?"

The missionary gave him a contemptuous look and without a word flung out of the room.

"You know Mr. Davidson very little if you think the fear of personal danger can stop him in the performance of his duty," said his wife.

She sat with her hands nervously clasped, a spot of colour on her high cheek-bones, listening to what was about to happen below. They all listened. They heard him clatter down the wooden stairs and throw open the door. The singing stopped suddenly, but the gramophone continued to bray out its vulgar tune. They heard Davidson's voice and then the noise of something heavy falling. The music stopped. He had hurled the gramophone on the floor. Then again they heard Davidson's voice, they could not make out the words, then Miss Thompson's, loud and shrill, then a confused clamour as though several people were shouting together at

the top of their lungs. Mrs. Davidson gave a little gasp, and
she clenched her hands more tightly. Dr. Macphail looked
uncertainly from her to his wife. He did not want to go down,
but he wondered if they expected him to. Then there was
something that sounded like a scuffle. The noise now was
more distinct. It might be that Davidson was being thrown
out of the room. The door was slammed. There was a moment's silence and they heard Davidson come up the stairs
again. He went to his room.

"I think I'll go to him," said Mrs. Davidson.

She got up and went out.

"If you want me, just call," said Mrs. Macphail, and then
when the other was gone: "I hope he isn't hurt."

"Why couldn't he mind his own business?" said Dr. Macphail.

They sat in silence for a minute or two and then they both
started, for the gramophone began to play once more, de-
fiantly, and mocking voices shouted hoarsely the words of an
obscene song.

Next day Mrs. Davidson was pale and tired. She complained of headache, and she looked old and wizened. She
told Mrs. Macphail that the missionary had not slept at all;
he had passed the night in a state of frightful agitation and
at five had got up and gone out. A glass of beer had been
thrown over him and his clothes were stained and stinking.
But a sombre fire glowed in Mrs. Davidson's eyes when she
spoke of Miss Thompson.

"She'll bitterly rue the day when she flouted Mr. Davidson," she said. "Mr. Davidson has a wonderful heart and no
one who is in trouble has ever gone to him without being
comforted, but he has no mercy for sin, and when his right-
eous wrath is excited he's terrible."

"Why, what will he do?" asked Mrs. Macphail.

"I don't know, but I wouldn't stand in that creature's shoes
for anything in the world."

Mrs. Macphail shuddered. There was something positively
alarming in the triumphant assurance of the little woman's
manner. They were going out together that morning, and
they went down the stairs side by side. Miss Thompson's

door was open, and they saw her in a bedraggled dressing-gown, cooking something in a chafing-dish.

"Good morning," she called. "Is Mr. Davidson better this morning?"

They passed her in silence, with their noses in the air, as if she did not exist. They flushed, however, when she burst into a shout of derisive laughter. Mrs. Davidson turned on her suddenly.

"Don't you dare to speak to me," she screamed. "If you insult me I shall have you turned out of here."

"Say, did I ask Mr. Davidson to visit with me?"

"Don't answer her," whispered Mrs. Macphail hurriedly. They walked on till they were out of earshot.

"She's brazen, brazen," burst from Mrs. Davidson.

Her anger almost suffocated her.

And on their way home they met her strolling towards the quay. She had all her finery on. Her great white hat with its vulgar, showy flowers was an affront. She called out cheerily to them as they went by, and a couple of American sailors who were standing there grinned as the ladies set their faces to an icy stare. They got in just before the rain began to fall again.

"I guess she'll get her fine clothes spoilt," said Mrs. Davidson with a bitter sneer.

Davidson did not come in till they were half way through dinner. He was wet through, but he would not change. He sat, morose and silent, refusing to eat more than a mouthful, and he stared at the slanting rain. When Mrs. Davidson told him of their two encounters with Miss Thompson he did not answer. His deepening frown alone showed that he had heard.

"Don't you think we ought to make Mr. Horn turn her out of here?" asked Mrs. Davidson. "We can't allow her to insult us."

"There doesn't seem to be any other place for her to go," said Macphail.

"She can live with one of the natives."

"In weather like this a native hut must be a rather uncomfortable place to live in."

"I lived in one for years," said the missionary.

When the little native girl brought in the fried bananas

which formed the sweet they had every day, Davidson turned to her.

"Ask Miss Thompson when it would be convenient for me to see her," he said.

The girl nodded shyly and went out.

"What do you want to see her for, Alfred?" asked his wife.

"It's my duty to see her. I won't act till I've given her every chance."

"You don't know what she is. She'll insult you."

"Let her insult me. Let her spit on me. She has an immortal soul, and I must do all that is in my power to save it."

Mrs. Davidson's ears rang still with the harlot's mocking laughter. "She's gone too far."

"Too far for the mercy of God?" His eyes lit up suddenly and his voice grew mellow and soft. "Never. The sinner may be deeper in sin than the depth of hell itself, but the love of the Lord Jesus can reach him still."

The girl came back with the message.

"Miss Thompson's compliments and as long as Rev. Davidson don't come in business hours she'll be glad to see him any time."

The party received it in stony silence, and Dr. Macphail quickly effaced from his lips the smile which had come upon them. He knew his wife would be vexed with him if he found Miss Thompson's effrontery amusing.

They finished the meal in silence. When it was over the two ladies got up and took their work. Mrs. Macphail was making another of the innumerable comforters which she had turned out since the beginning of the war, and the doctor lit his pipe. But Davidson remained in his chair and with abstracted eyes stared at the table. At last he got up and without a word went out of the room. They heard him go down and they heard Miss Thompson's defiant "Come in" when he knocked at the door. He remained with her for an hour. And Dr. Macphail watched the rain. It was beginning to get on his nerves. It was not like our soft English rain that drops gently on the earth; it was unmerciful and somehow terrible; you felt in it the malignancy of the primitive powers of nature. It did not pour, it flowed. It was like a deluge from heaven, and it rattled on the roof of corrugated iron with a steady persistence that was maddening. It seemed to have a fury of its own. And sometimes you felt that you must scream if it did not stop, and then suddenly you felt powerless, as though your bones had suddenly become soft; and you were miserable and hopeless.

Macphail turned his head when the missionary came back. The two women looked up.

"I've given her every chance. I have exhorted her to repent. She is an evil woman."

He paused, and Dr. Macphail saw his eyes darken and his pale face grow hard and stern.

"Now I shall take the whips with which the Lord Jesus drove the usurers and money changers out of the Temple of the Most High."

He walked up and down the room. His mouth was close set, and his black brows were frowning. "If she fled to the uttermost parts of the earth I should pursue her."

With a sudden movement he turned round and strode out of the room. They heard him go downstairs again.

"What is he going to do?" asked Mrs. Macphail.

"I don't know." Mrs. Davidson took off her *pince-nez* and wiped them. "When he is on the Lord's work I never ask him questions." She sighed a little.

"What's the matter?"

"He'll wear himself out. He doesn't know what it is to spare himself."

Dr. Macphail learnt the first results of the missionary's activity from the half-caste trader in whose house they lodged. He stopped the doctor when he passed the store and came out to speak to him on the stoop. His fat face was worried.

"The Rev. Davidson has been at me for letting Miss Thompson have a room here," he said, "but I didn't know what she was when I rented it to her. When people come and ask if I can rent them a room all I want to know is if they've the money to pay for it. And she paid me for hers a week in advance."

Dr. Macphail did not want to commit himself.

"When all's said and done it's your house. We're very much obliged to you for taking us in at all."

Horn looked at him doubtfully. He was not certain yet how definitely Macphail stood on the missionary's side.

"The missionaries are in with one another," he said, hesitatingly. "If they get it in for a trader he may just as well shut up his store and quit."

"Did he want you to turn her out?"

"No, he said so long as she behaved herself he couldn't ask me to do that. He said he wanted to be just to me. I promised she shouldn't have no more visitors. I've just been and told her."

"How did she take it?"

"She gave me Hell."

The trader squirmed in his old ducks. He had found Miss Thompson a rough customer.

"Oh, well, I daresay she'll get out. I don't suppose she wants to stay here if she can't have anyone in."

"There's nowhere she can go, only a native house, and no native'll take her now, not now that the missionaries have got their knife in her."

Dr. Macphail looked at the falling rain. "Well, I don't suppose it's any good waiting for it to clear up."

In the evening when they sat in the parlour Davidson talked to them of his early days at college. He had had no means and had worked his way through by doing odd jobs during the vacations. There was silence downstairs. Miss Thompson was sitting in her little room alone. But suddenly the gramophone began to play. She had set it on in defiance, to cheat her loneliness, but there was no one to sing, and it had a melancholy note. It was like a cry for help. Davidson took no notice. He was in the middle of a long anecdote and without change of expression went on. The gramophone continued. Miss Thompson put on one reel after another. It looked as though the silence of the night were getting on her nerves. It was breathless and sultry. When the Macphails went to bed they could not sleep. They lay side by side with their eyes wide open, listening to the cruel singing of the mosquitoes outside their curtain.

"What's that?" whispered Mrs. Macphail at last.

They heard a voice, Davidson's voice, through the wooden partition. It went on with a monotonous, earnest insistence.

He was praying aloud. He was praying for the soul of Miss Thompson.

Two or three days went by. Now when they passed Miss Thompson on the road she did not greet them with ironic cordiality or smile; she passed with her nose in the air, a sulky look on her painted face, frowning, as though she did not see them. The trader told Macphail that she had tried to get lodging elsewhere, but had failed. In the evening she played through the various reels of her gramophone, but the pretence of mirth was obvious now. The ragtime had a cracked, heart-broken rhythm as though it were a one-step of despair. When she began to play on Sunday Davidson sent Horn to beg her to stop at once since it was the Lord's day. The reel was taken off and the house was silent except for the steady pattering of the rain on the iron roof.

"I think she's getting a bit worked up," said the trader next day to Macphail. "She don't know what Mr. Davidson's up to and it makes her scared."

Macphail had caught a glimpse of her that morning and it struck him that her arrogant expression had changed. There was in her face a hunted look. The half-caste gave him a sidelong glance.

"I suppose you don't know what Mr. Davidson is doing about it?" he hazarded.

"No, I don't."

It was singular that Horn should ask him that question, for he also had the idea that the missionary was mysteriously at work. He had an impression that he was weaving a net around the woman, carefully, systematically, and suddenly, when everything was ready would pull the strings tight.

"He told me to tell her," said the trader, "that if at any time she wanted him she only had to send and he'd come."

"What did she say when you told her that?"

"She didn't say nothing. I didn't stop. I just said what he said I was to and then I beat it. I thought she might be going to start weepin'."

"I have no doubt the loneliness is getting on her nerves," said the doctor. "And the rain—that's enough to make any-one jumpy," he continued irritably. "Doesn't it ever stop in this confounded place?"

"It goes on pretty steady in the rainy season. We have three hundred inches in the year. You see, it's the shape of the bay. It seems to attract the rain from all over the Pacific."

"Damn the shape of the bay," said the doctor.

He scratched his mosquito bites. He felt very short-tempered. When the rain stopped and the sun shone, it was like a hothouse, seething, humid, sultry, breathless, and you had a strange feeling that everything was growing with a savage violence. The natives, blithe and childlike by reputation, seemed then, with their tattooing and their dyed hair, to have something sinister in their appearance; and when they pattered along at your heels with their naked feet you looked back instinctively. You felt they might at any moment come behind you swiftly and thrust a long knife between your shoulder blades. You could not tell what dark thoughts lurked behind their wide-set eyes. They had a little the look of ancient Egyptians painted on a temple wall, and there was about them the terror of what is immeasurably old.

The missionary came and went. He was busy, but the Macphails did not know what he was doing. Horn told the doctor that he saw the governor every day, and once Davidson mentioned him.

"He looks as if he had plenty of determination," he said, "but when you come down to brass tacks he has no backbone."

"I suppose that means he won't do exactly what you want," suggested the doctor facetiously.

The missionary did not smile. "I want him to do what's right. It shouldn't be necessary to persuade a man to do that."

"But there may be differences of opinion about what is right."

"If a man had a gangrenous foot would you have patience with anyone who hesitated to amputate it?"

"Gangrene is a matter of fact."

"And Evil?"

What Davidson had done soon appeared. The four of them had just finished their midday meal, and they had not yet separated for the siesta which the heat imposed on the ladies and on the doctor. Davidson had little patience with the

just now. I went to see the governor yesterday afternoon, but I couldn't get to him. I saw the secretary, and he told me I'd got to take that boat and that was all there was to it. I just had to see the governor, so I waited outside his house this morning, and when he come out I spoke to him. He didn't want to speak to me, I'll say, but I wouldn't let him shake me off, and at last he said he hadn't no objection to my staying here till the next boat to Sydney if the Rev. Davidson will stand for it."

She stopped and looked at Dr. Macphail anxiously.

"I don't know exactly what I can do," he said.

"Well, I thought maybe you wouldn't mind asking him. I swear to God I won't start anything here if he'll just only let me stay. I won't go out of the house if that'll suit him. It's no more'n a fortnight."

"I'll ask him."

"He won't stand for it," said Horn. "He'll have you out on Tuesday, so you may as well make up your mind to it."

"Tell him I can get work in Sydney, straight stuff, I mean. 'Tain't asking very much."

"I'll do what I can."

"And come and tell me right away, will you? I can't set down to a thing till I get the dope one way or the other."

It was not an errand that much pleased the doctor, and, characteristically perhaps, he went about it indirectly. He told his wife what Miss Thompson had said to him and asked her to speak to Mrs. Davidson. The missionary's attitude seemed rather arbitrary and it could do no harm if the girl were allowed to stay in Pago-Pago another fortnight. But he was not prepared for the result of his diplomacy. The missionary came to him straightway.

"Mrs. Davidson tells me that Thompson ha~ ~~ ~~ ~~ speaking to you."

Dr. Macphail, thus directly tackl~ ~~ ~~ ~~. He felt his temsentment at being forced out i~co, ~~ ~~ ~~ ~~ if she goes to per rising, and he flushed ~ere it's ~~ and so long as she

"I don't see that it ~ ~~ it's dashed hard to per-
Sydney rather th~ ~~ ~~
promises to ~ ~~
secute h~

The missionary fixed him with his stern eyes.

"Why is she unwilling to go back to San Francisco?"

"I didn't enquire," answered the doctor with some asperity. "And I think one does better to mind one's own business."

Perhaps it was not a very tactful answer.

"The governor has ordered her to be deported by the first boat that leaves the island. He's only done his duty and I will not interfere. Her presence is a peril here."

"I think you're very harsh and tyrannical."

The two ladies looked up at the doctor with some alarm, but they need not have feared a quarrel, for the missionary smiled gently.

"I'm terribly sorry you should think that of me, Dr. Macphail. Believe me, my heart bleeds for that unfortunate woman, but I'm only trying to do my duty."

The doctor made no answer. He looked out of the window sullenly. For once it was not raining and across the bay you saw nestling among the trees the huts of a native village.

"I think I'll take advantage of the rain stopping to go out," he said.

"Please don't bear me malice because I can't accede to your wish," said Davidson, with a melancholy smile. "I respect you very much, doctor, and I should be sorry if you thought ill of me."

"I have no doubt you have a sufficiently good opinion of yourself to bear mine with equanimity," he retorted.

"That's one on me," chuckled Davidson.

When Dr. Macphail, vexed with himself because he had been unci... to no purpose, went downstairs, Miss Thompson was waiting... sh... him with her door ajar.

"Well," I'm so... "have you spoken to him?"

"Yes, I'm... at her in... on't do anything," he answered, not looking at her in...

But then he gave... her. He saw that her... rassment.

shock of dismay. And s... k glance, for a sob broke from "But don't give up ho... te with fear. It gave him a

...d an idea.

...'s a shame the way

ormed a very favorable opinion of Mr. Davidson, but I am bound to confess that he was within his rights in pointing out to me the danger that the presence of a woman of Miss Thompson's character was to a place like this where a number of enlisted men are stationed among a native population."

He got up and Dr. Macphail was obliged to do so too.

"I must ask you to excuse me. I have an engagement. Please give my respects to Mrs. Macphail."

The doctor left him crest-fallen. He knew that Miss Thompson would be waiting for him, and unwilling to tell her himself that he had failed, he went into the house by the back door and sneaked up the stairs as though he had something to hide.

At supper he was silent and ill-at-ease, but the missionary was jovial and animated. Dr. Macphail thought his eyes rested on him now and then with triumphant good-humour. It struck him suddenly that Davidson knew of his visit to the governor and of its ill success. But how on earth could he have heard of it? There was something sinister about the power of that man. After supper he saw Horn on the verandah and, as though to have a casual word with him, went out.

"She wants to know if you've seen the governor," the trader whispered.

"Yes. He wouldn't do anything. I'm awfully sorry, I can't do anything more."

"I knew he wouldn't. They daren't go against the missionaries."

"What are you talking about?" said Davidson affably, coming out to join them.

"I was just saying there was no chance of your getting over to ʼia for at least another week," said the trader glibly.

He left Davidson and the two men returned into the parlour.

Mr. Davidson. Presently ʼoted one hour after each meal to recreation.

"Come in," saiʼ ʼ knock was heard at the door.

The door was not ʼavidson, in her sharp voice.

saw Miss Thompson ʼhe got up and opened it. They change in her appearanʼ ʼt the threshold. But the longer the flaunting hussy ʼordinary. This was no ʼed at them in the

slothful habit. The door was suddenly flung open and Miss Thompson came in. She looked round the room and then went up to Davidson.

"You low-down skunk, what have you been saying about me to the governor?"

She was spluttering with rage. There was a moment's pause. Then the missionary drew forward a chair.

"Won't you be seated, Miss Thompson? I've been hoping to have another talk with you."

"You poor low-life bastard." She burst into a torrent of insult, foul and insolent. Davidson kept his grave eyes on her.

"I'm indifferent to the abuse you think fit to heap on me, Miss Thompson," he said, "but I must beg you to remember that ladies are present."

Tears by now were struggling with her anger. Her face was red and swollen as though she were choking.

"What has happened?" asked Dr. Macphail.

"A feller's just been in here and he says I gotter beat it on the next boat."

Was there a gleam in the missionary's eyes? His face remained impassive.

"You could hardly expect the governor to let you stay here under the circumstances."

"You done it," she shrieked. "You can't kid me. You done it."

"I don't want to deceive you. I urged the governor to take the only possible step consistent with his obligations."

"Why couldn't you leave me be? I wasn't doin' you no harm."

"You may be sure that if you had I should be the last man to resent it."

"Do you think I want to stay on in this poor imitation of a burg? I don't look no busher, do I?"

"In that case I don't see what cause of complaint you have," he answered.

She gave an inarticulate cry of rage and flung out of the room. There was a short silence.

"It's a relief to know that the governor has acted at last," said Davidson finally. "He's a weak man and he shilly-shallied. He said she was only here for a fortnight anyway, and if she went on to Apia that was under British jurisdiction and had nothing to do with him." The missionary sprang to his feet and strode across the room.

"It's terrible the way the men who are in authority seek to evade their responsibility. They speak as though evil that was out of sight ceased to be evil. The very existence of that woman is a scandal and it does not help matters to shift it to another of the islands. In the end I had to speak straight from the shoulder."

Davidson's brow lowered, and he protruded his firm chin. He looked fierce and determined.

"What do you mean by that?"

"Our mission is not entirely without influence at Washington. I pointed out to the governor that it wouldn't do him any good if there was a complaint about the way he managed things here."

"When has she got to go?" asked the doctor, after a pause.

"The San Francisco boat is due here from Sydney next Tuesday. She's to sail on that."

That was in five days' time. It was next day, when he was coming back from the hospital where for want of something better to do Macphail spent most of his mornings, that the half-caste stopped him as he was going upstairs.

"Excuse me, Dr. Macphail, Miss Thompson's sick. Will you have a look at her?"

"Certainly." Horn led him to her room. She was sitting in a chair idly, neither reading nor sewing, staring in front of her. She wore her white dress and the large hat with the flowers on it. Macphail noticed that her skin was yellow and muddy under her powder, and her eyes were heavy.

"I'm sorry to hear you're not well," he said.

"Oh, I ain't sick really. I just said that, because I just had to see you. I've got to clear on a boat that's going to 'Frisco."

She looked at him and he saw that her eyes were suddenly startled. She opened and clenched her hands spasmodically. The trader stood at the door, listening.

"So I understand," said the doctor.

She gave a little gulp.

"I guess it ain't very convenient for me to go to 'Frisco

just now. I went to see the governor yesterday afternoon, but I couldn't get to him. I saw the secretary, and he told me I'd got to take that boat and that was all there was to it. I just had to see the governor, so I waited outside his house this morning, and when he come out I spoke to him. He didn't want to speak to me, I'll say, but I wouldn't let him shake me off, and at last he said he hadn't no objection to my staying here till the next boat to Sydney if the Rev. Davidson will stand for it."

She stopped and looked at Dr. Macphail anxiously.

"I don't know exactly what I can do," he said.

"Well, I thought maybe you wouldn't mind asking him. I swear to God I won't start anything here if he'll just only let me stay. I won't go out of the house if that'll suit him. It's no more'n a fortnight."

"I'll ask him."

"He won't stand for it," said Horn. "He'll have you out on Tuesday, so you may as well make up your mind to it."

"Tell him I can get work in Sydney, straight stuff, I mean. 'Tain't asking very much."

"I'll do what I can."

"And come and tell me right away, will you? I can't set down to a thing till I get the dope one way or the other."

It was not an errand that much pleased the doctor, and, characteristically perhaps, he went about it indirectly. He told his wife what Miss Thompson had said to him and asked her to speak to Mrs. Davidson. The missionary's attitude seemed rather arbitrary and it could do no harm if the girl were allowed to stay in Pago-Pago another fortnight. But he was not prepared for the result of his diplomacy. The missionary came to him straightway.

"Mrs. Davidson tells me that Thompson has been speaking to you."

Dr. Macphail, thus directly tackled, had the shy man's resentment at being forced out into the open. He felt his temper rising, and he flushed.

"I don't see that it can make any difference if she goes to Sydney rather than to San Francisco, and so long as she promises to behave while she's here it's dashed hard to persecute her."

The missionary fixed him with his stern eyes.

"Why is she unwilling to go back to San Francisco?"

"I didn't enquire," answered the doctor with some asperity. "And I think one does better to mind one's own business."

Perhaps it was not a very tactful answer.

"The governor has ordered her to be deported by the first boat that leaves the island. He's only done his duty and I will not interfere. Her presence is a peril here."

"I think you're very harsh and tyrannical."

The two ladies looked up at the doctor with some alarm, but they need not have feared a quarrel, for the missionary smiled gently.

"I'm terribly sorry you should think that of me, Dr. Macphail. Believe me, my heart bleeds for that unfortunate woman, but I'm only trying to do my duty."

The doctor made no answer. He looked out of the window sullenly. For once it was not raining and across the bay you saw nestling among the trees the huts of a native village.

"I think I'll take advantage of the rain stopping to go out," he said.

"Please don't bear me malice because I can't accede to your wish," said Davidson, with a melancholy smile. "I respect you very much, doctor, and I should be sorry if you thought ill of me."

"I have no doubt you have a sufficiently good opinion of yourself to bear mine with equanimity," he retorted.

"That's one on me," chuckled Davidson.

When Dr. Macphail, vexed with himself because he had been uncivil to no purpose, went downstairs, Miss Thompson was waiting for him with her door ajar.

"Well," she said, "have you spoken to him?"

"Yes, I'm sorry, he won't do anything," he answered, not looking at her in his embarrassment.

But then he gave her a quick glance, for a sob broke from her. He saw that her face was white with fear. It gave him a shock of dismay. And suddenly he had an idea.

"But don't give up hope yet. I think it's a shame the way

they're treating you and I'm going to see the governor myself."

"Now?"

He nodded. Her face brightened.

"Say, that's real good of you. I'm sure he'll let me stay if
you speak for me. I just won't do a thing I didn't ought all
the time I'm here."

Dr. Macphail hardly knew why he had made up his mind
to appeal to the governor. He was perfectly indifferent to
Miss Thompson's affairs, but the missionary had irritated
him, and with him temper was a smouldering thing. He found
the governor at home. He was a large, handsome man, a
sailor, with a grey toothbrush moustache; and he wore a
spotless uniform of white drill.

"I've come to see you about a woman who's lodging in the
same house as we are," he said. "Her name's Thompson."

"I guess I've heard nearly enough about her, Dr. Macphail," said the governor, smiling. "I've given her the order
to get out next Tuesday and that's all I can do."

"I wanted to ask you if you couldn't stretch a point and
let her stay here till the boat comes in from San Francisco
so that she can go to Sydney. I will guarantee her good behavior."

The governor continued to smile, but his eyes grew small
and serious. "I'd be very glad to oblige you, Dr. Macphail,
but I've given the order and it must stand."

The doctor put the case as reasonably as he could, but
now the governor ceased to smile at all. He listened sullenly,
with averted gaze. Macphail saw that he was making no impression.

"I'm sorry to cause any lady inconvenience, but she'll have
to sail on Tuesday and that's all there is to it."

"But what difference can it make?"

"Pardon me, doctor, but I don't feel called upon to explain
my official actions except to the proper authorities."

Macphail looked at him shrewdly. He remembered Davidson's hint that he had used threats, and in the governor's
attitude he read a singular embarrassment.

"Davidson's a damned busybody," he said hotly.

"Between ourselves, Dr. Macphail, I don't say that I have

formed a very favorable opinion of Mr. Davidson, but I am bound to confess that he was within his rights in pointing out to me the danger that the presence of a woman of Miss Thompson's character was to a place like this where a number of enlisted men are stationed among a native population."

He got up and Dr. Macphail was obliged to do so too.

"I must ask you to excuse me. I have an engagement. Please give my respects to Mrs. Macphail."

The doctor left him crest-fallen. He knew that Miss Thompson would be waiting for him, and unwilling to tell her himself that he had failed, he went into the house by the back door and sneaked up the stairs as though he had something to hide.

At supper he was silent and ill-at-ease, but the missionary was jovial and animated. Dr. Macphail thought his eyes rested on him now and then with triumphant good-humour. It struck him suddenly that Davidson knew of his visit to the governor and of its ill success. But how on earth could he have heard of it? There was something sinister about the power of that man. After supper he saw Horn on the verandah and, as though to have a casual word with him, went out.

"She wants to know if you've seen the governor," the trader whispered.

"Yes. He wouldn't do anything. I'm awfully sorry, I can't do anything more."

"I knew he wouldn't. They daren't go against the missionaries."

"What are you talking about?" said Davidson affably, coming out to join them.

"I was just saying there was no chance of your getting over to Apia for at least another week," said the trader glibly.

He left them, and the two men returned into the parlour. Mr. Davidson devoted one hour after each meal to recreation. Presently a timid knock was heard at the door.

"Come in," said Mrs. Davidson, in her sharp voice.

The door was not opened. She got up and opened it. They saw Miss Thompson standing at the threshold. But the change in her appearance was extraordinary. This was no longer the flaunting hussy who had jeered at them in the road, but a broken, frightened woman. Her hair, as a rule so elaborately arranged, was tumbling untidily over her neck. She wore bedroom slippers and a skirt and blouse. They were unfresh and bedraggled. She stood at the door with the tears streaming down her face and did not dare to enter.

"What do you want?" said Mrs. Davidson harshly.

"May I speak to Mr. Davidson?" she said in a choking voice. The missionary rose and went towards her.

"Come right in, Miss Thompson," he said in cordial tones. "What can I do for you?"

She entered the room. "Say, I'm sorry for what I said to you the other day an' for—for everythin' else. I guess I was a bit lit up. I beg pardon."

"Oh, it was nothing. I guess my back's broad enough to bear a few hard words."

She stepped towards him with a movement that was horribly cringing. "You've got me beat. I'm all in. You won't make me go back to 'Frisco?"

His genial manner vanished and his voice grew on a sudden hard and stern. "Why don't you want to go back there?"

She cowered before him.

"I guess my people live there. I don't want them to see me like this. I'll go anywhere else you say."

"Why don't you want to go back to San Francisco?"

"I've told you."

He leaned forward, staring at her, and his great, shining eyes seemed to try to bore into her soul. He gave a sudden gasp. "The penitentiary."

She screamed, and then she fell at his feet, clasping his legs.

"Don't send me back there. I swear to you before God I'll be a good woman. I'll give all this up."

She burst into a torrent of confused supplication and the tears coursed down her painted cheeks. He leaned over her and, lifting her face, forced her to look at him.

"Is that it, the penitentiary?"

"I beat it before they could get me," she gasped. "If the bulls grab me it's three years for mine."

He let go his hold of her and she fell in a heap on the floor, sobbing bitterly. Dr. Macphail stood up.

"This alters the whole thing," he said. "You can't make her go back when you know this. Give her another chance. She wants to turn over a new leaf."

"I'm going to give her the finest chance she's ever had. If she repents let her accept her punishment."

She misunderstood the words and looked up. There was a gleam of hope in her heavy eyes. "You'll let me go?"

"No. You shall sail for San Francisco on Tuesday."

She gave a groan of horror and then burst into low, hoarse shrieks which sounded hardly human, and she beat her head passionately on the ground. Dr. Macphail sprang to her and lifted her up.

"Come on, you mustn't do that. You'd better go to your room and lie down. I'll get you something."

He raised her to her feet and partly dragging her, partly carrying her, got her downstairs. He was furious with Mrs. Davidson and with his wife because they made no effort to help. The half-caste was standing on the landing and with his assistance he managed to get her on the bed. She was moaning and crying. She was almost insensible. He gave her a hypodermic injection. He was hot and exhausted when he went upstairs again. "I've got her to lie down."

The two women and Davidson were in the same positions as when he had left them. They could not have moved or spoken since he went.

"I was waiting for you," said Davidson, in a strange, distant voice. "I want you all to pray with me for the soul of our erring sister."

He took the Bible off a shelf, and sat down at the table at which they had supped. It had not been cleared, and he pushed the tea-pot out of the way. In a powerful voice, resonant and deep, he read to them the chapter in which is narrated the meeting of Jesus Christ with the woman taken in adultery.

"Now kneel with me and let us pray for the soul of our dear sister, Sadie Thompson."

He burst into a long, passionate prayer in which he implored God to have mercy on the sinful woman. Mrs. Macphail and Mrs. Davidson knelt with covered eyes. The doctor, taken by surprise, awkward and sheepish, knelt too. The missionary's prayer had a savage eloquence. He was extraordinarily moved, and as he spoke the tears ran down his cheeks. Outside, the pitiless rain fell, fell steadily, with a fierce malignity that was all too human.

At last he stopped. He paused for a moment and said:

"We will now repeat the Lord's prayer."

They said it and then, following him, they rose from their knees. Mrs. Davidson's face was pale and restful. She was comforted and at peace, but the Macphails felt suddenly bashful. They did not know which way to look.

"I'll just go down and see how she is now," said Dr. Macphail.

When he knocked at her door it was opened for him by Horn. Miss Thompson was in a rocking-chair, sobbing quietly.

"What are you doing there?" exclaimed Macphail. "I told you to lie down."

"I can't lie down. I want to see Mr. Davidson."

"My poor child, what do you think is the good of it? You'll never move him."

"He said he'd come if I sent for him."

Macphail motioned to the trader.

"Go and fetch him."

He waited with her in silence while the trader went upstairs. Davidson came in.

"Excuse me for asking you to come here," she said, looking at him sombrely.

"I was expecting you to send for me. I knew the Lord would answer my prayer."

They stared at one another for a moment and then she looked away. She kept her eyes averted when she spoke.

"I've been a bad woman. I want to repent."

"Thank God! thank God! He has heard our prayers."

He turned to the two men.

"Leave me alone with her. Tell Mrs. Davidson that our prayers have been answered."

They went out and closed the door behind them.

"Gee whizz," said the trader.

That night Dr. Macphail could not get to sleep till late, and when he heard the missionary come upstairs he looked at his watch. It was two o'clock. But even then he did not go to bed at once, for through the wooden partition that separated their rooms he heard him praying aloud, till he himself, exhausted, fell asleep.

When he saw him next morning he was surprised at his appearance. He was paler than ever, tired, but his eyes shone with an inhuman fire. It looked as though he were filled with an overwhelming joy.

"I want you to go down presently and see Sadie," he said. "I can't hope that her body is better, but her soul—her soul is transformed."

The doctor was feeling wan and nervous.

"You were with her very late last night," he said.

"Yes, she couldn't bear to have me leave her."

"You look as pleased as Punch," the doctor said irritably.

Davidson's eyes shone with ecstasy.

"A great mercy has been vouchsafed me. Last night I was privileged to bring a lost soul to the loving arms of Jesus."

Miss Thompson was again in the rocking-chair. The bed had not been made. The room was in disorder. She had not troubled to dress herself, but wore a dirty dressing-gown, and her hair was tied in a sluttish knot. She had given her face a dab with a wet towel, but it was all swollen and creased with crying. She looked a drab.

She raised her eyes dully when the doctor came in. She was cowed and broken. "Where's Mr. Davidson?" she asked.

"He'll come presently if you want him," answered Macphail acidly. "I came here to see how you were."

"Oh, I guess I'm O.K. You needn't worry about that."

"Have you had anything to eat?"

"Horn brought me some coffee."

She looked anxiously at the door.

"D'you think he'll come down soon? I feel as if it wasn't so terrible when he's with me."

"Are you still going on Tuesday?"

"Yes, he says I've got to go. Please tell him to come right along. You can't do me any good. He's the only one as can help me now."

"Very well," said Dr. Macphail.

During the next three days the missionary spent almost all his time with Sadie Thompson. He joined the others only to have his meals. Dr. Macphail noticed that he hardly ate.

"He's wearing himself out," said Mrs. Davidson pitifully. "He'll have a breakdown if he doesn't take care, but he won't spare himself."

She herself was white and pale. She told Mrs. Macphail that she had no sleep. When the missionary came upstairs from Miss Thompson he prayed till he was exhausted, but even then he did not sleep for long. After an hour or two he got up and dressed himself, and went for a tramp along the bay. He had strange dreams.

"This morning he told me that he'd been dreaming about the mountains of Nebraska," said Mrs. Davidson.

"That's curious," said Dr. Macphail.

He remembered seeing them from the windows of the train when he crossed America. They were like huge mole-hills, rounded and smooth, and they rose from the plain abruptly. Dr. Macphail remembered how it struck him that they were like a woman's breasts.

Davidson's restlessness was intolerable even to himself. But he was buoyed up by a wonderful exhilaration. He was tearing out by the roots the last vestiges of sin that lurked in the hidden corners of that poor woman's heart. He read with her and prayed with her.

"It's wonderful," he said to them one day at supper. "It's a true rebirth. Her soul, which was black as night, is now pure and white like the new-fallen snow. I am humble and afraid. Her remorse for all her sins is beautiful. I am not worthy to touch the hem of her garment."

"Have you the heart to send her back to San Francisco?" said the doctor. "Three years in an American prison. I should have thought you might have saved her from that?"

"Ah, but don't you see? It's necessary. Do you think my heart doesn't bleed for her? I love her as I love my wife and my sister. All the time that she is in prison I shall suffer all the pain that she suffers."

"Bunkum," cried the doctor impatiently.

"You don't understand because you're blind. She's sinned, and she must suffer. I know what she'll endure. She'll be starved and tortured and humiliated. I want her to accept the punishment of man as a sacrifice to God. I want her to accept it joyfully. She has an opportunity which is offered to very few of us. God is very good and very merciful."

Davidson's voice trembled with excitement. He could hardly articulate the words that tumbled passionately from his lips.

"All day I pray with her and when I leave her I pray again, I pray with all my might and main, so that Jesus may grant her this great mercy. I want to put in her heart the passionate desire to be punished so that at the end, even if I offered to let her go, she would refuse. I want her to feel that the bitter punishment of prison is the thank-offering that she places at the feet of our Blessed Lord, who gave his life for her."

The days passed slowly. The whole household, intent on the wretched, tortured woman downstairs, lived in a state of unnatural excitement. She was like a victim that was being prepared for the savage rites of a bloody idolatry. Her terror numbed her. She could not bear to let Davidson out of her sight; it was only when he was with her that she had courage, and she hung upon him with a slavish dependence. She cried a great deal, and she read the Bible, and prayed. Sometimes she was exhausted and apathetic. Then she did indeed look forward to her ordeal, for it seemed to offer an escape, direct and concrete, from the anguish she was enduring. She could not bear much longer the vague terrors which now assailed her. With her sins she had put aside all personal vanity, and she slopped about her room, unkempt and dishevelled, in her tawdry dressing-gown. She had not taken off her night-dress for four days, nor put on stockings. Her room was littered and untidy. Meanwhile the rain fell with a cruel persistence. You felt that the heavens must at last be empty of water, but still it poured down, straight and heavy, with a maddening iteration, on the iron roof. Everything was damp and clammy. There was mildew on the walls and on the boots that stood on the floor. Through the sleepless nights the mosquitoes droned their angry chant.

"If it would only stop raining for a single day it wouldn't be so bad," said Dr. Macphail.

They all looked forward to the Tuesday when the boat for San Francisco was to arrive from Sydney. The strain was intolerable. So far as Dr. Macphail was concerned, his pity and his resentment were alike extinguished by his desire to be rid of the unfortunate woman. The inevitable must be accepted. He felt he would breathe more freely when the ship had sailed. Sadie Thompson was to be escorted on board by a clerk in the governor's office. This person called on the Monday evening and told Miss Thompson to be prepared at eleven in the morning. Davidson was with her.

"I'll see that everything is ready. I mean to come on board with her myself." Miss Thompson did not speak.

When Dr. Macphail blew out his candle and crawled cautiously under his mosquito curtains, he gave a sigh of relief.

"Well, thank God that's over. By this time to-morrow she'll be gone."

"Mrs. Davidson will be glad too. She says he's wearing himself to a shadow," said Mrs. Macphail. "She's a different woman."

"Who?"

"Sadie. I should never have thought it possible. It makes one humble."

Dr. Macphail did not answer, and presently he fell asleep. He was tired out, and he slept more soundly than usual.

He was awakened in the morning by a hand placed on his arm, and, starting up, saw Horn by the side of his bed. The trader put his finger on his mouth to prevent any exclamation from Dr. Macphail and beckoned him to come. As a rule he wore shabby ducks, but now he was barefoot and wore only the *lava-lava* of the natives. He looked suddenly savage, and Dr. Macphail, getting out of bed, saw that he was heavily tattooed. Horn made him a sign to come on to the verandah. Dr. Macphail got out of bed and followed the trader out.

"Don't make a noise," he whispered. "You're wanted. Put on a coat and some shoes. Quick."

Dr. Macphail's first thought was that something had happened to Miss Thompson.

"What is it? Shall I bring my instruments?"

"Hurry, please, hurry."

Dr. Macphail crept back into the bedroom, put on a waterproof over his pyjamas, and a pair of rubber-soled shoes. He rejoined the trader, and together they tiptoed down the stairs. The door leading out to the road was open and at it were standing half a dozen natives.

"What is it?" repeated the doctor.

"Come along with me," said Horn.

He walked out and the doctor followed him. The natives came after them in a little bunch. They crossed the road and came on to the beach. The doctor saw a group of natives standing round some object at the water's edge. They hurried along, a couple of dozen yards perhaps, and the natives opened out as the doctor came up. The trader pushed him forwards. Then he saw, lying half in the water and half out, a dreadful object, the body of Davidson. Dr. Macphail bent down—he was not a man to lose his head in an emergency— and turned the body over. The throat was cut from ear to ear, and in the right hand was still the razor with which the deed was done.

"He's quite cold," said the doctor. "He must have been dead some time."

"One of the boys saw him lying there on his way to work just now and came and told me. Do you think he did it himself?"

"Yes. Someone ought to go for the police."

Horn said something in the native tongue, and two youths started off.

"We must leave him here till they come," said the doctor.

"They mustn't take him into my house. I won't have him in my house."

"You'll do what the authorities say," replied the doctor sharply. "In point of fact I expect they'll take him to the mortuary."

They stood waiting where they were. The trader took a cigarette from a fold in his *lava-lava* and gave one to Dr. Macphail. They smoked while they stared at the corpse. Dr. Macphail could not understand.

"Why do you think he did it?" asked Horn.

The doctor shrugged his shoulders. In a little while native police came along, under the charge of a marine, with a stretcher, and immediately afterwards a couple of naval officers and a naval doctor. They managed everything in a businesslike manner.

"What about the wife?" said one of the officers.

"Now that you've come I'll go back to the house and get some things on. I'll see that it's broken to her. She'd better not see him till he's been fixed up a little."

"I guess that's right," said the naval doctor.

When Dr. Macphail went back he found his wife nearly dressed.

"Mrs. Davidson's in a dreadful state about her husband," she said to him as soon as he appeared. "He hasn't been to bed all night. She heard him leave Miss Thompson's room at two, but he went out. If he's been walking about since then he'll be absolutely dead."

Dr. Macphail told her what had happened and asked her to break the news to Mrs. Davidson.

"But why did he do it?" she asked, horror-stricken.

"I don't know."

"But I can't. I can't."

"You must." She gave him a frightened look and went out. He heard her go into Mrs. Davidson's room. He waited a minute to gather himself together and then began to shave and wash. When he was dressed he sat down on the bed and waited for his wife. At last she came.

"She wants to see him," she said.

"They've taken him to the mortuary. We'd better go down with her. How did she take it?"

"I think she's stunned. She didn't cry. But she's trembling like a leaf."

"We'd better go at once."

When they knocked at her door Mrs. Davidson came out. She was very pale, but dry-eyed. To the doctor she seemed unnaturally composed. No word was exchanged, and they set out in silence down the road. When they arrived at the mortuary Mrs. Davidson spoke.

"Let me go in and see him alone."

They stood aside. A native opened a door for her and closed it behind her. They sat down and waited. One or two white men came and talked to them in undertones. Dr. Macphail told them again what he knew of the tragedy. At last the door was quietly opened and Mrs. Davidson came out. Silence fell upon them.

"I'm ready to go back now," she said.

Her voice was hard and steady. Dr. Macphail could not understand the look in her eyes. Her pale face was very stern. They walked back slowly, never saying a word, and at last they came round the bend on the other side of which stood their house. Mrs. Davidson gave a gasp, and for a moment they stopped still. An incredible sound assaulted their ears. The gramophone which had been silent for so long was playing, playing ragtime loud and harsh.

"What's that?" cried Mrs. Macphail with horror.

"Let's go on," said Mrs. Davidson.

They walked up the steps and entered the hall. Miss Thompson was standing at her door, chatting with a sailor. A sudden change had taken place in her. She was no longer the cowed drudge of the last days. She was dressed in all her finery, in her white dress, with the high shiny boots over which her fat legs bulged in her cotton stockings; her hair was elaborately arranged; and she wore that enormous hat covered with gaudy flowers. Her face was painted, her eyebrows were boldly black, and her lips were scarlet. She held herself erect. She was the flaunting queen that they had known at first. As they came in she broke into a loud, jeering laugh; and then, when Mrs. Davidson involuntarily stopped, she collected the spittle in her mouth and spat. Mrs. Davidson cowered back, and two red spots rose suddenly to her cheeks. Then, covering her face with her hands, she broke away and ran quickly up the stairs. Dr. Macphail was outraged. He pushed past the woman into her room.

"What the devil are you doing?" he cried. "Stop that damned machine."

He went up to it and tore the record off. She turned on him.

"Say, doc, you can that stuff with me. What the hell are you doin' in my room?"

"What do you mean?" he cried. "What d'you mean?"

She gathered herself together. No one could describe the scorn of her expression or the contemptuous hatred she put into her answer.

"You men! You filthy, dirty pigs! You're all the same, all of you. Pigs! Pigs!"

Dr. Macphail gasped. He understood.

RING LARDNER *(1885–1933)*

HAIRCUT

I GOT *another* barber that comes over from Carterville and helps me out Saturdays, but the rest of the time I can get along all right alone. You can see for yourself that this ain't no New York City and besides that, most of the boys works all day and don't have no leisure to drop in here and get themselves prettied up.

You're a newcomer, ain't you? I thought I hadn't seen you round before. I hope you like it good enough to stay. As I say, we ain't no New York City or Chicago, but we have pretty good times. Not as good, though, since Jim Kendall got killed. When he was alive, him and Hod Meyers used to keep this town in an uproar. I bet they was more laughin' done here than any town its size in America.

Jim was comical, and Hod was pretty near a match for him. Since Jim's gone, Hod tries to hold his end up just the same as ever, but it's tough goin' when you ain't got nobody to kind of work with.

They used to be plenty fun in here Saturdays. This place is jam-packed Saturdays, from four o'clock on. Jim and Hod would show up right after their supper, round six o'clock. Jim would set himself down in that big chair, nearest the blue spittoon. Whoever had been settin' in that chair, why they'd get up when Jim come in and give it to him.

You'd of thought it was a reserved seat like they have sometimes in a theayter. Hod would generally always stand or walk up and down, or some Saturdays, of course, he'd be settin' in this chair part of the time, gettin' a haircut.

Well, Jim would set there a w'ile without openin' his mouth only to spit, and then finally he'd say to me, "Whitey," —my right name, that is, my right first name, is Dick, but everybody round here calls me Whitey—Jim would say,

"Whitey, your nose looks like a rosebud tonight. You must of been drinkin' some of your aw de cologne."

So I'd say, "No, Jim, but you look like you'd been drinkin' somethin' of that kind or somethin' worse."

Jim would have to laugh at that, but then he'd speak up and say, "No, I ain't had nothin' to drink, but that ain't sayin' I wouldn't like somethin'. I wouldn't even mind if it was wood alcohol."

Then Hod Meyers would say, "Neither would your wife." That would set everybody to laughin' because Jim and his wife wasn't on very good terms. She'd of divorced him only they wasn't no chance to get alimony and she didn't have no way to take care of herself and the kids. She couldn't never understand Jim. He *was* kind of rough, but a good fella at heart.

Him and Hod had all kinds of sport with Milt Sheppard. I don't suppose you've seen Milt. Well, he's got an Adam's apple that looks more like a mushmelon. So I'd be shavin' Milt and when I'd start to shave down here on his neck, Hod would holler, "Hey, Whitey, wait a minute! Before you cut into it, let's make up a pool and see who can guess closest to the number of seeds."

And Jim would say, "If Milt hadn't of been so hoggish, he'd of ordered a half a cantaloupe instead of a whole one and it might not of stuck in his throat."

All the boys would roar at this and Milt himself would force a smile, though the joke was on him. Jim certainly was a card!

There's his shavin' mug, settin' on the shelf, right next to Charley Vail's. "Charles M. Vail." That's the druggist. He comes in regular for his shave, three times a week. And Jim's is the cup next to Charley's. "James H. Kendall." Jim won't need no shavin' mug no more, but I'll leave it there just the same for old time's sake. Jim certainly was a character!

Years ago, Jim used to travel for a canned goods concern over in Carterville. They sold canned goods. Jim had the whole northern half of the State and was on the road five days out of every week. He'd drop in here Saturdays and tell his experiences for that week. It was rich.

I guess he paid more attention to playin' jokes than makin'

sales. Finally the concern let him out and he come right home here and told everybody he'd been fired instead of sayin' he'd resigned like most fellas would of.

It was a Saturday and the shop was full and Jim got up out of that chair and says, "Gentlemen, I got an important announcement to make. I been fired from my job."

Well, they asked him if he was in earnest and he said he was and nobody could think of nothin' to say till Jim finally broke the ice himself. He says, "I been sellin' canned goods and now I'm canned goods myself."

You see, the concern he'd been workin' for was a factory that made canned goods. Over in Carterville. And now Jim said he was canned himself. He was certainly a card!

Jim had a great trick that he used to play w'ile he was travelin'. For instance, he'd be ridin' on a train and they'd come to some little town like, well, like, we'll say, like Benton. Jim would look out the train window and read the signs on the stores.

For instance, they'd be a sign, "Henry Smith, Dry Goods." Well, Jim would write down the name and the name of the town and when he got to wherever he was goin' he'd mail back a postal card to Henry Smith at Benton and not sign no name to it, but he'd write on the card, well, somethin' like "Ask your wife about that book agent that spent the afternoon last week," or "Ask your Missus who kept her from gettin' lonesome the last time you was in Carterville." And he'd sign the card, "A Friend."

Of course, he never knew what really come of none of those jokes, but he could picture what *probably* happened and that was enough.

Jim didn't work very steady after he lost his position with the Carterville people. What he did earn, doin' odd jobs round town, why he spent pretty near all of it on gin and his family might of starved if the stores hadn't of carried them along. Jim's wife tried her hand at dressmakin', but they ain't nobody goin' to get rich makin' dresses in this town.

As I say, she'd of divorced Jim, only she seen that she couldn't support herself and the kids and she was always hopin' that some day Jim would cut out his habits and give her more than two or three dollars a week.

They was a time when she would go to whoever he was workin' for and ask them to give her his wages, but after she done this once or twice, he beat her to it by borrowin' most of his pay in advance. He told it all round town, how he had outfoxed his Missus. He certainly was a caution!

But he wasn't satisfied with just outwittin' her. He was sore the way she had acted, tryin' to grab off his pay. And he made up his mind he'd get even. Well, he waited till Evans's Circus was advertised to come to town. Then he told his wife and two kiddies that he was goin' to take them to the circus. The day of the circus, he told them he would get the tickets and meet them outside the entrance to the tent.

Well, he didn't have no intentions of bein' there or buyin' tickets or nothin'. He got full of gin and laid round Wright's poolroom all day. His wife and kids waited and waited and of course he didn't show up. His wife didn't have a dime with her, or nowhere else, I guess. So she finally had to tell the kids it was all off and they cried like they wasn't never goin' to stop.

Well, it seems, w'ile they was cryin', Doc Stair came along and he asked what was the matter, but Mrs. Kendall was stubborn and wouldn't tell him, but the kids told him and he insisted on takin' them and their mother in to the show. Jim found this out afterwards and it was one reason why he had it in for Doc Stair.

Doc Stair come here about a year and a half ago. He's a mighty handsome young fella and his clothes always look like he has them made to order. He goes to Detroit two or three times a year and w'ile he's there he must have a tailor take his measure and then make him a suit to order. They cost pretty near twice as much, but they fit a whole lot better than if you just bought them in a store.

For a w'ile everybody was wonderin' why a young doctor like Doc Stair should come to a town like this where we already got old Doc Gamble and Doc Foote that's both been here for years and all the practice in town was always divided between the two of them.

Then they was a story got round that Doc Stair's gal had throwed him over, a gal up in the Northern Peninsula somewheres, and the reason he come here was to hide himself away and forget it. He said himself that he thought they wasn't nothin' like general practice in a place like ours to fit a man to be a good all round doctor. And that's why he'd came.

Anyways, it wasn't long before he was makin' enough to live on, though they tell me that he never dunned nobody for what they owed him, and the folks here certainly has got the owin' habit, even in my business. If I had all that was comin' to me for just shaves alone, I could go to Carterville and put up at the Mercer for a week and see a different picture every night. For instance, they's old George Purdy—but I guess I shouldn't ought to be gossipin'.

Well, last year, our coroner died, died of the flu. Ken Beatty, that was his name. He was the coroner. So they had to choose another man to be coroner in his place and they picked Doc Stair. He laughed at first and said he didn't want it, but they made him take it. It ain't no job that anybody would fight for and what a man makes out of it in a year would just about buy seeds for their garden. Doc's the kind, though, that can't say no to nothin' if you keep at him long enough.

But I was goin' to tell you about a poor boy we got here in town—Paul Dickson. He fell out of a tree when he was about ten years old. Lit on his head and it done somethin' to him and he ain't never been right. No harm in him, but just silly. Jim Kendall used to call him cuckoo; that's a name Jim had for anybody that was off their head, only he called people's head their bean. That was another of his gags, callin' head bean and callin' crazy people cuckoo. Only poor Paul ain't crazy, but just silly.

You can imagine that Jim used to have all kinds of fun with Paul. He'd send him to the White Front Garage for a left-handed monkey wrench. Of course they ain't no such a thing as a left-handed monkey wrench.

And once we had a kind of a fair here and they was a baseball game between the fats and the leans and before the game started Jim called Paul over and sent him way down to Schrader's hardware store to get a key for the pitcher's box.

They wasn't nothing in the way of gags that Jim couldn't think up, when he put his mind to it.

Poor Paul was always kind of suspicious of people, maybe on account of how Jim had kept foolin' him. Paul wouldn't have much to do with anybody only his own mother and Doc Stair and a girl here in town named Julie Gregg. That is, she ain't a girl no more, but pretty near thirty or over.

When Doc first came to town, Paul seemed to feel like here was a real friend and he hung round Doc's office most of the w'ile; the only time he wasn't there was when he'd go home to eat or sleep or when he seen Julie Gregg doin' her shoppin'.

When he looked out Doc's window and seen her, he'd run downstairs and join her and tag along with her to the different stores. The poor boy was crazy about Julie and she always treated him mighty nice and made him feel like he was welcome, though of course it wasn't nothin' but pity on her side.

Doc done all he could to improve Paul's mind and he told me once that he really thought the boy was gettin' better, that they was times when he was as bright and sensible as anybody else.

But I was goin' to tell you about Julie Gregg. Old Man Gregg was in the lumber business, but got to drinkin' and lost the most of his money and when he died, he didn't leave nothin' but the house and just enough insurance for the girl to skimp along on.

Her mother was a kind of a half invalid and didn't hardly ever leave the house. Julie wanted to sell the place and move somewheres else after the old man died, but the mother said she was born here and would die here. It was tough on Julie, as the young people round this town—well, she's too good for them.

She's been away to school and Chicago and New York and different places and they ain't no subject she can't talk on, where you take the rest of the young folks here and you mention anything to them outside of Gloria Swanson or

Tommy Meighan and they think you're delirious. Did you see Gloria in Wages of Virtue? You missed somethin'!

Well, Doc Stair hadn't been here more than a week when he come in one day to get shaved and I recognized who he was as he had been pointed out to me, so I told him about my old lady. She's been ailin' for a couple years and either Doc Gamble or Doc Foote, neither one, seemed to be helpin' her. So he said he would come out and see her, but if she was able to get out herself, it would be better to bring her to his office where he could make a completer examination.

So I took her to his office and w'ile I was waitin' for her in the reception room, in come Julie Gregg. When somebody comes in Doc Stair's office, they's a bell that rings in his inside office so he can tell they's somebody to see him.

So he left my old lady inside and come out to the front office and that's the first time him and Julie met and I guess it was what they call love at first sight. But it wasn't fifty-fifty. This young fella was the slickest lookin' fella she'd ever seen in this town and she went wild over him. To him she was just a young lady that wanted to see the doctor.

She'd come on about the same business I had. Her mother had been doctorin' for years with Doc Gamble and Doc Foote and with no results. So she'd heard they was a new doc in town and decided to give him a try. He promised to call and see her mother that same day.

I said a minute ago that it was love at first sight on her part. I'm not only judgin' by how she acted afterwards but how she looked at him that first day in his office. I ain't no mind reader, but it was wrote all over her face that she was gone.

Now Jim Kendall, besides bein' a jokesmith and a pretty good drinker, well, Jim was quite a lady-killer. I guess he run pretty wild durin' the time he was on the road for them Carterville people, and besides that, he'd had a couple little affairs of the heart right here in town. As I say, his wife would of divorced him, only she couldn't.

But Jim was like the majority of men, and women, too, I guess. He wanted what he couldn't get. He wanted Julie Gregg and worked his head off tryin' to land her. Only he'd of said bean instead of head.

Well, Jim's habits and his jokes didn't appeal to Julie and of course he was a married man, so he didn't have no more chance than, well, than a rabbit. That's an expression of Jim's himself. When somebody didn't have no chance to get elected or somethin', Jim would always say they didn't have no more chance than a rabbit.

He didn't make no bones about how he felt. Right in here, more than once, in front of the whole crowd, he said he was stuck on Julie and anybody that could get her for him was welcome to his house and his wife and kids included. But she wouldn't have nothin' to do with him; wouldn't even speak to him on the street. He finally seen he wasn't gettin' nowheres with his usual line so he decided to try the rough stuff. He went right up to her house one evenin' and when she opened the door he forced his way in and grabbed her. But she broke loose and before he could stop her, she run in the next room and locked the door and phoned to Joe Barnes. Joe's the marshal. Jim could hear who she was phonin' to and he beat it before Joe got there.

Joe was an old friend of Julie's pa. Joe went to Jim the next day and told him what would happen if he ever done it again.

I don't know how the news of this little affair leaked out. Chances is that Joe Barnes told his wife and she told somebody else's wife and they told their husband. Anyways, it did leak out and Hod Meyers had the nerve to kid Jim about it, right here in this shop. Jim didn't deny nothin' and kind of laughed it off and said for us all to wait; that lots of people had tried to make a monkey out of him, but he always got even.

Meanw'ile everybody in town was wise to Julie's bein' wild mad over the Doc. I don't suppose she had any idear how her face changed when him and her was together; of course she couldn't of, or she'd of kept away from him. And she didn't know that we was all noticin' how many times she made excuses to go up to his office or pass it on the other side of the street and look up in his window to see if he was there. I felt sorry for her and so did most other people.

Hod Meyers kept rubbin' it into Jim about how the Doc

had cut him out. Jim didn't pay no attention to the kiddin' and you could see he was plannin' one of his jokes.

One trick Jim had was the knack of changin' his voice. He could make you think he was a girl talkin' and he could mimic any man's voice. To show you how good he was along this line, I'll tell you the joke he played on me once.

You know, in most towns of any size, when a man is dead and needs a shave, why the barber that shaves him soaks him five dollars for the job; that is, he don't soak *him*, but whoever ordered the shave. I just charge three dollars because personally I don't mind much shavin' a dead person. They lay a whole lot stiller than live customers. The only thing is that you don't feel like talkin' to them and you get kind of lonesome.

Well, about the coldest day we ever had here, two years ago last winter, the phone rung at the house w'ile I was home to dinner and I answered the phone and it was a woman's voice and she said she was Mrs. John Scott and her husband was dead and would I come out and shave him.

Old John had always been a good customer of mine. But they live seven miles out in the country, on the Streeter road. Still I didn't see how I could say no.

So I said I would be there, but would have to come in a jitney and it might cost three or four dollars besides the price of the shave. So she, or the voice, it said that was all right, so I got Frank Abbott to drive me out to the place and when I got there, who should open the door but old John himself! He wasn't no more dead than, well, than a rabbit.

It didn't take no private detective to figure out who had played me this little joke. Nobody could of thought it up but Jim Kendall. He certainly was a card!

I tell you this incident just to show you how he could disguise his voice and make you believe it was somebody else talkin'. I'd of swore it was Mrs. Scott had called me. Anyways, some woman.

Well, Jim waited till he had Doc Stair's voice down pat; then he went after revenge.

He called Julie up on a night when he knew Doc was over in Carterville. She never questioned but what it was Doc's voice. Jim said he must see her that night; he couldn't wait no longer to tell her somethin'. She was all excited and told him to come to the house. But he said he was expectin' an important long distance call and wouldn't she please forget her manners for once and come to his office. He said they couldn't nothin' hurt her and nobody would see her and he just *must* talk to her a little w'ile. Well, poor Julie fell for it.

Doc always keeps a night light in his office, so it looked to Julie like they was somebody there.

Meanw'ile Jim Kendall had went to Wright's poolroom, where they was a whole gang amusin' themselves. The most of them had drank plenty of gin, and they was a rough bunch even when sober. They was always strong for Jim's jokes and when he told them to come with him and see some fun they give up their card games and pool games and followed along.

Doc's office is on the second floor. Right outside his door they's a flight of stairs leadin' to the floor above. Jim and his gang hid in the dark behind these stairs.

Well, Julie come up to Doc's door and rung the bell and they was nothin' doin'. She rung it again and she rung it seven or eight times. Then she tried the door and found it locked. Then Jim made some kind of a noise and she heard it and waited a minute, and then she says, "Is that you, Ralph?" Ralph is Doc's first name.

They was no answer and it must of came to her all of a sudden that she'd been bunked. She pretty near fell downstairs and the whole gang after her. They chased her all the way home, hollerin', "Is that you, Ralph?" and "Oh, Ralphie, dear, is that you?" Jim says he couldn't holler it himself, as he was laughin' too hard.

Poor Julie! She didn't show up here on Main Street for a long, long time afterward.

And of course Jim and his gang told everybody in town, everybody but Doc Stair. They was scared to tell him, and he might of never knowed only for Paul Dickson. The poor cuckoo, as Jim called him, he was here in the shop one night when Jim was still gloatin' yet over what he'd done to Julie. And Paul took in as much of it as he could understand and he run to Doc with the story.

It's a cinch Doc went up in the air and swore he'd make Jim suffer. But it was a kind of a delicate thing, because if it got out that he had beat Jim up, Julie was bound to hear of it and then she'd know that Doc knew and of course knowin' that he knew would make it worse for her than ever. He was goin' to do somethin', but it took a lot of figurin'.

Well, it was a couple of days later when Jim was here in the shop again, and so was the cuckoo. Jim was goin' duck-shootin' the next day and had come in lookin' for Hod Meyers to go with him. I happened to know that Hod had went over to Carterville and wouldn't be home till the end of the week. So Jim said he hated to go alone and he guessed he would call it off. Then poor Paul spoke up and said if Jim would take him he would go along. Jim thought a w'ile and then he said, well, he guessed a half-wit was better than nothin'.

I suppose he was plottin' to get Paul out in the boat and play some joke on him, like pushin' him in the water. Anyways, he said Paul could go. He asked him had he ever shot a duck and Paul said no, he'd never even had a gun in his hands. So Jim said he could set in the boat and watch him and if he behaved himself, he might lend him his gun for a couple of shots. They made a date to meet in the mornin' and that's the last I seen of Jim alive.

Next mornin', I hadn't been open more than ten minutes when Doc Stair come in. He looked kind of nervous. He asked me had I seen Paul Dickson. I said no, but I knew where he was, out duck-shootin' with Jim Kendall. So Doc says that's what he had heard, and he couldn't understand it because Paul had told him he wouldn't never have no more to do with Jim as long as he lived.

He said Paul had told him about the joke Jim had played on Julie. He said Paul had asked him what he thought of the joke and the Doc had told him that anybody that would do a thing like that ought not to be let live.

I said it had been a kind of a raw thing, but Jim just couldn't resist no kind of a joke, no matter how raw. I said I thought he was all right at heart, but just bubblin' over with mischief. Doc turned and walked out.

At noon he got a phone call from old John Scott. The lake where Jim and Paul had went shootin' is on John's place. Paul had came runnin' up to the house a few minutes before and said they'd been an accident. Jim had shot a few ducks and then give the gun to Paul and told him to try his luck. Paul hadn't never handled a gun and he was nervous. He was shakin' so hard that he couldn't control the gun. He let fire and Jim sunk back in the boat, dead.

Doc Stair, bein' the coroner, jumped in Frank Abbott's flivver and rushed out to Scott's farm. Paul and old John was down on the shore of the lake. Paul had rowed the boat to shore, but they'd left the body in it, waitin' for Doc to come.

Doc examined the body and said they might as well fetch it back to town. They was no use leavin' it there or callin' a jury, as it was a plain case of accidental shootin'.

Personally I wouldn't never leave a person shoot a gun in the same boat I was in unless I was sure they knew somethin' about guns. Jim was a sucker to leave a new beginner have his gun, let alone a half-wit. It probably served Jim right, what he got. But still we miss him round here. He certainly was a card!

Comb it wet or dry?

IVAN BUNIN *(1870–1953)*

THE GENTLEMAN FROM SAN FRANCISCO

Translated by A. Yarmolinsky

"Alas, alas, that great city Babylon, that mighty city!"
—REVELATION

THE GENTLEMAN from San Francisco—neither at Naples nor on Capri could any one recall his name—with his wife and daughter, was on his way to Europe, where he intended to stay for two whole years, solely for the pleasure of it.

He was firmly convinced that he had a full right to a rest, enjoyment, a long comfortable trip, and what not. This conviction had a two-fold reason: first he was rich, and second, despite his fifty-eight years, he was just about to enter the stream of life's pleasures. Until now he had not really lived, but simply existed, to be sure—fairly well, yet putting off his fondest hopes for the future. He toiled unweariedly—the Chinese, whom he imported by thousands for his works, knew full well what it meant,—and finally he saw that he had made much, and that he had nearly come up to the level of those whom he had once taken as a model, and he decided to catch his breath. The class of people to which he belonged was in the habit of beginning its enjoyment of life with a trip to Europe, India, Egypt. He made up his mind to do the same. Of course, it was first of all himself that he desired to reward for the years of toil, but he was also glad for his wife and daughter's sake. His wife was never distinguished by any extraordinary impressionability, but then, all elderly American women are ardent travelers. As for his daughter, a girl of marriageable age, and somewhat sickly,—travel was the very thing she needed. Not to speak of the benefit to her health, do not happy meetings occur during travels? Abroad, one may chance to sit at the same table with a prince, or examine frescoes side by side with a multi-millionaire.

The itinerary the Gentleman from San Francisco planned out was an extensive one. In December and January he expected to relish the sun of southern Italy, monuments of antiquity, the tarantella, serenades of wandering minstrels, and that which at his age is felt most keenly—the love, not entirely disinterested though, of young Neapolitan girls. The Carnival days he planned to spend at Nice and Monte Carlo, which at that time of the year is the meeting-place of the choicest society, the society upon which depend all the blessings of civilization: the cut of dress suits, the stability of thrones, the declaration of wars, the prosperity of hotels. Some of these people passionately give themselves over to automobile and boat races, others to roulette, others, again, busy themselves with what is called flirtation, and others shoot pigeons, which soar so beautifully from the dove-cote, hover a while over the emerald lawn, on the background of the forget-me-not colored sea, and then suddenly hit the ground, like little white lumps. Early March he wanted to devote to Florence, and at Easter, to hear the Miserere in

Rome. His plans also included Venice, Paris, bull-baiting at
Seville, bathing on the British Islands, also Athens, Constan-
tinople, Palestine, Egypt, and even Japan, of course, on the
way back. . . . And at first things went very well indeed.

It was the end of November, and all the way to Gibraltar
the ship sailed across seas which were either clad by icy darkness or swept by storms carrying wet snow. But there were no
accidents, and the vessel did not even roll. The passengers—
all people of consequence—were numerous, and the steamer,
the famous "Atlantis," resembled the most expensive European hotel with all improvements; a night refreshment-bar,
Oriental baths, even a newspaper of its own. The manner of
living was a most aristocratic one; passengers rose early,
awakened by the shrill voice of a bugle, filling the corridors
at the gloomy hour when the day broke slowly and sulkily
over the grayish-green watery desert, which rolled heavily in
the fog. After putting on their flannel pajamas, they took
coffee, chocolate, cocoa; they seated themselves in marble
baths, went through their exercises, whetting their appetites
and increasing their sense of well-being, dressed for the day,
and had their breakfast. Till eleven o'clock they were supposed to stroll on the deck, breathing in the chill freshness of
the ocean, or they played table-tennis, or other games which
arouse the appetite. At eleven o'clock a collation was served
consisting of sandwiches and bouillon, after which people
read their newspapers, quietly waiting for luncheon, which
was more nourishing and varied than the breakfast. The next
two hours were given to rest; all the decks were crowded
then with steamer chairs, on which the passengers, wrapped
in plaids, lay stretched, dozing lazily, or watching the cloudy
sky and the foamy-fringed water hillocks flashing beyond the
sides of the vessel. At five o'clock, refreshed and gay, they
drank strong, fragrant tea; at seven the sound of the bugle
announced a dinner of nine courses. . . . Then the Gentleman from San Francisco, rubbing his hands in an onrush of
vital energy, hastened to his luxurious state-room to dress.

In the evening, all the decks of the "Atlantis" yawned in
the darkness, shone with their innumerable fiery eyes, and a
multitude of servants worked with increased feverishness in
the kitchens, dish-washing compartments, and wine-cellars.

The ocean, which heaved about the sides of the ship, was dreadful, but no one thought of it. All had faith in the controlling power of the captain, a red-headed giant, heavy and very sleepy, who, clad in a uniform with broad golden stripes, looked like a huge idol, and but rarely emerged, for the benefit of the public, from his mysterious retreat. On the forecastle, the siren gloomily roared or screeched in a fit of mad rage, but few of the diners heard the siren: its hellish voice was covered by the sounds of an excellent string orchestra, which played ceaselessly and exquisitely in a vast hall, decorated with marble and spread with velvety carpets. The hall was flooded with torrents of light, radiated by crystal lustres and gilt chandeliers; it was filled with a throng of bejeweled ladies in low-necked dresses, of men in dinner-coats, graceful waiters, and deferential maîtres-d'hôtel. One of these,—who accepted wine orders exclusively—wore a chain on his neck like some lord-mayor. The evening dress, and the ideal linen made the Gentleman from San Francisco look very young. Dry-skinned, of average height, strongly, though irregularly built, glossy with thorough washing and cleaning, and moderately animated, he sat in the golden splendor of this palace. Near him stood a bottle of amber-colored Johannisberger, and goblets of most delicate glass and of varied sizes, surmounted by a frizzled bunch of fresh hyacinths. There was something Mongolian in his yellowish face with its trimmed silvery moustache; his large teeth glimmered with gold fillings, and his strong, bald head had a dull glow, like old ivory. His wife, a big, broad and placid woman, was dressed richly, but in keeping with her age. Complicated, but light, transparent, and innocently immodest was the dress of his daughter, tall and slender, with magnificent hair gracefully combed; her breath was sweet with violet-scented tablets, and she had a number of tiny and most delicate pink dimples near her lips and between her slightly-powdered shoulder blades. . . .

The dinner lasted two whole hours, and was followed by dances in the dancing hall, while the men—the Gentleman from San Francisco among them—made their way to the refreshment bar, where Negroes in red jackets and with eyeballs like shelled hard-boiled eggs, waited on them. There, with their feet on tables, smoking Havana cigars, and drinking themselves purple in the face, they settled the destinies of nations on the basis of the latest political and stock-exchange news. Outside, the ocean tossed up black mountains with a thud; and the snow-storm hissed furiously in the rigging grown heavy with slush; the ship trembled in every limb, struggling with the storm and ploughing with difficulty the shifting and seething mountainous masses that threw far and high their foaming tails; the siren groaned in agony, choked by storm and fog; the watchmen in their towers froze and almost went out of their minds under the superhuman stress of attention. Like the gloomy and sultry mass of the inferno, like its last, ninth circle, was the submersed womb of the steamer, where monstrous furnaces yawned with red-hot open jaws, and emitted deep, hooting sounds, and where the stokers, stripped to the waist, and purple with reflected flames, bathed in their own dirty, acid sweat. And here, in the refreshment-bar, carefree men, with their feet, encased in dancing shoes, on the table, sipped cognac and liqueurs, swam in waves of spiced smoke, and exchanged subtle remarks, while in the dancing-hall everything sparkled and radiated light, warmth and joy. The couples now turned around in a waltz, now swayed in the tango; and the music, sweetly shameless and sad, persisted in its ceaseless entreaties. . . . There were many persons of note in this magnificent crowd: an ambassador, a dry, modest old man; a great millionaire, shaved, tall, of an indefinite age, who, in his old-fashioned dress-coat, looked like a prelate; also a famous Spanish writer; and an international belle, already slightly faded and of dubious morals. There was also among them a loving pair, exquisite and refined, whom everybody watched with curiosity and who did not conceal their bliss; he danced only with her, sang—with great skill—only to her accompaniment, and they were so charming, so graceful. The captain alone knew that they had been hired by the company at a good salary to play at love, and that they had been sailing now on one, now on another steamer, for quite a long time.

In Gibraltar everybody was gladdened by the sun, and by the weather which was like early spring. A new passenger appeared aboard the "Atlantis" and aroused everybody's interest. It was the crown-prince of an Asiatic state, who traveled incognito, a small man, very nimble, though looking as if made of wood, broad-faced, narrow-eyed, in gold-rimmed glasses, somewhat disagreeable because of his long moustache, which was sparse like that of a corpse, but otherwise—charming, plain, modest. In the Mediterranean the breath of winter was again felt. The seas were heavy and motley like a peacock's tail and the waves stirred up by the gay gusts of the tramontane tossed their white crests under a sparkling and perfectly clear sky. Next morning, the sky grew paler and the skyline misty. Land was near. Then Ischia and Capri came in sight, and one could descry, through an opera-glass, Naples, looking like pieces of sugar strewn at the foot of an indistinct dove-colored mass, and above them, a snow-covered chain of distant mountains. The decks were crowded, many ladies and gentlemen put on light-furcoats; Chinese servants, bandy-legged youths—with pitch black braids down to the heels and with girlish, thick eyelashes,—always quiet and speaking in a whisper, were carrying to the foot of the staircases, plaid wraps, canes, and crocodile-leather valises and handbags. The daughter of the Gentleman from San Francisco stood near the prince, who, by a happy chance, had been introduced to her the evening before, and feigned to be looking steadily at something far-off, which he was pointing out to her, while he was, at the same time, explaining something, saying something rapidly and quietly. He was so small that he looked like a boy among other men, and he was not handsome at all. And then there was something strange about him; his glasses, derby and coat were most commonplace, but there was something horse-like in the hair of his sparse moustache, and the thin, tanned skin of his flat face looked as though it were somewhat stretched and varnished. But the girl listened to him, and so great was her excitement that she could hardly grasp the meaning of his words, her heart palpitated with incomprehensible rapture and with pride that he was standing and speaking with her and nobody else. Everything about him was different; his dry hands, his clean skin, under which flowed ancient kingly blood, even his light shoes and his European dress, plain, but singularly tidy—everything hid an inexplicable fascination and engendered thoughts of love. And the Gentleman from San Francisco, himself, in a silk-hat, grey leggings, patent leather shoes, kept eyeing the famous beauty who was standing near him, a tall, stately blonde, with eyes painted according to the latest Parisian fashion, and a tiny, bent peeled-off pet-dog, to whom she addressed herself. And the daughter, in a kind of vague perplexity, tried not to notice him.

Like all wealthy Americans he was very liberal when traveling, and believed in the complete sincerity and good-will of those who so painstakingly fed him, served him day and night, anticipating his slightest desire, protected him from dirt and disturbance, hauled things for him, hailed carriers, and delivered his luggage to hotels. So it was everywhere, and it had to be so at Naples. Meanwhile, Naples grew and came nearer. The musicians, with their shining brass instruments, had already formed a group on the deck, and all of a sudden deafened everybody with the triumphant sounds of a ragtime march. The giant captain, in his full uniform appeared on the bridge and like a gracious Pagan idol, waved his hands to the passengers,—and it seemed to the Gentleman from San Francisco,—as it did to all the rest,—that for him alone thundered the march, so greatly loved by proud America, and that him alone did the captain congratulate on the safe arrival. And when the "Atlantis" had finally entered the port and all its many-decked mass leaned against the quay, and the gangplank began to rattle heavily,—what a crowd of porters, with their assistants, in caps with golden galloons, what a crowd of various boys and husky ragamuffins with pads of colored postal cards attacked the Gentleman from San Francisco, offering their services! With kindly contempt he grinned at these beggars, and, walking towards the automobile of the hotel where the prince might stop, muttered between his teeth, now in English, now in Italian—"Go away! Via . . ."

Immediately, life at Naples began to follow a set routine. Early in the morning breakfast was served in the gloomy dining-room, swept by a wet draught from the open windows looking upon a stony garden, while outside the sky was cloudy and cheerless, and a crowd of guides swarmed at the door of the vestibule. Then came the first smiles of the warm roseate sun, and from the high suspended balcony, a broad vista unfolded itself: Vesuvius, wrapped to its base in radiant morning vapors; the pearly ripple, touched to silver, of the bay, the delicate outline of Capri in the skyline; tiny asses dragging two-wheeled buggies along the soft, sticky embankment, and detachments of little soldiers marching somewhere to the tune of cheerful and defiant music.

Next on the day's program was a slow automobile ride along crowded, narrow, and damp corridors of streets, between high, many-windowed buildings. It was followed by visits to museums, lifelessly clean and lighted evenly and pleasantly, but as though with the dull light cast by snow;— then to churches, cold, smelling of wax, always alike; a majestic entrance, closed by a ponderous, leather curtain, and inside—a vast void, silence, quiet flames of seven-branched candlesticks, sending forth a red glow from where they stood at the farther end, on the bedecked altar,—a lonely, old woman lost among the dark wooden benches, slippery gravestones under the feet, and somebody's "Descent from the Cross," infallibly famous. At one o'clock—luncheon, on the mountain of San-Martius, where at noon the choicest people gathered, and where the daughter of the Gentleman from San Francisco once almost fainted with joy, because it seemed to her that she saw the Prince in the hall, although she had learned from the newspapers that he had temporarily left for Rome. At five o'clock it was customary to take tea at the hotel, in a smart *salon*, where it was far too warm because of the carpets and the blazing fireplaces; and then came dinnertime—and again did the mighty, commanding voice of the gong resound throughout the building, again did silk rustle and the mirrors reflect files of ladies in low-necked dresses ascending the staircases, and again the splendid palatial dining hall opened with broad hospitality, and again the musicians' jackets formed red patches on the estrade, and the black figures of the waiters swarmed around the maître-d'hôtel, who, with extraordinary skill, poured a thick pink soup into plates. . . . As everywhere, the dinner was the crown of the day. People dressed for it as for a wedding, and so abundant was it in food, wines, mineral waters, sweets and fruits, that about eleven o'clock in the evening chamber-maids would carry to all the rooms hot-water bags.

That year, however, December did not happen to be a very propitious one. The doormen were abashed when people spoke to them about the weather, and shrugged their shoulders guiltily, mumbling that they could not recollect such a year, although, to tell the truth, that it was not the first year they mumbled those words, usually adding that "things are terrible everywhere"; that unprecedented showers and storms had broken out on the Riviera, that it was snowing in Athens, that Aetna, too, was all blocked up with snow, and glowed brightly at night, and that tourists were fleeing from Palermo to save themselves from the cold spell. . . .

That winter, the morning sun daily deceived Naples; to-ward noon the sky would invariably grow gray, and a light rain would begin to fall, growing thicker and duller. Then the palms at the hotel-porch glistened disagreeably like wet tin, the town appeared exceptionally dirty and congested, the museums too monotonous, the cigars of the drivers in their rubber raincoats, which flattened in the wind like wings, in-tolerably stinking, and the energetic flapping of their whips over their thin-necked nags—obviously false. The shoes of the signors, who cleaned the street-car tracks, were in a frightful state, the women who splashed in the mud, with black hair unprotected from the rain, were ugly and short legged, and the humidity mingled with the foul smell of rot-ting fish, that came from the foaming sea, was simply dis-heartening. And so, early-morning quarrels began to break out between the Gentleman from San Francisco and his wife; and their daughter now grew pale and suffered from head-aches, and now became animated, enthusiastic over every-thing, and at such times was lovely and beautiful. Beautiful were the tender, complex feelings which her meeting with the ungainly man aroused in her,—the man in whose veins flowed unusual blood, for, after all, it does not matter what in par-ticular stirs up a maiden's soul: money, or fame, or nobility of birth. . . . Everybody assured the tourists that it was quite different at Sorrento and on Capri, that lemon-trees were blossoming there, that it was warmer and sunnier there, the morals purer, and the wine less adulterated. And the family from San Francisco decided to set out with all their luggage for Capri. They planned to settle down at Sorrento, but first to visit the island, tread the stones where stood Tiberius's palaces, examine the fabulous wonders of the Blue Grotto, and listen to the bagpipers of Abruzzi, who roam about the island during the whole month preceding Christmas and sing the praises of the Madonna.

On the day of departure—a very memorable day for the family from San Francisco—the sun did not appear even in the morning. A heavy winter fog covered Vesuvius down to its very base and hung like a gray curtain low over the leaden surge of the sea, hiding it completely at a distance of half a mile. Capri was completely out of sight, as though it had never existed on this earth. And the little steamboat which was making for the island tossed and pitched so fiercely that the family lay prostrated on the sofas in the miserable cabin of the little steamer, with their feet wrapped in plaids and their eyes shut because of their nausea. The older lady suffered, as she thought, most; several times she was overcome with sea-sickness, and it seemed to her that she was dying, but the chambermaid, who repeatedly brought her the basin, and who for many years, in heat and in cold, had been tossing on these waves, ever on the alert, ever kindly to all,—the chambermaid only laughed. The lady's daughter was frightfully pale and kept a slice of lemon between her teeth. Not even the hope of an unexpected meeting with the prince of Sorrento, where he planned to arrive on Christmas, served to cheer her. The Gentleman from San Francisco, who was lying on his back, dressed in a large overcoat and a big cap, did not loosen his jaws throughout the voyage. His face grew dark, his moustache white, and his head ached heavily; for the last few days, because of the bad weather, he had drunk far too much in the evenings.

And the rain kept on beating against the rattling window panes, and water dripped down from them on the sofas; the howling wind attacked the masts, and sometimes, aided by a heavy sea, it laid the little steamer on its side, and then something below rolled about with a rattle.

While the steamer was anchored at Castellammare and Sorrento, the situation was more cheerful; but even here the ship rolled terribly, and the coast with all its precipices, gardens and pines, with its pink and white hotels and hazy mountains clad in curling verdure, flew up and down as if it were on swings. The rowboats hit against the sides of the steamer, the sailors and the deck passengers shouted at the top of their voices, and somewhere a baby screamed as if it were being crushed to pieces. A wet wind blew through the door, and from a wavering barge flying the flag of the Hotel Royal, an urchin kept on unwearyingly shouting "Kgoyal-all Hotel Kgoyal-all . . ." inviting tourists. And the Gentleman from San Francisco felt like the old man that he was,— and it was with weariness and animosity that he thought of all these "Royals," "Splendids," "Excelsiors," and of all those greedy bugs, reeking with garlic, who are called Italians. Once, during a stop, having opened his eyes and half-risen from the sofa, he noticed in the shadow of the rock beach a heap of stone huts, miserable, mildewed through and through, huddled close by the water, near boats, rags, tin-boxes, and brown fishing nets,—and as he remembered that this was the very Italy he had come to enjoy, he felt a great despair. . . . Finally, in twilight, the black mass of the island began to grow nearer, as though burrowed through at the base by red fires, the wind grew softer, warmer, more fragrant; from the dock-lanterns huge golden serpents flowed down the tame waves which undulated like black oil. . . . Then, suddenly, the anchor rumbled and fell with a splash into the water, the fierce yells of the boatman filled the air,— and at once everyone's heart grew easy. The electric lights in the cabin grew more brilliant, and there came a desire to eat, drink, smoke, move. . . . Ten minutes later the family from San Francisco found themselves in a large ferry-boat; fifteen minutes later they trod the stones of the quay, and then seated themselves in a small lighted car, which, with a buzz, started to ascend the slope, while vineyard stakes, half-ruined stone fences, and wet, crooked lemon-trees, in spots shielded by straw sheds, with their glimmering orange-colored fruit and thick glossy foliage, were sliding down past the open car windows. . . . After rain, the earth smells sweetly in Italy, and each of her islands has a fragrance of its own. The Island of Capri was dark and damp on that evening.

But for a while it grew animated and lit up, in spots, as
always in the hour of the steamer's arrival. On the top of the
hill, at the station of the *funioulairo*, there stood already the
crowd of those whose duty it was to receive properly the
Gentleman from San Francisco. The rest of the tourists
hardly deserved any attention. There were a few Russians,
who had settled on Capri, untidy, absent-minded people, absorbed in their bookish thoughts, spectacled, bearded, with
the collars of their cloth overcoats raised. There was also a
company of long-legged, long-necked, round-headed German
youths in Tyrolean costume, and with linen bags on their
backs, who need no one's services, are everywhere at home,
and are by no means liberal in their expenses. The Gentleman from San Francisco, who kept quietly aloof from both
the Russians and the Germans, was noticed at once. He and
his ladies were hurriedly helped from the car, a man ran before them to show them the way, and they were again surrounded by boys and those thickset Caprean peasant women,
who carry on their heads the trunks and valises of wealthy
travelers. Their tiny, wooden foot-stools rapped against the
pavement of the small square, which looked almost like an
opera square, and over which an electric lantern swung in the
damp wind; the gang of urchins whistled like birds and
turned somersaults, and as the Gentleman from San Francisco passed among them, it all looked like a stage scene; he
went first under some kind of mediaeval archway, beneath
houses huddled close together, and then along a steep echo-
ing lane which led to the hotel entrance, flooded with light.
At the left, a palm tree raised its tuft above the flat roofs,
and higher up, blue stars burned in the black sky. And again
things looked as though it was in honor of the guests from
San Francisco that the stony damp little town had awakened
on its rocky island in the Mediterranean, that it was they
who had made the owner of the hotel so happy and beaming, and that the Chinese gong, which had sounded the call
to dinner through all the floors as soon as they entered the
lobby, had been waiting only for them.

The owner, an elegant young man, who met the guests
with a polite and exquisite bow, for a moment startled the
Gentleman from San Francisco. Having caught sight of him,

the Gentleman from San Francisco suddenly recollected that on the previous night, among other confused images which disturbed his sleep, he had seen this very man. His vision resembled the hotel keeper to a dot, had the same head, the same hair, shining and scrupulously combed, and wore the same frock-coat with rounded skirts. Amazed, he almost stopped for a while. But as there was not a mustard-seed of what is called mysticism in his heart, his surprise subsided at once; in passing the corridor of the hotel he jestingly told his wife and daughter about this strange coincidence of dream and reality. His daughter alone glanced at him with alarm, longing suddenly compressed her heart, and such a strong feeling of solitude on this strange, dark island seized her that she almost began to cry. But, as usual, she said nothing about her feeling to her father.

A person of high dignity, REX XVII, who had spent three entire weeks on Capri, had just left the island, and the guests from San Francisco were given the apartments he had occupied. At their disposal was put the most handsome and skillful chambermaid, a Belgian, with a figure rendered slim and firm by her corset, and with a starched cap, shaped like a small, indented crown; and they had the privilege of being served by the most well-appearing and portly footman, a black, fiery-eyed Sicilian, and by the quickest waiter, the small, stout Luigi, who was a fiend at cracking jokes and had changed many places in his life. Then the maître-d'hôtel, a Frenchman, gently rapped at the door of the American gentleman's room. He came to ask whether the gentleman and the ladies would dine, and in case they would, which he did not doubt, to report that there was to be had that day lobsters, roast beef, asparagus, pheasants, etc., etc.

The floor was still rocking under the Gentleman from San Francisco—so sea-sick had the wretched Italian steamer made him—yet, he slowly, though awkwardly, shut the window which had banged when the maître-d'hôtel entered, and which let in the smell of the distant kitchen and wet flowers in the garden, and answered with slow distinctiveness, that they would dine, that their table must be placed farther away from the door, in the depth of the hall, that

they would have local wine and champagne, moderately dry
and but slightly cooled. The maître-d'hôtel approved the
words of the guest in various intonations, which all meant,
however, only one thing; there is and can be no doubt that
the desires of the Gentleman from San Francisco are right,
and that everything would be carried out, in exact con-
formity with his words. At last he inclined his head and
asked delicately: "Is that all, sir?"

And having received in reply a slow "Yes," he added that
to-day they were going to have the tarantella danced in the
vestibule by Carmela and Giuseppe, known to all Italy and
to "the entire world of tourists."

"I saw her on post-card pictures," said the Gentleman
from San Francisco in a tone of voice which expressed nothing. "And this Giuseppe, is he her husband?"

"Her cousin, sir," answered the maître-d'hôtel.

The Gentleman from San Francisco tarried a little, evidently musing on something, but said nothing, then dismissed
him with a nod of his head.

Then he started making preparations, as though for a
wedding: he turned on all the electric lamps, and filled the
mirrors with reflections of light and the sheen of furniture,
and opened trunks; he began to shave and to wash himself,
and the sound of his bell was heard every minute in the corridor, crossing with other impatient calls which came from
the rooms of his wife and daughter. Luigi, in his red apron,
with the ease characteristic of stout people, made funny
faces at the chambermaids, who were dashing by with the
buckets in their hands, making them laugh until the tears
came. He rolled head over heels to the door, and, tapping
with his knuckles, asked with feigned timidity and with an
obsequiousness which he knew how to render idiotic:

"Ha sonata, Signore?" (Did you ring, sir?)

And from behind the door a slow, grating, insultingly polite voice answered: "Yes, come in."

What did the Gentleman from San Francisco think and
feel on that evening forever memorable to him? It must be
said frankly; absolutely nothing exceptional. The trouble is
that everything on this earth appears too simple. Even had
he felt anything deep in his heart, a premonition that some-

thing was going to happen, he would have imagined that
it was not going to happen so soon, at least not at once.
Besides, as is usually the case just after sea-sickness is over,
he was very hungry, and he anticipated with real delight
the first spoonful of soup, and the first gulp of wine; therefore, he was performing the habitual process of dressing, in
a state of excitement which left no time for reflection.

Having shaved and washed himself, and dexterously put
in place a few false teeth, he then, standing before the
mirror, moistened and vigorously plastered what was left
of his thick pearly-colored hair, close to his tawny-yellow
skull. Then he put on, with some effort, a tight-fitting under-
shirt of cream-colored silk, fitted tight to his strong, aged
body with its waist swelling out because of an abundant
diet; and he pulled black silk socks and patent-leather dancing shoes on his dry feet with their fallen arches. Squatting
down, he set right his black trousers, drawn high by means
of silk suspenders, adjusted his snow-white shirt with its
bulging front, put the buttons into the shining cuffs, and
began the painful process of hunting up the front button
under the hard collar. The floor was still swaying under
him, the tips of his fingers hurt terribly, the button at times
painfully pinched the flabby skin in the depression under
his Adam's apple, but he persevered, and finally, with his
eyes shining from the effort, his face blue because of the
narrow collar which squeezed his neck, he triumphed over
the difficulties—and all exhausted, he sat down before the
pier-glass, his reflected image repeating itself in all the
mirrors.

"It's terrible!" he muttered, lowering his strong, bald
head and making no effort to understand what was terrible;
then, with a careful and habitual gesture, he examined his
short fingers with gouty callosities in the joints, and their
large, convex, almond-colored nails, and repeated with conviction, "It's terrible!"

But here the stentorian voice of the second gong sounded
throughout the house, as in a heathen temple. And having
risen hurriedly, the Gentleman from San Francisco drew
his tie more taut and firm around his collar, and pulled together his abdomen by means of a tight waistcoat, put on

a dinner-coat, set to rights the cuffs, and for the last time he examined himself in the mirror. . . . This Carmella, tawny as a mulatto, with fiery eyes, in a dazzling dress in which orange-color predominated, must be an extraordinary dancer, —it occurred to him. And cheerfully leaving his room, he walked on the carpet, to his wife's chamber, and asked in a loud tone of voice if they would be long.

"In five minutes, papa!" answered cheerfully and gaily a girlish voice. "I am combing my hair."

"Very well," said the Gentleman from San Francisco.

And thinking of her wonderful hair, streaming on her shoulders, he slowly walked down along corridors and stair-cases, spread with red velvet carpets,—looking for the li-brary. The servants he met hugged the walls, and he walked by as if not noticing them. An old lady, late for dinner, already bowed with years, with milk-white hair, yet bare-necked, in a light-gray silk dress, hurried at top speed, but she walked in a mincing, funny, hen-like manner, and he easily overtook her. At the glass door of the dining hall where the guests had already gathered and started eating, he stopped before the table crowded with boxes of matches and Egyptian cigarettes, took a great Manila cigar, and threw three liras on the table. On the winter veranda he glanced into the open window; a stream of soft air came to him from the darkness, the top of the old palm loomed up before him afar-off, with its boughs spread among the stars and looking gigantic, and the distant even noise of the sea reached his ear. In the library-room, snug, quiet, a German in round silver-bowed glasses and with crazy, won-dering eyes—stood turning the rustling pages of a news-paper. Having coldly eyed him, the Gentleman from San Francisco seated himself in a deep leather arm-chair near a lamp under a green hood, put on his pince-nez and twitching his head because of the collar which choked him, hid him-self from view behind a newspaper. He glanced at a few headlines, read a few lines about the interminable Balkan war, and turned over the page with an habitual gesture. Suddenly, the lines blazed up with a glassy sheen, the veins of his neck swelled, his eyes bulged out, the pince-nez fell from his nose. . . . He dashed forward, wanted to swallow air—and made a wild, rattling noise; his lower jaw dropped, dropped on his shoulder and began to shake, the shirt-front bulged out,—and the whole body, writhing, the heels catching in the carpet, slowly fell to the floor in a desperate struggle with an invisible foe. . . .

Had not the German been in the library, this frightful accident would have been quickly and adroitly hushed up. The body of the Gentleman from San Francisco would have been rushed away to some far corner—and none of the guests would have known of the occurrence. But the German dashed out of the library with outcries and spread the alarm all over the house. And many rose from their meal, upsetting chairs, others growing pale, ran along the corridors to the library, and the question, asked in many languages, was heard: "What is it? What has happened?" And no one was able to answer it clearly, no one understood anything, for until this very day men still wonder most at death and most absolutely refuse to believe in it. The owner rushed from one guest to another, trying to keep back those who were running and soothe them with hasty assurances, that this was nothing, a mere trifle, a little fainting-spell by which a Gentleman from San Francisco, had been overcome. But no one listened to him, many saw how the footman and waiters tore from the gentleman his tie, collar, waistcoat, the rumpled evening coat, and even—for no visible reason—the dancing shoes from his black-silk-covered feet. And he kept on writhing. He obstinately struggled with death, he did not want to yield to the foe that attacked him so unexpectedly and grossly. He shook his head, emitted rattling sounds like one throttled, and turned up his eyeballs like one drunk with wine. When he was hastily brought into Number Forty-three,—the smallest, worst, dampest, and coldest room at the end of the lower corridor,—and stretched on the bed,—his daughter came running, her hair falling over her shoulders, the skirts of her dressing-gown thrown open, with bare breasts raised by the corset. Then came his wife, big, heavy, almost completely dressed for dinner, her mouth round with terror.

In a quarter of an hour all was again in good trim at the hotel. But the evening was irreparably spoiled. Some tourists returned to the dining-hall and finished their dinner, but they kept silent, and it was obvious that they took the accident as a personal insult, while the owner went from one guest to another, shrugging his shoulders in impotent and appropriate irritation, feeling like one innocently victimized, assuring everyone that he understood perfectly well "how disagreeable this is," and giving his word that he would take all "the measures that are within my power" to do away with the trouble. Yet it was found necessary to cancel the tarantella. The unnecessary electric lamps were put out, most of the guests left for the beer-hall, and it grew so quiet in the hotel that one could distinctly hear the tick-tock of the clock in the lobby, where a lonely parrot babbled something in its expressionless manner, stirring in its cage, and trying to fall asleep with its paw clutching the upper perch in a most absurd manner. The Gentleman from San Francisco lay stretched in a cheap iron bed, under coarse woolen blankets, dimly lighted by a single gas-burner fastened in the ceiling. An ice-bag slid down on his wet, cold forehead. His blue, already lifeless face grew gradually cold; the hoarse, rattling noise which came from his mouth, lighted by the glimmer of the golden fillings, gradually weakened. It was not the Gentleman from San Francisco that was emitting those weird sounds; he was no more,—someone else did it. His wife and daughter, the doctor, the servants were standing and watching him apathetically. Suddenly, that which they expected and feared happened. The rattling sound ceased. And slowly, slowly, in everybody's sight a pallor stole over the face of the dead man, and his features began to grow thinner and more luminous, beautiful with the beauty that he had long shunned and that became him well. . . .

The proprietor entered. "Gia e morto," whispered the doctor to him. The proprietor shrugged his shoulders indifferently. The older lady, with tears slowly running down her cheeks, approached him and said timidly that now the deceased must be taken to his room.

"O no, madam," answered the proprietor politely, but without any amiability and not in English, but in French. He was no longer interested in the trifle which the guests from San Francisco could now leave at his cash-office. "This is absolutely impossible," he said, and added in the form of an explanation that he valued this apartment highly, and if he satisfied her desire, this would become known all over Capri and the tourists would begin to avoid it.

The girl, who had looked at him strangely, sat down, and with her handkerchief to her mouth, began to cry. Her mother's tears dried up at once, and her face flared up. She raised her tone, began to demand, using her own language and still unable to realize that the respect for her was absolutely gone. The proprietor, with polite dignity, cut her short: "If madam does not like the ways of this hotel, he dare not detain her." And he firmly announced that the corpse must leave the hotel that very day, at dawn, that the police had been informed, that an agent would call immediately and attend to all the necessary formalities. . . . "It is possible to get on Capri at least a plain coffin?" madam asks. . . . Unfortunately not; by no means, and as for making one, there will be no time. It will be necessary to arrange things some other way. . . . For instance, he gets English soda-water in big, oblong boxes. . . . The partitions could be taken out from such a box. . . .

By night, the whole hotel was asleep. A waiter opened the window in Number Forty-three—it faced a corner of the garden where a consumptive banana-tree grew in the shadow of a high stone wall set with broken glass on the top—turned out the electric light, locked the door, and went away. The deceased remained alone in the darkness. Blue stars looked down at him from the black sky, the cricket in the wall started his melancholy, care-free song. In the dimly lighted corridor two chambermaids were sitting on the window-sill, mending something. Then Luigi came in, in slippered feet, with a heap of clothes on his arm.

"*Pronto!*"—he asked in a stage whisper, as if greatly concerned, directing his eyes toward the terrible door, at the end of the corridor. And waving his free hand in that direction, "*Partenza!*" he cried out in a whisper, as if seeing off a train,—and the chambermaids, choking with noiseless laughter, put their heads on each other's shoulders.

Then, stepping softly, he ran to the door, slightly rapped

at it, and inclining his ear, asked most obsequiously in a subdued tone of voice: "Ha sonata, Signore?"

And, squeezing his throat and thrusting his lower jaw forward, he answered himself in a drawling, grating, sad voice, as if from behind the door: "Yes, come in. . . ."

At dawn, when the window panes in Number Forty-three grew white, and a damp wind rustled in the leaves of the banana-tree, when the pale-blue morning sky rose and stretched over Capri, and the sun, rising from behind the distant mountains of Italy, touched into gold the pure, clearly outlined summit of Monte Solaro, when the masons, who mended the paths for the tourists on the island, went out to their work,—an oblong box was brought to room Number Forty-three. Soon it grew very heavy and painfully pressed against the knees of the assistant doorman who was conveying it in a one-horse carriage along the white high-road which wound on the slopes, among stone fences and vineyards, all the way down to the seacoast. The driver, a sickly man, with red eyes, in an old short-sleeved coat and in worn-out shoes, had a drunken headache; all night long he had played dice at the eatinghouse—and he kept on flogging his vigorous little horse. According to Sicilian custom, the animal was heavily burdened with decorations: all sorts of bells tinkled on the bridle, which was ornamented with colored woolen fringes; there were bells also on the edge of the high saddle; and a bird's feather, two feet long, stuck in the trimmed crest of the horse, nodded up and down. The driver kept silence: he was depressed by his wrongheadedness and vices, by the fact that last night he had lost in gambling all the copper coins with which his pockets had been full,—neither more nor less than four liras and forty centesimi. But on such a morning, when the air is so fresh, and the sea stretches nearby, and the sky is serene with a morning serenity,—a headache passes rapidly and one becomes carefree again. Besides, the driver was also somewhat cheered by the unexpected earnings which the Gentleman from San Francisco, who bumped his dead head against the walls of the box behind his back, had brought him. The little steamer, shaped like a great bug, which lay far down, on the tender and brilliant blue filling to the brim

the Neapolitan bay, was blowing the signal of departure,—
and the sounds swiftly resounded all over Capri. Every bend
of the island, every ridge and stone was seen as distinctly as
if there were no air between heaven and earth. Near the
quay the driver was overtaken by the head doorman who
conducted in an auto the wife and daughter of the Gentleman from San Francisco. Their faces were pale and their
eyes sunken with tears and a sleepless night. And in ten
minutes the little steamer was again stirring up the water
and picking its way toward Sorrento and Castellammare, carrying the American family away from Capri forever. . . .
Meanwhile, peace and rest were restored on the island.

Two thousand years ago there had lived on that island a
man who became utterly entangled in his own brutal and
filthy actions. For some unknown reason he usurped the
rule over millions of men and found himself bewildered by
the absurdity of this power, while the fear that someone
might kill him unawares, made him commit deeds inhuman
beyond all measure. And mankind has forever retained his
memory, and those who, taken together, now rule the world,
as incomprehensibly and, essentially, as cruelly as he did,—
come from all the corners of the earth to look at the rem-
nants of the stone house he inhabited, which stands on one
of the steepest cliffs of the island. On that wonderful morning the tourists, who had come to Capri for precisely that
purpose, were still asleep in the various hotels, but tiny
long-eared asses under red saddles were already being led
to the hotel entrances. Americans and Germans, men and
women, old and young, after having arisen and breakfasted
heartily, were to scramble on them, and the old beggar-
women of Capri, with sticks in their sinewy hands, were
again to run after them along stony, mountainous paths,
all the way up to the summit of Monte Tiberia. The dead
old man from San Francisco, who had planned to keep the
tourists company but who had, instead, only scared them by
reminding them of death, was already shipped to Naples,
and soothed by this, the travelers slept soundly, and silence
reigned over the island. The stores in the little town were
still closed, with the exception of the fish and greens market
on the tiny square. Among the plain people who filled it,

going about their business, stood idly by, as usual, Lorenzo,
a tall old boatman, a carefree reveller and once a handsome
man, famous all over Italy, who had many times served as
a model for painters. He had brought and already sold—
for a song—two big sea-crawfish, which he had caught at
night and which were rustling in the apron of Don Cataldo,
the cook of the hotel where the family from San Francisco
had been lodged,—and now Lorenzo could stand calmly
until nightfall, wearing princely airs, showing off his rags,
his clay pipe with its long reed mouth-piece, and his red
woolen cap, tilted on one ear. Meanwhile, among the precipices of Monte Solare, down the ancient Phoenician road,
cut in the rocks in the form of a gigantic staircase, two
Abruzzi mountaineers were coming from Anacapri. One
carried under his leather mantle a bagpipe, a large goat's
skin with two pipes; the other, something in the nature of
a wooden flute. They walked, and the entire country, joyous, beautiful, sunny, stretched below them; the rocky shoulders of the island, which lay at their feet, the fabulous blue
in which it swam, the shining morning vapors over the
sea westward, beneath the dazzling sun, and the wavering
masses of Italy's mountains, both near and distant, whose
beauty human word is powerless to render. . . . Midway
they slowed up. Overshadowing the road stood, in a grotto
of the rock wall of Monte Solare, the Holy Virgin, all
radiant, bathed in the warmth and the splendor of the sun.
The rust of her snow-white plaster-of-Paris vestures and
queenly crown was touched into gold, and there were meekness and mercy in her eyes raised toward the heavens, toward the eternal and beatific abode of her thrice-blessed
Son. They bared their heads, applied the pipes to their lips,
and praises flowed on, candid and humbly-joyous, praises
to the sun and the morning, to Her, the Immaculate Inter-
cessor for all who suffer in this evil and beautiful world,
and to Him who had been born of her womb in the cavern
of Bethlehem, in a hut of lowly shepherds in distant Judea.
    As for the body of the dead Gentleman from San Fran-
cisco, it was on its way home, to the shores of the New
World, where a grave awaited it. Having undergone many
humiliations and suffered much human neglect, having wan-

dered about a week from one port warehouse to another, it finally got on that same famous ship which had brought the family, such a short while ago and with such a pomp, to the Old World. But now he was concealed from the living: in a tar-coated coffin he was lowered deep into the black hold of the steamer. And again did the ship set out on its far sea journey. At night it sailed by the island of Capri, and, for those who watched it from the island, its lights slowly disappearing in the dark sea, it seemed infinitely sad. But there, on the vast steamer, in its lighted halls shining with brilliance and marble, a noisy dancing party was going on, as usual.

On the second and the third night there was again a ball —this time in mid-ocean, during the furious storm sweeping over the ocean, which roared like a funeral mass and rolled up mountainous seas fringed with mourning silvery foam. The Devil, who from the rocks of Gibraltar, the stony gateway of two worlds, watched the ship vanish into night and storm, could hardly distinguish from behind the snow the innumerable fiery eyes of the ship. The Devil was as huge as a cliff, but the ship was even bigger, a many-storied, many-stacked giant, created by the arrogance of the New Man with the old heart. The blizzard battered the ship's rigging and its broadnecked stacks, whitened with snow, but it remained firm, majestic—and terrible. On its uppermost deck, amidst a snowy whirlwind there loomed up in loneliness the cozy, dimly lighted cabin, where, only half awake, the vessel's ponderous pilot reigned over its entire mass, bearing the semblance of a pagan idol. He heard the wailing moans and the furious screeching of the siren, choked by the storm, but the nearness of that which was behind the wall and which in the last account was incomprehensible to him, removed his fears. He was reassured by the thought of the large, armored cabin, which now and then was filled with mysterious rumbling sounds and with the dry creaking of blue fires, flaring up and exploding around a man with a metallic headpiece, who was eagerly catching the indistinct voices of the vessels that hailed him, hundreds of miles away. At the very bottom, in the under-water womb of the "Atlantis," the huge masses of tanks and various other machines, their steel parts shining dully, wheezed with steam and oozed hot water and oil; here was the gigantic kitchen, heated by hellish furnaces, where the motion of the vessel was being generated; here seethed those forces terrible in their concentration which were transmitted to the keel of the vessel, and into that endless round tunnel, which was lighted by electricity, and looked like a gigantic cannon barrel, where slowly, with a punctuality and certainty that crushes the human soul, a colossal shaft was revolving in its oily nest, like a living monster stretching in its lair. As for the middle part of the "Atlantis," its warm, luxurious cabins, dining-rooms, and halls, they radiated light and joy, were astir with a chattering smartly-dressed crowd, were filled with the fragrance of fresh flowers, and resounded with a string orchestra. And again did the slender supple pair of hired lovers painfully turn and twist and at times clash convulsively amid the splendor of lights, silks, diamonds, and bare feminine shoulders: she—a sinfully modest pretty girl, with lowered eyelashes and an innocent hair-dressing, he— a tall young man, with black hair, looking as if it were pasted, pale with powder, in most exquisite patent-leather shoes, in a narrow, long-skirted dresscoat,—a beautiful man resembling a leech. And no one knew that this couple had long since been weary of torturing themselves with a feigned beatific torture under the sounds of shamefully-melancholy music; nor did any one know what lay deep, deep, beneath them, on the very bottom of the hold, in the neighborhood of the gloomy and sultry maw of the ship, that heavily struggled with the ocean, the darkness, and the storm. . . .

Saki *(H. H. Munro 1870–1916)*

TOBERMORY

It was a chill, rain-washed afternoon of a late August day,
that indefinite season when partridges are still in security or
cold storage, and there is nothing to hunt—unless one is
bounded on the north by the Bristol Channel, in which case
one may lawfully gallop after fat red stags. Lady Blemley's
house-party was not bounded on the north by the Bristol
Channel, hence there was a full gathering of her guests
round the tea-table on this particular afternoon. And, in
spite of the blankness of the season and the triteness of the
occasion, there was no trace in the company of that fatigued
restlessness which means a dread of the pianola and a subdued hankering for auction bridge. The undisguised open-
mouthed attention of the entire party was fixed on the
homely negative personality of Mr. Cornelius Appin. Of all
her guests, he was the one who had come to Lady Blemley
with the vaguest reputation. Some one had said he was
"clever," and he had got his invitation in the moderate expectation, on the part of his hostess, that some portion at
least of his cleverness would be contributed to the general
entertainment. Until tea-time that day she had been unable
to discover in what direction, if any, his cleverness lay. He
was neither a wit nor a croquet champion, a hypnotic force
nor a begetter of amateur theatricals. Neither did his exterior suggest the sort of man in whom women are willing to
pardon a generous measure of mental deficiency. He had
subsided into mere Mr. Appin, and the Cornelius seemed a
piece of transparent baptismal bluff. And now he was claiming to have launched on the world a discovery beside which
the invention of gunpowder, of the printing-press, and of
steam locomotion were inconsiderable trifles. Science had
made bewildering strides in many directions during recent

decades, but this thing seemed to belong to the domain of miracle rather than to scientific achievement.

"And do you really ask us to believe," Sir Wilfrid was saying, "that you have discovered a means for instructing animals in the art of human speech, and that dear old Tobermory has proved your first successful pupil?"

"It is a problem at which I have worked for the last seventeen years," said Mr. Appin, "but only during the last eight or nine months have I been rewarded with glimmerings of success. Of course I have experimented with thousands of animals, but latterly only with cats, those wonderful creatures which have assimilated themselves so marvellously with our civilization while retaining all their highly developed feral instincts. Here and there among cats one comes across an outstanding superior intellect, just as one does among the ruck of human beings, and when I made the acquaintance of Tobermory a week ago I saw at once that I was in contact with a 'Beyond-cat' of extraordinary intelligence. I had gone far along the road to success in recent experiments; with Tobermory, as you call him, I have reached the goal."

Mr. Appin concluded his remarkable statement in a voice which he strove to divest of a triumphant inflection. No one said "Rats," though Clovis's lips moved in a monosyllabic contortion which probably invoked those rodents of disbelief.

"And do you mean to say," asked Miss Resker, after a slight pause, "that you have taught Tobermory to say and understand easy sentences of one syllable?"

"My dear Miss Resker," said the wonder-worker patiently, "one teaches little children and savages and backward adults in that piecemeal fashion; when one has once solved the problem of making a beginning with an animal of highly developed intelligence one has no need for those halting methods. Tobermory can speak our language with perfect correctness."

This time Clovis very distinctly said, "Beyond-rats!" Sir Wilfrid was more polite, but equally sceptical.

"Hadn't we better have the cat in and judge for ourselves?" suggested Lady Blemley.

Sir Wilfrid went in search of the animal, and the company settled themselves down to the languid expectation of witnessing some more or less adroit drawing-room ventriloquism.

In a minute Sir Wilfrid was back in the room, his face white beneath its tan and his eyes dilated with excitement.

"By Gad, it's true!"

His agitation was unmistakably genuine, and his hearers started forward in a thrill of awakened interest.

Collapsing into an armchair he continued breathlessly: "I found him dozing in the smoking-room, and called out to him to come for his tea. He blinked at me in his usual way, and I said, 'Come on, Toby; don't keep us waiting'; and, by Gad! he drawled out in a most horribly natural voice that he'd come when he dashed well pleased! I nearly jumped out of my skin!"

Appin had preached to absolutely incredulous hearers; Sir Wilfrid's statement carried instant conviction. A Babel-like chorus of startled exclamation arose, amid which the scientist sat mutely enjoying the first fruit of his stupendous discovery.

In the midst of the clamour Tobermory entered the room and made his way with velvet tread and studied unconcern across the group seated round the tea-table.

A sudden hush of awkwardness and constraint fell on the company. Somehow there seemed an element of embarrassment in addressing on equal terms a domestic cat of acknowledged mental ability.

"Will you have some milk, Tobermory?" asked Lady Blemley in a rather strained voice.

"I don't mind if I do," was the response, couched in a tone of even indifference. A shiver of suppressed excitement went through the listeners, and Lady Blemley might be excused for pouring out the saucerful of milk rather unsteadily.

"I'm afraid I've spilt a good deal of it," she said apologetically.

"After all, it's not my Axminster," was Tobermory's rejoinder.

Another silence fell on the group, and then Miss Resker,

in her best district-visitor manner, asked if the human language had been difficult to learn. Tobermory looked squarely at her for a moment and then fixed his gaze serenely on the middle distance. It was obvious that boring questions lay outside his scheme of life.

"What do you think of human intelligence?" asked Mavis Pellington lamely.

"Of whose intelligence in particular?" asked Tobermory coldly.

"Oh, well, mine for instance," said Mavis, with a feeble laugh.

"You put me in an embarrassing position," said Tobermory, whose tone and attitude certainly did not suggest a shred of embarrassment. "When your inclusion in this house-party was suggested Sir Wilfrid protested that you were the most brainless woman of his acquaintance, and that there was a wide distinction between hospitality and the care of the feeble-minded. Lady Blemley replied that your lack of brain-power was the precise quality which had earned you your invitation, as you were the only person she could think of who might be idiotic enough to buy their old car. You know, the one they call 'The Envy of Sisyphus,' because it goes quite nicely up-hill if you push it."

Lady Blemley's protestations would have had greater effect if she had not casually suggested to Mavis only that morning that the car in question would be just the thing for her down at her Devonshire home.

Major Barfield plunged in heavily to effect a diversion.

"How about your carryings-on with the tortoise-shell puss up at the stables, eh?"

The moment he had said it every one realized the blunder.

"One does not usually discuss these matters in public," said Tobermory frigidly. "From a slight observation of your ways since you've been in this house I should imagine you'd find it inconvenient if I were to shift the conversation on to your own little affairs."

The panic which ensued was not confined to the Major.

"Would you like to go and see if cook has got your dinner ready?" suggested Lady Blemley hurriedly, affecting to ignore the fact that it wanted at least two hours to Tobermory's dinner-time.

"Thanks," said Tobermory, "not quite so soon after my tea. I don't want to die of indigestion."

"Cats have nine lives, you know," said Sir Wilfrid heartily.

"Possibly," answered Tobermory; "but only one liver."

"Adelaide!" said Mrs. Cornett, "do you mean to encourage that cat to go out and gossip about us in the servants' hall?"

The panic had indeed become general. A narrow ornamental balustrade ran in front of most of the bedroom windows at the Towers, and it was recalled with dismay that this had formed a favourite promenade for Tobermory at all hours, whence he could watch the pigeons—and heaven knew what else besides. If he intended to become reminiscent in his present out-spoken strain the effect would be something more than disconcerting. Mrs. Cornett, who spent much time at her toilet table, and whose complexion was reputed to be of a nomadic though punctual disposition, looked as ill at ease as the Major. Miss Scrawen, who wrote fiercely sensuous poetry and led a blameless life, merely displayed irritation; if you are methodical and virtuous in private you don't necessarily want every one to know it. Bertie van Tahn, who was so depraved at seventeen that he had long ago given up trying to be any worse, turned a dull shade of gardenia white, but he did not commit the error of dashing out of the room like Odo Finsberry, a young gentleman who was understood to be reading for the Church and who was possibly disturbed at the thought of scandals he might hear concerning other people. Clovis had the presence of mind to maintain a composed exterior; privately he was calculating how long it would take to procure a box of fancy mice through the agency of the *Exchange and Mart* as a species of hush-money.

Even in a delicate situation like the present, Agnes Resker could not endure to remain too long in the background.

"Why did I ever come down here?" she asked dramatically.

Tobermory immediately accepted the opening.

"Judging by what you said to Mrs. Cornett on the croquet-lawn yesterday, you were out for food. You described

the Blemleys as the dullest people to stay with that you
knew, but said they were clever enough to employ a first-
rate cook; otherwise they'd find it difficult to get any one to
come down a second time."

"There's not a word of truth in it! I appeal to Mrs. Cornett——" exclaimed the discomfited Agnes.

"Mrs. Cornett repeated your remark afterwards to Bertie
van Tahn," continued Tobermory, "and said, 'That woman
is a regular Hunger Marcher; she'd go anywhere for four
square meals a day,' and Bertie van Tahn said——"

At this point the chronicle mercifully ceased. Tobermory
had caught a glimpse of the big yellow Tom from the Rectory working his way through the shrubbery towards the
stable wing. In a flash he had vanished through the open
French window.

With the disappearance of his too brilliant pupil Cornelius
Appin found himself beset by a hurricane of bitter upbraid-
ing, anxious inquiry, and frightened entreaty. The responsibility for the situation lay with him, and he must prevent
matters from becoming worse. Could Tobermory impart his
dangerous gift to other cats? was the first question he had
to answer. It was possible, he replied, that he might have
initiated his intimate friend the stable puss into his new
accomplishment, but it was unlikely that his teaching could
have taken a wider range as yet.

"Then," said Mrs. Cornett, "Tobermory may be a valuable cat and a great pet; but I'm sure you'll agree, Adelaide,
that both he and the stable cat must be done away with
without delay."

"You don't suppose I've enjoyed the last quarter of an
hour, do you?" said Lady Blemley bitterly. "My husband
and I are very fond of Tobermory—at least, we were before
this horrible accomplishment was infused into him; but now,
of course, the only thing is to have him destroyed as soon as
possible."

"We can put some strychnine in the scraps he always gets
at dinner-time," said Sir Wilfrid, "and I will go and drown
the stable cat myself. The coachman will be very sore at
losing his pet, but I'll say a very catching form of mange

has broken out in both cats and we're afraid of it spreading
to the kennels."

"But my great discovery!" expostulated Mr. Appin; "after
all my years of research and experiment——"

"You can go and experiment on the short-horns at the
farm, who are under proper control," said Mrs. Cornett, "or
the elephants at the Zoological Gardens. They're said to be
highly intelligent, and they have this recommendation, that
they don't come creeping about our bedrooms and under
chairs, and so forth."

An archangel ecstatically proclaiming the Millennium,
and finding that it clashed unpardonably with Henley and
would have to be indefinitely postponed, could hardly have
felt more crestfallen than Cornelius Appin at the reception
of his wonderful achievement. Public opinion, however, was
against him—in fact, had the general voice been consulted
on the subject it is probable that a strong minority vote
would have been in favor of including him in the strychnine
diet.

Defective train arrangements and a nervous desire to see
matters brought to a finish prevented an immediate dispersal
of the party, but dinner that evening was not a social success. Sir Wilfrid had had rather a trying time with the stable
cat and subsequently with the coachman. Agnes Resker
ostentatiously limited her repast to a morsel of dry toast,
which she bit as though it were a personal enemy; while
Mavis Pellington maintained a vindictive silence throughout
the meal. Lady Blemley kept up a flow of what she hoped
was conversation, but her attention was fixed on the doorway. A plateful of carefully dosed fish scraps was in readiness on the sideboard, but sweets and savoury and dessert
went their way, and no Tobermory appeared either in the
dining-room or kitchen.

The sepulchral dinner was cheerful compared with the
subsequent vigil in the smoking-room. Eating and drinking
had at least supplied a distraction and cloak to the prevailing embarrassment. Bridge was out of the question in the
general tension of nerves and tempers, and after Odo Finsberry had given a lugubrious rendering of "Melisande in the
Wood" to a frigid audience, music was tacitly avoided. At

eleven the servants went to bed, announcing that the small window in the pantry had been left open as usual for Tobermory's private use. The guests read steadily through the current batch of magazines, and fell back gradually on the "Badminton Library" and bound volumes of *Punch*. Lady Blemley made periodic visits to the pantry, returning each time with an expression of listless depression which forestalled questioning.

At two o'clock Clovis broke the dominating silence.

"He won't turn up tonight. He's probably in the local newspaper office at the present moment, dictating the first instalment of his reminiscences. Lady What's-her-name's book won't be in it. It will be the event of the day."

Having made this contribution to the general cheerfulness, Clovis went to bed. At long intervals the various members of the house-party followed his example.

The servants taking round the early tea made a uniform announcement in reply to a uniform question. Tobermory had not returned.

Breakfast was, if anything, a more unpleasant function than dinner had been, but before its conclusion the situation was relieved. Tobermory's corpse was brought in from the shrubbery, where a gardener had just discovered it. From the bites on his throat and the yellow fur which coated his claws it was evident that he had fallen in unequal combat with the big Tom from the Rectory.

By midday most of the guests had quitted the Towers, and after lunch Lady Blemley had sufficiently recovered her spirits to write an extremely nasty letter to the Rectory about the loss of her valuable pet.

Tobermory had been Appin's one successful pupil, and he was destined to have no successor. A few weeks later an elephant in the Dresden Zoological Garden, which had shown no previous signs of irritability, broke loose and killed an Englishman who had apparently been teasing it. The victim's name was variously reported in the papers as Oppin and Eppelin, but his front name was faithfully rendered Cornelius.

"If he was trying German irregular verbs on the poor beast," said Clovis, "he deserved all he got."

W. W. Jacobs (1863–1943)

THE MONKEY'S PAW

Without, the night was cold and wet, but in the small parlor of Lakesnam Villa the blinds were drawn and the fire burned brightly. Father and son were at chess, the former, who possessed ideas about the game involving radical changes, putting his king into such sharp and unnecessary perils that it even provoked comment from the white-haired old lady knitting placidly by the fire.

"Hark at the wind," said Mr. White, who, having seen a fatal mistake after it was too late, was amiably desirous of preventing his son from seeing it.

"I'm listening," said the latter, grimly surveying the board as he stretched out his hand. "Check."

"I should hardly think that he'd come tonight," said his father, with his hand poised over the board.

"Mate," replied the son.

"That's the worst of living so far out," bawled Mr. White, with sudden and unlooked-for violence; "of all the beastly, slushy, out-of-the-way places to live in, this is the worst. Pathway's a bog, and the road's a torrent. I don't know what people are thinking about. I suppose because only two houses on the road are let, they think it doesn't matter."

"Never mind, dear," said his wife soothingly; "perhaps you'll win the next one."

Mr. White looked up sharply, just in time to intercept a knowing glance between mother and son. The words died away on his lips, and he hid a guilty grin in his thin gray beard.

"There he is," said Herbert White, as the gate banged to loudly and heavy footsteps came toward the door.

The old man rose with hospitable haste, and opening the

door, was heard condoling with the new arrival. The new arrival also condoled with himself, so that Mrs. White said, "Tut, tut!" and coughed gently as her husband entered the room, followed by a tall burly man, beady of eye and rubicund of visage.

"Sergeant-Major Morris," he said, introducing him.

The sergeant-major shook hands, and taking the proffered seat by the fire, watched contentedly while his host got out whisky and tumblers and stood a small copper kettle on the fire.

At the third glass his eyes got brighter, and he began to talk, the little family circle regarding with eager interest this visitor from distant parts, as he squared his broad shoulders in the chair and spoke of strange scenes and doughty deeds, of wars and plagues and strange peoples.

"Twenty-one years of it," said Mr. White, nodding at his wife and son. "When he went away he was a slip of a youth in the warehouse. Now look at him."

"He don't look to have taken much harm," said Mrs. White politely.

"I'd like to go to India myself," said the old man, "just to look round a bit, you know."

"Better where you are," said the sergeant-major, shaking his head. He put down the empty glass and, sighing softly, shook it again.

"I should like to see those old temples and fakirs and jugglers," said the old man. "What was that you started telling me the other day about a monkey's paw or something, Morris?"

"Nothing," said the soldier hastily. "Leastways, nothing worth hearing."

"Monkey's paw?" said Mrs. White curiously.

"Well, it's just a bit of what you might call magic, perhaps," said the sergeant-major off-handedly.

His three listeners leaned forward eagerly. The visitor absent-mindedly put his empty glass to his lips and then set it down again. His host filled it for him.

"To look at," said the sergeant-major, fumbling in his pocket, "it's just an ordinary little paw, dried to a mummy."

He took something out of his pocket and proffered it. Mrs.

White drew back with a grimace, but her son, taking it, examined it curiously.

"And what is there special about it?" inquired Mr. White, as he took it from his son and, having examined it, placed it upon the table.

"It had a spell put on it by an old fakir," said the sergeant-major, "a very holy man. He wanted to show that fate ruled people's lives, and that those who interfered with it did so to their sorrow. He put a spell on it so that three separate men could each have three wishes from it."

His manner was so impressive that his hearers were conscious that their light laughter jarred somewhat.

"Well, why don't you have three, sir?" said Herbert White cleverly.

The soldier regarded him in the way that middle age is wont to regard presumptuous youth. "I have," he said quietly, and his blotchy face whitened.

"And did you really have the three wishes granted?" asked Mrs. White.

"I did," said the sergeant-major, and his glass tapped against his strong teeth.

"And has anybody else wished?" inquired the old lady.

"The first man had his three wishes, yes," was the reply. "I don't know what the first two were, but the third was for death. That's how I got the paw."

His tones were so grave that a hush fell upon the group. "If you've had your three wishes, it's no good to you now, then, Morris," said the old man at last. "What do you keep it for?"

The soldier shook his head. "Fancy, I suppose," he said slowly. "I did have some idea of selling it, but I don't think I will. It has caused enough mischief already. Besides, people won't buy. They think it's a fairy tale, some of them, and those who do think anything of it want to try it first and pay me afterward."

"If you could have another three wishes," said the old man, eyeing him keenly, "would you have them?"

"I don't know," said the other. "I don't know."

He took the paw, and dangling it between his front finger

and thumb, suddenly threw it upon the fire. White, with a slight cry, stooped down and snatched it off.

"Better let it burn," said the soldier solemnly.

"If you don't want it, Morris," said the old man, "give it to me."

"I won't," said his friend doggedly. "I threw it on the fire. If you keep it, don't blame me for what happens. Pitch it on the fire again, like a sensible man."

The other shook his head and examined his new possession closely. "How do you do it?" he inquired.

"Hold it up in your right hand and wish aloud," said the sergeant-major, "but I warn you of the consequences."

"Sounds like the *Arabian Nights*," said Mrs. White, as she rose and began to set the supper. "Don't you think you might wish for four pairs of hands for me?"

Her husband drew the talisman from his pocket and then all three burst into laughter as the sergeant-major, with a look of alarm on his face, caught him by the arm. "If you must wish," he said gruffly, "wish for something sensible."

Mr. White dropped it back into his pocket, and placing chairs, motioned his friend to the table. In the business of supper the talisman was partly forgotten, and afterward the three sat listening in an enthralled fashion to a second installment of the soldier's adventures in India.

"If the tale about the monkey paw is not more truthful than those he has been telling us," said Herbert, as the door closed behind their guest, just in time for him to catch the last train, "we shan't make much out of it."

"Did you give him anything for it, father?" inquired Mrs. White, regarding her husband closely.

"A trifle," said he, coloring slightly. "He didn't want it, but I made him take it. And he pressed me again to throw it away."

"Likely," said Herbert, with pretended horror. "Why, we're going to be rich, and famous, and happy. Wish to be an emperor, father, to begin with; then you can't be hen-pecked."

He darted round the table, pursued by the maligned Mrs. White armed with an antimacassar.

Mr. White took the paw from his pocket and eyed it dubi-

ously. "I don't know what to wish for, and that's a fact," he
said slowly. "It seems to me I've got all I want."

"If you only cleared the house, you'd be quite happy,
wouldn't you?" said Herbert, with his hand on his shoulder.
"Well, wish for two hundred pounds, then; that'll just do it."

His father, smiling shamefacedly at his own credulity,
held up the talisman, as his son, with a solemn face somewhat marred by a wink at his mother, sat down at the piano
and struck a few impressive chords.

"I wish for two hundred pounds," said the old man distinctly.

A fine crash from the piano greeted the words, interrupted
by a shuddering cry from the old man. His wife and son
ran toward him.

"It moved," he cried, with a glance of disgust at the object as it lay on the floor. "As I wished it twisted in my
hands like a snake."

"Well, I don't see the money," said his son, as he picked
it up and placed it on the table, "and I bet I never shall."

"It must have been your fancy, father," said his wife, regarding him anxiously.

He shook his head. "Never mind, though; there's no harm
done, but it gave me a shock all the same."

They sat down by the fire again while the two men finished their pipes. Outside, the wind was higher than ever,
and the old man started nervously at the sound of a door
banging upstairs. A silence unusual and depressing settled
upon all three, which lasted until the old couple rose to retire for the night.

"I expect you'll find the cash tied up in a big bag in the
middle of your bed," said Herbert, as he bade them good
night, "and something horrible squatting up on top of the
wardrobe watching you as you pocket your ill-gotten gains."

II

In the brightness of the wintry sun next morning as it
streamed over the breakfast table Herbert laughed at his
fears. There was an air of prosaic wholesomeness about the
room which it had lacked on the previous night, and the

dirty, shriveled little paw was pitched on the sideboard with a carelessness which betokened no great belief in its virtues.

"I suppose all old soldiers are the same," said Mrs. White. "The idea of our listening to such nonsense! How could wishes be granted in these days? And if they could, how could two hundred pounds hurt you, father?"

"Might drop on his head from the sky," said the frivolous Herbert.

"Morris said the things happened so naturally," said his father, "that you might if you so wished attribute it to coincidence."

"Well, don't break into the money before I come back," said Herbert, as he rose from the table. "I'm afraid it'll turn you into a mean, avaricious man, and we shall have to disown you."

His mother laughed, and followed him to the door, watched him down the road, and returning to the breakfast table, was very happy at the expense of her husband's credulity. All of which did not prevent her from scurrying to the door at the postman's knock, nor prevent her from referring somewhat shortly to retired sergeant-majors of bibulous habits when she found that the post brought a tailor's bill.

"Herbert will have some more of his funny remarks, I expect, when he comes home," she said, as they sat at dinner.

"I dare say," said Mr. White, pouring himself out some beer; "but for all that, the thing moved in my hand; that I'll swear to."

"You thought it did," said the old lady soothingly.

"I say it did," replied the other. "There was no thought about it. I had just— What's the matter?"

His wife made no reply. She was watching the mysterious movements of a man outside, who, peering in an undecided fashion at the house, appeared to be trying to make up his mind to enter. In mental connection with the two hundred pounds, she noticed that the stranger was well dressed and wore a silk hat of glossy newness. Three times he paused at the gate, and then walked on again. The fourth time he stood with his hand upon it, and then with sudden resolution flung it open and walked up the path. Mrs. White at the same moment placed her hands behind her, and hurriedly unfastening the strings of her apron, put that useful article of apparel beneath the cushion of her chair.

She brought the stranger, who seemed ill at ease, into the room. He gazed furtively at Mrs. White, and listened in a preoccupied fashion as the old lady apologized for the appearance of the room, and her husband's coat, a garment which he usually reserved for the garden. She then waited as patiently as her sex would permit for him to broach his business, but he was at first strangely silent.

"I—was asked to call," he said at last, and stooped and picked a piece of cotton from his trousers. "I came from Maw and Meggins."

The old lady started. "Is anything the matter?" she asked breathlessly. "Has anything happened to Herbert? What is it? What is it?"

Her husband interposed. "There, there, mother," he said hastily. "Sit down, and don't jump to conclusions. You've not brought bad news, I'm sure, sir," and he eyed the other wistfully.

"I'm sorry——" began the visitor.

"Is he hurt?" demanded the mother.

The visitor bowed in assent. "Badly hurt," he said quietly, "but he is not in any pain."

"Oh, thank God!" said the old woman, clasping her hands. "Thank God for that! Thank——"

She broke off suddenly as the sinister meaning of the assurance dawned upon her and she saw the awful confirmation of her fears in the other's averted face. She caught her breath, and turning to her slower-witted husband, laid her trembling old hand upon his. There was a long silence.

"He was caught in the machinery," said the visitor at length, in a low voice.

"Caught in the machinery," repeated Mr. White, in a dazed fashion, "yes."

He sat staring blackly out at the window, and taking his wife's hand between his own, pressed it as he had been wont to do in their old courting days nearly forty years before.

"He was the only one left to us," he said, turning gently to the visitor. "It is hard."

The other coughed, and rising, walked slowly to the window. "The firm wished me to convey their sincere sympathy with you in your great loss," he said, without looking around. "I beg that you will understand I am only their servant and merely obeying orders."

There was no reply; the old woman's face was white, her eyes staring, and her breath inaudible; on the husband's face was a look such as his friend the sergeant might have carried into his first action.

"I was to say that Maw and Meggins disclaim all responsibility," continued the other. "They admit no liability at all, but in consideration of your son's services they wish to present you with a certain sum as compensation."

Mr. White dropped his wife's hand, and rising to his feet, gazed with a look of horror at his visitor. His dry lips shaped the words, "How much?"

"Two hundred pounds," was the answer.

Unconscious of his wife's shriek, the old man smiled faintly, put out his hands like a sightless man, and dropped, a senseless heap to the floor.

III

In the huge new cemetery, some two miles distant, the old people buried their dead, and came back to a house steeped in shadow and silence. It was all over so quickly that at first they could hardly realize it, and remained in a state of expectation as though of something else to happen—something else which was to lighten this load, too heavy for old hearts to bear. But the days passed, and expectation gave place to resignation—the hopeless resignation of the old, sometimes miscalled apathy. Sometimes they hardly exchanged a word, for now they had nothing to talk about, and their days were long to weariness.

It was about a week after that that the old man, waking suddenly in the night, stretched out his hand and found himself alone. The room was in darkness, and the sound of subdued weeping came from the window. He raised himself in bed and listened.

"Come back," he said tenderly. "You will be cold."

"It is colder for my son," said the old woman, and wept afresh.

The sound of her sobs died away on his ears. The bed was warm, and his eyes heavy with sleep. He dozed fitfully, and then slept until a sudden wild cry from his wife awoke him with a start.

"The monkey's paw!" she cried wildly. "The monkey's paw!"

He started up in alarm. "Where? Where is it? What's the matter?"

She came stumbling across the room toward him. "I want it," she said quietly. "You've not destroyed it?"

"It's in the parlor, on the bracket," he replied, marvelling. "Why?"

She cried and laughed together, and bending over, kissed his cheek.

"I only just thought of it," she said hysterically. "Why didn't I think of it before? Why didn't you think of it?"

"Think of what?" he questioned.

"The other two wishes," she replied rapidly. "We've only had one."

"Was not that enough?" he demanded fiercely.

"No," she cried triumphantly; "we'll have one more. Go down and get it quickly, and wish our boy alive again."

The man sat up in bed and flung the bedclothes from his quaking limbs. "Good God, you are mad!" he cried, aghast.

"Get it," she panted; "get it quickly, and wish— Oh, my boy, my boy!"

Her husband struck a match and lit the candle. "Get back to bed," he said unsteadily. "You don't know what you are saying."

"We had the first wish granted," said the old woman feverishly; "why not the second?"

"A coincidence," stammered the old man.

"Go and get it and wish," cried the old woman, and dragged him toward the door.

He went down in the darkness, and felt his way to the parlor, and then to the mantelpiece. The talisman was in its place, and a horrible fear that the unspoken wish might bring his mutilated son before him ere he could escape from the room seized upon him, and he caught his breath as he found that he had lost the direction of the door. His brow cold with sweat, he felt his way round the table, and groped along the wall until he found himself in the small passage with the unwholesome thing in his hand.

Even his wife's face seemed changed as he entered the room. It was white and expectant, and to his fears seemed to have an unnatural look upon it. He was afraid of her.

"Wish!" she cried, in a strong voice.

"It is foolish and wicked," he faltered.

"Wish!" repeated his wife.

He raised his hand. "I wish my son alive again."

The talisman fell to the floor, and he regarded it shudderingly. Then he sank trembling into a chair as the old woman, with burning eyes, walked to the window and raised the blind.

He sat until he was chilled with the cold, glancing occasionally at the figure of the old woman peering through the window. The candle end, which had burnt below the rim of the china candlestick, was throwing pulsating shadows on the ceiling and walls, until, with a flicker larger than the rest, it expired. The old man, with an unspeakable sense of relief at the failure of the talisman, crept back to his bed, and a minute or two afterward the old woman came silently and apathetically beside him.

Neither spoke, but both lay silently listening to the ticking of the clock. A stair creaked, and a squeaky mouse scurried noisily through the wall. The darkness was oppressive, and after lying for some time screwing up his courage, the husband took the box of matches, and striking one, went down stairs for a candle.

At the foot of the stairs the match went out, and he paused to strike another, and at the same moment a knock, so quiet and stealthy as to be scarcely audible, sounded on the front door.

The matches fell from his hand. He stood motionless, his breath suspended until the knock was repeated. Then he turned and fled swiftly back to his room, and closed the door behind him. A third knock sounded through the house.

"*What's that?*" cried the old woman, starting up.

"A rat," said the old man, in shaking tones—"a rat. It passed me on the stairs."

His wife sat up in bed listening. A loud knock resounded through the house.

"It's Herbert!" she screamed. "It's Herbert!"

She ran to the door, but her husband was before her, and catching her by the arm, held her tightly.

"What are you going to do?" he whispered hoarsely.

"It's my boy; it's Herbert!" she cried, struggling mechanically. "I forgot it was two miles away. What are you holding me for? Let go. I must open the door."

"For God's sake don't let it in," cried the old man, trembling.

"You're afraid of your own son," she cried, struggling. "Let me go. I'm coming, Herbert; I'm coming."

There was another knock, and another. The old woman with a sudden wrench broke free and ran from the room. Her husband followed to the landing, and called after her appealingly as she hurried downstairs. He heard the chain rattle back and the bottom bolt drawn slowly and stiffly from the socket. Then the old woman's voice, strained and panting.

"The bolt," she cried loudly. "Come down. I can't reach it."

But her husband was on his hands and knees groping wildly on the floor in search of the paw. If he could only find it before the thing outside got in. A perfect fusillade of knocks reverberated through the house, and he heard the scraping of a chair as his wife put it down in the passage against the door. He heard the creaking of the bolt as it came slowly back, and at the same moment he found the monkey's paw, and frantically breathed his third and last wish.

The knocking ceased suddenly, although the echoes of it were still in the house. He heard the chair drawn back and the door opened. A cold wind rushed up the staircase, and a long loud wail of disappointment and misery from his wife gave him courage to run down to her side, and then to the gate beyond. The street lamp flickering opposite shone on a quiet and deserted road.

O. HENRY (1862–1910)

A MUNICIPAL REPORT

The cities are full of pride,
Challenging each to each—
This from her mountainside,
That from her burthened beach.
RUDYARD KIPLING

Fancy a novel about Chicago or Buffalo, let us say, or Nashville, Tennessee! There are just three big cities in the United States that are "story cities"—New York, of course, New Orleans, and, best of the lot, San Francisco.

—FRANK NORRIS

EAST IS EAST, and West is San Francisco, according to Californians. Californians are a race of people; they are not merely inhabitants of a State. They are the Southerners of the West. Now, Chicagoans are no less loyal to their city; but when you ask them why, they stammer and speak of lake fish and the new Odd Fellows Building. But Californians go into detail.

Of course they have, in the climate, an argument that is good for half an hour while you are thinking of your coal bills and heavy underwear. But as soon as they come to mistake your silence for conviction, madness comes upon them, and they picture the city of the Golden Gate as the Bagdad of the New World. So far, as a matter of opinion, no refutation is necessary. But dear cousins all (from Adam and Eve descended), it is a rash one who will lay his finger on the map and say: "In this town there can be no romance—what could happen here?" Yes, it is a bold and a rash deed to challenge in one sentence history, romance, and Rand and McNally.

NASHVILLE.—*A city, port of delivery, and the capital of the State of Tennessee, is on the Cumberland River and on the N. C. & St. L. and the L. & N. railroads. This city is regarded as the most important educational center in the South.*

I stepped off the train at 8 P.M. Having searched the thesaurus in vain for adjectives, I must, as a substitution, hie me to comparison in the form of a recipe.

Take of London fog 30 parts; malaria 10 parts; gas leaks 20 parts; dewdrops gathered in a brick yard at sunrise 25 parts; odor of honeysuckle 15 parts. Mix.

The mixture will give you an approximate conception of a Nashville drizzle. It is not so fragrant as a moth-ball nor so thick as pea-soup; but 'tis enough—'twill serve.

I went to a hotel in a tumbril. It required strong self-suppression for me to keep from climbing to the top of it and giving an imitation of Sidney Carton. The vehicle was drawn by beasts of a bygone era and driven by something dark and emancipated.

I was sleepy and tired, so when I got to the hotel I hurriedly paid it the fifty cents it demanded (with appropriate lagniappe, I assure you). I knew its habits; and I did not want to hear it prate about its old "marster" or anything that happened "befo' de wah."

The hotel was one of the kind described as "renovated." That means $20,000 worth of new marble pillars, tiling, electric lights and brass cuspidors in the lobby, and a new L. & N. time table and a lithograph of Lookout Mountain in each one of the great rooms above. The management was without reproach, the attention full of exquisite Southern courtesy, the service was as slow as the progress of a snail and as good-humored as Rip Van Winkle. The food was worth traveling a thousand miles for. There is no other hotel in the world where you can get such chicken livers *en brochette*.

At dinner I asked a Negro waiter if there was anything doing in town. He pondered gravely for a minute, and then replied: "Well, boss, I don't really reckon there's anything at all doin' after sundown."

Sundown had been accomplished; it had been drowned in the drizzle long before. So that spectacle was denied me. But

I went forth upon the streets in the drizzle to see what might be here.

It is built on undulating grounds; and the streets are lighted by electricity at a cost of $32,470 per annum.

As I left the hotel there was a race riot. Down upon me charged a company of freedmen, or Arabs, or Zulus, armed with—no, I saw with relief that they were not rifles, but whips. And I saw dimly a caravan of black, clumsy vehicles; and at the reassuring shouts, "Kyar you anywhere in the town, boss, fuh fifty cents," I reasoned that I was merely a "fare" instead of a victim.

I walked through long streets, all leading uphill. I wondered how those streets ever came down again. Perhaps they didn't until they were "graded." On a few of the "main streets" I saw lights in stores here and there; saw street cars go by conveying worthy burghers hither and yon; saw people pass engaged in the art of conversation, and heard a burst of semi-lively laughter issuing from a soda-water and ice-cream parlor. The streets other than "main" seemed to have enticed upon their borders houses consecrated to peace and domesticity. In many of them lights shone behind discreetly drawn window shades, in a few pianos tinkled orderly and irreproachable music. There was, indeed, little "doing." I wished I had come before sundown. So I returned to my hotel.

In November, 1864, the Confederate General Hood advanced against Nashville, where he shut up a National force under General Thomas. The latter then sallied forth and defeated the Confederates in a terrible conflict.

All my life I have heard of, admired, and witnessed the fine marksmanship of the South in its peaceful conflicts in the tobacco-chewing regions. But in my hotel a surprise awaited me. There were twelve bright, new, imposing, capacious brass cuspidors in the great lobby, tall enough to be called urns and so wide-mouthed that the crack pitcher of a lady baseball team should have been able to throw a ball into one of them at five paces distant. But, although a terrible battle had raged and was still raging, the enemy had not suffered. Bright, new, imposing, capacious, untouched, they stood. But, shades of Jefferson Brick! the tile floor—the beau-

tiful tile floor! I could not avoid thinking of the battle of
Nashville, and trying to draw, as is my foolish habit, some
deductions about hereditary marksmanship.

Here I first saw Major (by misplaced courtesy) Wentworth Caswell. I knew him for a type the moment my eyes
suffered from the sight of him. A rat has no geographical
habitat. My old friend, A. Tennyson, said, as he so well said
almost everything:

> Prophet, curse me the blabbing lip,
> And curse me the British vermin, the rat.

Let us regard the word "British" as interchangeable *ad
lib.* A rat is a rat.

This man was hunting about the hotel lobby like a starved
dog that had forgotten where he had buried a bone. He had
a face of great acreage, red, pulpy, and with a kind of sleepy
massiveness like that of Buddha. He possessed one single
virtue—he was very smoothly shaven. The mark of the beast
is not indelible upon a man until he goes about with a stub-
ble. I think that if he had not used his razor that day I
would have repulsed his advances, and the criminal calendar
of the world would have been spared the addition of one
murder.

I happened to be standing within five feet of a cuspidor
when Major Caswell opened fire upon it. I had been observ-
ant enough to perceive that the attacking force was using
Gatlings instead of squirrel rifles, so I sidestepped so promptly
that the major seized the opportunity to apologize to a non-
combatant. He had the blabbing lip. In four minutes he
had become my friend and had dragged me to the bar.

I desire to interpolate here that I am a Southerner. But I
am not one by profession or trade. I eschew the string tie, the
slouch hat, the Prince Albert, the number of bales of cotton
destroyed by Sherman, and plug chewing. When the orchestra plays "Dixie" I do not cheer. I slide a little lower on the
leather-cornered seat and, well, order another Würzburger
and wish that Longstreet had—but what's the use?

Major Caswell banged the bar with his fist, and the first
gun at Fort Sumter re-echoed. When he fired the last one at
Appomattox I began to hope. But then he began on family
trees, and demonstrated that Adam was only a third cousin

of a collateral branch of the Caswell family. Genealogy disposed of, he took up, to my distaste, his private family matters. He spoke of his wife, traced her descent back to Eve,
and profanely denied any possible rumor that she may have
had relations in the land of Nod.

By this time I began to suspect that he was trying to obscure by noise the fact that he had ordered the drinks, on
the chance that I would be bewildered into paying for them.
But when they were down he crashed a silver dollar loudly
upon the bar. Then, of course, another serving was obliga-
tory. And when I had paid for that I took leave of him
brusquely; for I wanted no more of him. But before I had
obtained my release he had prated loudly of an income that
his wife received, and showed a handful of silver money.

When I got my key at the desk the clerk said to me
courteously: "If that man Caswell has annoyed you, and if
you would like to make a complaint, we will have him
ejected. He is a nuisance, a loafer, and without any known
means of support, although he seems to have some money
most of the time. But we don't seem to be able to hit upon
any means of throwing him out legally."

"Why, no," said I, after some reflection; "I don't see my
way clear to making a complaint. But I would like to place
myself on record as asserting that I do not care for his
company. Your town," I continued, "seems to be a quiet one.
What manner of entertainment, adventure, or excitement
have you to offer to the stranger within your gates?"

"Well, sir," said the clerk, "there will be a show here next
Thursday. It is—I'll look it up and have the announcement
sent up to your room with ice water. Good night."

After I went up to my room I looked out the window. It
was only about ten o'clock, but I looked upon a silent town.
The drizzle continued, spangled with dim lights, as far apart
as currants in a cake sold at the Ladies' Exchange.

"A quiet place," I said to myself, as my first shoe struck
the ceiling of the occupant of the room beneath mine. "Nothing of the life here that gives color and good variety to the
cities in the East and West. Just a good, ordinary, humdrum,
business town."

Nashville occupies a foremost place among the manufac-

turing centers of the country. It is the fifth boot and shoe market in the United States, the largest candy and cracker manufacturing city in the South, and does an enormous wholesale dry goods, grocery, and drug business.

I must tell you how I came to be in Nashville, and I assure you the digression brings as much tedium to me as it does to you. I was traveling elsewhere on my own business, but I had a commission from a Northern literary magazine to stop over there and establish a personal connection between the publication and one of its contributors, Azalea Adair.

Adair (there was no clue to the personality except the handwriting) had sent in some essays (lost art!) and poems that had made the editors swear approvingly over their one o'clock luncheon. So they had commissioned me to round up said Adair and corner by contract his or her output at two cents a word before some other publisher offered her ten or twenty.

At nine o'clock the next morning, after my chicken livers *en brochette* (try them if you can find that hotel), I strayed out into the drizzle, which was still on for an unlimited run. At the first corner I came upon Uncle Cæsar. He was a stalwart Negro, older than the pyramids, with gray wool and a face that reminded me of Brutus, and a second afterwards of the late King Cettiwayo. He wore the most remarkable coat that I ever had seen or expect to see. It reached to his ankles and had once been a Confederate gray in color. But rain and sun and age had so variegated it that Joseph's coat, beside it, would have faded to a pale monochrome. I must linger with that coat, for it has to do with the story—the story that is so long in coming, because you can hardly expect anything to happen in Nashville.

Once it must have been the military coat of an officer. The cape of it had vanished, but all adown its front it had been frogged and tasseled magnificently. But now the frogs and tassels were gone. In their stead had been patiently stitched (I surmised by some surviving "black mammy") new frogs made of cunningly twisted common hempen twine. This twine was frayed and disheveled. It must have been added to the coat as a substitute for vanished splendors, with tasteless but painstaking devotion, for it followed faithfully the curves of the long-missing frogs. And, to complete the comedy and pathos of the garment, all its buttons were gone save one. The second button from the top alone remained. The coat was fastened by other twine strings tied through the buttonholes and other holes rudely pierced in the opposite side. There was never such a weird garment so fantastically bedecked and of so many mottled hues. The lone button was the size of a half-dollar, made of yellow horn and sewed on with coarse twine.

This Negro stood by a carriage so old that Ham himself might have started a hack line with it after he left the ark with the two animals hitched to it. As I approached he threw open the door, drew out a feather duster, waved it without using it, and said in deep, rumbling tones: "Step right in, suh; ain't a speck of dust in it—jus' got back from a funeral, suh."

I inferred that on such gala occasions carriages were given an extra cleaning. I looked up and down the street and perceived that there was little choice among the vehicles for hire that lined the curb. I looked in my memorandum book for the address of Azalea Adair.

"I want to go to 861 Jessamine Street," I said, and was about to step into the hack. But for an instant the thick, long, gorilla-like arm of the Negro barred me. On his massive and saturnine face a look of sudden suspicion and enmity flashed for a moment. Then, with quickly returning conviction, he asked blandishingly: "What are you gwine there for, boss?"

"What is that to you?" I asked, a little sharply.

"Nothin', suh, jus' nothin'. Only it's a lonesome kind of part of town and few folks ever has business out there. Step right in. The seats is clean—jes' got back from a funeral, suh."

A mile and a half it must have been to our journey's end. I could hear nothing but the fearful rattle of the ancient hack over the uneven brick paving; I could smell nothing but the drizzle, now further flavored with coal smoke and something like a mixture of tar and oleander blossoms. All I could see through the streaming windows were two rows of dim houses.

The city has an area of 10 square miles; 181 miles of streets, of which 137 miles are paved; a system of water-works that cost $2,000,000 with 77 miles of mains.

Eight-sixty-one Jessamine Street was a decayed mansion. Thirty yards back from the street it stood, out-merged in a splendid grove of trees and untrimmed shrubbery. A row of box bushes overflowed and almost hid the paling fence from sight: the gate was kept closed by a rope noose that encircled the gate post and the first paling of the gate. But when you got inside you saw that 861 was a shell, a shadow, a ghost of former grandeur and excellence. But in the story, I have not yet got inside.

When the hack had ceased from rattling and the weary quadrupeds come to a rest I handed my jehu his fifty cents with an additional quarter, feeling a glow of conscious generosity as I did so. He refused it.

"It's two dollars, suh," he said.

"How's that?" I asked. "I plainly heard you call out at the hotel, 'Fifty cents to any part of the town.'"

"It's two dollars, suh," he repeated obstinately. "It's a long ways from the hotel."

"It is within the city limits and well within them," I argued. "Don't think that you have picked up a greenhorn Yankee. Do you see those hills over there?" I went on, pointing toward the east (I could not see them, myself, for the drizzle); "well, I was born and raised on their other side. You old fool nigger, can't you tell people from other people when you see 'em?"

The grim face of King Cettiwayo softened. "Is you from the South, suh? I reckon it was them shoes of yourn fooled me. They is somethin' sharp in the toes for a Southern gen'-l'man to wear."

"Then the charge is fifty cents, I suppose?" said I, inexorably.

His former expression, a mingling of cupidity and hostility, returned, remained ten seconds, and vanished.

"Boss," he said, "fifty cents is right; but I *needs* two dollars, suh; I'm *obleeged* to have two dollars. I ain't *demandin'* it now, suh; after I knows whar you's from; I'm jus' sayin' that I *has* to have two dollars tonight and business is mighty po'."

Peace and confidence settled upon his heavy features. He had been luckier than he had hoped. Instead of having picked up a greenhorn, ignorant of rates, he had come upon an inheritance.

"You confounded old rascal," I said, reaching down to my pocket, "you ought to be turned over to the police."

For the first time I saw him smile. He knew; *he knew;* HE KNEW.

I gave him two one-dollar bills. As I handed them over I noticed that one of them had seen parlous times. Its upper right-hand corner was missing, and it had been torn through in the middle, but joined again. A strip of blue tissue paper, pasted over the split, preserved its negotiability.

Enough of the African bandit for the present: I left him happy, lifted the rope, and opened the creaky gate.

The house, as I said, was a shell. A paint brush had not touched it in twenty years. I could not see why a strong wind should not have bowled it over like a house of cards until I looked again at the trees that hugged it close—the trees that saw the battle of Nashville and still drew their protecting branches around it against storm and enemy and cold.

Azalea Adair, fifty years old, white-haired, a descendant of the cavaliers, as thin and frail as the house she lived in, robed in the cheapest and cleanest dress I ever saw, with an air as simple as a queen's, received me.

The reception room seemed a mile square, because there was nothing in it except some rows of books, on unpainted white-pine bookshelves, a cracked marble-topped table, a rag rug, a hairless horsehair sofa, and two or three chairs. Yes, there was a picture on the wall, a colored crayon drawing of a cluster of pansies. I looked around for the portrait of Andrew Jackson and the pine cone hanging basket but they were not there.

Azalea Adair and I had conversation, a little of which will be repeated to you. She was a product of the old South, gently nurtured in the sheltered life. Her learning was not broad, but was deep and of splendid originality in its somewhat narrow scope. She had been educated at home, and her knowledge of the world was derived from inference and by inspiration. Of such is the precious, small group of essayists made. While she talked to me I kept brushing my fingers, trying, unconsciously, to rid them guiltily of the absent dust from the half-calf backs of Lamb, Chaucer, Hazlitt, Marcus Aurelius, Montaigne, and Hood. She was exquisite, she was a valuable discovery. Nearly everybody nowadays knows too much—oh, so much too much—of real life.

I could perceive clearly that Azalea Adair was very poor. A house and a dress she had, not much else, I fancied. So, divided between my duty to the magazine and my loyalty to the poets and essayists who fought Thomas in the valley of the Cumberland, I listened to her voice which was like a harpsichord's, and found that I could not speak of contracts. In the presence of the nine Muses and the three Graces one hesitated to lower the topic to two cents. There would have to be another colloquy after I had regained my commercialism. But I spoke of my mission, and three o'clock of the next afternoon was set for the discussion of the business proposition.

"Your town," I said, as I began to make ready to depart (which is the time for smooth generalities) "seems to be a quiet, sedate place. A home town, I should say, where few things out of the ordinary ever happen."

It carries on an extensive trade in stoves and hollow ware with the West and South, and its flouring mills have a daily capacity of more than 2,000 barrels.

Azalea Adair seemed to reflect. "I have never thought of it that way," she said, with a kind of sincere intensity that seemed to belong to her. "Isn't it in the still, quiet places that things do happen? I fancy that when God began to create the earth on the first Monday morning one could have leaned out one's window and heard the drops of mud splashing from His trowel as He built up the everlasting hills. What did the noisiest project in the world—I mean the building of the tower of Babel—result in finally? A page and a half of Esperanto in the *North American Review*."

"Of course," said I, platitudinously, "human nature is the same everywhere; but there is more color—er—more drama and movement and—er—romance in some cities than in others."

"On the surface," said Azalea Adair. "I have traveled many times around the world in a golden airship wafted on two wings—print and dreams. I have seen (on one of my imaginary tours) the Sultan of Turkey bowstring with his own hands one of his wives who had uncovered her face in public. I have seen a man in Nashville tear up his theater tickets because his wife was going out with her face covered —with rice powder. In San Francisco's Chinatown I saw the slave girl Sing Yee dipped slowly, inch by inch, in boiling almond oil to make her swear she would never see her American lover again. She gave in when the boiling oil had reached three inches above her knee. At a euchre party in East Nashville the other night I saw Kitty Morgan cut dead by seven of her schoolmates and lifelong friends because she had married a house painter. The boiling oil was sizzling as high as her heart; but I wish you could have seen the fine little smile that she carried from table to table. Oh, yes, it is a humdrum town. Just a few miles of red brick houses and mud and stores and lumber yards."

Someone had knocked hollowly at the back of the house. Azalea Adair breathed a soft apology and went to investigate the sound. She came back in three minutes with brightened eyes, a faint flush on her cheeks, and ten years lifted from her shoulders.

"You must have a cup of tea before you go," she said, "and a sugar cake."

She reached and shook a little iron bell. In shuffled a small Negro girl about twelve, barefoot, not very tidy, glowering at me with thumb in mouth and bulging eyes.

Azalea Adair opened a tiny, worn purse and drew out a dollar bill, a dollar bill with the upper right-hand corner missing, torn in two pieces and pasted together again with a strip of blue tissue paper. It was one of those bills I had given the piratical Negro—there was no doubt of it.

"Go up to Mr. Baker's store on the corner, Impy," she said, handing the girl the dollar bill, "and get a quarter of a pound of tea—the kind he always sends me—and ten cents' worth of sugar cakes. Now, hurry. The supply of tea in the house happens to be exhausted," she explained to me.

Impy left by the back way. Before the scrape of her hard, bare feet had died away on the back porch, a wild shriek—I was sure it was hers—filled the hollow house. Then the deep, gruff tones of an angry man's voice mingled with the girl's further squeals and unintelligible words.

Azalea Adair rose without surprise or emotion and disappeared. For two minutes I heard the hoarse rumble of the man's voice; then something like an oath and a slight scuffle, and she returned calmly to her chair.

"This is a roomy house," she said, "and I have a tenant for part of it. I am sorry to have to rescind my invitation to tea. It is impossible to get the kind I always use at the store. Perhaps tomorrow Mr. Baker will be able to supply me."

I was sure that Impy had not had time to leave the house. I inquired concerning street-car lines and took my leave. After I was well on my way I remembered that I had not learned Azalea Adair's name. But tomorrow would do.

That same day I started in on the course of iniquity that this uneventful city forced upon me. I was in the town only two days, but in that time I managed to lie shamelessly by telegraph, and to be an accomplice—after the fact, if that is the correct legal term—to a murder.

As I rounded the corner nearest my hotel the Afrite coachman of the polychromatic, nonpareil coat seized me, swung open the dungeony door of his peripatetic sarcophagus, flirted his feather duster and began his ritual: "Step right in, boss. Carriage is clean—jus' got back from a funeral. Fifty cents to any——"

And then he knew me and grinned broadly. " 'Scuse me, boss; you is de gen'l'man what rid out with me dis mawnin'. Thank you kindly, suh."

"I am going out to 861 again tomorrow afternoon at three," said I, "and if you will be here, I'll let you drive me. So you know Miss Adair?" I concluded, thinking of my dollar bill.

"I belonged to her father, Judge Adair, suh," he replied.

"I judge that she is pretty poor," I said. "She hasn't much money to speak of, has she?"

For an instant I looked again at the fierce countenance of King Cettiwayo, and then he changed back to an extortionate old Negro hack driver.

"She ain't gwine to starve, suh," he said, slowly. "She has reso'ces, suh; she has reso'ces."

"I shall pay you fifty cents for the trip," said I.

"Dat is puffectly correct, suh," he answered, humbly. "I jus' *had* to have dat two dollars dis mawnin', boss."

I went to the hotel and lied by electricity. I wired the magazine: "A. Adair holds out for eight cents a word."

The answer that came back was: "Give it to her quick, you duffer."

Just before dinner "Major" Wentworth Caswell bore down upon me with the greetings of a long-lost friend. I have seen few men whom I have so instantaneously hated, and of whom it was so difficult to be rid. I was standing at the bar when he invaded me; therefore I could not wave the white ribbon in his face. I would have paid gladly for the drinks, hoping thereby, to escape another; but he was one of those despicable, roaring, advertising bibbers who must have brass bands and fireworks attend upon every cent that they waste in their follies.

With an air of producing millions he drew two one-dollar bills from a pocket and dashed one of them upon the bar. I looked once more at the dollar bill with the upper right-hand corner missing, torn through the middle, and patched with a strip of blue tissue paper. It was my dollar bill again. It could have been no other.

I went up to my room. The drizzle and the monotony of a dreary, eventless Southern town had made me tired and listless. I remember that just before I went to bed I mentally disposed of the mysterious dollar bill (which might have formed the clue to a tremendously fine detective story of San Francisco) by saying to myself sleepily: "Seems as if a lot of people here own stock in the Hack-Drivers' Trust. Pays dividends promptly, too. Wonder if——" Then I fell asleep.

King Cettiwayo was at his post the next day, and rattled my bones over the stones out to 861. He was to wait and rattle me back again when I was ready.

Azalea Adair looked paler and cleaner and frailer than she had looked on the day before. After she had signed the contract at eight cents per word she grew still paler and began to slip out of her chair. Without much trouble I managed to get her up on the antediluvian horsehair sofa and then I ran out to the sidewalk and yelled to the coffee-colored Pirate to bring a doctor. With a wisdom that I had not suspected in him, he abandoned his team and struck off up the street afoot, realizing the value of speed. In ten minutes he returned with a grave, gray-haired, and capable man of medicine. In a few words (worth much less than eight cents each) I explained to him my presence in the hollow house of mystery. He bowed with stately understanding, and turned to the old Negro.

"Uncle Cæsar," he said, calmly, "run up to my house and ask Miss Lucy to give you a cream pitcher full of fresh milk and half a tumbler of port wine. And hurry back. Don't drive —run. I want you to get back some time this week."

It occurred to me that Dr. Merriman also felt a distrust as to the speeding powers of the land-pirate's steeds. After Uncle Cæsar was gone, lumberingly, but swiftly, up the street, the doctor looked me over with great politeness and as much careful calculation until he had decided that I might do.

"It is only a case of insufficient nutrition," he said. "In other words, the result of poverty, pride, and starvation. Mrs. Caswell has many devoted friends who would be glad to aid her, but she will accept nothing except from that old Negro, Uncle Cæsar, who was once owned by her family."

"Mrs. Caswell!" said I, in surprise. And then I looked at the contract and saw that she had signed it "Azalea Adair Caswell."

"I thought she was Miss Adair," I said.

"Married to a drunken, worthless loafer, sir," said the doctor. "It is said that he robs her even of the small sums that her old servant contributes toward her support."

When the milk and wine had been brought the doctor soon revived Azalea Adair. She sat up and talked of the beauty of the autumn leaves that were then in season and their height of color. She referred lightly to her fainting seizure as the outcome of an old palpitation of the heart. Impy fanned her as she lay on the sofa. The doctor was due elsewhere, and I followed him to the door. I told him that it was within my power and intentions to make a reasonable advance of money to Azalea Adair on future contributions to the magazine, and he seemed pleased.

"By the way," he said, "perhaps you would like to know that you have had royalty for a coachman. Old Cæsar's grandfather was a king in Congo. Cæsar himself has royal ways, as you may have observed."

As the doctor was moving off I heard Uncle Cæsar's voice inside: "Did he git bofe of dem two dollars from you, Mis' Zalea?"

"Yes, Cæsar," I heard Azalea Adair answer, weakly. And then I went in and concluded business negotiations with our contributor. I assumed the responsibility of advancing fifty dollars, putting it as a necessary formality in binding our bargain. And then Uncle Cæsar drove me back to the hotel.

Here ends all of the story as far as I can testify as a witness. The rest must be only bare statements of facts.

At about six o'clock I went out for a stroll. Uncle Cæsar was at his corner. He threw open the door of his carriage, flourished his duster, and began his depressing formula: "Step right in, suh. Fifty cents to anywhere in the city—hack's puffickly clean, suh—jus' got back from a funeral——"

And then he recognized me. I think his eyesight was getting bad. His coat had taken on a few more faded shades of color, the twine strings were more frayed and ragged, the last remaining button—the button of yellow horn—was gone. A motley descendant of kings was Uncle Cæsar!

About two hours later I saw an excited crowd besieging the front of the drug store. In a desert where nothing happens this was manna; so I wedged my way inside. On an extemporized couch of empty boxes and chairs was stretched the mortal corporeality of Major Wentworth Caswell. A doctor was testing him for the mortal ingredient. His decision was that it was conspicuous by its absence.

The erstwhile Major had been found dead on a dark street and brought by curious and ennuied citizens to the drug store. The late human being had been engaged in terrific battle—the details showed that. Loafer and reprobate though he had been, he had been also a warrior. But he had lost. His hands were yet clinched so tightly that his fingers would not be opened. The gentle citizens who had known him stood about and searched their vocabularies to find some good words, if it were possible, to speak of him. One kind-looking man said, after much thought: "When 'Cas' was about fo'teen he was one of the best spellers in the school."

While I stood there the fingers of the right hand of "the man that was," which hung down the side of a white pine box, relaxed, and dropped something at my feet. I covered it with one foot quietly, and a little later on I picked it up and pocketed it. I reasoned that in his last struggle his hand must have seized that object unwittingly and held it in a death grip.

At the hotel that night the main topic of conversation, with the possible exceptions of politics and prohibition, was the demise of Major Caswell. I heard one man say to a group of listeners:

"In my opinion, gentlemen, Caswell was murdered by some of these no-account niggers for his money. He had fifty dollars this afternoon which he showed to several gentlemen in the hotel. When he was found the money was not on his person."

I left the city the next morning at nine, and as the train was crossing the bridge over the Cumberland River I took out of my pocket a yellow horn overcoat button the size of a fifty-cent piece, with grayed ends of coarse twine hanging from it, and cast it out of the window into the slow, muddy waters below. *I wonder what's doing in Buffalo!*

ANTON P. CHEKHOV *(1860–1904)*

THE DARLING

OLENKA, the daughter of the retired collegiate assessor Plemyanikov, was sitting on the back-door steps of her house doing nothing. It was hot, the flies were nagging and teasing, and it was pleasant to think that it would soon be evening. Dark rain clouds were gathering from the east, wafting a breath of moisture every now and then.

Kukin, who roomed in the wing of the same house, was standing in the yard looking up at the sky. He was the manager of the Tivoli, an open-air theatre.

"Again," he said despairingly. "Rain again. Rain, rain, rain! Every day rain! As though to spite me. I might as well stick my head into a noose and be done with it. It's ruining me. Heavy losses every day!" He wrung his hands, and continued, addressing Olenka: "What a life, Olga Semyonovna! It's enough to make a man weep. He works, he does his best, his very best, he tortures himself, he passes sleepless nights, he thinks and thinks and thinks how to do everything just right. And what's the result? He gives the public the best operetta, the very best pantomime, excellent artists. But do they want it? Have they the least appreciation of it? The public is rude. The public is a great boor. The public wants a circus, a lot of nonsense, a lot of stuff. And there's the weather. Look! Rain almost every evening. It began to rain on the tenth of May, and it's kept it up through the whole of June. It's simply awful. I can't get any audiences, and don't I have to pay rent? Don't I have to pay the actors?"

The next day towards evening the clouds gathered again, and Kukin said with an hysterical laugh:

"Oh, I don't care. Let it do its worst. Let it drown the whole theatre, and me, too. All right, no luck for me in this

235

world or the next. Let the actors bring suit against me and drag me to court. What's the court? Why not Siberia at hard labour, or even the scaffold? Ha, ha, ha!"

It was the same on the third day.

Olenka listened to Kukin seriously, in silence. Sometimes tears would rise to her eyes. At last Kukin's misfortune touched her. She fell in love with him. He was short, gaunt, with a yellow face, and curly hair combed back from his forehead, and a thin tenor voice. His features puckered all up when he spoke. Despair was ever inscribed on his face. And yet he awakened in Olenka a sincere, deep feeling.

She was always loving somebody. She couldn't get on without loving somebody. She had loved her sick father, who sat the whole time in his armchair in a darkened room, breathing heavily. She had loved her aunt, who came from Brianska once or twice a year to visit them. And before that, when a pupil at the progymnasium, she had loved her French teacher. She was a quiet, kind-hearted, compassionate girl, with a soft gentle way about her. And she made a very healthy, wholesome impression. Looking at her full, rosy cheeks, at her soft white neck with the black mole, and at the good naïve smile that always played on her face when something pleasant was said, the men would think, "Not so bad," and would smile too; and the lady visitors, in the middle of the conversation, would suddenly grasp her hand and exclaim, "You darling!" in a burst of delight.

The house, hers by inheritance, in which she had lived from birth, was located at the outskirts of the city on the Gypsy Road, not far from the Tivoli. From early evening till late at night she could hear the music in the theatre and the bursting of the rockets; and it seemed to her that Kukin was roaring and battling with his fate and taking his chief enemy, the indifferent public, by assault. Her heart melted softly, she felt no desire to sleep, and when Kukin returned home towards morning, she tapped on her window-pane, and through the curtains he saw her face and one shoulder and the kind smile she gave him.

He proposed to her, and they were married. And when he had a good look at her neck and her full vigorous shoulders, he clapped his hands and said: "You darling!"

He was happy. But it rained on their wedding-day, and the expression of despair never left his face.

They got along well together. She sat in the cashier's box, kept the theatre in order, wrote down the expenses, and paid out the salaries. Her rosy cheeks, her kind naïve smile, like a halo around her face, could be seen at the cashier's window, behind the scenes, and in the café. She began to tell her friends that the theatre was the greatest, the most important, the most essential thing in the world, that it was the only place to obtain true enjoyment in and become humanised and educated.

"But do you suppose the public appreciates it?" she asked. "What the public wants is the circus. Yesterday Vanichka and I gave *Faust Burlesqued,* and almost all the boxes were empty. If we had given some silly nonsense, I assure you, the theatre would have been overcrowded. Tomorrow we'll put *Orpheus in Hades* on. Do come."

Whatever Kukin said about the theatre and the actors, she repeated. She spoke, as he did, with contempt of the public, of its indifference to art, of its boorishness. She meddled in the rehearsals, corrected the actors, watched the conduct of the musicians; and when an unfavourable criticism appeared in the local paper, she wept and went to the editor to argue with him.

The actors were fond of her and called her "Vanichka and I" and "the darling." She was sorry for them and lent them small sums. When they bilked her, she never complained to her husband; at the utmost she shed a few tears.

In winter, too, they got along nicely together. They leased a theatre in the town for the whole winter and sublet it for short periods to a Little Russian theatrical company, to a conjuror and to the local amateur players.

Olenka grew fuller and was always beaming with contentment; while Kukin grew thinner and yellower and complained of his terrible losses, though he did fairly well the whole winter. At night he coughed, and she gave him raspberry syrup and lime water, rubbed him with eau de Cologne, and wrapped him up in soft coverings.

"You are my precious sweet," she said with perfect sincerity, stroking his hair. "You are such a dear."

At Lent he went to Moscow to get his company together, and, while without him, Olenka was unable to sleep. She sat at the window the whole time, gazing at the stars. She likened herself to the hens that are also uneasy and unable to sleep when their rooster is out of the coop. Kukin was detained in Moscow. He wrote he would be back during Easter Week, and in his letters discussed arrangements already for the Tivoli. But late one night, before Easter Monday, there was an ill-omened knocking at the wicket-gate. It was like a knocking on a barrel—boom, boom, boom! The sleepy cook ran barefooted, plashing through the puddles, to open the gate.

"Open the gate, please," said some one in a hollow bass voice. "I have a telegram for you."

Olenka had received telegrams from her husband before; but this time, somehow, she was numbed with terror. She opened the telegram with trembling hands and read:

"Ivan Petrovich died suddenly to-day. Awaiting propt orders for wuneral Tuesday."

That was the way the telegram was written—"wuneral" —and another unintelligible word—"propt." The telegram was signed by the manager of the opera company.

"My dearest!" Olenka burst out sobbing. "Vanichka, my dearest, my sweetheart. Why did I ever meet you? Why did I ever get to know you and love you? To whom have you abandoned your poor Olenka, your poor, unhappy Olenka?"

Kukin was buried on Tuesday in the Vagankov Cemetery in Moscow. Olenka returned home on Wednesday; and as soon as she entered her house she threw herself on her bed and broke into such loud sobbing that she could be heard in the street and in the neighbouring yards.

"The darling!" said the neighbours, crossing themselves. "How Olga Semyonovna, the poor darling, is grieving!"

Three months afterwards Olenka was returning home from mass, downhearted and in deep mourning. Beside her walked a man also returning from church, Vasily Pustovalov, the manager of the merchant Babakayev's lumber-yard. He was wearing a straw hat, a white vest with a gold chain, and looked more like a landowner than a business man.

"Everything has its ordained course, Olga Semyonovna,"

he said sedately, with sympathy in his voice. "And if any one near and dear to us dies, then it means it was God's will and we should remember that and bear it with submission."

He took her to the wicket-gate, said good-bye and went away. After that she heard his sedate voice the whole day; and on closing her eyes she instantly had a vision of his dark beard. She took a great liking to him. And evidently he had been impressed by her, too; for, not long after, an elderly woman, a distant acquaintance, came in to have a cup of coffee with her. As soon as the woman was seated at table she began to speak about Pustovalov—how good he was, what a steady man, and any woman could be glad to get him as a husband. Three days later Pustovalov himself paid Olenka a visit. He stayed only about ten minutes, and spoke little, but Olenka fell in love with him, fell in love so desperately that she did not sleep the whole night and burned as with fever. In the morning she sent for the elderly woman. Soon after, Olenka and Pustovalov were engaged, and the wedding followed.

Pustovalov and Olenka lived happily together. He usually stayed in the lumber-yard until dinner, then went out on business. In his absence Olenka took his place in the office until evening, attending to the book-keeping and despatching the orders.

"Lumber rises twenty per cent every year nowadays," she told her customers and acquaintances. "Imagine, we used to buy wood from our forests here. Now Vanichka has to go every year to the government of Mogilev to get wood. And what a tax!" she exclaimed, covering her cheeks with her hands in terror. "What a tax!"

She felt as if she had been dealing in lumber for ever so long, that the most important and essential thing in life was lumber. There was something touching and endearing in the way she pronounced the words "beam," "joist," "plank," "stave," "lath," "gun-carriage," "clamp." At night she dreamed of whole mountains of boards and planks, long, endless rows of wagons conveying the wood somewhere, far, far from the city. She dreamed that a whole regiment of beams, 36 ft. x 5 in., were advancing in an upright position to do battle against the lumber-yard; that the beams and joists and clamps were knocking against each other, emitting the sharp crackling reports of dry wood, that they were all falling and then rising again, piling on top of each other. Olenka cried out in her sleep, and Pustovalov said to her gently:

"Olenka, my dear, what is the matter? Cross yourself."

Her husband's opinions were all hers. If he thought the room was too hot, she thought so too. If he thought business was dull, she thought business was dull. Pustovalov was not fond of amusements and stayed home on holidays, she did the same.

"You are always either at home or in the office," said her friends. "Why don't you go to the theatre or to the circus, darling?"

"Vanichka and I never go to the theatre," she answered sedately. "We have work to do, we have no time for nonsense. What does one get out of going to the theatre?"

On Saturdays she and Pustovalov went to vespers, and on holidays to early mass. On returning home they walked side by side with rapt faces, an agreeable smell emanating from both of them and her silk dress rustling pleasantly. At home they drank tea with milk-bread and various jams, and then ate pie. Every day at noontime there was an appetising odour in the yard and outside the gate of cabbage soup, roast mutton, or duck; and, on fast days, of fish. You couldn't pass the gate without being seized by an acute desire to eat. The samovar was always boiling on the office table, and customers were treated to tea and biscuits. Once a week the married couple went to the baths and returned with red faces, walking side by side.

"We are getting along very well, thank God," said Olenka to her friends. "God grant that all should live as well as Vanichka and I."

When Pustovalov went to the government of Mogilev to buy wood, she was dreadfully homesick for him, did not sleep nights, and cried. Sometimes the veterinary surgeon of the regiment, Smirnov, a young man who lodged in the wing of her house, came to see her evenings. He related incidents, or they played cards together. This distracted her. The most interesting of his stories were those of his own life. He was married and had a son; but he had separated from his wife because she had deceived him, and now he hated her and sent her forty rubles a month for his son's support. Olenka sighed, shook her head, and was sorry for him.

"Well, the Lord keep you," she said, as she saw him off to the door by candlelight. "Thank you for coming to kill time with me. May God give you health. Mother in Heaven!" She spoke very sedately, very judiciously, imitating her husband. The veterinary surgeon had disappeared behind the door when she called out after him: "Do you know, Vladimir Platonych, you ought to make up with your wife. Forgive her, if only for the sake of your son. The child understands everything, you may be sure."

When Pustovalov returned, she told him in a low voice about the veterinary surgeon and his unhappy family life; and they sighed and shook their heads, and talked about the boy who must be homesick for his father. Then, by a strange association of ideas, they both stopped before the sacred images, made genuflections, and prayed to God to send them children.

And so the Pustovalovs lived for six full years, quietly and peaceably, in perfect love and harmony. But once in the winter Vasily Andreyich, after drinking some hot tea, went out into the lumber-yard without a hat on his head, caught a cold and took sick. He was treated by the best physicians, but the malady progressed, and he died after an illness of four months. Olenka was again left a widow.

"To whom have you left me, my darling?" she wailed after the funeral. "How shall I live now without you, wretched creature that I am. Pity me, good people, pity me, fatherless and motherless, all alone in the world!"

She went about dressed in black and weepers, and she gave up wearing hats and gloves for good. She hardly left the house except to go to church and to visit her husband's grave. She almost led the life of a nun.

It was not until six months had passed that she took off the weepers and opened her shutters. She began to go out occasionally in the morning to market with her cook. But how she lived at home and what went on there, could only be surmised. It could be surmised from the fact that she was seen in her little garden drinking tea with the veterinarian while he read the paper out loud to her, and also from the fact that once on meeting an acquaintance at the post-office, she said to her:

"There is no proper veterinary inspection in our town. That is why there is so much disease. You constantly hear of people getting sick from the milk and becoming infected by the horses and cows. The health of domestic animals ought really to be looked after as much as that of human beings."

She repeated the veterinarian's words and held the same opinions as he about everything. It was plain that she could not exist a single year without an attachment, and she found her new happiness in the wing of her house. In any one else this would have been condemned; but no one could think ill of Olenka. Everything in her life was so transparent. She and the veterinary surgeon never spoke about the change in their relations. They tried, in fact, to conceal it, but unsuccessfully; for Olenka could have no secrets. When the surgeon's colleagues from the regiment came to see him, she poured tea, and served the supper, and talked to them about the cattle plague, the hoof and mouth disease, and the municipal slaughter houses. The surgeon was dreadfully embarrassed, and after the visitors had left, he caught her hand and hissed angrily:

"Didn't I ask you not to talk about what you don't understand? When we doctors discuss things, please don't mix in. It's getting to be a nuisance."

She looked at him in astonishment and alarm, and asked:

"But, Volodichka, what *am* I to talk about?" And she threw her arms round his neck, with tears in her eyes, and begged him not to be angry. And they were both happy.

But their happiness was of short duration. The veterinary surgeon went away with his regiment to be gone for good, when it was transferred to some distant place almost as far as Siberia, and Olenka was left alone.

Now she was completely alone. Her father had long been dead, and his armchair lay in the attic covered with dust and minus one leg. She got thin and homely, and the people who met her on the street no longer looked at her as they had used to, nor smiled at her. Evidently her best years were over, past and gone, and a new, dubious life was to begin which it were better not to think about.

In the evening Olenka sat on the steps and heard the music playing and the rockets bursting in the Tivoli; but it no longer aroused any response in her. She looked listlessly into the yard, thought of nothing, wanted nothing, and when night came on, she went to bed and dreamed of nothing but the empty yard. She ate and drank as though by compulsion.

And what was worst of all, she no longer held any opinions. She saw and understood everything that went on around her, but she could not form an opinion about it. She knew of nothing to talk about. And how dreadful not to have opinions! For instance, you see a bottle, or you see that it is raining, or you see a muzhik riding by in a wagon. But what the bottle or the rain or the muzhik are for, or what the sense of them all is, you cannot tell—you cannot tell, not for a thousand rubles. In the days of Kukin and Pustovalov and then of the veterinary surgeon, Olenka had had an explanation for everything, and would have given her opinion freely no matter about what. But now there was the same emptiness in her heart and brain as in her yard. It was as galling and bitter as a taste of wormwood.

Gradually the town grew up all around. The Gypsy Road had become a street, and where the Tivoli and the lumber-yard had been, there were now houses and a row of side streets. How quickly time flies! Olenka's house turned gloomy, the roof rusty, the shed slanting. Dock and thistles overgrew the yard. Olenka herself had aged and grown homely. In the summer she sat on the steps, and her soul was empty and dreary and bitter. When she caught the breath of spring, or when the wind wafted the chime of the cathedral bells, a sudden flood of memories would pour over her, her heart would expand with a tender warmth, and the tears would stream down her cheeks. But that lasted only a moment. Then would come emptiness again, and the feeling, What is the use of living? The black kitten Bryska rubbed up against her and purred softly, but the little creature's caresses left Olenka untouched. That was not what she needed. What she needed was a love that would absorb her whole being, her reason, her whole soul, that would give her ideas, an object in life, that would warm her aging blood. And she shook the black kitten off her skirt angrily, saying:

"Go away! What are you doing here?"

And so day after day, year after year not a single joy, not a single opinion. Whatever Marva, the cook, said was all right.

One hot day in July, towards evening, as the town cattle were being driven by, and the whole yard was filled with clouds of dust, there was suddenly a knocking at the gate. Olenka herself went to open it, and was dumbfounded to behold the veterinarian Smirnov. He had turned grey and was dressed as a civilian. All the old memories flooded into her soul, she could not restrain herself, she burst out crying, and laid her head on Smirnov's breast without saying a word. So overcome was she that she was totally unconscious of how they walked into the house and seated themselves to drink tea.

"My darling!" she murmured, trembling with joy. "Vladimir Platonych, from where has God sent you?"

"I want to settle here for good," he told her. "I have resigned my position and have come here to try my fortune as a free man and lead a settled life. Besides, it's time to send my boy to the gymnasium. He is grown up now. You know, my wife and I have become reconciled."

"Where is she?" asked Olenka.

"At the hotel with the boy. I am looking for lodgings."

"Good gracious, bless you, take my house. Why won't my house do? Oh, dear! Why, I won't ask any rent of you," Olenka burst out in the greatest excitement, and began to cry again. "You live here, and the wing will be enough for me. Oh, Heavens, what a joy!"

The very next day the roof was being painted and the walls whitewashed, and Olenka, arms akimbo, was going about the yard superintending. Her face brightened with her old smile. Her whole being revived and freshened, as though she had awakened from a long sleep. The veterinarian's wife and child arrived. She was a thin, plain woman, with a crabbed expression. The boy Sasha, small for his ten years of age, was a chubby child, with clear blue eyes and dimples in his cheeks. He made for the kitten the instant he entered the yard, and the place rang with his happy laughter.

"Is that your cat, auntie?" he asked Olenka. "When she has little kitties, please give me one. Mama is awfully afraid of mice."

Olenka chatted with him, gave him tea, and there was a sudden warmth in her bosom and a soft gripping at her heart, as though the boy were her own son.

In the evening, when he sat in the dining-room studying his lessons, she looked at him tenderly and whispered to herself:

"My darling, my pretty. You are such a clever child, so good to look at."

"An island is a tract of land entirely surrounded by water," he recited.

"An island is a tract of land," she repeated—the first idea asseverated with conviction after so many years of silence and mental emptiness.

She now had her opinions, and at supper discussed with Sasha's parents how difficult the studies had become for the children at the gymnasium, but how, after all, a classical education was better than a commercial course, because when you graduated from the gymnasium then the road was open to you for any career at all. If you chose to, you could become a doctor, or, if you wanted to, you could become an engineer.

Sasha began to go to the gymnasium. His mother left on a visit to her sister in Kharkov and never came back. The father was away every day inspecting cattle, and sometimes was gone three whole days at a time, so that Sasha, it seemed to Olenka, was utterly abandoned, was treated as if he were quite superfluous, and must be dying of hunger. So she transferred him into the wing along with herself and fixed up a little room for him there.

Every morning Olenka would come into his room and find him sound asleep with his hand tucked under his cheek, so quiet that he seemed not to be breathing. What a shame to have to wake him, she thought.

"Sashenka," she said sorrowingly, "get up, darling. It's time to go to the gymnasium."

He got up, dressed, said his prayers, then sat down to drink tea. He drank three glasses of tea, ate two large cracknels and half a buttered roll. The sleep was not yet out of him, so he was a little cross.

"You don't know your fable as you should, Sashenka," said Olenka, looking at him as though he were departing on a long journey. "What a lot of trouble you are. You must try hard and learn, dear, and mind your teachers."

"Oh, let me alone, please," said Sasha.

Then he went down the street to the gymnasium, a little fellow wearing a large cap and carrying a satchel on his back. Olenka followed him noiselessly.

"Sashenka," she called.

He looked round and she shoved a date or a caramel into his hand. When he reached the street of the gymnasium, he turned around and said, ashamed of being followed by a tall, stout woman: "You had better go home, aunt. I can go the rest of the way myself."

She stopped and stared after him until he had disappeared into the school entrance.

Oh, how she loved him! Not one of her other ties had been so deep. Never before had she given herself so completely, so disinterestedly, so cheerfully as now that her maternal instincts were all aroused. For this boy, who was not hers, for the dimples in his cheeks and for his big cap, she would have given her life, given it with joy and with tears of rapture. Why? Ah, indeed, why?

When she had seen Sasha off to the gymnasium, she returned home quietly, content, serene, overflowing with love. Her face, which had grown younger in the last half year, smiled and beamed. People who met her were pleased as they looked at her.

"How are you, Olga Semyonovna, darling? How are you getting on, darling?"

"The gymnasium course is very hard nowadays," she told at the market. "It's no joke. Yesterday the first class had a fable to learn by heart, a Latin translation, and a problem. How is a little fellow to do all that?"

And she spoke of the teacher and the lessons and the textbooks, repeating exactly what Sasha said about them.

At three o'clock they had dinner. In the evening they prepared the lessons together, and Olenka wept with Sasha over the difficulties. When she put him to bed, she lingered a long time making the sign of the cross over him and muttering a prayer. And when she lay in bed, she dreamed of the faraway, misty future when Sasha would finish his studies and become a doctor or an engineer, have a large house of his own, with horses and a carriage, marry and have children. She would fall asleep still thinking of the same things, and tears would roll down her cheeks from her closed eyes. And the black cat would lie at her side purring: "Mrr, mrr, mrr."

Suddenly there was a loud knocking at the gate. Olenka woke up breathless with fright, her heart beating violently. Half a minute later there was another knock.

"A telegram from Kharkov," she thought, her whole body in a tremble. "His mother wants Sasha to come to her in Kharkov. Oh, great God!"

She was in despair. Her head, her feet, her hands turned cold. There was no unhappier creature in the world, she felt. But another minute passed, she heard voices. It was the veterinarian coming home from the club.

"Thank God," she thought. The load gradually fell from her heart, she was at ease again. And she went back to bed, thinking of Sasha who lay fast asleep in the next room and sometimes cried out in his sleep:

"I'll give it to you! Get away! Quit your scrapping!"

Robert Louis Stevenson *(1850–1894)*

A LODGING FOR THE NIGHT

It was late in November, 1456. The snow fell over Paris with rigorous, relentless persistency; sometimes the wind made a sally and scattered it in flying vortices; sometimes there was a lull, and flake after flake descended out of the black night air, silent, circuitous, interminable. To poor people, looking up under moist eyebrows, it seemed a wonder where it all came from. Master Francis Villon had propounded an alternative that afternoon, at a tavern window: was it only Pagan Jupiter plucking geese upon Olympus? or were the holy angels moulting? He was only a poor Master of Arts, he went on; and as the questions somewhat touched upon divinity, he durst not venture to conclude. A silly old priest from Montargis, who was among the company, treated the young rascal to a bottle of wine in honor of the jest and grimaces with which it was accompanied, and swore on his own white beard that he had been just such another irreverent dog when he was Villon's age.

The air was raw and pointed, but not far below freezing; and the flakes were large, damp, and adhesive. The whole city was sheeted up. An army might have marched from end to end and not a footfall given the alarm. If there were any belated birds in heaven, they saw the island like a large white patch, and the bridges like slim white spars, on the black ground of the river. High up overhead the snow settled among the tracery of the cathedral towers. Many a niche was drifted full; many a statue wore a long white bonnet on its grotesque or sainted head. The gargoyles had been transformed into great false noses, drooping towards the point. The crockets were like upright pillows swollen on one side. In the intervals of the wind, there was a dull sound of dripping about the precincts of the church.

The cemetery of St. John had taken its own share of the snow. All the graves were decently covered; tall white house-tops stood around in grave array; worthy burghers were long ago in bed, benightcapped like their domiciles, there was no light in all the neighborhood but a little peep from a lamp that hung swinging in the church choir, and tossed the shadows to and fro in time to its oscillations. The clock was hard on ten when the patrol went by with halberds and a lantern, beating their hands; and they saw nothing suspicious about the cemetery of St. John.

Yet there was a small house, backed up against the ceme-tery wall, which was still awake, and awake to evil purpose, in that snoring district. There was not much to betray it from without; only a stream of warm vapor from the chim-ney-top, a patch where the snow melted on the roof, and a few half-obliterated footprints at the door. But within, be-hind the shuttered windows, Master Francis Villon, the poet, and some of the thievish crew with whom he consorted, were keeping the night alive and passing round the bottle.

A great pile of living embers diffused a strong and ruddy glow from the arched chimney. Before this straddled Dom Nicolas, the Picardy monk, with his skirts picked up and his fat legs bared to the comfortable warmth. His dilated shadow cut the room in half; and the firelight only escaped on either side of his broad person, and in a little pool be-tween his outspread feet. His face had the beery, bruised appearance of the continual drinker's; it was covered with a network of congested veins, purple in ordinary circum-stances, but now pale violet, for even with his back to the fire the cold pinched him on the other side. His cowl had half fallen back, and made a strange excrescence on either side of his bull neck. So he straddled, grumbling, and cut the room in half with the shadow of his portly frame.

On the right, Villon and Guy Tabary were huddled to-gether over a scrap of parchment; Villon making a ballade which he was to call the "Ballade of Roast Fish," with Tabary spluttering admiration at his shoulder. The poet was a rag of a man, dark, little, and lean, with hollow cheeks and thin black locks. He carried his four-and-twenty years with feverish animation. Greed had made folds about his eyes, evil smiles had puckered his mouth. The wolf and pig struggled together in his face. It was an eloquent, sharp, ugly, earthly countenance. His hands were small and prehensile, with fingers knotted like a cord; and they were continually flickering in front of him in violent and expressive pantomime. As for Tabary, a broad, complacent, admiring imbecility breathed from his squash nose and slobbering lips: he had become a thief, just as he might have become the most decent of burgesses, by the imperious chance that rules the lives of human geese and human donkeys.

At the monk's other hand, Montigny and Thevenin Pensete played a game of chance. About the first there clung some flavor of good birth and training, as about a fallen angel; something long, lithe, and courtly in the person; something aquiline and darkling in the face. Thevenin, poor soul, was in great feather: he had done a good stroke of knavery that afternoon in the Faubourg St. Jacques, and all night he had been gaining from Montigny. A flat smile illuminated his face; his bald head shone rosily in a garland of red curls; his little protuberant stomach shook with silent chucklings as he swept in his gains.

"Doubles or quits?" said Thevenin.

Montigny nodded grimly.

"*Some may prefer to dine in state,*" wrote Villon. "*On bread and cheese on silver plate.* Or, or—help me out, Guido!"

Tabary giggled.

"*Or parsley on a golden dish,*" scribbled the poet.

The wind was freshening without; it drove the snow before it, and sometimes raised its voice in a victorious whoop, and made sepulchral grumblings in the chimney. The cold was growing sharper as the night went on. Villon, protruding his lips, imitated the gust with something between a whistle and a groan. It was an eerie, uncomfortable talent of the poet's, much detested by the Picardy monk.

"Can't you hear it rattle in the gibbet?" said Villon. "They are all dancing the devil's jig on nothing, up there. You may dance, my gallants, you'll be none the warmer! Whew! what a gust! Down went somebody just now! A medlar the fewer on the three-legged medlar-tree—I say,

Dom Nicolas, it'll be cold to-night on the St. Denis Road?" he asked.

Dom Nicolas winked both his big eyes, and seemed to choke upon his Adam's apple. Montfaucon, the great grisly Paris gibbet, stood hard by the St. Denis Road, and the pleasantry touched him on the raw. As for Tabary, he laughed immoderately over the medlars; he had never heard anything more light-hearted; and he held his sides and crowed. Villon fetched him a fillip on the nose, which turned his mirth into an attack of coughing.

"Oh, stop that row," said Villon, "and think of rhymes to 'fish.'"

"Doubles or quits," said Montigny doggedly.

"With all my heart," quoth Thevenin.

"Is there any more in that bottle?" asked the monk.

"Open another," said Villon. "How do you ever hope to fill that big hogshead, your body, with little things like bottles? And how do you expect to get to heaven? How many angels, do you fancy, can be spared to carry up a single monk from Picardy? Or do you think yourself another Elias—and they'll send the coach for you?"

"*Hominibus impossibile,*" replied the monk as he filled his glass. Tabary was in ecstasies.

Villon filliped his nose again.

"Laugh at my jokes, if you like," he said.

"It was very good," objected Tabary.

Villon made a face at him. "Think of rhymes to 'fish,'" he said. "What have you to do with Latin? You'll wish you knew none of it at the great assizes, when the devil calls for Guido Tabary, clericus—the devil with the hump-back and red-hot finger-nails. Talking of the devil," he added in a whisper, "look at Montigny!"

All three peered covertly at the gamester. He did not seem to be enjoying his luck. His mouth was a little to a side; one nostril nearly shut, and the other much inflated. The black dog was on his back, as people say, in terrifying nursery metaphor; and he breathed hard under the gruesome burden.

"He looks as if he could knife him," whispered Tabary, with round eyes.

The monk shuddered, and turned his face and spread his open hands to the red embers. It was the cold that thus affected Dom Nicolas, and not any excess of moral sensibility.

"Come now," said Villon—"about this ballade. How does it run so far?" And beating time with his hand, he read it aloud to Tabary.

They were interrupted at the fourth rhyme by a brief and fatal movement among the gamesters. The round was completed, and Thevenin was just opening his mouth to claim another victory, when Montigny leaped up, swift as an adder, and stabbed him to the heart. The blow took effect before he had time to utter a cry, before he had time to move. A tremor or two convulsed his frame; his hands opened and shut, his heels rattled on the floor; then his head rolled backward over one shoulder with the eyes wide open; and Thevenin Pensete's spirit had returned to Him who made it.

Every one sprang to his feet; but the business was over in two twos. The four living fellows looked at each other in rather a ghastly fashion; the dead man contemplating a corner of the roof with a singular and ugly leer.

"My God!" said Tabary; and he began to pray in Latin.

Villon broke out into hysterical laughter. He came a step forward and ducked a ridiculous bow at Thevenin, and laughed still louder. Then he sat down suddenly, all of a heap, upon a stool, and continued laughing bitterly, as though he would shake himself to pieces.

Montigny recovered his composure first.

"Let's see what he has about him," he remarked, and he picked the dead man's pockets with a practised hand, and divided the money into four equal portions on the table.

"There's for you," he said.

The monk received his share with a deep sigh, and a single stealthy glance at the dead Thevenin, who was beginning to sink into himself and topple sideways off the chair.

"We're all in for it," cried Villon, swallowing his mirth. "It's a hanging job for every man jack of us that's here—not to speak of those who aren't." He made a shocking gesture in the air with his raised right hand, and put out his tongue and threw his head on one side, so as to counterfeit the appearance of one who has been hanged. Then he pocketed his share of the spoil, and executed a shuffle with his feet as if to restore the circulation.

Tabary was the last to help himself; he made a dash at the money, and retired to the other end of the apartment.

Montigny stuck Thevenin upright in the chair, and drew out the dagger, which was followed by a jet of blood.

"You fellows had better be moving," he said, as he wiped the blade on his victim's doublet.

"I think we had," returned Villon, with a gulp. "Damn his fat head!" he broke out. "It sticks in my throat like phlegm. What right has a man to have red hair when he is dead?" And he fell all of a heap again upon the stool, and fairly covered his face with his hands.

Montigny and Dom Nicolas laughed aloud, even Tabary feebly chiming in.

"Cry baby," said the monk.

"I always said he was a woman," added Montigny, with a sneer. "Sit up, can't you?" he went on, giving another shake to the murdered body. "Tread out the fire, Nick!"

But Nick was better employed; he was quietly taking Villon's purse, as the poet sat, limp and trembling, on the stool where he had been making a ballade not three minutes before. Montigny and Tabary dumbly demanded a share of the booty, which the monk silently promised as he passed the little bag into the bosom of his gown. In many ways an artistic nature unfits a man for practical existence.

No sooner had the theft been accomplished than Villon shook himself, jumped to his feet, and began helping to scatter and extinguish the embers. Meanwhile Montigny opened the door and cautiously peered into the street. The coast was clear; there was no meddlesome patrol in sight. Still it was judged wiser to slip out severally; and as Villon was himself in a hurry to escape from the neighbourhood of the dead Thevenin, and the rest were in a still greater hurry to get rid of him before he should discover the loss of his money, he was the first by general consent to issue forth into the street.

The wind had triumphed and swept all the clouds from

heaven. Only a few vapours, as thin as moonlight, fleeted rapidly across the stars. It was bitter cold; and by a common optical effect, things seemed almost more definite than in the broadest daylight. The sleeping city was absolutely still; a company of white hoods, a field full of little alps, below the twinkling stars. Villon cursed his fortune. Would it were still snowing! Now, wherever he went, he left an indelible trail behind him on the glittering streets; wherever he went he was still tethered to the house by the cemetery of St. John; wherever he went he must weave, with his own plodding feet, the rope that bound him to the crime and would bind him to the gallows. The leer of the dead man came back to him with a new significance. He snapped his fingers as if to pluck up his own spirits, and choosing a street at random, stepped boldly forward in the snow.

Two things preoccupied him as he went: the aspect of the gallows at Montfaucon in this bright, windy phase of the night's existence, for one; and for another, the look of the dead man with his bald head and garland of red curls. Both struck cold upon his heart, and he kept quickening his pace as if he could escape from unpleasant thoughts by mere fleetness of foot. Sometimes he looked back over his shoulder with a sudden nervous jerk; but he was the only moving thing in the white streets, except when the wind swooped round a corner and threw up the snow, which was beginning to freeze, in spouts of glittering dust.

Suddenly he saw, a long way before him, a black clump and a couple of lanterns. The clump was in motion, and the lanterns swung as though carried by men walking. It was a patrol. And though it was merely crossing his line of march he judged it wiser to get out of eyeshot as speedily as he could. He was not in the humor to be challenged, and he was conscious of making a very conspicuous mark upon the snow. Just on his left hand there stood a great hotel, with some turrets and a large porch before the door; it was half ruinous, he remembered, and had long stood empty; and so he made three steps of it, and jumped into the shelter of the porch. It was pretty dark inside, after the glimmer of the snowy streets, and he was groping forward with outspread hands, when he stumbled over some substance which offered an indescribable mixture of resistances, hard and soft, firm and loose. His heart gave a leap, and he sprang two steps back and stared dreadfully at the obstacle. Then he gave a little laugh of relief. It was only a woman, and she dead. He knelt beside her to make sure upon this latter point. She was freezing cold, and rigid like a stick. A little ragged finery fluttered in the wind about her hair, and her cheeks had been heavily rouged that same afternoon. Her pockets were quite empty; but in her stocking, underneath the garter, Villon found two of the small coins that went by the name of whites. It was little enough; but it was always something; and the poet was moved with a deep sense of pathos that she should have died before she had spent her money. That seemed to him a dark and pitiable mystery; and he looked from the coins in his hand to the dead woman, and back again to the coins, shaking his head over the riddle of man's life. Henry V of England, dying at Vincennes just after he had conquered France, and this poor jade cut off by a cold draught in a great man's doorway, before she had time to spend her couple of whites—it seemed a cruel way to carry on the world. Two whites would have taken such a little while to squander; and yet it would have been one more good taste in the mouth, one more smack of the lips, before the devil got the soul, and the body was left to birds and vermin. He would like to use all his tallow before the light was blown out and the lantern broken.

While these thoughts were passing through his mind, he was feeling, half mechanically, for his purse. Suddenly his heart stopped beating; a feeling of cold scales passed up the back of his legs, and a cold blow seemed to fall upon his scalp. He stood petrified for a moment; then he felt again with one feverish movement; and then his loss burst upon him, and he was covered at once with perspiration. To spendthrifts money is so living and actual—it is such a thin veil between them and their pleasures! There is only one limit to their fortune—that of time; and a spendthrift with only a few crowns is the Emperor of Rome until they are spent. For such a person to lose his money is to suffer the most shocking reverse, and fall from heaven to hell, from all to nothing, in a breath. And all the more if he has put his head in the halter for it; if he may be hanged to-morrow for that same purse, so dearly earned, so foolishly departed! Villon stood and cursed; he threw the two whites into the street; he shook his fist at heaven; he stamped, and was not horrified to find himself trampling the poor corpse. Then he began rapidly to retrace his steps towards the house beside the cemetery. He had forgotten all fear of the patrol, which was long gone by at any rate, and had no idea but that of his lost purse. It was in vain that he looked right and left upon the snow: nothing was to be seen. He had not dropped it in the streets. Had it fallen in the house? He would have liked dearly to go in and see; but the idea of the grisly occupant unmanned him. And he saw besides, as he drew near, that their efforts to put out the fire had been unsuccessful; on the contrary, it had broken into a blaze, and a changeful light played in the chinks of door and window, and revived his terror for the authorities and Paris gibbet.

He returned to the hotel with the porch, and groped about upon the snow for the money he had thrown away in his childish passion. But he could only find one white; the other had probably struck sideways and sunk deeply in. With a single white in his pocket, all his projects for a rousing night in some wild tavern vanished utterly away. And it was not only pleasure that fled laughing from his grasp; positive discomfort, positive pain, attacked him as he stood ruefully before the porch. His perspiration had dried upon him; and although the wind had now fallen, a binding frost was setting in stronger with every hour, and he felt benumbed and sick at heart. What was to be done? Late as was the hour, improbable as was success, he would try the house of his adopted father, the chaplain of St. Benoit.

He ran there all the way, and knocked timidly. There was no answer. He knocked again and again, taking heart with every stroke; and at last steps were heard approaching from within. A barred wicket fell open in the iron-studded door, and emitted a gush of yellow light. "Hold up your face to the wicket," said the chaplain from within.

"It's only me," whimpered Villon.

"Oh, it's only you, is it?" returned the chaplain; and he

cursed him with foul unpriestly oaths for disturbing him at such an hour, and bade him be off to hell, where he came from.

"My hands are blue to the wrist," pleaded Villon; "my feet are dead and full of twinges; my nose aches with the sharp air; the cold lies at my heart. I may be dead before morning. Only this once, father, and before God, I will never ask again!"

"You should have come earlier," said the ecclesiastic coolly. "Young men require a lesson now and then." He shut the wicket and retired deliberately into the interior of the house.

Villon was beside himself; he beat upon the door with his hands and feet, and shouted hoarsely after the chaplain.

"Wormy old fox!" he cried. "If I had my hand under your twist, I would send you flying headlong into the bottomless pit."

A door shut in the interior, faintly audible to the poet down long passages. He passed his hand over his mouth with an oath. And then the humor of the situation struck him, and he laughed and looked lightly up to heaven, where the stars seemed to be winking over his discomfiture.

What was to be done? It looked very like a night in the frosty streets. The idea of the dead woman popped into his imagination, and gave him a hearty fright; what had happened to her in the early night might very well happen to him before morning. And he so young! and with such immense possibilities of disorderly amusement before him! He felt quite pathetic over the notion of his own fate, as if it had been some one else's, and made a little imaginative vignette of the scene in the morning when they should find his body.

He passed all his chances under review, turning the white between his thumb and forefinger. Unfortunately he was on bad terms with some old friends who would once have taken pity on him in such a plight. He had lampooned them in verses; he had beaten and cheated them; and yet, now, when he was in so close a pinch, he thought there was at least one who might perhaps relent. It was a chance. It was worth trying at least, and he would go and see.

On the way, two little accidents happened to him which colored his musings in a very different manner. For, first, he fell in with the track of a patrol, and walked in it for some hundred yards, although it lay out of his direction. And this spirited him up; at least he had confused his trail; for he was still possessed with the idea of people tracking him all about Paris over the snow, and collaring him next morning before he was awake. The other matter affected him quite differently. He passed a street corner, where, not so long before, a woman and her child had been devoured by wolves. This was just the kind of weather, he reflected, when wolves might take it into their heads to enter Paris again; and a lone man in these deserted streets would run the chance of something worse than a mere scare. He stopped and looked upon the place with an unpleasant interest—it was a center where several lanes intersected each other, and held his breath to listen, lest he should detect some galloping black things on the snow or hear the sound of howling between him and the river. He remembered his mother telling him the story and pointing out the spot, while he was yet a child. His mother! If he only knew where she lived, he might make sure at least of shelter. He determined he would inquire upon the morrow; nay, he would go and see her too, poor old girl! So thinking, he arrived at his destination—his last hope for the night.

The house was quite dark, like its neighbors; and yet after a few taps, he heard a movement overhead, a door opening, and a cautious voice asking who was there. The poet named himself in a loud whisper, and waited, not without some trepidation, the result. Nor had he to wait long. A window was suddenly opened, and a pailful of slop splashed down upon the door-step. Villon had not been unprepared for something of the sort, and had put himself as much in shelter as the nature of the porch admitted; but for all that, he was deplorably drenched below the waist. His hose began to freeze almost at once. Death from cold and exposure stared him in the face; he remembered he was of phthisical tendency, and began coughing tentatively. But the gravity of the danger steadied his nerves. He stopped a few hundred yards from the door where he had been so rudely used, and reflected with his finger to his nose. He could only see one way of getting a lodging, and that was to take it. He had noticed a house not far away, which looked as if it might be easily broken into, and thither he betook himself promptly, entertaining himself on the way with the idea of a room still hot, with a table still loaded with the remains of supper, where he might pass the rest of the black hours and whence he should issue, on the morrow, with an armful of valuable plate. He even considered on what viands and what wines he should prefer; and as he was calling the roll of his favorite dainties, roast fish presented itself to his mind with an odd mixture of amusement and horror.

"I shall never finish that ballade," he thought to himself; and then, with another shudder at the recollection, "Oh, damn his fat head!" he repeated fervently, and spat upon the snow.

The house in question looked dark at first sight; but as Villon made a preliminary inspection in search of the handiest point of attack, a little twinkle of light caught his eye from behind a curtained window.

"The devil!" he thought. "People awake! Some student or some saint, confound the crew! Can't they get drunk and lie in bed snoring like their neighbors? What's the good of curfew, and poor devils of bell-ringers jumping at a rope's end in bell-towers? What's the use of day, if people sit up all night? The gripes to them!" He grinned as he saw where his logic was leading him. "Every man to his business, after all," added he, "and if they're awake, by the Lord, I may come by a supper honestly for once, and cheat the devil."

He went boldly to the door and knocked with an assured hand. On both previous occasions, he had knocked timidly and with some dread of attracting notice; but now when he had just discarded the thought of a burglarious entry, knocking at a door seemed a mighty simple and innocent proceeding. The sound of his blows echoed through the house with thin, phantasmal reverberations, as tho it were quite empty; but these had scarcely died away before a measured tread drew near, a couple of bolts were withdrawn, and one wing was opened broadly, as tho no guile or fear of guile were known to those within. A tall figure of a man, muscular and spare, but a little bent, confronted Villon. The head was massive in bulk, but finely sculptured; the nose blunt at the bottom, but refining upward to where it joined a pair of strong and honest eyebrows; the mouth and eyes surrounded with delicate markings, and the whole face based upon a thick white beard, boldly and squarely trimmed. Seen as it was by the light of a flickering hand-lamp, it looked perhaps nobler than it had a right to do; but it was a fine face, honorable rather than intelligent, strong, simple, and right-eous.

"You knock late, sir," said the old man in resonant, courteous tones.

Villon cringed and brought up many servile words of apology; at a crisis of this sort the beggar was uppermost in him, and the man of genius hid his head with confusion.

"You are cold," repeated the old man, "and hungry? Well, step in." And he ordered him into the house with a noble enough gesture.

"Some great seigneur," thought Villon, as his host, setting down the lamp on the flagged pavement of the entry, shot the bolts once more into their places.

"You will pardon me if I go in front," he said, when this was done; and he preceded the poet upstairs into a large apartment, warmed with a pan of charcoal and lit by a great lamp hanging from the roof. It was very bare of furniture: only some gold plate on a sideboard; some folios; and a stand of armor between the windows. Some smart tapestry hung upon the walls, representing the crucifixion of our Lord in one piece, and in another a scene of shepherds and shepherdesses by a running stream. Over the chimney was a shield of arms.

"Will you seat yourself," said the old man, "and forgive me if I leave you? I am alone in my house tonight, and if you are to eat I must forage for you myself."

No sooner was his host gone than Villon leaped from the chair on which he had just seated himself, and began examining the room, with the stealth and passion of a cat. He weighed the gold flagons in his hands, opened all the folios, and investigated the arms upon the shield, and the stuff with which the seats were lined. He raised the window curtains, and saw that the windows were set with rich stained glass in figures, so far as he could see, of martial import. Then he stood in the middle of the room, drew a long breath, and retaining it with puffed cheeks, looked round and round him, turning on his heels, as if to impress every feature of the apartment on his memory.

"Seven pieces of plate," he said. "If there had been ten, I would have risked it. A fine house, and a fine old master, so help me all the saints!"

And just then, hearing the old man's tread returning along the corridor, he stole back to his chair, and began humbly toasting his wet legs before the charcoal pan.

His entertainer had a plate of meat in one hand and a jug of wine in the other. He set down the plate upon the table, motioning Villon to draw in his chair, and going to the sideboard, brought back two goblets which he filled.

"I drink to your better fortune," he said, gravely touching Villon's cup with his own.

"To our better acquaintance," said the poet, growing bold. A mere man of the people would have been awed by the courtesy of the old seigneur, but Villon was hardened in that matter, he had made mirth for great lords before now, and found them as black rascals as himself. And so he devoted himself to the viands with a ravenous gusto, while the old man, leaning backward, watched him with steady, curious eyes.

"You have blood on your shoulder, my man," he said.

Montigny must have laid his wet right hand upon him as he left the house. He cursed Montigny in his heart.

"It was none of my shedding," he stammered.

"I had not supposed so," returned his host quietly. "A brawl?"

"Well, something of that sort," Villon admitted with a quaver.

"Perhaps a fellow murdered?"

"Oh, no, not murdered," said the poet, more and more confused. "It was all fair play—murdered by accident. I had no hand in it, God strike me dead!" he added fervently.

"One rogue fewer, I dare say," observed the master of the house.

"You may dare to say that," agreed Villon, infinitely relieved. "As big a rogue as there is between here and Jerusalem. He turned up his toes like a lamb. But it was a nasty
thing to look at. I dare say you've seen dead men in your
time, my lord?" he added glancing at the armor.

"Many," said the old man. "I have followed the wars, as
you imagine."

Villon laid down his knife and fork, which he had just
taken up again.

"Were any of them bald?" he asked.

"Oh, yes, and with hair as white as mine."

"I don't think I should mind the white so much," said
Villon. "His was red." And he had a return of his shuddering
and tendency to laughter, which he drowned with a great
draught of wine. "I'm a little put out when I think of it,"
he went on. "I knew him—damn him! And then the cold
gives a man fancies—or the fancies give a man cold, I don't
know which."

"Have you any money?" asked the old man.

"I have one white," returned the poet, laughing. "I got it
out of a dead jade's stocking in a porch. She was as dead as
Cæsar, poor wench, and as cold as a church, with bits of
ribbon sticking in her hair. This is a hard world in winter
for wolves and wenches and poor rogues like me."

"I," said the old man, "am Enguerrand de la Feuillée,
seigneur de Brisetout, bailly du Patatrac. Who and what
may you be?"

Villon rose and made a suitable reverence. "I am called
Francis Villon," he said, "a poor Master of Arts of this university. I know some Latin, and a great deal of vice. I can
make chansons, ballades, lais, virelais, and roundels, and I
am very fond of wine. I was born in a garret, and I shall not
improbably die upon the gallows. I may add, my lord, that
from this night forward I am your lordship's very obsequious
servant to command."

"No servant of mine," said the knight; "my guest for this
evening, and no more."

"A very grateful guest," said Villon politely, and he drank
in dumb show to his entertainer.

"You are shrewd," began the old man, tapping his forehead, "very shrewd; you have learning; you are a clerk; and yet you take a small piece of money off a dead woman in the street. Is it not a kind of theft?"

"It is a kind of theft much practised in the wars, my lord."

"The wars are the field of honor," returned the old man proudly. "There a man plays his life upon the cast; he fights in the name of his lord the king, his Lord God, and all their lordships the holy saints and angels."

"Put it," said Villon, "that I were really a thief, should I not play my life also, and against heavier odds?"

"For gain but not for honor."

"Gain?" repeated Villon with a shrug. "Gain! The poor fellow wants supper, and takes it. So does the soldier in a campaign. Why, what are all these requisitions we hear so much about? If they are not gain to those who take them, they are loss enough to the others. The men-at-arms drink by a good fire, while the burgher bites his nails to buy them wine and wood. I have seen a good many plowmen swinging on trees about the country; ay, I have seen thirty on one elm, and a very poor figure they made; and when I asked some one how all these came to be hanged, I was told it was because they could not scrape together enough crowns to satisfy the men-at-arms."

"These things are a necessity of war, which the low-born must endure with constancy. It is true that some captains drive overhard; there are spirits in every rank not easily moved by pity; and indeed many follow arms who are no better than brigands."

"You see," said the poet, "you cannot separate the soldier from the brigand; and what is a thief but an isolated brigand with circumspect manners? I steal a couple of mutton chops, without so much as disturbing people's sleep; the farmer grumbles a bit, but sups none the less wholesomely on what remains. You come up blowing gloriously on a trumpet, take away the whole sheep, and beat the farmer pitifully into the bargain. I have no trumpet; I am only Tom, Dick, or Harry; I am a rogue and a dog, and hanging's too good for me—with all my heart; but just ask the farmer which of us he prefers, just find out which of us he lies awake to curse on cold nights."

"Look at us two," said his lordship. "I am old, strong, and honored. If I were turned from my house to-morrow, hundreds would be proud to shelter me. Poor people would go out and pass the night in the streets with their children, if I merely hinted that I wished to be alone. And I find you up, wandering homeless, and picking farthings off dead women by the wayside! I fear no man and nothing; I have seen you tremble and lose countenance at a word. I wait God's summons contentedly in my own house, or, if it please the king to call me out again, upon the field of battle. You look for the gallows; a rough, swift death, without hope or honor. Is there no difference between these two?"

"As far as to the moon," Villon acquiesced. "But if I had been born lord of Brisetout, and you had been the poor scholar Francis, would the difference have been any the less? Should not I have been warming my knees at this charcoal pan, and would not you have been groping for farthings in the snow? Should not I have been the soldier, and you the thief?"

"A thief?" cried the old man. "I a thief! If you understood your words, you would repent them."

Villon turned out his hands with a gesture of inimitable impudence. "If your lordship had done me the honor to follow my argument!" he said.

"I do you too much honor in submitting to your presence," said the knight. "Learn to curb your tongue when you speak with old and honorable men, or some one hastier than I may reprove you in a sharper fashion." And he rose and paced the lower end of the apartment, struggling with anger and antipathy. Villon surreptitiously refilled his cup, and settled himself more comfortably in the chair, crossing his knees and leaning his head upon one hand and the elbow against the back of the chair. He was now replete and warm; and he was in nowise frightened for his host, having gaged him as justly as was possible between two such different characters. The night was far spent, and in a very comfortable fashion after all; and he felt morally certain of a safe departure on the morrow.

"Tell me one thing," said the old man, pausing in his walk. "Are you really a thief?"

"I claim the sacred rights of hospitality," returned the poet. "My lord, I am."

"You are very young," the knight continued.

"I should never have been so old," replied Villon, showing his fingers, "if I had not helped myself with these ten talents. They have been my nursing mothers and my nursing fathers."

"You may still repent and change."

"I repent daily," said the poet. "There are few people more given to repentance than poor Francis. As for change, let somebody change my circumstances. A man must continue to eat, if it were only that he may continue to repent."

"The change must begin in the heart," returned the old man solemnly.

"My dear lord," answered Villon, "do you really fancy that I steal for pleasure? I hate stealing, like any other piece of work or of danger. My teeth chatter when I see a gallows. But I must eat, I must drink, I must mix in society of some sort. What the devil! Man is not a solitary animal—*Cui Deus fœminam tradit*. Make me king's pantler—make me abbot of St. Denis; make me bailly of the Patatrac; and then I shall be changed indeed. But as long as you leave me the poor scholar Francis Villon, without a farthing, why, of course, I remain the same."

"The grace of God is all-powerful."

"I should be a heretic to question it," said Francis. "It has made you lord of Brisetout and bailly of the Patatrac; it has given me nothing but the quick wits under my hat and these ten toes upon my hands. May I help myself to wine? I thank you respectfully. By God's grace, you have a very superior vintage."

The lord of Brisetout walked to and fro with his hands behind his back. Perhaps he was not yet quite settled in his mind about the parallel between thieves and soldiers; perhaps Villon had interested him by some cross-thread of sympathy; perhaps his wits were simply muddled by so much unfamiliar reasoning; but whatever the cause, he somehow yearned to convert the young man to a better way of thinking, and could not make up his mind to drive him forth again into the street.

"There is something more than I can understand in this," he said at length. "Your mouth is full of subtleties, and the devil has led you very far astray; but the devil is only a very weak spirit before God's truth, and all his subtleties vanish at a word of true honor, like darkness at morning. Listen to me once more. I learned long ago that a gentleman should live chivalrously and lovingly to God, and the king, and his lady; and though I have seen many strange things done, I have still striven to command my ways upon that rule. It is not only written in all noble histories, but in every man's heart, if he will take care to read. You speak of food and wine, and I know very well that hunger is a difficult trial to endure; but you do not speak of other wants; you say nothing of honor, of faith to God and other men, of courtesy, of love without reproach. It may be that I am not very wise—and yet I think I am—but you seem to me like one who has lost his way and made a great error in life. You are attending to the little wants, and you have totally forgotten the great and only real ones, like a man who should be doctoring toothache on the Judgment Day. For such things as honor and love and faith are not only nobler than food and drink, but indeed I think we desire them more, and suffer more sharply for their absence. I speak to you as I think you will most easily understand me. Are you not, while careful to fill your belly, disregarding another appetite in your heart, which spoils the pleasure of your life and keeps you continually wretched?"

Villon was sensibly nettled under all this sermonizing. "You think I have no sense of honor!" he cried. "I'm poor enough, God knows! It's hard to see rich people with their gloves, and you blowing in your hands. An empty belly is a bitter thing, altho you speak so lightly of it. If you had had as many as I, perhaps you would change your tune. Anyway I'm a thief—make the most of that—but I'm not a devil from hell, God strike me dead. I would have you to know I've an honor of my own, as good as yours, though I don't prate about it all day long, as if it was a God's miracle to have any. It seems quite natural to me; I keep it in its box till it's wanted. Why now, look you here, how long have I been in this room with you? Did you not tell me you were alone in the house? Look at your gold plate! You're strong, if you like, but you're old and unarmed, and I have my knife. What did I want but a jerk of the elbow and here would have been you with the cold steel in your bowels, and there would have been me, linking in the streets, with an armful of golden cups! Did you suppose I hadn't wit enough to see that? And I scorned the action. There are your damned goblets, as safe as in a church; there are you, with your heart ticking as good as new; and here am I, ready to go out again as poor as I came in, with my one white that you threw in my teeth! And you think I have no sense of honor—God strike me dead!"

The old man stretched out his right arm. "I will tell you what you are," he said. "You are a rogue, my man, an impudent and black-hearted rogue and vagabond. I have passed an hour with you. Oh! believe me, I feel myself disgraced! And you have eaten and drunk at my table. But now I am sick at your presence; the day has come, and the night-bird should be off to his roost. Will you go before, or after?"

"Which you please," returned the poet, rising. "I believe you to be strictly honorable." He thoughtfully emptied his cup. "I wish I could add you were intelligent," he went on, knocking on his head with his knuckles. "Age! age! the brains stiff and rheumatic."

The old man preceded him from a point of self-respect. Villon followed, whistling, with his thumbs in his girdle.

"God pity you," said the lord of Brisetout at the door.

"Good-bye, papa," returned Villon with a yawn. "Many thanks for the cold mutton."

The door closed behind him. The dawn was breaking over the white roofs. A chill, uncomfortable morning ushered in the day. Villon stood and heartily stretched himself in the middle of the road.

"A very dull old gentleman," he thought. "I wonder what his goblets may be worth."

Guy de Maupassant *(1850–1893)*

THE NECKLACE

Translated by Ernest Boyd

SHE WAS one of those pretty and charming girls born, as though fate had blundered over her, into a family of artisans. She had no marriage portion, no expectations, no means of getting known, understood, loved, and wedded by a man of wealth and distinction; and she let herself be married off to a little clerk in the Ministry of Education.

Her tastes were simple because she had never been able to afford any other, but she was as unhappy as though she had married beneath her; for women have no caste or class, their beauty, grace, and charm serving them for birth or family. Their natural delicacy, their instinctive elegance, their nimbleness of wit, are their only mark of rank, and put the slum girl on a level with the highest lady in the land.

She suffered endlessly, feeling herself born for every delicacy and luxury. She suffered from the poorness of her house, from its mean walls, worn chairs, and ugly curtains. All these things, of which other women of her class would not even have been aware, tormented and insulted her. The sight of the little Breton girl who came to do the work in her little house aroused heart-broken regrets and hopeless dreams in her mind. She imagined silent antechambers, heavy with Oriental tapestries, lit by torches in lofty bronze sockets, with two tall footmen in knee-breeches sleeping in large armchairs, overcome by the heavy warmth of the stove. She imagined vast salons hung with antique silks, exquisite pieces of furniture supporting priceless ornaments, and small, charming, perfumed rooms, created just for little parties of intimate friends, men who were famous and sought after, whose homage roused every other woman's envious longings.

When she sat down for dinner at the round table covered with a three-days-old cloth, opposite her husband, who took the cover off the soup tureen, exclaimed delightedly: "Aha! Scotch broth! There's nothing better," she imagined delicate meals, gleaming silver, tapestries peopling the walls with folk of a past age and strange birds in faery forest; she imagined delicate food served in marvellous dishes, murmured gallantries, listened to with an inscrutable smile as one trifled with the rosy flesh of trout or wings of asparagus chicken.

She had no clothes, no jewels, nothing. And these were the only things she loved; she felt that she was made for them. She had longed so eagerly to charm, to be desired, to be wildly attractive and sought after.

She had a rich friend, an old school friend whom she refused to visit, because she suffered so keenly when she returned home. She would weep whole days, with grief, regret, despair, and misery.

One evening her husband came home with an exultant air, holding a large envelope in his hand.

"Here's something for you," he said.

Swiftly she tore the paper and drew out a printed card on which were these words: *The Minister of Education and Madame Ramponneau request the pleasure of the company of Monsieur and Madame Loisel at the Ministry on the evening of Monday, January the 18th.*

Instead of being delighted, as her husband hoped, she flung the invitation petulantly across the table, murmuring:

"What do you want me to do with this?"

"Why, darling, I thought you'd be pleased. You never go out, and this is a great occasion. I had tremendous trouble to get it. Everyone wants one; it's very select, and very few go to the clerks. You'll see all the really big people there."

She looked at him out of furious eyes, and said impatiently:

"And what do you suppose I am to wear at such an affair?"

He had not thought about it; he stammered:

"Why, the dress you go to the theatre in. It looks very nice, to me. . . ."

He stopped, stupefied and utterly at a loss when he saw that his wife was beginning to cry. Two large tears ran slowly down from the corners of her eyes towards the corners of her mouth.

"What's the matter with you? What's the matter with you?" he faltered.

But with a violent effort she overcame her grief and replied in a calm voice, wiping her wet cheeks:

"Nothing. Only I haven't a dress and so I can't go to this party. Give your invitation to some friend of yours whose wife will be turned out better than I shall."

He was heart-broken.

"Look here, Mathilde," he persisted. "What would be the cost of a suitable dress, which you could use on other occasions as well, something very simple?"

She thought for several seconds, reckoning up prices and also wondering for how large a sum she could ask without bringing upon herself an immediate refusal and an exclamation of horror from the careful-minded clerk.

At last she replied with some hesitation: "I don't know exactly, but I think I could do it on four hundred francs."

He grew slightly pale, for this was exactly the amount he had been saving for a gun, intending to get a little shooting next summer on the plain of Nanterre with some friends who went lark-shooting there on Sundays.

Nevertheless he said: "Very well. I'll give you four hundred francs. But try and get a really nice dress with the money."

The day of the party drew near, and Madame Loisel seemed sad, uneasy and anxious. Her dress was ready, however. One evening her husband said to her: "What's the matter with you? You've been very odd for the last three days."

"I'm utterly miserable at not having any jewels, not a single stone, to wear," she replied. "I shall look absolutely no one. I would almost rather not go to the party."

"Wear flowers," he said. "They're very smart at this time

of year. For ten francs you could get two or three gorgeous roses." She was not convinced.

"No . . . there's nothing so humiliating as looking poor in the middle of a lot of rich women."

"How stupid you are!" exclaimed her husband. "Go and see Madame Forestier and ask her to lend you some jewels. You know her quite well enough for that."

She uttered a cry of delight.

"That's true. I never thought of it."

Next day she went to see her friend and told her her trouble.

Madame Forestier went to her dressing-table, took up a large box, brought it to Madame Loisel, opened it, and said:

"Choose, my dear."

First she saw some bracelets, then a pearl necklace, then a Venetian cross in gold and gems, of exquisite workmanship. She tried the effect of the jewels before the mirror, hesitating, unable to make up her mind to leave them, to give them up. She kept on asking: "Haven't you anything else?"

"Yes. Look for yourself. I don't know what you would like best."

Suddenly she discovered, in a black satin case, a superb diamond necklace; her heart began to beat covetously. Her hands trembled as she lifted it. She fastened it round her neck, upon her high dress, and remained in ecstasy at sight of herself. Then, with hesitation, she asked in anguish:

"Could you lend me this, just this alone?"

"Yes, of course."

She flung herself on her friend's breast, embraced her frenziedly, and went away with her treasure.

The day of the party arrived. Madame Loisel was a success. She was the prettiest woman present, elegant, graceful, smiling, and quite above herself with happiness. All the men stared at her, inquired her name, and asked to be introduced to her. All the under-secretaries of state were eager to waltz with her. The Minister noticed her.

She danced madly, ecstatically, drunk with pleasure, with no thought for anything, in the triumph of her beauty, in the pride of her success, in a cloud of happiness made up of this universal homage and admiration, of the desires she had aroused, of the completeness of a victory so dear to her feminine heart.

She left about four o'clock in the morning. Since midnight her husband had been dozing in a deserted little room, in company with three other men whose wives were having a good time.

He threw over her shoulders the garments he had brought for them to go home in, modest everyday clothes, whose poorness clashed with the beauty of the ball dress. She was conscious of this and was anxious to hurry away, so that she would not be noticed by the other women putting on their costly furs. Loisel restrained her.

"Wait a little. You'll catch cold in the open. I'm going to fetch a cab."

But she did not listen to him and rapidly descended the staircase. When they were out in the street they could not find a cab; they began to look for one, shouting at the drivers whom they saw passing in the distance.

They walked down towards the Seine, desperate and shivering. At last they found on the quay one of those old night-prowling carriages which are only to be seen in Paris after dark, as though they were ashamed of their shabbiness in the daylight.

It brought them to their door in Rue des Martyrs, and sadly they walked up to their own apartment. It was the end, for her. As for him, he was thinking that he must be at the office at ten.

She took off the garments in which she had wrapped her shoulders, so as to set herself in all her glory before the mirror. But suddenly she uttered a cry. The necklace was no longer around her neck!

"What's the matter with you?" asked her husband, already half undressed.

She turned towards him in the utmost distress.

"I . . . I . . . I've no longer got Madame Forestier's necklace. . . ."

He stared with astonishment. "What! . . . Impossible!"

They searched in the folds of her dress, in the folds of the coat, in the pockets, everywhere. They could not find it.

"Are you sure that you still had it on when you came away from the ball?" he asked.

"Yes, I touched it in the hall at the Ministry."

"But if you had lost it in the street, we should have heard it fall."

"Yes. Probably we should. Did you take the number of the cab?"

"No. You didn't notice it, did you?"

"No."

They stared at one another, dumbfounded. At last Loisel put on his clothes again.

"I'll go over all the ground we walked," he said, "and see if I can find it."

And he went out. She remained in her evening clothes, lacking strength to get into bed, huddled on a chair, without volition or power of thought.

Her husband returned about seven. He had found nothing.

He went to the police station, to the newspapers, to offer a reward to the cab companies, everywhere that a ray of hope impelled him.

She waited all day long, in the same state of bewilderment at this fearful catastrophe.

Loisel came home at night, his face lined and pale; he had discovered nothing.

"You must write your friend," he said, "and tell her that you've broken the clasp of her necklace and are getting it mended. That will give us time to look about us."

She wrote at his dictation.

By the end of a week they had lost all hope.

Loisel, who had aged five years, declared:

"We must see about replacing the diamonds."

Next day they took the box which had held the necklace and went to the jewellers whose name was inside. He consulted his books.

"It was not I who sold this necklace, madame; I must have merely supplied the clasp."

Then they went from jeweller to jeweller, searching for

another necklace like the first, consulting their memories, both ill with remorse and anguish of mind.

In a shop at the Palais-Royal they found a string of diamonds which seemed to them exactly like the one they were looking for. It was worth forty thousand francs. They were allowed to have it for thirty-six thousand.

They begged the jeweller not to sell it for three days. And they arranged matters on the understanding that it would be taken back for thirty-four thousand francs, if the first one were found before the end of February.

Loisel possessed eighteen thousand francs left to him by his father. He intended to borrow the rest.

He did borrow it, getting a thousand from one man, five hundred from another, five louis here, three louis there. He gave notes of hand, entered into ruinous agreements, did business with usurers and the whole race of money-lenders. He mortgaged the whole remaining years of his existence, risked his signature without even knowing if he could honour it, and, appalled at the agonising face of the future, at the black misery about to fall upon him, at the prospect of every possible physical privation and mortal torture, he went to get the new necklace and put down upon the jeweller's counter thirty-six thousand francs.

When Madame Loisel took back the necklace to Madame Forestier, the latter said to her in a chilly voice:

"You ought to have brought it back sooner; I might have needed it."

She did not, as her friend had feared, open the case. If she had noticed the substitution, what would she have thought? What would she have said? Would she not have taken her for a thief?

Madame Loisel came to know the ghastly life of abject poverty. Right from the start she played her part heroically. This fearful debt must be paid off. She would pay it. The servant was dismissed. They changed their apartment; they took a garret under the roof.

She came to know the heavy work of the house, the hateful duties of the kitchen. She washed the plates, wearing out her pink nails on the coarse pottery and the bottoms of pans.

She washed the dirty linen, the shirts and dish-cloths, and hung them out to dry on a string; every morning she took the dustbin down into the street and carried up the water, stopping on each landing to get her breath. And, clad like a poor woman, she went to the fruiterer, to the grocer, to the butcher, a basket on her arm, haggling, insulted, fighting for every wretched halfpenny of her money.

Every month notes had to be paid off, others to be renewed, time to be gained.

Her husband worked in the evenings at putting straight a merchant's accounts, and often at night he did copying at twopence halfpenny a page.

And this life lasted ten years.

At the end of ten years everything was paid off, everything, the usurers' charges and the accumulation of superimposed interest.

Madame Loisel looked old now. She had become like all the other strong, hard, coarse women of poor households. Her hair was badly done, her skirts were awry, her hands were red. She spoke in a shrill voice, and the water slopped all over the floor when she scrubbed it. But sometimes, when her husband was at the office, she sat down by the window and thought of that evening long ago, of the ball at which she had been so beautiful and so much admired.

What would have happened if she had never lost those jewels? Who knows? Who knows? How strange life is, how fickle! How little is needed to ruin or to save!

One Sunday, as she had gone for a walk along the Champs-Elysées to freshen herself after the labours of the week, she caught sight suddenly of a woman who was taking a child out for a walk. It was Madame Forestier, still young, still beautiful, still attractive.

Madame Loisel was conscious of some emotion. Should she speak to her? Yes, certainly. And now that she had paid, she would tell her all. Why not?

She went up to her. "Good morning, Jeanne."

The other did not recognise her, and was surprised at being thus familiarly addressed by a poor woman. "But . . . madame . . ." she stammered. "I don't know . . . you must be making a mistake."

"No . . . I am Mathilde Loisel."

Her friend uttered a cry. "Oh! . . . my poor Mathilde, how you have changed! . . ."

"Yes, I've had some hard times since I saw you last; and many sorrows . . . and all on your account."

"On my account! . . . How was that?"

"You remember the diamond necklace you lent me for the ball at the Ministry?"

"Yes. Well?"

"Well, I lost it."

"How could you? Why, you brought it back."

"I brought you another one just like it. And for the last ten years we have been paying for it. You realise it wasn't easy for us; we had no money . . . Well, it's paid for at last, and I'm mighty glad."

Madame Forestier had halted. "You say you bought a diamond necklace to replace mine?"

"Yes. You hadn't noticed it? They were very much alike." And she smiled in proud and innocent happiness.

Madame Forestier, deeply moved, took her two hands. "Oh, my poor Mathilde! But mine was imitation. It was worth at the very most only five hundred francs! . . ."

ANATOLE FRANCE (1844–1924)

THE PROCURATOR OF JUDÆA

Translated by Frederick Chapman

L. AELIUS LAMIA, born in Italy of illustrious parents, had not yet discarded the *toga prætexta* when he set out for the schools of Athens to study philosophy. Subsequently he took up his residence at Rome, and in his house on the Esquiline, amid a circle of youthful wastrels, abandoned himself to licentious courses. But being accused of engaging in criminal relations with Lepida, the wife of Sulpicius Quirinus, a

man of consular rank, and being found guilty, he was exiled
by Tiberius Cæsar. At that time he was just entering his
twenty-fourth year. During the eighteen years that his exile lasted he traversed Syria, Palestine, Cappadocia, and
Armenia, and made prolonged visits to Antioch, Cæsarea,
and Jerusalem. When, after the death of Tiberius, Caius was
raised to the purple, Lamia obtained permission to return to
Rome. He even regained a portion of his possessions. Ad-
versity had taught him wisdom.

He avoided all intercourse with the wives and daughters
of Roman citizens, made no efforts towards obtaining office,
held aloof from public honours, and lived a secluded life in
his house on the Esquiline. Occupying himself with the task
of recording all the remarkable things he had seen during his
distant travels, he turned, as he said, the vicissitudes of his
years of expiation into a diversion for his hours of rest. In
the midst of these calm employments, alternating with as-
siduous study of the works of Epicurus, he recognized with
a mixture of surprise and vexation that age was stealing
upon him. In his sixty-second year, being afflicted with an
illness which proved in no slight degree troublesome, he decided to have recourse to the waters at Baiæ. The coast at
that point, once frequented by the halcyon, was at this date
the resort of the wealthy Roman, greedy of pleasure. For a
week Lamia lived alone, without a friend in the brilliant
crowd. Then one day, after dinner, an inclination to which
he yielded urged him to ascend the incline, which, covered
with vines that resembled bacchantes, looked out upon the
waves.

Having reached the summit he seated himself by the side
of a path beneath a terebinth, and let his glances wander
over the lovely landscape. To his left, livid and bare, the
Phlegræan plain stretched out towards the ruins of Cumæ.
On his right, Cape Misenum plunged its abrupt spur beneath the Tyrrhenian sea. Beneath his feet luxurious Baiæ,
following the graceful outline of the coast, displayed its gardens, its villas thronged with statues, its porticos, its marble
terraces along the shores of the blue ocean where the dol-
phins sported. Before him, on the other side of the bay, on
the Campanian coast, gilded by the already sinking sun,

gleamed the temples which far away rose above the laurels of Posilippo, whilst on the extreme horizon Vesuvius looked forth smiling.

Lamia drew from a fold of his toga a scroll containing the *Treatise upon Nature*, extended himself upon the ground, and began to read. But the warning cries of a slave necessitated his rising to allow of the passage of a litter which was being carried along the narrow pathway through the vineyards. The litter being uncurtained, permitted Lamia to see stretched upon the cushions as it was borne nearer to him the figure of an elderly man of immense bulk, who, supporting his head on his hand, gazed out with a gloomy and disdainful expression. His nose, which was aquiline, and his chin, which was prominent, seemed desirous of meeting across his lips, and his jaws were powerful.

From the first moment Lamia was convinced that the face was familiar to him. He hesitated a moment before the name came to him. Then suddenly hastening towards the litter with a display of surprise and delight—

"Pontius Pilate!" he cried. "The gods be praised who have permitted me to see you once again!"

The old man gave a signal to the slaves to stop, and cast a keen glance upon the stranger who had addressed him.

"Pontius, my dear host," resumed the latter, "have twenty years so far whitened my hair and hollowed my cheeks that you no longer recognize your friend Ælius Lamia?"

At this time Pontius Pilate dismounted from the litter as actively as the weight of his years and the heaviness of his gait permitted him, and embraced Ælius Lamia again and again.

"Gods! what a treat it is to me to see you once more! But, alas, you call up memories of those long-vanished days when I was Procurator of Judæa in the province of Syria. Why, it must be thirty years ago that I first met you. It was at Cæsarea, whither you came to drag out your weary term of exile. I was fortunate enough to alleviate it a little, and out of friendship, Lamia, you followed me to that depressing place Jerusalem, where the Jews filled me with bitterness and disgust. You remained for more than ten years my guest and my companion, and in converse about Rome and things Roman we both of us managed to find consolation—you for your misfortunes, and I for my burdens of State."

Lamia embraced him afresh.

"You forget two things, Pontius; you are overlooking the facts that you used your influence on my behalf with Herod Antipas, and that your purse was freely open to me."

"Let us not talk of that," replied Pontius, "since after your return to Rome you sent me by one of your freedmen a sum of money which repaid me with usury."

"Pontius, I could never consider myself out of your debt by the mere payment of money. But tell me, have the gods fulfilled your desires? Are you in the enjoyment of all the happiness you deserve? Tell me about your family, your fortunes, your health."

"I have withdrawn to Sicily, where I possess estates, and where I cultivate wheat for the market. My eldest daughter, my best-loved Pontia, who has been left a widow, lives with me, and directs my household. The gods be praised, I have preserved my mental vigour; my memory is not in the least degree enfeebled. But old age always brings in its train a long procession of griefs and infirmities. I am cruelly tormented with gout. And at this very moment you find me on my way to the Phlegræan plain in search of a remedy for my sufferings. From that burning soil, whence at night flames burst forth, proceed acrid exhalations of sulphur, which, so they say, ease the pains and restore suppleness to the joints. At least, the physicians assure me that it is so."

"May you find it so in your case, Pontius! But, despite the gout and its burning torments, you scarcely look as old as myself, although in reality you must be my senior by ten years. Unmistakably you have retained a greater degree of vigour than I ever possessed, and I am overjoyed to find you looking so hale. Why, dear friend, did you retire from the public service before the customary age? Why, on resigning your governorship in Judæa, did you withdraw to a voluntary exile on your Sicilian estates? Give me an account of your doings from the moment that I ceased to be a witness of them. You were preparing to suppress a Samaritan rising when I set out for Cappadocia, where I hoped to draw some profit from the breeding of horses and mules. I have not seen you since then. How did that expedition succeed? Pray tell me. Everything interests me that concerns you in any way."

Pontius Pilate sadly shook his head.

"My natural disposition," he said, "as well as a sense of duty, impelled me to fulfill my public responsibilities, not merely with diligence, but even with ardour. But I was pursued by unrelenting hatred. Intrigues and calumnies cut short my career in its prime, and the fruit it should have looked to bear has withered away. You ask me about the Samaritan insurrection. Let us sit down on this hillock. I shall be able to give you an answer in a few words. Those occurrences are as vividly present to me as if they had happened yesterday.

"A man of the people, of persuasive speech—there are many such to be met with in Syria—induced the Samaritans to gather together in arms on Mount Gerizim (which in that country is looked upon as a holy place) under the promise that he would disclose to their sight the sacred vessels which in the ancient days of Evander and our father, Æneas, had been hidden away by an eponymous hero, or rather a tribal deity, named Moses. Upon this assurance the Samaritans rose in rebellion; but having been warned in time to forestall them, I dispatched detachments of infantry to occupy the mountain, and stationed cavalry to keep the approaches to it under observation.

"These measures of prudence were urgent. The rebels were already laying siege to the town of Tyrathaba, situated at the foot of Mount Gerizim. I easily dispersed them, and stifled the as yet scarcely organized revolt. Then, in order to give a forcible example with as few victims as possible, I handed over to execution the leaders of the rebellion. But you are aware, Lamia, in what strait dependence I was kept by the proconsul Vitellius, who governed Syria not in, but against the interests of Rome, and looked upon the provinces of the empire as territories which could be farmed out to tetrarchs. The head-men among the Samaritans, in their resentment against me, came and fell at his feet lamenting. To listen to them, nothing had been further from their thoughts than to disobey Cæsar. It was I who had provoked the rising, and it was purely in order to withstand my vio-

lence that they had gathered together round Tyrathaba.
Vitellius listened to their complaints, and handing over the
affairs of Judæa to his friend Marcellus, commanded me to
go and justify my proceedings before the Emperor himself.
With a heart overflowing with grief and resentment I took
ship. Just as I approached the shores of Italy, Tiberius,
worn out with age and cares of empire, died suddenly on
the selfsame Cape Misenum, whose peak we see from this
very spot magnified in the mists of evening. I demanded
justice of Caius, his successor, whose perception was naturally acute, and who was acquainted with Syrian affairs. But
marvel with me, Lamia, at the maliciousness of fortune, resolved on my discomfiture. Caius then had in his suite at
Rome the Jew Agrippa, his companion, the friend of his
childhood, whom he cherished as his own eyes. Now Agrippa
favoured Vitellius, inasmuch as Vitellius was the enemy of
Antipas, whom Agrippa pursued with his hatred. The Emperor adopted the prejudices of his beloved Asiatic, and refused even to listen to me. There was nothing for me to do
but bow beneath the stroke of unmerited misfortune. With
tears for my meat and gall for my portion, I withdrew to my
estates in Sicily, where I should have died of grief if my
sweet Pontia had not come to console her father. I have
cultivated wheat, and succeeded in producing the fullest
ears in the whole province. But now my life is ended; the
future will judge between Vitellius and me."

"Pontius," replied Lamia, "I am persuaded that you acted
towards the Samaritans according to the rectitude of your
character, and solely in the interests of Rome. But were you
not perchance on that occasion a trifle too much influenced
by that impetuous courage which has always swayed you?
You will remember that in Judæa it often happened that I
who, younger than you, should naturally have been more
impetuous than you, was obliged to urge you to clemency
and suavity."

"Suavity towards the Jews!" cried Pontius Pilate. "Although you have lived amongst them, it seems clear that you
ill understand those enemies of the human race. Haughty
and at the same time base, combining an invincible obstinacy with a despicably mean spirit, they weary alike your

love and your hatred. My character, Lamia, was formed
upon the maxims of the divine Augustus. When I was appointed Procurator of Judæa, the world was already pene-
trated with the majestic ideal of the *pax romana*. No longer,
as in the days of our internecine strife, were we witnesses
to the sack of a province for the aggrandisement of a proconsul. I knew where my duty lay. I was careful that my
actions should be governed by prudence and moderation.
The gods are my witnesses that I was resolved upon mildness, and upon mildness only. Yet what did my benevolent
intentions avail me? You were at my side, Lamia, when, at
the outset of my career as ruler, the first rebellion came to
a head. Is there any need for me to recall the details to you?
The garrison had been transferred from Cæsarea to take up
its winter quarters at Jerusalem. Upon the ensigns of the
legionaries appeared the presentment of Cæsar. The inhabitants of Jerusalem, who did not recognize the indwelling
divinity of the Emperor, were scandalized at this, as though,
when obedience is compulsory, it were not less abject to
obey a god than a man. The priests of their nation appeared
before my tribunal imploring me with supercilious humility
to have the ensigns removed from within the holy city. Out
of reverence for the divine nature of Cæsar and the majesty
of the empire, I refused to comply. Then the rabble made
common cause with the priests, and all around the pretorium
portentous cries of supplication arose. I ordered the soldiers
to stack their spears in front of the towers of Antonia, and
to proceed, armed only with sticks like lictors, to disperse
the insolent crowd. But, heedless of blows, the Jews continued their entreaties, and the more obstinate amongst them
threw themselves on the ground and, exposing their throats
to the rods, deliberately courted death. You were a witness
of my humiliation on that occasion, Lamia. By the order of
Vitellius I was forced to send the insignia back to Cæsarea.
That disgrace I had certainly not merited. Before the immortal gods I swear that never once during my term of office
did I flout justice and the laws. But I am grown old. My
enemies and detractors are dead. I shall die unavenged. Who
will now retrieve my character?"

He moaned and lapsed into silence. Lamia replied—

"That man is prudent who neither hopes nor fears anything from the uncertain events of the future. Does it matter in the least what estimate men may form of us hereafter? We ourselves are after all our own witnesses, and our own judges. You must rely, Pontius Pilate, on the testimony you yourself bear to your own rectitude. Be content with your now personal respect and that of your friends. For the rest, we know that mildness by itself will not suffice for the work of government. There is but little room in the actions of public men for that indulgence of human frailty which the philosophers recommend."

"We'll say no more at present," said Pontius. "The sulphureous fumes which rise from Phlegræan plain are more powerful when the ground which exhales them is still warm beneath the sun's rays. I must hasten on. Adieu! But now that I have rediscovered a friend, I should wish to take advantage of my good fortune. Do me the favour, Ælius Lamia, to give me your company at supper at my house tomorrow. My house stands on the seashore, at the extreme end of the town in the direction of Misenum. You will easily recognize it by the porch which bears a painting representing Orpheus surrounded by tigers and lions, whom he is charming with the strains from his lyre.

"Till to-morrow, Lamia," he repeated, as he climbed once more into his litter. "To-morrow we will talk about Judæa."

The following day at the supper hour Lamia presented himself at the house of Pontius Pilate. Two couches only were in readiness for occupants. Creditably but simply equipped, the table held a silver service in which were set out beccaficos in honey, thrushes, oysters from the Lucrine lake, and lampreys from Sicily. As they proceeded with their repast, Pontius and Lamia interchanged inquiries with one another about their ailments, the symptoms of which they described at considerable length, mutually emulous of communicating the various remedies which had been recommended to them. Then, congratulating themselves on being thrown together once more at Baiæ, they vied with one another in praise of the beauty of that enchanting coast and the mildness of the climate they enjoyed. Lamia was enthusiastic about the charms of the courtesans who frequented the seashore laden with golden ornaments and trailing draperies of barbaric broidery. But the aged Procurator deplored the ostentation with which by means of trumpery jewels and filmy garments foreigners and even enemies of the empire beguiled the Romans of their gold. After a time they turned to the subject of the great engineering feats that had been accomplished in the country; the prodigious bridge constructed by Caius between Puteoli and Baiæ, and the canals which Augustus excavated to convey the waters of the ocean to Lake Avernus and the Lucrine lake.

"I also," said Pontius, with a sigh, "I also wished to set afoot public works of great utility. When, for my sins, I was appointed Governor of Judæa, I conceived the idea of furnishing Jerusalem with an abundant supply of pure water by means of an aqueduct. The elevation of the levels, the proportionate capacity of the various parts, the gradient for the brazen reservoirs to which the distribution pipes were to be fixed—I had gone into every detail, and decided everything for myself with the assistance of mechanical experts. I had drawn up regulations for the superintendents so as to prevent individuals from making unauthorized depredations. The architects and the workmen had their instructions. I gave orders for the commencement of operations. But far from viewing with satisfaction the construction of that conduit, which was intended to carry to their town upon its massive arches not only water but health, the inhabitants of Jerusalem gave vent to lamentable outcries. They gathered tumultuously together, exclaiming against the sacrilege and impiousness, and, hurling themselves upon the workmen, scattered the foundation stones. Can you picture to yourself, Lamia, a filthier set of barbarians? Nevertheless, Vitellius decided in their favour, and I received orders to put a stop to the work."

"It is a knotty point," said Lamia, "how far one is justified in devising things for the commonweal against the will of the populace."

Pontius Pilate continued as though he had not heard this interruption. "Refuse an aqueduct! What madness! But whatever is of Roman origin is distasteful to the Jews. In their eyes we are an unclean race, and our very presence appears a profanation to them. You will remember that they would never venture to enter the pretorium for fear of defiling themselves, and that I was consequently obliged to discharge my magisterial functions in an open-air tribunal on that marble pavement your feet so often trod.

"They fear us and they despise us. Yet is not Rome the mother and warden of all those peoples who nestle smiling upon her venerable bosom? With her eagles in the van, peace and liberty have been carried to the very confines of the universe. Those whom we have subdued we look on as our friends, and we leave those conquered races, nay, we secure to them the permanence of their customs and their laws. Did Syria, aforetime rent asunder by its rabble of petty kings, ever even begin to taste of peace and prosperity until it submitted to the armies of Pompey? And when Rome might have reaped a golden harvest as the price of her goodwill, did she lay hands on the hoards that swell the treasuries of barbaric temples? Did she despoil the shrine of Cybele at Pessinus, or the Morimene and Cilician sanctuaries of Jupiter, or the temple of the Jewish god at Jerusalem? Antioch, Palmyra, and Apamea, secure despite their wealth, and no longer in dread of the wandering Arab of the desert, have erected temples to the genius of Rome and the divine Cæsar. The Jews alone hate and withstand us. They withhold their tribute till it is wrested from them, and obstinately rebel against military service."

"The Jews," replied Lamia, "are profoundly attached to their ancient customs. They suspected you, unreasonably I admit, of a desire to abolish their laws and change their usages. Do not resent it, Pontius, if I say that you did not always act in such a way as to disperse their unfortunate illusion. It gratified you, despite your habitual self-restraint, to play upon their fears, and more than once have I seen you betray in their presence the contempt with which their beliefs and religious ceremonies inspired you. You irritated them particularly by giving instructions for the sacerdotal garments and ornaments of their high priest to be kept in ward by your legionaries in the Antonine tower. One must admit that though they have never risen like us to an appreciation of things divine, the Jews celebrate rites which their very antiquity renders venerable."

Pontius Pilate shrugged his shoulders.

"They have very little exact knowledge of the nature of the gods," he said. "They worship Jupiter, yet they abstain from naming him or erecting a statue of him. They do not even adore him under the semblance of a rude stone, as certain of the Asiatic peoples are wont to do. They know nothing of Apollo, of Neptune, of Mars, nor of Pluto, nor of any goddess. At the same time, I am convinced that in days gone by they worshipped Venus. For even to this day their women bring doves to the altar as victims; and you know as well as I that the dealers who trade beneath the arcades of their temple supply those birds in couples for sacrifice. I have even been told that on one occasion some madman proceeded to overturn the stalls bearing these offerings, and their owners with them. The priests raised an outcry about it, and looked on it as a case of sacrilege. I am of the opinion that their custom of sacrificing turtle-doves was instituted in honour of Venus. Why are you laughing, Lamia?"

"I was laughing," said Lamia, "at an amusing idea which, I hardly know how, just occurred to me. I was thinking that perchance some day the Jupiter of the Jews might come to Rome and vent his fury upon you. Why should he not? Asia and Africa have already enriched us with a considerable number of gods. We have seen temples in honour of Isis and the dog-faced Anubis erected in Rome. In the public squares, and even on the race-courses, you may run across the Bona Dea of the Syrians mounted on an ass. And did you never hear how, in the reign of Tiberius, a young patrician passed himself off as the horned Jupiter of the Egyptians, Jupiter Ammon, and in this disguise procured the favours of an illustrious lady who was too virtuous to deny anything to a god? Beware, Pontius, lest the invisible Jupiter of the Jews disembark some day on the quay at Ostia!"

At the idea of a god coming out of Judæa a fleeting smile played over the severe countenance of the Procurator. Then he replied gravely—

"How would the Jews manage to impose their sacred law on outside peoples when they are in a perpetual state of

tumult amongst themselves as to the interpretation of that
law? You have seen them yourselves, Lamia, in the public
squares, split up into twenty rival parties, with staves in
their hands, abusing each other and clutching one another
by the beard. You have seen them on the steps of the temple, tearing their filthy garments as a symbol of lamenta-
tion, with some wretched creature in a frenzy of prophetic
exaltation in their midst. They have never realized that it
is possible to discuss peacefully and with an even mind those
matters concerning the divine which yet are hidden from
the profane and wrapped in uncertainty. For the nature of
the immortal gods remains hidden from us, and we cannot
arrive at a knowledge of it. Though I am of opinion, none
the less, that it is a prudent thing to believe in the provi-
dence of the gods. But the Jews are devoid of philosophy,
and cannot tolerate any diversity of opinions. On the contrary, they judge worthy of the extreme penalty all those
who on divine subjects profess opinions opposed to their law.
And as, since the genius of Rome has towered over them,
capital sentences pronounced by their own tribunals can
only be carried out with the sanction of the proconsul or the
procurator, they harry the Roman magistrate at any hour to
procure his signature to their baleful decrees, they besiege
the pretorium with their cries of 'Death!' A hundred times,
at least, have I known them, mustered, rich and poor together, all united under their priests, make a furious on-
slaught on my ivory chair, seizing me by the skirts of my
robe, by the thongs of my sandals, and all to demand of me
—nay, to exact from me—the death sentence on some unfortunate whose guilt I failed to perceive, and as to whom
I could only pronounce that he was as mad as his accusers.
A hundred times, do I say! Not a hundred, but every day
and all day. Yet it was my duty to execute their law as if it
were ours, since I was appointed by Rome not for the de-
struction, but for the upholding of their customs, and over
them I had the power of the rod and the axe. At the outset
of my term of office I endeavoured to persuade them to hear
reason; I attempted to snatch their miserable victims from
death. But this show of mildness only irritated them the
more; they demanded their prey, fighting around me like a

horde of vultures with wing and beak. Their priests reported
to Cæsar that I was violating their law, and their appeals,
supported by Vitellius, drew down upon me a severe repri-
mand. How many times did I long, as the Greeks used to
say, to dispatch accusers and accused in one convoy to the
crows!

"Do not imagine, Lamia, that I nourish the rancour of
the discomfited, the wrath of the superannuated, against a
people which in my person has prevailed against both Rome
and tranquillity. But I foresee the extremity to which sooner
or later they will reduce us. Since we cannot govern them, we
shall be driven to destroy them. Never doubt it. Always in a
state of insubordination, brewing rebellion in their inflam-
matory minds, they will one day burst forth upon us with a
fury beside which the wrath of the Numidians and the mut-
terings of the Parthians are mere child's play. They are se-
cretly nourishing preposterous hopes, and madly premedi-
tating our ruin. How can it be otherwise, when, on the
strength of an oracle, they are living in expectation of the
coming of a prince of their own blood whose kingdom shall
extend over the whole earth? There are no half measures
with such a people. They must be exterminated. Jerusalem
must be laid waste to the very foundation. Perchance, old as
I am, it may be granted me to behold the day when her walls
shall fall and the flames shall envelop her houses, when her
inhabitants shall pass under the edge of the sword, when salt
shall be strewn on the place where once the temple stood.
And in that day I shall at length be justified."

Lamia exerted himself to lead the conversation back to a
less acrimonious note.

"Pontius," he said, "it is not difficult for me to understand
both your long-standing resentment and your sinister fore-
bodings. Truly, what you have experienced of the character
of the Jews is nothing to their advantage. But I lived in
Jerusalem as an interested onlooker, and mingled freely with
the people, and I succeeded in detecting certain obscure virtues in these rude folk which were altogether hidden from
you. I have met Jews who were all mildness, whose simple
manners and faithfulness of heart recalled to me what our
poets have related concerning the Spartan lawgiver. And you

yourself, Pontius, have seen perish beneath the cudgels of your legionaries simple-minded men who have died for a cause they believed to be just without revealing their names. Such men do not deserve our contempt. I am saying this because it is desirable in all things to preserve moderation and an even mind. But I own that I never experienced any lively sympathy for the Jews. The Jewesses, on the contrary, I found extremely pleasing. I was young then, and the Syrian women stirred all my senses to response. Their ruddy lips, their liquid eyes that shone in the shade, their sleepy gaze pierced me to the very marrow. Painted and stained, smelling of nard and myrrh, steeped in odours, their physical attractions are both rare and delightful."

Pontius listened impatiently to these praises.

"I was not the kind of man to fall into the snares of the Jewish women," he said; "and since you have opened the subject yourself, Lamia, I was never able to approve of your laxity. If I did not express with sufficient emphasis formerly how culpable I held you for having intrigued at Rome with the wife of a man of consular rank, it was because you were then enduring heavy penance for your misdoings. Marriage from the patrician point of view is a sacred tie; it is one of the institutions which are the support of Rome. As to foreign women and slaves, such relations as one may enter into with them would be of little account were it not that they habituate the body to a humiliating effeminacy. Let me tell you that you have been too liberal in your offerings to the Venus of the Market-place; and what, above all, I blame in you is that you have not married in compliance with the law and given children to the Republic, as every good citizen is bound to do."

But the man who had suffered exile under Tiberius was no longer listening to the venerable magistrate. Having tossed off his cup of Falernian, he was smiling at some image visible to his eye alone.

After a moment's silence he resumed in a very deep voice, which rose in pitch by little and little—

"With what languorous grace they dance, those Syrian women! I knew a Jewess at Jerusalem who used to dance in a poky little room, on a threadbare carpet, by the light of

one smoky little lamp, waving her arms as she clanged her
cymbals. Her loins arched, her head thrown back, and, as
it were, dragged down by the weight of her heavy red hair,
her eyes swimming with voluptuousness, eager, languishing,
compliant, she would have made Cleopatra herself grow pale
with envy. I was in love with her barbaric dances, her voice
—a little raucous and yet so sweet—her atmosphere of in-
cense, the semi-somnolescent state in which she seemed to
live. I followed her everywhere. I mixed with the vile rabble
of soldiers, conjurers, and extortioners with which she was
surrounded. One day, however, she disappeared, and I saw
her no more. Long did I seek her in disreputable alleys and
taverns. It was more difficult to learn to do without her than
to lose the taste for Greek wine. Some months after I lost
sight of her, I learned by chance that she had attached herself to a small company of men and women who were fol-
lowers of a young Galilean thaumaturgist. His name was
Jesus; he came from Nazareth, and he was crucified for
some crime, I don't quite know what. Pontius, do you remember anything about the man?"

Pontius Pilate contracted his brows, and his hand rose to
his forehead in the attitude of one who probes the deeps of
memory. Then after a silence of some seconds—

"Jesus?" he murmured, "Jesus—of Nazareth? I cannot call
him to mind."

MARK TWAIN *(1835–1910)*

THE CELEBRATED JUMPING FROG
OF CALAVERAS COUNTY

IN COMPLIANCE with the request of a friend of mine, who
wrote me from the East, I called on good-natured, garrulous
old Simon Wheeler, and inquired after my friend's friend,
Leonidas W. Smiley, as requested to do, and I hereunto
append the result. I have a lurking suspicion that *Leonidas*

W. Smiley is a myth, that my friend never knew such a personage; and that he only conjectured that, if I asked old Wheeler about him, it would remind him of his infamous *Jim* Smiley, and he would go to work and bore me nearly to death with some infernal reminiscence of him as long and tedious as it should be useless to me. If that was the design, it certainly succeeded.

I found Simon Wheeler dozing comfortably by the barroom stove of the old, dilapidated tavern in the ancient mining camp of Angel's, and I noticed that he was fat and baldheaded, and had an expression of winning gentleness and simplicity upon his tranquil countenance. He roused up and gave me good-day. I told him a friend of mine had commissioned me to make some inquiries about a cherished companion of his boyhood named *Leonidas W.* Smiley—*Rev. Leonidas W.* Smiley—a young minister of the Gospel, who he had heard was at one time a resident of Angel's Camp. I added, that, if Mr. Wheeler could tell me anything about this Rev. *Leonidas* W. Smiley, I would feel under many obligations to him.

Simon Wheeler backed me into a corner and blockaded me there with his chair, and then sat me down and reeled off the monotonous narrative which follows this paragraph. He never smiled, he never frowned, he never changed his voice from the gentle-flowing key to which he tuned the initial sentence, he never betrayed the slightest suspicion of enthusiasm; but all through the interminable narrative there ran a vein of impressive earnestness and sincerity, which showed me plainly that, so far from his imagining that there was anything ridiculous or funny about his story, he regarded it as a really important matter, and admitted its two heroes as men of transcendent genius in *finesse*. To me, the spectacle of a man drifting serenely along through such a queer yarn without ever smiling, was exquisitely absurd. As I said before, I asked him to tell me what he knew of Rev. *Leonidas* W. Smiley, and he replied as follows. I let him go on in his own way, and never interrupted him once:

There was a feller here once by the name of *Jim* Smiley, in the winter of '49—or maybe it was the spring of '50—I don't recollect exactly, somehow, though what makes me

think it was one or the other is because I remember the big
flume wasn't finished when he first came to the camp; but
anyway, he was the curiousest man about always betting on
anything that turned up you ever see, if he could get anybody to bet on the other side; and if he couldn't, he'd change
sides. Any way what suited the other man would suit him—
any way just so's he got a bet, *he* was satisfied. But still he
was lucky, uncommon lucky—he most always come out winner. He was always ready and laying for a chance; there
couldn't be no solit'ry thing mentioned but that feller'd offer to bet on it, and take any side you please, as I was just
telling you. If there was a horse-race, you'd find him flush,
or you'd find him busted at the end of it; if there was a
dog-fight, he'd bet on it; if there was a cat-fight, he'd bet on
it; if there was a chicken-fight, he'd bet on it; why, if there
was two birds setting on a fence, he would bet you which
one would fly first; or if there was a camp meeting, he would
be there reg'lar, to bet on Parson Walker, which he judged
to be the best exhorter about here, and so he was, too, and
a good man. If he even seen a straddle-bug start to go any-
wheres, he would bet you how long it would take him to get
wherever he was going to, and if you took him up, he would
foller that straddle-bug to Mexico but what he would find
out where he was bound for and how long he was on the
road. Lot of the boys here had seen that Smiley, and can
tell you about him. Why, it never made no difference to *him*
—he would bet on *any*thing—the dangedest feller. Parson
Walker's wife laid very sick once, for a good while, and it
seemed as if they warn't going to save her; but one morning he came in, and Smiley asked how she was, and he said
she was considerable better—thank the Lord for his inf'nit
mercy—and coming on so smart that, with the blessing of
Prov'dence, she'd get well yet; and Smiley, before he
thought, says, "Well, I'll risk two-and-a-half that she don't,
anyway."

Thish-yer Smiley had a mare—the boys called her the
fifteen-minute nag, but that was only in fun, you know, because, of course, she was faster than that—and he used to
win money on that horse, for all she was so slow and always
had the asthma, or the distemper, or the consumption, or

something of that kind. They used to give her two or three hundred yards start, and then pass her under way; but always at the fag-end of the race she'd get excited and desperate-like, and come cavorting and straddling up, and scattering her legs around limber, sometimes in the air, and sometimes out to one side amongst the fences, and kicking up m-o-r-e dust, and raising m-o-r-e racket with her coughing and sneezing and blowing her nose—and always fetch up at the stand just about a neck ahead, as near as you could cipher it down.

And he had a little small bull pup, that to look at him you'd think he wan't worth a cent but to set around and look ornery and lay for a chance to steal something. But as soon as money was up on him, he was a different dog; his under-jaw'd begin to stick out like the fo'castle of a steamboat, and his teeth would uncover, and shine savage like the furnaces. And a dog might tackle him, and bullyrag him, and bite him, and throw him over his shoulder two or three times, and Andrew Jackson—which was the name of the pup—Andrew Jackson would never let on but what *he* was satisfied, and hadn't expected nothing else—and the bets being doubled and doubled on the other side all the time, till the money was all up; and then all of a sudden he would grab that other dog jest by the j'int of his hind leg and freeze to it—not claw, you understand, but only jest grip and hang on till they throwed up the sponge, if it was a year. Smiley always come out winner on that pup, till he harnessed a dog once that didn't have no hind legs, because they'd been sawed off by a circular saw, and when the thing had gone along far enough, and the money was all up, and he come to make a snatch for his pet holt, he saw in a minute how he'd been imposed on, and how the other dog had him in the door, so to speak, and he 'peared surprised, and then he looked sorter discouraged-like, and didn't try no more to win the fight, and so he got shucked out bad. He give Smiley a look, as much to say his heart was broke and it was *his* fault for putting up a dog that hadn't no hind legs for him to take holt of, which was his main dependence in a fight, and then he limped off a piece and laid down and died. It was a good pup, was that Andrew Jackson, and would have made a name for hisself if he'd lived, for the stuff was in him, and he had genius—I know it, because he hadn't no opportunities to speak of, and it don't stand to reason that a dog could make such a fight as he could under them circumstances, if he hadn't no talent. It always makes me feel sorry when I think of that last fight of his'n, and the way it turned out.

Well, thish-yer Smiley had rat-tarriers, and chicken-cocks, and tomcats, and all them kind of things, till you couldn't rest, and you couldn't fetch nothing for him to bet on but he'd match you. He ketched a frog one day, and took him home, and said he cal'klated to edercate him; and so he never done nothing for these three months but set in his back yard and learn that frog to jump. And you bet you he *did* learn him, too. He'd give him a little punch behind, and the next minute you'd see that frog whirling in the air like a doughnut—see him turn one summerset, or maybe a couple, if he got a good start, and come down flat-footed and all right, like a cat. He got him up so in the matter of catching flies, and kept him in practice so constant, that he'd nail a fly every time as far as he could see him. Smiley said all a frog wanted was education, and he could do most anything —and I believe him. Why, I've seen him set Dan'l Webster down here on this floor—Dan'l Webster was the name of the frog—and sing out, "Flies, Dan'l, flies!" and quicker'n you could wink, he'd spring straight up, and snake a fly off'n the counter there, and flop down on the floor again as solid as a gob of mud, and fall to scratching the side of his head with his hind foot as indifferent as if he hadn't no idea he's been doin' any more'n any frog might do. You never see a frog so modest and straight-for'ard as he was, for all he was so gifted. And when it come to fair and square jumping on the dead level, he could get over more ground at one straddle than any animal of his breed you ever see. Jumping on a dead level was his strong suit, you understand; and when it come to that, Smiley would ante up money on him as long as he had a red. Smiley was monstrous proud of his frog, and well he might be, for fellers that had traveled and been everywhere all said he laid over any frog that ever *they* see.

Well, Smiley kept the beast in a little lattice box, and he used to fetch him downtown sometimes and lay for a bet.

One day a feller—a stranger in the camp, he was—come across him with his box, and says:

"What might it be that you've got in the box?"

And Smiley says, sorter indifferent like, "It might be a parrot, or it might be a canary, maybe, but it ain't—it's only just a frog."

An' the feller took it, and looked at it careful, and turned it round this way and that, and says, "H'm—so 'tis. Well, what's *he* good for?"

"Well," Smiley says, easy and careless, "he's good enough for *one* thing, I should judge—he can outjump any frog in Calaveras county."

The feller took the box again, and took another long, particular look, and gave it back to Smiley, and says, very deliberate, "Well, I don't see no p'ints about that frog that's any better'n any other frog."

"Maybe you don't," Smiley says. "Maybe you understand frogs, and maybe you don't understand 'em; maybe you've had experience, and maybe you ain't only a amature, as it were. Anyways, I've got *my* opinion, and I'll risk forty dollars that he can outjump any frog in Calaveras county."

And the feller studied a minute, and then says, kinder sad like, "Well, I'm only a stranger here, and I ain't got no frog; but if I had a frog, I'd bet you."

And then Smiley says, "That's all right—that's all right— if you'll hold my box a minute, I'll go and get you a frog." And so the feller took the box, and put up his forty dollars along with Smiley's, and set down to wait.

So he set there a good while thinking and thinking to his-self, and then he got the frog out and prized his mouth open and took a teaspoon and filled him full of quail shot—filled him pretty near up to his chin—and set him on the floor. Smiley he went to the swamp and slopped around in the mud for a long time, and finally he ketched a frog, and fetched him in, and give him to this feller, and says:

"Now, if you're ready, set him alongside of Dan'l, with his forepaws just even with Dan'l, and I'll give the word." Then he says, "One—two—three—jump!" and him and the feller touched up the frogs from behind, and the new frog hopped off, but Dan'l give a heave, and hysted up his shoulders—so—like a Frenchman, but it wasn't no use—he couldn't budge; he was planted as solid as an anvil, and he couldn't no more stir than if he was anchored out. Smiley was a good deal surprised, and he was disgusted too, but he didn't have no idea what the matter was, of course.

The feller took the money and started away; and when he was going out at the door, he sorter jerked his thumb over his shoulder—this way—at Dan'l, and says again, very deliberate, "Well, *I* don't see no p'ints about that frog that's any better'n any other frog."

Smiley he stood scratching his head and looking down at Dan'l a long time, and at last he says, "I do wonder what in the nation that frog throw'd off for—I wonder if there ain't something the matter with him—he 'pears to look mighty baggy, somehow." And he ketched Dan'l by the nap of the neck, and lifted him up and says, "Why, blame my cats, if he don't weigh five pounds!" and turned him upside down, and he belched out a double handful of shot. And then he see how it was, and he was the maddest man—he set the frog down and took out after that feller, but he never ketched him. And—

(Here Simon Wheeler heard his name called from the front yard, and got up to see what was wanted.) And turning to me as he moved away, he said: "Just set where you are, stranger, and rest easy—I ain't going to be gone a second."

But, by your leave, I did not think that a continuation of the history of the enterprising vagabond *Jim* Smiley would be likely to afford me much information concerning the Rev. *Leonidas. W.* Smiley, and so I started away.

At the door I met the sociable Wheeler returning, and he buttonholed me and recommenced: "Well, thish-yer Smiley had a yeller one-eyed cow that didn't have no tail, only jest a short stump like a bannanner, and—"

"Oh, hang Smiley and his afflicted cow!" I muttered, good-naturedly, and bidding the old gentleman good-day, I departed.

Bret Harte (1839–1902)

THE LUCK OF ROARING CAMP

There was commotion in Roaring Camp. It could not have been a fight, for in 1850 that was not novel enough to have called together the entire settlement. The ditches and claims were not only deserted, but "Tuttle's grocery" had contributed its gamblers, who, it will be remembered, calmly continued their game the day that French Pete and Kanaka Joe shot each other to death over the bar in the front room. The whole camp was collected before a rude cabin on the outer edge of the clearing. Conversation was carried on in a low tone, but the name of a woman was frequently repeated. It was a name familiar enough in the camp,—"Cherokee Sal."

Perhaps the less said of her the better. She was a coarse and, it is to be feared, a very sinful woman. But at that time she was the only woman in Roaring Camp, and was just then lying in sore extremity, when she most needed the ministration of her own sex. Dissolute, abandoned, and irreclaimable, she was yet suffering a martyrdom hard enough to bear even when veiled by sympathizing womanhood, but now terrible in her loneliness. The primal curse had come to her in that original isolation which must have made the punishment of the first transgression so dreadful. It was, perhaps, part of the expiation of her sin that, at a moment when she most lacked her sex's intuitive tenderness and care, she met only the half-contemptuous faces of her masculine associates. Yet a few of the spectators were, I think, touched by her sufferings. Sandy Tipton thought it was "rough on Sal," and, in the contemplation of her condition, for a moment rose superior to the fact that he had an ace and two bowers in his sleeve.

It will be seen also that the situation was novel. Deaths were by no means uncommon in Roaring Camp, but a birth was a new thing. People had been dismissed from the camp effectively, finally, and with no possibility of return; but this was the first time anybody had been introduced *ab initio*. Hence the excitement.

"You go in there, Stumpy," said a prominent citizen known as "Kentuck," addressing one of the loungers. "Go in there, and see what you kin do. You've had experience in them things."

Perhaps there was a fitness in the selection. Stumpy, in other climes, had been the putative head of two families; in fact, it was owing to some legal informality in these proceedings that Roaring Camp—a city of refuge—was indebted to his company. The crowd approved the choice, and Stumpy was wise enough to bow to the majority. The door closed on the extempore surgeon and midwife, and Roaring Camp sat down outside, smoked its pipe, and awaited the issue.

The assemblage numbered about a hundred men. One or two of these were actual fugitives from justice, some were criminal, and all were reckless. Physically they exhibited no indication of their past lives and character. The greatest scamp had a Raphael face, with a profusion of blonde hair; Oakhurst, a gambler, had the melancholy air and intellectual abstraction of a Hamlet; the coolest and most courageous man was scarcely over five feet in height, with a soft voice and an embarrassed, timid manner. The term "roughs" applied to them was a distinction rather than a definition. Perhaps in the minor details of fingers, toes, ears, etc., the camp may have been deficient, but these slight omissions did not detract from their aggregate force. The strongest man had but three fingers on his right hand; the best shot had but one eye.

Such was the physical aspect of the men that were dispersed around the cabin. The camp lay in a triangular valley between two hills and a river. The only outlet was a steep trail over the summit of a hill that faced the cabin, now illuminated by the rising moon. The suffering woman might have seen it from the rude bunk whereon she lay,—seen it winding like a silver thread until it was lost in the stars above.

A fire of withered pine boughs added sociability to the

gathering. By degrees the natural levity of Roaring Camp returned. Bets were freely offered and taken regarding the result. Three to five that "Sal would get through with it;" even that the child would survive; side bets as to the sex and complexion of the coming stranger. In the midst of an excited discussion an exclamation came from those nearest the door, and the camp stopped to listen. Above the swaying and moaning of the pines, the swift rush of the river, and the crackling of the fire rose a sharp, querulous cry,—a cry unlike anything heard before in the camp. The pines stopped moaning, the river ceased to rush, and the fire to crackle. It seemed as if Nature had stopped to listen too.

The camp rose to its feet as one man! It was proposed to explode a barrel of gunpowder; but in consideration of the situation of the mother, better counsels prevailed, and only a few revolvers were discharged; for whether owing to the rude surgery of the camp, or some other reason, Cherokee Sal was sinking fast. Within an hour she had climbed, as it were, that rugged road that led to the stars, and so passed out of Roaring Camp, its sin and shame, forever. I do not think that the announcement disturbed them much, except in speculation as to the fate of the child. "Can he live now?" we asked of Stumpy. The answer was doubtful. The only other being of Cherokee Sal's sex and maternal condition in the settlement was an ass. There was some conjecture as to fitness, but the experiment was tried. It was less problematical than the ancient treatment of Romulus and Remus, and apparently as successful.

When these details were completed, which exhausted another hour, the door was opened, and the anxious crowd of men, who had already formed themselves into a queue, entered in single file. Beside the low bunk or shelf, on which the figure of the mother was starkly outlined below the blankets, stood a pine table. On this a candle-box was placed, and within it, swathed in staring red flannel, lay the last arrival at Roaring Camp. Beside the candle-box was placed a hat. Its use was soon indicated. "Gentlemen," said Stumpy, with a singular mixture of authority and *ex officio* complacency,—"gentlemen will please pass in at the front door, round the table, and out at the back door. Them as wishes to

contribute anything toward the orphan will find a hat
handy." The first man entered with his hat on; he uncovered,
however, as he looked about him, and so unconsciously set
an example to the next. In such communities good and
bad actions are catching. As the procession filed in comments were audible,—criticisms addressed perhaps rather to
Stumpy in the character of showman: "Is that him?"
"Mighty small specimen;" "Hasn't more'n got the color;"
"Ain't bigger nor a derringer." The contributions were as
characteristic: A silver tobacco box; a doubloon; a navy
revolver, silver mounted; a gold specimen; a very beautifully
embroidered lady's handkerchief (from Oakhurst the gambler); a diamond breast-pin; a diamond ring (suggested by
the pin, with the remark from the giver that he "saw that pin
and went two diamonds better"); a sling-shot; a Bible (contributor not detected); a golden spur; a silver teaspoon
(the initials, I regret to say, were not the giver's); a pair of
surgeon's shears; a lancet; a Bank of England note for £5;
and about $200 in loose gold and silver coin. During these
proceedings Stumpy maintained a silence as impassive as
the dead on his left, a gravity as inscrutable as that of the
newly born on his right. Only one incident occurred to break
the monotony of the curious procession. As Kentuck bent
over the candle-box half curiously, the child turned, and, in
a spasm of pain, caught at his groping finger, and held it fast
for a moment. Kentuck looked foolish and embarrassed.
Something like a blush tried to assert itself in his weather-
beaten cheek. "The d—d little cuss!" he said, as he extricated his finger, with perhaps more tenderness and care
than he might have been deemed capable of showing. He
held that finger a little apart from its fellows as he went out,
and examined it curiously. The examination provoked the
same original remark in regard to the child. In fact, he
seemed to enjoy repeating it. "He rastled with my finger,"
he remarked to Tipton, holding up the member, "the d—d
little cuss!"

It was four o'clock before the camp sought repose. A light
burnt in the cabin where the watchers sat, for Stumpy did
not go to bed that night. Nor did Kentuck. He drank quite
freely, and related with great gusto his experience, invariably

ending with his characteristic condemnation of the new-comer. It seemed to relieve him of any unjust implication of sentiment, and Kentuck had the weaknesses of the nobler sex. When everybody else had gone to bed, he walked down to the river and whistled reflectingly. Then he walked up the gulch past the cabin, still whistling with demonstrative unconcern. At a large redwood-tree he paused and retraced his steps, and again passed the cabin. Half-way down to the river's bank he again paused, and then returned and knocked at the door. It was opened by Stumpy. "How goes it?" said Kentuck, looking past Stumpy toward the candle-box. "All serene!" replied Stumpy. "Anything up?" "Nothing." There was a pause—an embarrassing one—Stumpy still holding the door. Then Kentuck had recourse to his finger, which he held up to Stumpy. "Rastled with it,—the d—d little cuss," he said, and retired.

The next day Cherokee Sal had such rude sepulture as Roaring Camp afforded. After her body had been committed to the hillside, there was a formal meeting of the camp to discuss what should be done with her infant. A resolution to adopt it was unanimous and enthusiastic. But an animated discussion in regard to the manner and feasibility of providing for its wants at once sprang up. It was remarkable that the argument partook of none of those fierce personalities with which discussions were usually conducted at Roaring Camp. Tipton proposed that they should send the child to Red Dog,—a distance of forty miles,—where female attention could be procured. But the unlucky suggestion met with fierce and unanimous opposition. It was evident that no plan which entailed parting from their new acquisition would for a moment be entertained. "Besides," said Tom Ryder, "them fellows at Red Dog would swap it, and ring in somebody else on us." A disbelief in the honesty of other camps prevailed at Roaring Camp, as in other places.

The introduction of a female nurse in the camp also met with objection. It was argued that no decent woman could be prevailed upon to accept Roaring Camp as her home, and the speaker urged that "they didn't want any more of the other kind." This unkind allusion to the defunct mother, harsh as it may seem, was the first spasm of propriety,—the first

symptom of the camp's regeneration. Stumpy advanced
nothing. Perhaps he felt a certain delicacy in interfering with
the selection of a possible successor in office. But when
questioned, he averred stoutly that he and "Jinny"—the
mammal before alluded to—could manage to rear the child.
There was something original, independent, and heroic about
the plan that pleased the camp. Stumpy was retained. Certain articles were sent for to Sacramento. "Mind," said the
treasurer, as he pressed a bag of gold-dust into the expressman's hand, "the best that can be got,—lace, you know, and
filigree-work and frills,—d—n the cost!"

Strange to say, the child thrived. Perhaps the invigorating
climate of the mountain camp was compensation for material
deficiencies. Nature took the foundling to her broader breast.
In that rare atmosphere of the Sierra foothills,—that air
pungent with balsamic odor, that ethereal cordial at once
bracing and exhilarating,—he may have found food and
nourishment, or a subtle chemistry that transmuted ass's
milk to lime and phosphorus. Stumpy inclined to the belief
that it was the latter and good nursing. "Me and that ass,"
he would say, "has been father and mother to him! Don't
you," he would add, apostrophizing the helpless bundle before him, "never go back on us."

By the time he was a month old the necessity of giving him
a name became apparent. He had generally been known as
"The Kid," "Stumpy's Boy," "The Coyote" (an allusion to
his vocal powers), and even by Kentuck's endearing diminutive of "The d—d little cuss." But these were felt to be vague
and unsatisfactory, and were at last dismissed under another
influence. Gamblers and adventurers are generally supersti-
tious, and Oakhurst one day declared that the baby had
brought "the luck" to Roaring Camp. It was certain that of
late they had been successful. "Luck" was the name agreed
upon, with the prefix of Tommy for greater convenience. No
allusion was made to the mother, and the father was unknown. "It's better," said the philosophical Oakhurst, "to
take a fresh deal all round. Call him Luck, and start him
fair." A day was accordingly set apart for the christening.
What was meant by this ceremony the reader may imagine
who has already gathered some idea of the reckless irrever-

ence of Roaring Camp. The master of ceremonies was one "Boston," a noted wag, and the occasion seemed to promise the greatest facetiousness. This ingenious satirist had spent two days in preparing a burlesque of the Church service, with pointed local allusions. The choir was properly trained, and Sandy Tipton was to stand godfather. But after the procession had marched to the grove with music and banners, and the child had been deposited before a mock altar, Stumpy stepped before the expectant crowd. "It ain't my style to spoil fun, boys," said the little man, stoutly eying the faces around him, "but it strikes me that this thing ain't exactly on the squar. It's playing it pretty low down on this yer baby to ring in fun on him that he ain't goin' to understand. And ef there's goin' to be any godfathers round, I'd like to see who's got any better rights than me." A silence followed Stumpy's speech. To the credit of all humorists be it said that the first man to acknowledge its justice was the satirist thus stopped of his fun. "But," said Stumpy, quickly following up his advantage, "we're here for a christening, and we'll have it. I proclaim you Thomas Luck, according to the laws of the United States and the State of California, so help me God." It was the first time that the name of the Deity had been otherwise uttered than profanely in the camp. The form of christening was perhaps even more ludicrous than the satirist had conceived; but strangely enough, nobody saw it and nobody laughed. "Tommy" was christened as seriously as he would have been under a Christian roof, and cried and was comforted in as orthodox fashion.

And so the work of regeneration began in Roaring Camp. Almost imperceptibly a change came over the settlement. The cabin assigned to "Tommy Luck"—or "The Luck," as he was more frequently called—first showed signs of improvement. It was kept scrupulously clean and whitewashed. Then it was boarded, clothed, and papered. The rosewood cradle, packed eighty miles by mule, had, in Stumpy's way of putting it, "sorter killed the rest of the furniture." So the rehabilitation of the cabin became a necessity. The men who were in the habit of lounging in at Stumpy's to see "how 'The Luck' got on" seemed to appreciate the change, and in self-

defense the rival establishment of "Tuttle's grocery" bestirred itself and imported a carpet and mirrors. The reflections of the latter on the appearance of Roaring Camp tended
to produce stricter habits of personal cleanliness. Again
Stumpy imposed a kind of quarantine upon those who as-
pired to the honor and privilege of holding The Luck. It was
a cruel mortification to Kentuck—who, in the carelessness
of a large nature and the habits of frontier life, had begun
to regard all garments as a second cuticle, which, like a
snake's, only sloughed off through decay—to be debarred
this privilege for certain prudential reasons. Yet such was
the subtle influence of innovation that he thereafter appeared regularly every afternoon in a clean shirt and face
still shining from his ablutions. Nor were moral and social
sanitary laws neglected. "Tommy," who was supposed to
spend his whole existence in a persistent attempt to repose,
must not be disturbed by noise. The shouting and yelling,
which had gained the camp its infelicitous title, were not permitted within hearing distance of Stumpy's. The men con-
versed in whispers or smoked with Indian gravity. Profanity
was tacitly given up in these sacred precincts, and throughout the camp a popular form of expletive, known as "D—n
the luck!" and "Curse the luck!" was abandoned, as having
a new personal bearing. Vocal music was not interdicted,
being supposed to have a soothing, tranquilizing quality; and
one song, sung by "Man-o'-War Jack," an English sailor
from Her Majesty's Australian colonies, was quite popular
as a lullaby. It was a lugubrious recital of the exploits of
"the Arethusa, Seventy-four," in a muffled minor, ending
with a prolonged dying fall at the burden of each verse, "On
b-oo-o-ard of the Arethusa." It was a fine sight to see Jack
holding The Luck, rocking from side to side as if with the
motion of a ship, and crooning forth this naval ditty. Either
through the peculiar rocking of Jack or the length of his
song,—it contained ninety stanzas, and was continued with
conscientious deliberation to the bitter end,—the lullaby
generally had the desired effect. At such times the men
would lie at full length under the trees in the soft summer
twilight, smoking their pipes and drinking in the melodious
utterances. An indistinct idea that this was pastoral happi-

ness pervaded the camp. "This 'ere kind o' thing," said the Cockney Simmons, meditatively reclining on his elbow, "is 'evingly." It reminded him of Greenwich.

On the long summer days The Luck was usually carried to the gulch from whence the golden store of Roaring Camp was taken. There, on a blanket spread over pine boughs, he would lie while the men were working in the ditches below. Latterly there was a rude attempt to decorate this bower with flowers and sweet-smelling shrubs, and generally some one would bring him a cluster of wild honeysuckles, azaleas, or the painted blossoms of Las Mariposas. The men had suddenly awakened to the fact that there were beauty and significance in these trifles, which they had so long trodden carelessly beneath their feet. A flake of glittering mica, a fragment of variegated quartz, a bright pebble from the bed of the creek, became beautiful to eyes thus cleared and strengthened, and were invariably put aside for The Luck. It was wonderful how many treasures the woods and hillsides yielded that "would do for Tommy." Surrounded by playthings such as never child out of fairyland had before, it is to be hoped that Tommy was content. He appeared to be serenely happy, albeit there was an infantine gravity about him, a contemplative light in his round gray eyes, that sometimes worried Stumpy. He was always tractable and quiet, and it is recorded that once, having crept beyond his "corral,"—a hedge of tessellated pine boughs, which surrounded his bed,—he dropped over the bank on his head in the soft earth, and remained with his mottled legs in the air in that position for at least five minutes with unflinching gravity. He was extricated without a murmur. I hesitate to record the many other instances of his sagacity, which rest, unfortunately, upon the statements of prejudiced friends. Some of them were not without a tinge of superstition. "I crep' up the bank just now," said Kentuck one day, in a breathless state of excitement, "and dern my skin if he wasn't a-talking to a jaybird as was a-sittin' on his lap. There they was, just as free and sociable as anything you please, a-jawin' at each other just like two cherry-bums." Howbeit, whether creeping over the pine boughs or lying lazily on his back blinking at the leaves above him, to him the birds sang, the squirrels chattered, and the flowers bloomed. Nature was his nurse and playfellow. For him she would let slip between the leaves golden shafts of sunlight that fell just within his grasp; she would send wandering breezes to visit him with the balm of bay and resinous gum; to him the tall redwoods nodded familiarly and sleepily, the bumblebees buzzed, and the rooks cawed a slumbrous accompaniment.

Such was the golden summer of Roaring Camp. They were "flush times," and the luck was with them. The claims had yielded enormously. The camp was jealous of its privileges and looked suspiciously on strangers. No encouragement was given to immigration, and, to make their seclusion more perfect, the land on either side of the mountain wall that surrounded the camp they duly preempted. This, and a reputation for singular proficiency with the revolver, kept the reserve of Roaring Camp inviolate. The expressman—their only connecting link with the surrounding world—sometimes told wonderful stories of the camp. He would say, "They've a street up there in 'Roaring' that would lay over any street in Red Dog. They've got vines and flowers round their houses, and they wash themselves twice a day. But they're mighty rough on strangers, and they worship an Ingin baby."

With the prosperity of the camp came a desire for further improvement. It was proposed to build a hotel in the following spring, and to invite one or two decent families to reside there for the sake of The Luck, who might perhaps profit by female companionship. The sacrifice that this concession to the sex cost these men, who were fiercely skeptical in regard to its general virtue and usefulness, can only be accounted for by their affection for Tommy. A few still held out. But the resolve could not be carried into effect for three months, and the minority meekly yielded in the hope that something might turn up to prevent it. And it did.

The winter of 1851 will long be remembered in the foothills. The snow lay deep on the Sierras, and every mountain creek became a river, and every river a lake. Each gorge and gulch was transformed into a tumultuous watercourse that descended the hillsides, tearing down giant trees and scattering its drift and débris along the plain. Red Dog had been twice under water, and Roaring Camp had been forewarned.

"Water put the gold into them gulches," said Stumpy. "It's been here once and will be here again!" And that night the North Fork suddenly leaped over its banks and swept up the triangular valley of Roaring Camp.

In the confusion of rushing water, crashing trees, and crackling timber, and the darkness which seemed to flow with the water and blot out the fair valley, but little could be done to collect the scattered camp. When the morning broke, the cabin of Stumpy, nearest the river-bank, was gone. Higher up the gulch they found the body of its unlucky owner; but the pride, the hope, the joy, The Luck, of Roaring Camp had disappeared. They were returning with sad hearts when a shout from the bank recalled them.

It was a relief-boat from down the river. They had picked up, they said, a man and an infant, nearly exhausted, about two miles below. Did anybody know them, and did they belong here?

It needed but a glance to show them Kentuck lying there, cruelly crushed and bruised, but still holding The Luck of Roaring Camp in his arms. As they bent over the strangely assorted pair, they saw that the child was cold and pulseless. "He is dead," said one. Kentuck opened his eyes. "Dead?" he repeated feebly. "Yes, my man, and you are dying too." A smile lit the eyes of the expiring Kentuck. "Dying!" he repeated; "he's a-taking me with him. Tell the boys I've got The Luck with me now;" and the strong man, clinging to the frail babe as a drowning man is said to cling to a straw, drifted away into the shadowy river that flows forever to the unknown sea.

Leo N. Tolstoi *(1828–1910)*

GOD SEES THE TRUTH, BUT WAITS

In the town of Vladimir lived a young merchant named Ivan Dmitrich Aksionov. He had two shops and a house of his own.

Aksionov was a handsome, fair-haired, curly-headed fellow, full of fun, and very fond of singing. When quite a young man he had been given to drink, and was riotous when he had had too much; but after he married he gave up drinking, except now and then.

One summer Aksionov was going to the Nizhny Fair, and as he bade good-bye to his family, his wife said to him, "Ivan Dmitrich, do not start to-day; I have had a bad dream about you."

Aksionov laughed, and said, "You are afraid that when I get to the fair I shall go on a spree."

His wife replied: "I do not know what I am afraid of; all I know is that I had a bad dream. I dreamt you returned from the town, and when you took off your cap I saw that your hair was quite grey."

Aksionov laughed. "That's a lucky sign," said he. "See if I don't sell out all my goods, and bring you some presents from the fair."

So he said good-bye to his family, and drove away.

When he had travelled half-way, he met a merchant whom he knew, and they put up at the same inn for the night. They had some tea together, and then went to bed in adjoining rooms.

It was not Aksionov's habit to sleep late, and, wishing to travel while it was still cool, he aroused his driver before dawn, and told him to put in the horses.

Then he made his way across to the landlord of the inn

(who lived in a cottage at the back), paid his bill, and continued his journey.

When he had gone about twenty-five miles, he stopped for the horses to be fed. Aksionov rested awhile in the passage of the inn, then he stepped out into the porch, and, ordering a samovar to be heated, got out his guitar and began to play.

Suddenly a troika drove up with tinkling bells and an official alighted, followed by two soldiers. He came to Aksionov and began to question him, asking him who he was and whence he came. Aksionov answered him fully, and said, "Won't you have some tea with me?" But the official went on cross-questioning him and asking him, "Where did you spend last night? Were you alone, or with a fellow-merchant? Did you see the other merchant this morning? Why did you leave the inn before dawn?"

Aksionov wondered why he was asked all these questions, but he described all that had happened, and then added, "Why do you cross-question me as if I were a thief or a robber? I am travelling on business of my own, and there is no need to question me."

Then the official, calling the soldiers, said, "I am the police-officer of this district, and I question you because the merchant with whom you spent last night has been found with his throat cut. We must search your things."

They entered the house. The soldiers and the police-officer unstrapped Aksionov's luggage and searched it. Suddenly the officer drew a knife out of a bag, crying, "Whose knife is this?"

Aksionov looked, and seeing a blood-stained knife taken from his bag, he was frightened.

"How is it there is blood on this knife?"

Aksionov tried to answer, but could hardly utter a word, and only stammered: "I—don't know—not mine."

Then the police-officer said: "This morning the merchant was found in bed with his throat cut. You are the only person who could have done it. The house was locked from inside, and no one else was there. Here is this blood-stained knife in your bag, and your face and manner betray you!

Tell me how you killed him, and how much money you stole?"

Aksionov swore he had not done it; that he had not seen the merchant after they had had tea together; that he had no money except eight thousand rubles of his own, and that the knife was not his. But his voice was broken, his face pale, and he trembled with fear as though he were guilty.

The police-officer ordered the soldiers to bind Aksionov and to put him in the cart. As they tied his feet together and flung him into the cart, Aksionov crossed himself and wept. His money and goods were taken from him, and he was sent to the nearest town and imprisoned there. Enquiries as to his character were made in Vladimir. The merchants and other inhabitants of that town said that in former days he used to drink and waste his time, but that he was a good man. Then the trial came on: he was charged with murdering a merchant from Ryazan, and robbing him of twenty thousand rubles.

His wife was in despair, and did not know what to believe. Her children were all quite small; one was a baby at her breast. Taking them all with her, she went to the town where her husband was in jail. At first she was not allowed to see him; but after much begging, she obtained permission from the officials, and was taken to him. When she saw her husband in prison-dress and in chains, shut up with thieves and criminals, she fell down, and did not come to her senses for a long time. Then she drew her children to her, and sat down near him. She told him of things at home, and asked about what had happened to him. He told her all, and she asked, "What can we do now?"

"We must petition the Czar not to let an innocent man perish."

His wife told him that she had sent a petition to the Czar, but it had not been accepted.

Aksionov did not reply, but only looked downcast.

Then his wife said, "It was not for nothing I dreamt your hair had turned grey. You remember? You should not have started that day." And passing her fingers through his hair, she said: "Vanya dearest, tell your wife the truth; was it not you who did it?"

"So you, too, suspect me!" said Aksionov, and, hiding his face in his hands, he began to weep. Then a soldier came to say that the wife and children must go away; and Aksionov said good-bye to his family for the last time.

When they were gone, Aksionov recalled what had been said, and when he remembered that his wife also had suspected him, he said to himself, "It seems that only God can know the truth; it is to Him alone we must appeal, and from Him alone expect mercy."

And Aksionov wrote no more petitions; gave up all hope, and only prayed to God.

Aksionov was condemned to be flogged and sent to the mines. So he was flogged with a knot, and when the wounds made by the knot were healed, he was driven to Siberia with other convicts.

For twenty-six years Aksionov lived as a convict in Siberia. His hair turned white as snow, and his beard grew long, thin, and grey. All his mirth went; he stooped; he walked slowly, spoke little, and never laughed, but he often prayed.

In prison Aksionov learnt to make boots, and earned a little money, with which he bought *The Lives of the Saints*. He read this book when there was light enough in the prison; and on Sundays in the prison-church he read the lessons and sang in the choir; for his voice was still good.

The prison authorities liked Aksionov for his meekness, and his fellow-prisoners respected him: they called him "Grandfather," and "The Saint." When they wanted to petition the prison authorities about anything, they always made Aksionov their spokesman, and when there were quarrels among the prisoners they came to him to put things right, and to judge the matter.

No news reached Aksionov from his home, and he did not even know if his wife and children were still alive.

One day a fresh gang of convicts came to the prison. In the evening the old prisoners collected round the new ones and asked them what towns or villages they came from, and what they were sentenced for. Among the rest Aksionov sat down near the newcomers, and listened with downcast air to what was said.

One of the new convicts, a tall, strong man of sixty, with a closely-cropped grey beard, was telling the others what he had been arrested for.

"Well, friends," he said, "I only took a horse that was tied to a sledge, and I was arrested and accused of stealing. I said I had only taken it to get home quicker, and had then let it go; besides, the driver was a personal friend of mine. So I said, 'It's all right.' 'No,' said they, 'you stole it.' But how or where I stole it they could not say. I once really did something wrong, and ought by rights to have come here long ago, but that time I was not found out. Now I have been sent here for nothing at all. . . . Eh, but it's lies I'm telling you; I've been to Siberia before, but I did not stay long."

"Where are you from?" asked some one.

"From Vladimir. My family are of that town. My name is Makar, and they also call me Semyonich."

Aksionov raised his head and said: "Tell me, Semyonich, do you know anything of the merchants Aksionov of Vladimir? Are they still alive?"

"Know them? Of course I do. The Aksionovs are rich, though their father is in Siberia: a sinner like ourselves, it seems! As for you, Gran'dad, how did you come here?"

Aksionov did not like to speak of his misfortune. He only sighed, and said, "For my sins I have been in prison these twenty-six years."

"What sins?" asked Makar Semyonich.

But Aksionov only said, "Well, well—I must have deserved it!" He would have said no more, but his companions told the newcomers how Aksionov came to be in Siberia; how some one had killed a merchant, and had put the knife among Aksionov's things, and Aksionov had been unjustly condemned.

When Makar Semyonich heard this, he looked at Aksionov, slapped his own knee, and exclaimed, "Well, this is wonderful! Really wonderful! But how old you've grown, Gran'dad!"

The others asked him why he was so surprised, and where he had seen Aksionov before; but Makar Semyonich did not reply. He only said: "It's wonderful that we should meet here, lads!"

These words made Aksionov wonder whether this man knew who had killed the merchant; so he said, "Perhaps, Semyonich, you have heard of that affair, or maybe you've seen me before?"

"How could I help hearing? The world's full of rumours. But it's a long time ago, and I've forgotten what I heard."

"Perhaps you heard who killed the merchant?" asked Aksionov.

Makar Semyonich laughed and replied: "It must have been him in whose bag the knife was found! If some one else hid the knife there, 'He's not a thief till he's caught,' as the saying is. How could any one put a knife into your bag while it was under your head? It would surely have woke you up."

When Aksionov heard these words, he felt sure this was the man who had killed the merchant. He rose and went away. All that night Aksionov lay awake. He felt terribly unhappy, and all sorts of images rose in his mind. There was the image of his wife as she was when he parted from her to go to the fair. He saw her as if she were present; her face and her eyes rose before him; he heard her speak and laugh. Then he saw his children, quite little, as they were at that time: one with a little cloak on, another at his mother's breast. And then he remembered himself as he used to be—young and merry. He remembered how he sat playing the guitar in the porch of the inn where he was arrested, and how free from care he had been. He saw, in his mind, the place where he was flogged, the executioner, and the people standing around; the chains, the convicts, all the twenty-six years of his prison life, and his premature old age. The thought of it all made him so wretched that he was ready to kill himself.

"And it's all that villain's doing!" thought Aksionov. And his anger was so great against Makar Semyonich that he longed for vengeance, even if he himself should perish for it. He kept repeating prayers all night, but could get no peace. During the day he did not go near Makar Semyonich, nor even look at him.

A fortnight passed in this way. Aksionov could not sleep

at night, and was so miserable that he did not know what to do.

One night as he was walking about the prison he noticed some earth that came rolling out from under one of the shelves on which the prisoners slept. He stopped to see what it was. Suddenly Makar Semyonich crept out from under the shelf, and looked up at Aksionov with frightened face. Aksionov tried to pass without looking at him, but Makar seized his hand and told him that he had dug a hole under the wall, getting rid of the earth by putting it into his high-boots, and emptying it out every day on the road when the prisoners were driven to their work.

"Just you keep quiet, old man, and you shall get out too. If you blab, they'll flog the life out of me, but I will kill you first."

Aksionov trembled with anger as he looked at his enemy. He drew his hand away, saying, "I have no wish to escape, and you have no need to kill me; you killed me long ago! As to telling of you—I may do so or not, as God shall direct."

Next day, when the convicts were led out to work, the convoy soldiers noticed that one of the prisoners emptied some earth out of his boots. The prison was searched and the tunnel found. The Governor came and questioned all the prisoners to find out who had dug the hole. They all denied any knowledge of it. Those who knew would not betray Makar Semyonich, knowing he would be flogged almost to death. At last the Governor turned to Aksionov whom he knew to be a just man, and said: "You are a truthful old man; tell me, before God, who dug the hole?"

Makar Semyonich stood as if he were quite unconcerned, looking at the Governor and not so much as glancing at Aksionov. Aksionov's lips and hands trembled, and for a long time he could not utter a word. He thought, "Why should I screen him who ruined my life? Let him pay for what I have suffered. But if I tell, they will probably flog the life out of him, and maybe I suspect him wrongly. And, after all, what good would it be to me?"

"Well, old man," repeated the Governor, "tell me the truth: who has been digging under the wall?"

Aksionov glanced at Makar Semyonich, and said, "I cannot say, your honour. It is not God's will that I should tell! Do what you like with me; I am in your hands."

However much the Governor tried, Aksionov would say no more, and so the matter had to be left.

That night, when Aksionov was lying on his bed and just beginning to doze, some one came quietly and sat down on his bed. He peered through the darkness and recognized Makar.

"What more do you want of me?" asked Aksionov. "Why have you come here?"

Makar Semyonich was silent. So Aksionov sat up and said, "What do you want? Go away, or I will call the guard!"

Makar Semyonich bent close over Aksionov, and whispered, "Ivan Dmitrich, forgive me!"

"What for?" asked Aksionov.

"It was I who killed the merchant and hid the knife among your things. I meant to kill you too, but I heard a noise outside, so I hid the knife in your bag and escaped out of the window."

Aksionov was silent, and did not know what to say. Makar Semyonich slid off the bed-shelf and knelt upon the ground. "Ivan Dmitrich," said he, "forgive me! For the love of God, forgive me! I will confess that it was I who killed the merchant, and you will be released and can go to your home."

"It is easy for you to talk," said Aksionov, "but I have suffered for you these twenty-six years. Where could I go to now? . . . My wife is dead, and my children have forgotten me. I have nowhere to go. . . ."

Makar Semyonich did not rise, but beat his head on the floor. "Ivan Dmitrich, forgive me!" he cried. "When they flogged me with the knot it was not so hard to bear as it is to see you now . . . yet you had pity on me, and did not tell. For Christ's sake forgive me, wretch that I am!" And he began to sob.

When Aksionov heard him sobbing he, too, began to weep. "God will forgive you!" said he. "Maybe I am a hundred times worse than you." And at these words his heart grew light, and the longing for home left him. He no longer had any desire to leave the prison, but only hoped for his last hour to come.

In spite of what Aksionov had said, Makar Semyonich confessed his guilt. But when the order for his release came Aksionov was already dead.

EDGAR ALLAN POE *(1809–1849)*

THE CASK OF AMONTILLADO

THE THOUSAND injuries of Fortunato I had borne as I best could, but when he ventured upon insult, I vowed revenge. You, who so well know the nature of my soul, will not suppose, however, that I gave utterance to a threat. *At length* I would be avenged; this was a point definitely settled—but the very definitiveness with which it was resolved precluded the idea of risk. I must not only punish, but punish with impunity. A wrong is unredressed when retribution overtakes its redresser. It is equally unredressed when the avenger fails to make himself felt as such to him who has done the wrong.

It must be understood that neither by word nor deed had I given Fortunato cause to doubt my good will. I continued, as was my wont, to smile in his face, and he did not perceive that my smile *now* was at the thought of his immolation.

He had a weak point—this Fortunato—although in other regards he was a man to be respected and even feared. He prided himself on his connoisseurship in wine. Few Italians have the true virtuoso spirit. For the most part their enthusiasm is adopted to suit the time and opportunity to practise imposture upon the British and Austrian *millionaires*. In painting and gemmary Fortunato, like his countrymen, was a quack, but in the matter of old wines he was sincere. In this respect I did not differ from him materially;—I was skilful in the Italian vintages myself, and bought largely whenever I could.

It was about dusk, one evening during the supreme madness of the carnival season, that I encountered my friend. He accosted me with excessive warmth, for he had been drinking much. The man wore motley. He had on a tight-fitting parti-striped dress, and his head was surmounted by the conical cap and bells. I was so pleased to see him, that I thought I should never have done wringing his hand.

I said to him—"My dear Fortunato, you are luckily met. How remarkably well you are looking to-day! But I have received a pipe of what passes for Amontillado, and I have my doubts."

"How?" said he, "Amontillado? A pipe? Impossible! And in the middle of the carnival?"

"I have my doubts," I replied; "and I was silly enough to pay the full Amontillado price without consulting you in the matter. You were not to be found, and I was fearful of losing a bargain."

"Amontillado!"

"I have my doubts."

"Amontillado!"

"And I must satisfy them."

"Amontillado!"

"As you are engaged, I am on my way to Luchesi. If any one has a critical turn, it is he. He will tell me——"

"Luchesi cannot tell Amontillado from Sherry."

"And yet some fools will have it that his taste is a match for your own."

"Come, let us go."

"Whither?"

"To your vaults."

"My friend, no; I will not impose upon your good nature. I perceive you have an engagement. Luchesi——"

"I have no engagement; come."

"My friend, no. It is not the engagement, but the severe cold with which I perceive you are afflicted. The vaults are insufferably damp. They are encrusted with nitre."

"Let us go, nevertheless. The cold is merely nothing. Amontillado! You have been imposed upon; and as for Luchesi, he cannot distinguish Sherry from Amontillado."

Thus speaking, Fortunato possessed himself of my arm. Putting on a mask of black silk, and drawing a *roquelaure* closely about my person, I suffered him to hurry me to my palazzo.

There were no attendants at home; they had absconded to make merry in honour of the time. I had told them that I should not return until the morning, and had given them explicit orders not to stir from the house. These orders were sufficient, I well knew, to insure their immediate disappearance, one and all, as soon as my back was turned.

I took from their sconces two flambeaux, and giving one to Fortunato, bowed him through several suites of rooms to the archway that led into the vaults. I passed down a long and winding staircase, requesting him to be cautious as he followed. We came at length to the foot of the descent, and stood together on the damp ground of the catacombs of the Montresors.

The gait of my friend was unsteady, and the bells upon his cap jingled as he strode.

"The pipe," said he.

"It is farther on," said I; "but observe the white web-work which gleams from these cavern walls."

He turned towards me, and looked into my eyes with two filmy orbs that distilled the rheum of intoxication.

"Nitre?" he asked, at length.

"Nitre," I replied. "How long have you had that cough?"

"Ugh! ugh! ugh!—ugh! ugh! ugh!—ugh! ugh! ugh!—ugh! ugh! ugh!—ugh! ugh! ugh!"

My poor friend found it impossible to reply for many minutes.

"It is nothing," he said, at last.

"Come," I said, with decision, "we will go back; your health is precious. You are rich, respected, admired, beloved; you are happy, as once I was. You are a man to be missed. For me it is no matter. We will go back; you will be ill, and I cannot be responsible. Besides, there is Luchesi——"

"Enough," he said; "the cough is a mere nothing: it will not kill me. I shall not die of a cough."

"True—true," I replied; "and, indeed, I had no intention of alarming you unnecessarily—but you should use all proper caution. A draught of this Medoc will defend us from the damps."

Here I knocked off the neck of a bottle which I drew from a long row of its fellows that lay upon the mould.

"Drink," I said, presenting him the wine.

He raised it to his lips with a leer. He paused and nodded to me familiarly, while his bells jingled.

"I drink," he said, "to the buried that repose around us."

"And I to your long life."

He again took my arm, and we proceeded.

"These vaults," he said, "are extensive."

"The Montresors," I replied, "were a great and numerous family."

"I forget your arms."

"A huge human foot d'or, in a field azure; the foot crushes a serpent rampant whose fangs are imbedded in the heel."

"And the motto?"

"Nemo me impune lacessit." [1]

"Good!" he said.

The wine sparkled in his eyes and the bells jingled. My own fancy grew warm with the Medoc. We had passed through walls of piled bones, with casks and puncheons intermingling, into the inmost recesses of the catacombs. I paused again, and this time I made bold to seize Fortunato by an arm above the elbow.

"The nitre!" I said; "see, it increases. It hangs like moss upon the vaults. We are below the river's bed. The drops of moisture trickle among the bones. Come, we will go back ere it is too late. Your cough——"

"It is nothing," he said; "let us go on. But first, another draught of the Medoc." I broke and reached him a flagon of De Grâve. He emptied it at a breath. His eyes flashed with a fierce light. He laughed and threw the bottle upwards with a gesticulation I did not understand.

I looked at him in surprise. He repeated the movement—a grotesque one. "You do not comprehend?" he said.

"Not I," I replied.

"Then you are not of the brotherhood."

"How?"

"You are not of the masons."

[1] No one dare attack me with impunity (the motto of Scotland).

"Yes, yes," I said, "yes, yes."

"You? Impossible! A mason?"

"A mason," I replied.

"A sign," he said.

"It is this," I answered, producing a trowel from beneath the folds of my *roquelaure*.

"You jest," he exclaimed, recoiling a few paces. "But let us proceed to the Amontillado."

"Be it so," I said, replacing the tool beneath the cloak, and again offering him my arm. He leaned upon it heavily. We continued our route in search of the Amontillado. We passed through a range of low arches, descended, passed on, and descending again, arrived at a deep crypt, in which the foulness of the air caused our flambeaux rather to glow than flame.

At the most remote end of the crypt there appeared another less spacious. Its walls had been lined with human remains piled to the vault overhead, in the fashion of the great catacombs of Paris. Three sides of this interior crypt were still ornamented in this manner. From the fourth the bones had been thrown down, and lay promiscuously upon the earth, forming at one point a mound of some size. Within the wall thus exposed by the displacing of the bones, we perceived a still interior recess, in depth about four feet, in width three, in height six or seven. It seemed to have been constructed for no especial use within itself, but formed merely the interval between two of the colossal supports of the roof of the catacombs, and was backed by one of the circumscribing walls of solid granite.

It was in vain that Fortunato, uplifting his dull torch endeavored to pry into the depths of the recess. Its termination the feeble light did not enable us to see.

"Proceed," I said; "herein is the Amontillado. As for Luchesi——"

"He is an ignoramus," interrupted my friend, as he stepped unsteadily forward, while I followed immediately at his heels. In an instant he had reached the extremity of the niche, and finding his progress arrested by the rock, stood stupidly bewildered. A moment more and I had fettered him to the granite. In its surface were two iron staples, distant from each other about two feet, horizontally. From one of these depended a short chain, from the other a padlock. Throwing the links about his waist, it was but the work of a few seconds to secure it. He was too much astounded to resist. Withdrawing the key I stepped back from the recess.

"Pass your hand," I said, "over the wall; you cannot help feeling the nitre. Indeed it is *very* damp. Once more let me *implore* you to return. No? Then I must positively leave you. But I must first render you all the little attentions in my power."

"The Amontillado!" ejaculated my friend, not yet recovered from his astonishment.

"True," I replied; "the Amontillado."

As I said these words I busied myself among the pile of bones of which I have before spoken. Throwing them aside, I soon uncovered a quantity of building-stone and mortar. With these materials and with the aid of my trowel, I began vigorously to wall up the entrance of the niche.

I had scarcely laid the first tier of the masonry when I discovered that the intoxication of Fortunato had in a great measure worn off. The earliest indication I had of this was a low moaning cry from the depth of the recess. It was *not* the cry of a drunken man. There was then a long and obstinate silence. I laid the second tier, and the third, and the fourth; and then I heard the furious vibrations of the chain. The noise lasted for several minutes, during which, that I might hearken to it with the more satisfaction, I ceased my labours and sat down upon the bones. When at last the clanking subsided, I resumed the trowel, and finished without interruption the fifth, the sixth, and the seventh tier. The wall was now nearly upon a level with my breast. I again paused, and holding the flambeaux over the masonwork, threw a few feeble rays upon the figure within.

A succession of loud and shrill screams, bursting suddenly from the throat of the chained form, seemed to thrust me violently back. For a brief moment I hesitated—I trembled. Unsheathing my rapier, I began to grope with it about the recess; but the thought of an instant reassured me. I placed my hand upon the solid fabric of the catacombs, and felt satisfied. I reapproached the wall. I replied to the yells of him who clamoured. I re-echoed—I aided—I surpassed them in volume and in strength. I did this, and the clamourer grew still.

It was now midnight, and my task was drawing to a close. I had completed the eighth, the ninth, and the tenth tier. I had finished a portion of the last and the eleventh; there remained but a single stone to be fitted and plastered in. I struggled with its weight; I placed it partially in its destined position. But now there came from out the niche a low laugh that erected the hairs upon my head. It was succeeded by a sad voice, which I had difficulty in recognizing as that of the noble Fortunato. The voice said—

"Ha! ha! ha!—he! he! he!—a very good joke indeed—an excellent jest. We will have many a rich laugh about it at the palazzo—he! he! he!—over our wine—he! he! he!"

"The Amontillado!" I said.

"He! he! he!—he! he! he!—yes, the Amontillado. But is it not getting late? Will not they be awaiting us at the palazzo, the Lady Fortunato and the rest? Let us be gone."

"Yes," I said, "let us be gone."

"*For the love of God, Montresor!*"

"Yes," I said, "for the love of God!"

But to these words I hearkened in vain for a reply. I grew impatient. I called aloud; "Fortunato!"

No answer. I called again; "Fortunato!"

No answer still. I thrust a torch through the remaining aperture and let it fall within. There came forth in return only a jingling of the bells. My heart grew sick—on account of the dampness of the catacombs. I hastened to make an end of my labor. I forced the last stone into its position; I plastered it up. Against the new masonry I re-erected the old rampart of bones. For the half of a century no mortal has disturbed them. *In pace requiescat!*

Honoré de Balzac (1799-1850)

A PASSION IN THE DESERT

"The whole show is dreadful," she cried, coming out of the menagerie of M. Martin. She had just been looking at that daring speculator "working with his hyena"—to speak in the style of the program.

"By what means," she continued, "can he have tamed these animals to such a point as to be certain of their affection for——."

"What seems to you a problem," said I, interrupting, "is really quite natural."

"Oh!" she cried, letting an incredulous smile wander over her lips.

"You think that beasts are wholly without passions?" I asked her. "Quite the reverse; we can communicate to them all the vices arising in our own state of civilization."

She looked at me with an air of astonishment.

"Nevertheless," I continued, "the first time I saw M. Martin, I admit, like you, I did give vent to an exclamation of surprise. I found myself next to an old soldier with the right leg amputated, who had come in with me. His face had struck me. He had one of those intrepid heads, stamped with the seal of warfare, and on which the battles of Napoleon are written. Besides, he had that frank good-humored expression which always impresses me favorably. He was without doubt one of those troopers who are surprised at nothing, who find matter for laughter in the contortions of a dying comrade, who bury or plunder him quite light-heartedly, who stand intrepidly in the way of bullets; in fact, one of those men who waste no time in deliberation, and would not hesitate to make friends with the devil himself. After looking very attentively at the proprietor of the menagerie getting out of his box, my companion pursed up his lips with an air

323

of mockery and contempt, with that peculiar and expressive twist which superior people assume to show they are not taken in. Then when I was expatiating on the courage of M. Martin, he smiled, shook his head knowingly, and said, 'Well known.'

"How 'well known'?" I said. "If you would only explain to me the mystery I should be vastly obliged.

"After a few minutes, during which we made acquaintance, we went to dine at the first *restaurateur's* whose shop caught our eye. At dessert a bottle of champagne completely refreshed and brightened up the memories of this odd old soldier. He told me his story, and I said he had every reason to exclaim, 'Well known.' "

When she got home, she teased me to that extent and made so many promises, that I consented to communicate to her the old soldier's confidences. Next day she received the following episode of an epic which one might call "The Frenchman in Egypt."

During the expedition in Upper Egypt under General Desaix, a Provençal soldier fell into the hands of the Mangrabins, and was taken by these Arabs into the deserts beyond the falls of the Nile.

In order to place a sufficient distance between themselves and the French army, the Mangrabins made forced marches, and only rested during the night. They camped round a well overshadowed by palm trees under which they had previously concealed a store of provisions. Not surmising that the notion of flight would occur to their prisoner, they contented themselves with binding his hands, and after eating a few dates, and giving provender to their horses, went to sleep.

When the brave Provençal saw that his enemies were no longer watching him, he made use of his teeth to steal a scimitar, fixed the blade between his knees, and cut the cords which prevented using his hands; in a moment he was free. He at once seized a rifle and dagger, then taking the precaution to provide himself with a sack of dried dates, oats, and powder and shot, and to fasten a scimitar to his waist he leaped onto a horse, and spurred on vigorously in the direction where he thought to find the French army. So impatient was he to see a bivouac again that he pressed on the already tired courser at such speed that its flanks were lacerated with his spurs, and at last the poor animal died, leaving the Frenchman alone in the desert. After walking some time in the sand with all the courage of an escaped convict, the soldier was obliged to stop, as the day had already ended. In spite of the beauty of an oriental sky at night, he felt he had not strength enough to go on. Fortunately he had been able to find a small hill, on the summit of which a few palm trees shot up into the air; it was their verdure seen from afar which had brought hope and consolation to his heart. His fatigue was so great that he lay down upon a rock of granite, capriciously cut out like a camp-bed; there he fell asleep without taking any precaution to defend himself while he slept. He had made the sacrifice of his life. His last thought was one of regret. He repented having left the Mangrabins, whose nomad life seemed to smile on him now that he was afar from them and without help. He was awakened by the sun, whose pitiless rays fell with all their force on the granite and produced an intolerable heat—for he had had the stupidity to place himself inversely to the shadow thrown by the verdant majestic heads of the palm trees. He looked at the solitary trees and shuddered—they reminded him of the graceful shafts crowned with foliage which characterize the Saracen columns in the cathedral of Arles.

But when, after counting the palm trees, he cast his eye around him, the most horrible despair was infused into his soul. Before him stretched an ocean without limit. The dark sand of the desert spread farther than sight could reach in every direction, and glittered like steel struck with a bright light. It might have been a sea of looking-glass, or lakes melted together in a mirror. A fiery vapor carried up in streaks made a perpetual whirlwind over the quivering land. The sky was lit with an oriental splendor of insupportable purity, leaving naught for the imagination to desire. Heaven and earth were on fire.

The silence was awful in its wild and terrible majesty. Infinity, immensity, closed in upon the soul from every side. Not a cloud in the sky, not a breath in the air, not a flaw on the bosom of the sand, ever moving in diminutive waves; the horizon ended as at sea on a clear day, with one line of light, definite as the cut of a sword.

The Provençal threw his arms around the trunk of one of the palm trees, as though it were the body of a friend, and then in the shelter of the thin straight shadow that the palm cast upon the granite, he wept. Then sitting down he remained as he was, contemplating with profound sadness the implacable scene, which was all he had to look upon. He cried aloud, to measure the solitude. His voice, lost in the hollows of the hill, sounded faintly, and aroused no echo—the echo was in his own heart. The Provençal was twenty-two years old; he loaded his carbine.

"There'll be time enough," he said to himself, laying on the ground the weapon which alone could bring him deliverance.

Looking by turns at the black expanse and the blue expanse, the soldier dreamed of France—he smelt with delight the gutters of Paris—he remembered the towns through which he had passed, the faces of his fellow-soldiers, the most minute details of his life. His southern fancy soon showed him the stones of his beloved Provence, in the play of the heat which waved over the spread sheet of the desert. Fearing the danger of this cruel mirage, he went down the opposite side of the hill to that by which he had come up the day before. The remains of a rug showed that this place of refuge had at one time been inhabited; at a short distance he saw some palm trees full of dates. Then the instinct which binds us to life awoke again in his heart. He hoped to live long enough to await the passing of some Arabs, or perhaps he might hear the sound of cannon; for at this time Bonaparte was traversing Egypt.

This thought gave him new life. The palm tree seemed to bend with the weight of the ripe fruit. He shook some of it down. When he tasted this unhoped-for manna, he felt sure that the palms had been cultivated by a former inhabitant—the savory, fresh meat of the dates was proof of the care of his predecessor. He passed suddenly from dark despair to an almost insane joy. He went up again to the top of the hill, and spent the rest of the day in cutting down one of the sterile palm trees, which the night before had served him for shelter. A vague memory made him think of the animals of the desert; and in case they might come to drink at the spring, visible from the base of the rocks but lost farther down, he resolved to guard himself from their visits by placing a barrier at the entrance of his hermitage.

In spite of his diligence, and the strength which the fear of being devoured asleep gave him, he was unable to cut the palm in pieces, though he succeeded in cutting it down. At eventide the king of the desert fell; the sound of its fall resounded far and wide, like a sign in the solitude; the soldier shuddered as though he had heard some voice predicting woe.

But like an heir who does not long bewail a deceased parent, he tore off from this beautiful tree the tall broad green leaves which are its poetic adornment, and used them to mend the mat on which he was to sleep.

Fatigued by the heat and his work, he fell asleep under the red curtains of his wet cave.

In the middle of the night his sleep was troubled by an extraordinary noise; he sat up, and the deep silence around him allowed him to distinguish the alternative accents of a respiration whose savage energy could not belong to a human creature.

A profound terror, increased still further by the darkness, the silence, and his waking images, froze his heart within him. He almost felt his hair stand on end, when by straining his eyes to their utmost he perceived through the shadows two faint yellow lights. At first he attributed these lights to the reflection of his own pupils, but soon the vivid brilliance of the night aided him gradually to distinguish the objects around him in the cave, and he beheld a huge animal lying but two steps from him. Was it a lion, a tiger, or a crocodile?

The Provençal was not educated enough to know under what species his enemy ought to be classed; but his fright was all the greater, as his ignorance led him to imagine all terrors at once; he endured a cruel torture, noting every variation of the breathing close to him without daring to make the slightest movement. An odor, pungent like that of a fox, but more penetrating, profounder—so to speak—filled the cave, and when the Provençal became sensible of this, his terror reached its height, for he could not longer doubt the proximity of a terrible companion, whose royal dwelling served him for shelter.

Presently the reflection of the moon, descending on the horizon, lit up the den, rendering gradually visible and resplendent the spotted skin of a panther.

The lion of Egypt slept, curled up like a big dog, the peaceful possessor of a sumptuous niche at the gate of an hotel; its eyes opened for a moment and closed again; its face was turned toward the man. A thousand confused thoughts passed through the Frenchman's mind; first he thought of killing it with a bullet from his gun, but he saw there was not enough distance between them for him to take proper aim—the shot would miss the mark. And if it were to wake!—the thought made his limbs rigid. He listened to his own heart beating in the midst of the silence, and cursed the too violent pulsations which the flow of blood brought on, fearing to disturb that sleep which allowed him time to think of some means of escape.

Twice he placed his hand on his scimitar, intending to cut off the head of his enemy; but the difficulty of cutting the stiff, short hair compelled him to abandon this daring project. To miss would be to die for *certain*, he thought; he preferred the chances of fair fight, and made up his mind to wait till morning; the morning did not leave him long to wait.

He could now examine the panther at ease; its muzzle was smeared with blood.

"She's had a good dinner," he thought, without troubling himself as to whether her feast might have been on human flesh. "She won't be hungry when she gets up."

It was a female. The fur on her belly and flanks was glistening white; many small marks like velvet formed beautiful bracelets round her feet; her sinuous tail was also white, ending with black rings; the overpart of her dress, yellow like unburnished gold, very lissom and soft, had the characteristic blotches in the form of rosettes, which distinguish the panther from every other feline species.

This tranquil and formidable hostess snored in an attitude as graceful as that of a cat lying on a cushion. Her blood-stained paws, nervous and well-armed, were stretched out before her face, which rested upon them, and from which radiated her straight, slender whiskers, like threads of silver.

If she had been like that in a cage, the Provençal would doubtless have admired the grace of the animal, and the vigorous contrasts of vivid color which gave her robe an imperial splendor; but just then his sight was troubled by her sinister appearance.

The presence of the panther, even asleep, could not fail to produce the effect which the magnetic eyes of the serpent are said to have on the nightingale.

For a moment the courage of the soldier began to fail before this danger, though no doubt it would have risen at the mouth of a cannon charged with shell. Nevertheless, a bold thought brought daylight to his soul and sealed up the source of the cold sweat which sprang forth on his brow. Like men driven to bay who defy death and offer their body to the smiter, so he, seeing in this merely a tragic episode, resolved to play his part with honor to the last.

"The day before yesterday the Arabs would have killed me perhaps," he said; so considering himself as good as dead already, he waited bravely, with excited curiosity, his enemy's awakening.

When the sun appeared, the panther suddenly opened her eyes; then she put out her paws with energy, as if to stretch them and get rid of cramp. At last she yawned, showing the formidable apparatus of her teeth and pointed tongue, rough as a file.

"A regular *petite maîtresse*," thought the Frenchman, seeing her roll herself about so softly and coquettishly. She licked off the blood which stained her paws and muzzle, and scratched her head with reiterated gestures full of prettiness. "All right, make a little toilet," the Frenchman said to himself, beginning to recover his gaiety with his courage; "we'll say good morning to each other presently," and he seized the small, short dagger which he had taken from the Mangrabins. At this moment the panther turned her head toward the man and looked at him fixedly without moving.

The rigidity of her metallic eyes and their insupportable luster made him shudder, especially when the animal walked toward him. But he looked at her caressingly, staring into her eyes in order to magnetize her, and let her come quite close to him; then with a movement both gentle and amorous, as though he were caressing the most beautiful of women, he passed his hand over her whole body, from the head to the tail, scratching the flexible vertebrae which divided the panther's yellow back. The animal waved her tail voluptuously, and her eyes grew gentle; and when for the third time the Frenchman accomplished this interesting flattery, she gave forth one of those purrings by which our cats express their pleasure; but this murmur issued from a throat so powerful and so deep, that it resounded through the cave like the last vibrations of an organ in a church. The man, understanding the importance of his caresses, redoubled them in such a way as to surprise and stupefy his imperious courtesan. When he felt sure of having extinguished the ferocity of his capricious companion, whose hunger had so fortunately been satisfied the day before, he got up to go out of the cave; the panther let him go out, but when he had reached the summit of the hill she sprang with the lightness of a sparrow hopping from twig to twig, and rubbed herself against his legs, putting up her back after the manner of all the race of cats. Then regarding her guest with eyes whose glare had softened a little, she gave vent to that wild cry which naturalists compare to the grating of a saw.

"She is exacting," said the Frenchman, smilingly.

He was bold enough to play with her ears; he caressed her belly and scratched her head as hard as he could.

When he saw that he was successful, he tickled her skull with the point of his dagger, watching for the right moment to kill her, but the hardness of her bones made him tremble for his success.

The sultana of the desert showed herself gracious to her slave; she lifted her head, stretched out her neck, and manifested her delight by the tranquillity of her attitude. It suddenly occurred to the soldier that to kill this savage princess with one blow he must poignard her in the throat.

He raised the blade, when the panther, satisfied no doubt, laid herself gracefully at his feet, and cast up at him glances in which, in spite of their natural fierceness, were mingled confusedly a kind of good-will. The poor Provençal ate his dates, leaning against one of the palm trees, and casting his eyes alternately on the desert in quest of some liberator and on his terrible companion to watch her uncertain clemency.

The panther looked at the place where the date stones fell, and every time that he threw one down her eyes expressed an incredible mistrust.

She examined the man with an almost commercial prudence. However, this examination was favorable to him, for when he had finished his meager meal she licked his boots with her powerful rough tongue, brushing off with marvellous skill the dust gathered in the creases.

"Ah, but when she's really hungry!" thought the Frenchman. In spite of the shudder this thought caused him, the soldier began to measure curiously the proportions of the panther, certainly one of the most splendid specimens of its race. She was three feet high and four feet long without counting her tail; this powerful weapon, rounded like a cudgel, was nearly three feet long. The head, large as that of a lioness, was distinguished by a rare expression of refinement. The cold cruelty of a tiger was dominant, it was true, but there was also a vague resemblance to the face of a sensual woman. Indeed, the face of this solitary queen had something of the gaiety of a drunken Nero: she had satiated herself with blood, and she wanted to play.

The soldier tried if he might walk up and down, and the panther left him free, contenting herself with following him with her eyes, less like a faithful dog than a big Angora cat, observing everything, and every movement of her master.

When he looked around, he saw, by the spring, the remains of his horse; the panther had dragged the carcass all that way; about two-thirds of it had been devoured already. The sight reassured him.

It was easy to explain the panther's absence, and the respect she had had for him while he slept. The first piece of good luck emboldened him to tempt the future, and he conceived the wild hope of continuing on good terms with the panther during the entire day, neglecting no means of taming her, and remaining in her good graces.

He returned to her, and had the unspeakable joy of seeing

her wag her tail with an almost imperceptible movement at
his approach. He sat down then, without fear, by her side,
and they began to play together; he took her paws and
muzzle, pulled her ears, rolled her over on her back, stroked
her warm, delicate flanks. She let him do whatever he liked,
and when he began to stroke the hair on her feet she drew
her claws in carefully.

The man, keeping the dagger in one hand, thought to
plunge it into the belly of the too-confiding panther, but he
was afraid that he would be immediately strangled in her
last convulsive struggle; besides, he felt in his heart a sort of
remorse which bid him respect a creature that had done him
no harm. He seemed to have found a friend, in a boundless
desert; half unconsciously he thought of his first sweetheart, whom he had nicknamed "Mignonne" by way of contrast, because she was so atrociously jealous that all the
time of their love he was in fear of the knife with which she
had always threatened him.

This memory of his early days suggested to him the idea
of making the young panther answer to this name, now that
he began to admire with less terror her swiftness, suppleness,
and softness. Toward the end of the day he had familiarized
himself with his perilous position; he now almost liked the
painfulness of it. At last his companion had got into the
habit of looking up at him whenever he cried in a falsetto
voice, "Mignonne."

At the setting of the sun Mignonne gave, several times
running, a profound melancholy cry. "She's been well
brought up," said the light-hearted soldier; "she says her
prayers." But this mental joke only occurred to him when
he noticed what a pacific attitude his companion remained
in. "Come, *ma petite blonde*, I'll let you go to bed first," he
said to her, counting on the activity of his own legs to run
away as quickly as possible, directly she was asleep, and seek
another shelter for the night.

The soldier waited with impatience the hour of his flight,
and when it had arrived he walked vigorously in the direction of the Nile; but hardly had he made a quarter of a
league in the sand when he heard the panther bounding after

him, crying with that saw-like cry more dreadful even than the sound of her leaping.

"Ah!" he said, "then she's taken a fancy to me; she has never met any one before, and it is really quite flattering to have her first love." That instant the man fell into one of those movable quicksands so terrible to travellers and from which it is impossible to save oneself. Feeling himself caught, he gave a shriek of alarm; the panther seized him with her teeth by the collar, and, springing vigorously backward, drew him as if by magic out of the whirling sand.

"Ah, Mignonne!" cried the soldier, caressing her enthusiastically; "we're bound together for life and death—but no jokes, mind!" and he retraced his steps.

From that time the desert seemed inhabited. It contained a being to whom the man could talk, and whose ferocity was rendered gentle by him, though he could not explain to himself the reason for their strange friendship. Great as was the soldier's desire to stay upon guard, he slept.

On awakening he could not find Mignonne; he mounted the hill, and in the distance saw her springing toward him after the habit of these animals, who cannot run on account of the extreme flexibility of the vertebral column. Mignonne arrived, her jaws covered with blood; she received the wonted caress of her companion, showing with much purring how happy it made her. Her eyes, full of languor, turned still more gently than the day before toward the Provençal who talked to her as one would to a tame animal.

"Ah! Mademoiselle, you are a nice girl, aren't you? Just look at that! so we like to be made much of, don't we? Aren't you ashamed of yourself? So you have been eating some Arab or other, have you? that doesn't matter. They're animals just the same as you are; but don't you take to eating Frenchmen, or I shan't like you any longer."

She played like a dog with its master, letting herself be rolled over, knocked about, and stroked, alternately; sometimes she herself would provoke the soldier, putting up her paw with a soliciting gesture.

Some days passed in this manner. This companionship permitted the Provençal to appreciate the sublime beauty of the desert; now that he had a living thing to think about, alternations of fear and quiet, and plenty to eat, his mind became filled with contrast and his life began to be diversified.

Solitude revealed to him all her secrets, and enveloped him in her delights. He discovered in the rising and setting of the sun sights unknown to the world. He knew what it was to tremble when he heard over his head the hiss of a bird's wing, so rarely did they pass, or when he saw the clouds, changing and many-colored travellers, melt one into another. He studied in the night time the effect of the moon upon the ocean of sand, where the simoom made waves swift of movement and rapid in their change. He lived the life of the Eastern day, marvelling at its wonderful pomp; then, after having revelled in the sight of a hurricane over the plain where the whirling sands made red, dry mists and death-bearing clouds, he would welcome the night with joy, for then fell the healthful freshness of the stars, and he listened to imaginary music in the skies. Then solitude taught him to unroll the treasures of dreams. He passed whole hours in remembering mere nothings, and comparing his present life with his past.

At last he grew passionately fond of the panther; for some sort of affection was a necessity.

Whether it was that his will powerfully projected had modified the character of his companion, or whether, because she found abundant food in her predatory excursions in the desert, she respected the man's life, he began to fear for it no longer, seeing her so well tamed.

He devoted the greater part of his time to sleep, but he was obliged to watch like a spider in its web that the moment of his deliverance might not escape him, if any one should pass the line marked by the horizon. He had sacrificed his shirt to make a flag with, which he hung at the top of a palm tree, whose foliage he had torn off. Taught by necessity, he found the means of keeping it spread out, by fastening it with little sticks; for the wind might not be blowing at the moment when the passing traveller was looking through the desert.

It was during the long hours, when he had abandoned hope, that he amused himself with the panther. He had come to learn the different inflections of her voice, the expressions of her eyes; he had studied the capricious patterns of all the rosettes which marked the gold of her robe. Mignonne was not even angry when he took hold of the tuft at the end of her tail to count her rings, those graceful ornaments which glittered in the sun like jewelry. It gave him pleasure to contemplate the supple, fine outlines of her form, the whiteness of her belly, the graceful pose of her head. But it was especially when she was playing that he felt most pleasure in looking at her; the agility and youthful lightness of her movements were a continual surprise to him; he wondered at the supple way in which she jumped and climbed, washed herself and arranged her fur, crouched down and prepared to spring. However rapid her spring might be, however slippery the stone she was on, she would always stop short at the word "Mignonne."

One day, in a bright mid-day sun, an enormous bird coursed through the air. The man left his panther to look at this new guest; but after waiting a moment the deserted sultana growled deeply.

"My goodness! I do believe she's jealous," he cried, seeing her eyes become hard again; "the soul of Virginie has passed into her body; that's certain."

The eagle disappeared into the air, while the soldier admired the curved contour of the panther.

But there was such youth and grace in her form! she was beautiful as a woman! the blond fur of her robe mingled well with the delicate tints of faint white which marked her flanks.

The profuse light cast down by the sun made this living gold, these russet markings, to burn in a way to give them an indefinable attraction.

The man and the panther looked at one another with a look full of meaning; the coquette quivered when she felt her friend stroke her head; her eyes flashed like lightning—then she shut them tightly.

"She has a soul," he said, looking at the stillness of this queen of the sands, golden like them, white like them, solitary and burning like them.

"Well," she said, "I have read your plea in favor of beasts;

but how did two so well adapted to understand each other end?"

"Ah, well! you see, they ended as all great passions do end —by a misunderstanding. For some reason *one* suspects the other of treason; they don't come to an explanation through pride, and quarrel and part from sheer obstinacy."

"Yet sometimes at the best moments a single word or a look is enough—but anyhow go on with your story."

"It's horribly difficult, but you will understand, after what the old villain told me over his champagne.

"He said—'I don't know if I hurt her, but she turned round, as if enraged, and with her sharp teeth caught hold of my leg—gently, I daresay; but I, thinking she would devour me, plunged my dagger into her throat. She rolled over, giving a cry that froze my heart; and I saw her dying, still looking at me without anger. I would have given all the world—my cross even, which I had not got then—to have brought her to life again. It was as though I had murdered a real person; and the soldiers who had seen my flag, and were come to my assistance, found me in tears.'

" 'Well sir,' he said, after a moment of silence, 'since then I have been in war in Germany, in Spain, in Russia, in France; I've certainly carried my carcass about a good deal, but never have I seen anything like the desert. Ah! yes, it is very beautiful!'

" 'What did you feel there?' I asked him.

" 'Oh! that can't be described, young man. Besides, I am not always regretting my palm trees and my panther. I should have to be very melancholy for that. In the desert, you see, there is everything, and nothing.'

" 'Yes, but explain——'

" 'Well,' he said, with an impatient gesture, 'it is God without mankind.' "